The King's Evil

The King's Evil

EDWARD MARSTON

This edition first published in 2010 by
Allison & Busby Limited
13 Charlotte Mews
London, W1T 4EJ
www.allisonandbusby.com

A CIP catalogue record for this book is available from
the British Library.

First published in the UK in 1999.

10 9 8 7 6 5 4 3 2 1

ISBN 978-0-7490-0897-0

Typeset in 10.5/15 pt Sabon by
Allison & Busby Ltd.

The paper used for this Allison & Busby publication
has been produced from trees that have been legally sourced
from well-managed and credibly certified forests.

Printed and bound in the UK by
CPI Bookmarque, Croydon, CR0 4TD

EDWARD MARSTON was born and brought up in South Wales. A full-time writer for over thirty years, he has worked in radio, film, television and the theatre and is a former chairman of the Crime Writers' Association. Prolific and highly successful, he is equally at home writing children's books or literary criticism, plays or biographies. *The King's Evil* is the first book in the series featuring architect Christopher Redmayne and the Puritan constable Jonathan Bale, set in Restoration London.

www.edwardmarston.com

Available from
ALLISON & BUSBY

The Christopher Redmayne series
The King's Evil
The Amorous Nightingale
The Repentant Rake
The Frost Fair
The Parliament House
The Painted Lady

The Inspector Robert Colbeck series
The Railway Detective
The Excursion Train
The Railway Viaduct
The Iron Horse
Murder on the Brighton Express
The Silver Locomotive Mystery
Railway to the Grave
Blood on the Line

The Captain Rawson series
Soldier of Fortune
Drums of War
Fire and Sword
Under Siege

*To Louis Silverstein and
Monty Montee of Phoenix, Arizona.
Good friends and bibliophiles supreme.*

'O! lay that hand upon me
Adored Caesar! and my faith is such,
I shall be heal'd, if that my KING but touch.
The Evill is not yours: my sorrow sings,
Mine is the Evill, but the cure, the KINGS.'

ROBERT HERRICK

'I was yesterday in many meetings of the principal Cittizens,
whose houses are laid in ashes, who in stead of complaining,
discoursed almost of nothing, but of a survey of London,
and a dessein for rebuilding.'

HENRY OLDENBURG'S LETTER TO
ROBERT BOYLE, 10TH SEPTEMBER 1666

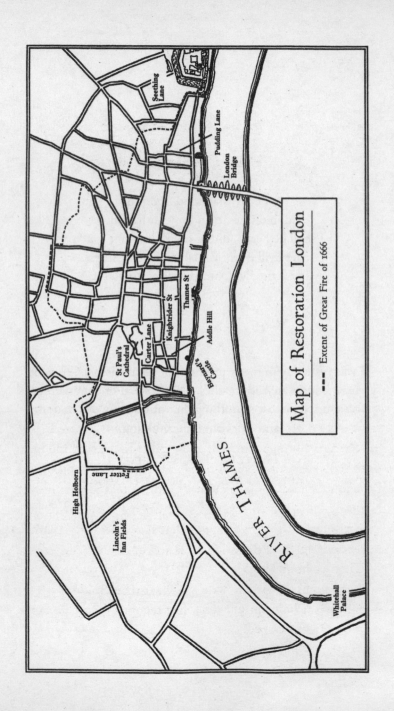

Map of Restoration London

--- Extent of Great Fire of 1666

RIVER THAMES

Whitehall Palace

Lincoln's Inn Fields

High Holborn

Fetter Lane

St Paul's Cathedral

Carter Lane

Knightrider St

Thames St

Addle Hill

Baynard's Castle

Seething Lane

Pudding Lane

London Bridge

PROLOGUE

The month of September had scarcely begun when a new disaster struck an already beleaguered city. London had been savaged without mercy by the Great Plague, frozen to the marrow by a cold winter then blistered in a hot, dry, unrelenting summer which bred drought, discontent and fresh outbreaks of virulent disease. Even the oldest inhabitants of the capital could not recall a more intense period of suffering but they consoled themselves – between weary curses at a malign Fate – with the thought that they had now endured misery enough and that their situation could only improve.

Then came the fire.

It brought Jonathan Bale awake in the middle of the night. He sat bolt upright for a few seconds then clambered unwillingly out of bed.

'What ails you?' asked his wife, stirring in the dark.

'Nothing, Sarah,' he said.

'Then why have you got up?'

'Go back to sleep. I did not mean to wake you.'

'Are you unwell, Jonathan?'

'No,' he said, putting a reassuring hand on her arm. 'I am in good health – thank God – though it is as much your doing as the Almighty's. I am blessed in a wife who cooks and cares for me so wondrously well. You have earned your rest, Sarah. Take it. Sleep on.'

'How can I when you are so disturbed?'

'I am not disturbed.'

'Then why did you wake up with such a start?'

'I must have had a bad dream.'

'You never have dreams of any kind,' she said, sitting up in bed and stifling a yawn. 'I am the dreamer in the family. Every night is filled with them. But not you. Your mind seems to have no fancies. Now tell me what is going on.'

'Nothing that need upset you,' he soothed.

'Tell me.'

'In the morning, perhaps. Not now.'

'Stop trying to fob me off.'

'Sarah—'

'And I'll not be Sarah'd into silence,' she warned with a tired smile. 'I have not been married to you all these years without learning your ways and your moods. You are a man who sleeps soundly in his bed. Much too soundly at times for I have had to rouse you more than once of a morning. Only something very unusual could have made you wake up of a sudden like that. What was it?'

'I do not know,' he said with a shrug, 'and that is the truth of it, Sarah. I simply do not know.'

Jonathan Bale was a big, solid, serious man whose frame seemed to fill the small bedchamber. Now in his late thirties, he still retained the muscles which he had developed during his years as a shipwright and, despite the excellence of his wife's cooking, there was not a superfluous ounce of fat on his body. The same could not be said of Sarah. Motherhood had rounded her hips and filled out her thighs, buttocks and breasts. A good appetite helped to complete the transformation of a slim, attractive young woman into a plump but still comely matron. Jonathan had marked no change in her. To his loving eye, she was still the same Sarah Teague whom he had met and married nine years earlier.

He sat on the bed and slipped a comforting arm around her.

'There is no point in the two of us losing sleep,' he said.

'Neither of us need lose it. Come back to bed.'

'No, Sarah. Not yet. You lie down again.'

'Not until you tell me what this is all about.'

'I have told you. I honestly do not know.'

'When you came awake, you let out a little yell.'

'Did I?'

'What provoked it?'

'I have no idea.'

'Was it fear? Pain? Foreboding?'

'I wish I knew,' he sighed. 'It was almost as if someone shook me awake. There was a sense of alarm. I felt that I was being summoned.'

'You are not on duty now, Jonathan.'

'A constable is always on duty.'

'Even in the middle of the night?'

'If he is called, Sarah.'

'But what on earth has called you?'

'That is what I intend to find out.'

He kissed her gently on the forehead then eased her back down on the pillow before crossing to the window. Opening the shutters, he looked out into the unrelieved blackness of Addle Hill. Familiar smells assaulted his nostrils and the open sewer which ran down the lane was especially pungent on a warm night. Dogs roamed and foraged, cats fought a distant battle over territory. Footsteps dragged laboriously as a drunken reveller tried to stagger home. But there was nothing to be seen beyond the vague outlines of the buildings opposite. All was exactly as he would have expected to find it at such an hour yet Jonathan Bale remained quietly perturbed. Instinct told him that something was amiss. It troubled him that he could not detect what it was. He stayed at the window until his eyes grew more accustomed to the darkness and allowed him to take a fuller inventory of the lane. He could even pick out the inn sign of the White Swan now and the massive bulk of Baynard's Castle emerged from the gloom like a cliff face.

But nothing untoward came into view. The city was peaceful.

Sarah was torn between fatigue and impatience.

'Well?' she asked.

'Nothing,' he said, closing the shutters. 'I was mistaken.'

'Good.'

'It must have been a dream, after all.'

'Just come back to bed.'

'I will.' He climbed in beside her and pulled the bedsheet over him. 'I am sorry that I woke you,' he said, giving her an affectionate peck on the cheek. 'Good night, Sarah.'

'Good night.'

Nestling into him, she was asleep within minutes but her husband remained wide awake. He had an overwhelming sense of being needed to fight some undisclosed emergency. It made him fretful. London, his birthplace and home, the sovereign city which he loved so much and helped to patrol so conscientiously, was in grave danger yet he was unable to go to its aid. His frustration steadily grew until he had to fight to contain it. London was imperilled. While his wife surrendered once more to the sweetness of her dreams, Jonathan Bale's fevered mind was restlessly pacing the streets of the capital in search of the latest terror.

CHAPTER ONE

The fire was cunning. It was no more than a dying ember in a Pudding Lane bakehouse when Thomas Farriner, the proprietor, checked his oven and the five other hearths on the premises before retiring to bed at midnight on that first Saturday of the month. Having deceived the practised eye of the baker, the fire rekindled itself with glee and crept stealthily around the ground floor of the house until it had wrapped every stick of furniture in its hot embrace. By the time the occupants caught their first whiff of smoke, it was far too late. Leaping from their beds, they found their descent cut off by a burning staircase so they were forced to escape through an upstairs window and along the gutter to a neighbouring house. Not all of them made the rooftop journey. Frightened at the prospect of a hazardous climb, the maidservant chose to remain in her room and was slowly roasted to death.

The fire tasted flesh. There was no holding it now.

Enlisting the aid of a sharp northeast wind, it sent a shower of sparks across Pudding Lane and into the coach-yard of the Star Inn, setting alight the heaps of hay and straw piled against the wooden galleries. Word was immediately sent to the Lord Mayor. Sir Thomas Bludworth, roused from his slumbers at his home in Maiden Lane, rode irritably to the scene to survey the fire. It caused him no undue tremors. What he saw was nothing more than a typical local blaze which would soon spend itself and leave only limited damage behind. It did not justify any official action from him.

'Pish!' he said with contempt. 'A woman might piss it out.'

And he returned swiftly to his bed with a clear conscience.

But the contents of every chamber pot in England could not have doused the fire now. It mocked the Sabbath with the flames of Hell and turned a day of rest into a continuous ordeal. Wafted by the rising wind, the fire was carried irresistibly across the cobbles of Pudding Lane and down towards the timber sheds and stalls of Fish Street Hill. The littered alleys which led from Thames Street to the river were soon ablaze and the stacks of wood and coal on the wharves made a suicide pact with the bales of goods in the warehouses and with the barrels of tallow oil and spirits in the cellars, flinging themselves onto the flames and turning a troublesome fire into a raging inferno. Houses, tenements, shops, inns, stables and even churches were alight. When the indifferent Lord Mayor was hauled once more from his complacent bed, dozens of buildings had already been destroyed and the fire was spreading relentlessly.

Billingsgate Ward was in a state of utter chaos. The narrow streets and alleys made it a most difficult part of the city in which to fight a fire. Householders were in a complete quandary, not knowing whether to flee with whatever they could carry or try to beat back the flames. The noise was indescribable. The few fire engines which were rushed to the scene proved hopelessly inadequate and the leather buckets of water which were thrown on the blaze produced no more than hisses of derision. Heat and smoke drove the firefighters back with brutal unconcern. They had lost the battle at its very outset. Roaring in triumph, the fire revelled in its invincibility. No part of the city was safe now.

When the alarm was raised, Jonathan Bale was three-quarters of a mile away in Baynard's Castle Ward but he heard it clearly. Bells were rung, drums were beaten and pandemonium was carried freely on the wind. He jumped out of his bed and rushed to the window, flinging back the shutters to look up at a sky which was brightly illumined by the false dawn of a fire. This was the crisis which had brought him so rudely awake earlier on. He groped for his clothes.

'What is it?' murmured his wife, still half asleep.

'A fire,' he said.

'Where?'

'On the other side of the city. I must help to fight it.'

'But it is not in your parish.'

'I am needed, Sarah.'

'Let someone else take care of it.'

'I have to go.'

'Now?'

'At once.'

'Why?'

It was a rhetorical question. Jonathan Bale's sense of duty knew no boundaries. Wherever and whenever an emergency arose, he would lend his assistance without a second thought. Other constables stayed strictly within the bounds of their own parish and few ventured outside their respective wards but Jonathan was different. Imbued with ideals of civic responsibility, he treated the whole of London as his territory. If the city was under threat in any way, he would race to its defence.

When he was dressed, he gave his wife a hurried kiss before letting himself out of the house. Long strides took him around the first corner into Thames Street and he headed eastward. The bending thoroughfare with its tall buildings on both sides obscured the fire from him at first but its glare guided his footsteps. Distant panic gradually increased in volume. Still in night attire, a few people were stumbling out of their houses to ask what was going on. They showed curiosity rather than apprehension, secure in the knowledge that the fire was much too far away to affect them or their property. The further he went, the more people he encountered and Jonathan was soon having to pick his way through a small crowd.

The sky was now lit as if by a noonday sun. He was over halfway there when he heard the full-throated roar of the fire. Eager to reach the scene, Jonathan broke into a trot and dodged the anxious citizens who now poured out of their homes in disarray as they sensed an impending catastrophe. Thames Street was turning into a cauldron of fear and confusion. Men shouted, women screamed, children cried and animals expressed their own alarm. The noise was deafening and an acrid smell grew fouler with each second. Jonathan ran on through the commotion. He was soon having to buffet a path with his broad shoulders. Fire was an ever-present menace in London and, in his time, he had seen many but none of them compared in scale and ferocity with the blaze which now confronted him.

When he rounded a bend, he saw a sheet of yellow flame advancing slowly towards him, eating its way along Thames Street with a voracious appetite and swallowing everything down to the riverfront. Smoke billowed in the swirling wind. A series of violent explosions went off as the fire found new stocks of combustible material in yards, cellars and warehouses. Jonathan came to an abrupt halt and stared in horror at the grotesque firework display. Expecting a degree of danger, he was instead looking into the jaws of death. This crisis was potentially more threatening than the Great Plague and far more immediate.

The fire was still some distance away but its warm fingers were already bestowing lascivious caresses on his face. Jonathan gritted his teeth and moved on. Thames Street was in turmoil. The panic-stricken families who tumbled out of their houses were met by the first fleeing victims of the fire. Carts, coaches and packhorses bore the most precious possessions of those whose homes were already doomed. People unable to afford transport of any kind simply carried what they could in their arms. Jonathan saw a man bent double under the weight of a heavy sack and an old lady staggering along with a spinning wheel. Two small children dragged their meagre belongings over the cobbles in a tattered bedsheet. Three men lugged a stout oak table.

When he got closer to the blaze, Jonathan saw the most stark evidence yet of its power. Even the rats were leaving, darting out of their hiding places in wild profusion and joining the general exodus. Three of them scampered uncaringly over the constable's shoes. Cats and dogs bade clamorous farewells as they scuttled away but not all animals were fortunate enough to escape. Crazed horses kicked and neighed in burning stables. A donkey brayed for mercy in the heart of the fire. A goat was trapped in a blazing garden and searched feverishly for an exit. Geese honked in a locked shed. Chickens clucked their noisy requiems. Pigeons too slow to leave their perches found their wings singed as soon as they took to the air and they plummeted to instant death. Creatures who lived in thatch, crevice or timber were extinguished with callous delight. No living thing was spared.

Jonathan paused to assess where he could be most useful. The fire engines were defunct and it was left to chains of men, passing buckets of water along, to continue the fight. Heat was now so fierce that they were pushed further and further back. When water was hurled, it did not even reach the flames in some cases. Braving the pain, Jonathan took his turn at the head of a chain, snatching a leather bucket from the man behind him and flinging its contents at the blazing doorway of a house. His bucket was exchanged for a full one and he emptied that at the same target. It was all to no avail. Whipped up by the wind, the fire was spreading with increased fury. It was clear that buckets of water would never contain the blaze, still less quell it. There was an additional problem. The dry summer had left water levels very low and there was an unsteady flow from the conduits. Buckets took longer than usual to fill and Jonathan was soon having to wait minutes for a fresh supply of water to be passed along to him. The fire raged on inexorably.

The building suddenly crumbled to the ground in front of them and forced them to jump back. The man beside Jonathan – a tall, thin, wiry individual with rolling eyes – flung up his arms in despair.

'It is hopeless!' he wailed.

'The fire must be checked,' said Jonathan. 'They must pull down a row of houses in its path and create a firebreak.'

'The Lord Mayor has forbidden it.'

'Why?'

'He fears the cost involved in rebuilding.'

'Would he rather lose the entire city?'

'Sir Thomas would not give the order.'

'Somebody must,' insisted Jonathan. 'Where did the fire start?'

'Who knows?' said the man. 'I was fast asleep when the alarm was raised. By the time I got here, Fish Street Hill was ablaze and the houses at the northern end of the bridge were alight. In the past half-hour, we have been driven back a hundred yards or more. We are powerless.'

'Fire posts must be set up at once.'

'Tell that to the Lord Mayor.'

'More water!'

'What is the point?'

'We must fight on!' urged Jonathan, exhorting the others

in the chain. 'More water there! Keep the buckets coming! We must not give in. Something may yet be saved.'

It was a forlorn hope. Though he tossed gallons of water at the fire, he made no discernible impact. It blazed up defiantly in front of him and encroached on both sides. Hysteria mounted. Many people fled west along the crowded thoroughfare but most scurried towards the river with their belongings, hoping to put the broad back of the Thames between themselves and certain extinction, only to find the myriad boats and lighters already filled with frightened refugees. Quick to take advantage of the situation, watermen doubled and trebled their prices before rowing their passengers to the uncertain safety of Bankside. When they scrambled ashore with their money, their furniture, their musical instruments and anything else they had salvaged, they looked back at a fire which seemed to engulf the whole of the riverfront from London Bridge to Dowgate and beyond. Flames danced madly on the water as the Thames mirrored the calamity.

Jonathan Bale struggled on against impossible odds for well over an hour. His hair was singed, his face was running with perspiration and holes had been burnt in his coat by flying sparks. His whole body ached and smarted but he would not give up. Only when the water supply ceased did he have any respite. He looked down the long line of exhausted bodies between him and the conduit.

'More water!' he ordered, panting from his exertions.

'There is none!' called a voice at the far end. 'It has dried up.'

'How?'

'Someone must have cut into the pipe further up to fill buckets of their own. There is barely a trickle down here.'

'We have done all we can, my friend,' gasped the man next to Jonathan. 'We must look to our own salvation.'

'There is too much to do here. That is why I came.'

'Where do you live?'

'On Addle Hill.'

'Near Baynard's Castle?'

'Yes.'

The man was surprised. 'You came all this way to help?'

'I was needed.'

'You and a thousand like you are needed, my friend, but there would still not be enough of us to put out this fire. I'll home to Cornhill. I have done my share here. It is time to worry about my own house. Do likewise.'

'The fire will never reach Addle Hill,' said Jonathan.

'Do not be so sure,' warned the other. 'If this wind holds, the blaze will spread all the way to the Palace of Westminster to burn the royal breeches. And so it should,' he added with bitter reproach, 'for the King is the true cause of this fire.'

'That is treasonable talk.'

'It is the plain truth.'

'Fires are caused by folly and neglect.'

'The King's folly and the King's neglect.'

'I will not listen to such nonsense.'

'Then look around you,' urged the man, waving an arm. 'See for yourself. This is no ordinary fire. It is a judgement on us. King Charles and his vile Court have corrupted the whole of London. The fire has been sent to purge the city. We must all suffer for his sins.' He gave Jonathan a nudge. 'Go home, my friend. Return to Addle Hill. Protect your family. Save yourself while you still may. Nothing can stop this blaze now.'

The man staggered off. Jonathan watched him go and reflected on what he had said. His position as a constable obliged him to reprimand the fellow but he had considerable sympathy with the view expressed. England was ruled once more by a Stuart king. A monarchy which Jonathan had been pleased to see ended was now emphatically restored. As a result, London was indeed a wicked city and nobody was better placed to see the extent of its depravity than someone who patrolled the streets in the office of constable. Jonathan was a God-fearing man who always sought guidance from above and he was bound to wonder if the conflagration really was a sign of divine anger. There were Biblical precedents of cities being punished for their corruption.

The problem was that the innocent would suffer along with the guilty. Jonathan thought about his wife and children, still asleep, quite unaware that their blameless lives might be under threat. Their safety came first. He had to get back to them. The fire now raged totally out of control and buildings were crashing to the ground all around him. Smoke stung his eyes and caught in his throat. Scorching heat pushed him back like a giant hand.

Chaos reached a new pitch and he was heavily jostled in the ensuing tumult. Brushing some sparks from the sleeve of his coat, Jonathan pushed his way through the seething mass of bodies and trotted back down Thames Street in a futile attempt to outrun disaster.

CHAPTER TWO

Christopher Redmayne could not believe what he saw. On the journey from Oxford, they encountered a number of people who had fled from London but their tales of woe smacked too much of wild exaggeration to be taken seriously. The evidence of their own eyes robbed Christopher and his companions of their scepticism. They were still miles away when they caught their first glimpse of the rising smoke which sullied the clear blue sky and hung over the city like a pall. The travellers reined in their horses to stare open-mouthed at the phenomenon ahead of them. It was truly incredible. London was destroyed. The most vibrant city in Europe had been burnt to the ground.

As they considered the dreadful implications, everyone was struck dumb. It was minutes before an anguished voice shattered the silence.

'Dear God!' exclaimed Christopher. 'How did this happen?'

He had joined the others for security on the journey but he now spurned all thoughts of safety. Kicking his horse into life, he rode off at a steady canter to cover the remaining distance alone. Anxieties crowded in on him. What of his own house? Had that perished in the blaze? Were his possessions burnt to a cinder? His precious drawings lost? Was Jacob, his servant, still alive? Did the fire reach his brother's house? Where *was* Henry Redmayne? And what of Christopher's friends? His neighbours? His parish church? What happened to all those magnificent buildings he so admired and from which he drew his inspiration?

How much of his London survived?

As he rode towards the smoking ruin, his mind was also ablaze.

The consequences of the Great Fire were soon all too apparent. Desultory groups of refugees trudged past him to uncertain destinations. The outer reaches of the city seemed to have been colonised by gipsies for there was hardly a spare patch of land which did not have its tents or its makeshift huts. Some families had no shelter whatsoever and simply sat by the roadside amid their vestigial belongings. Fires had been lit to cook food. Water was drawn from every stream or pond. A sense of fatigue pervaded the whole scene. Less than a week earlier, these same people all had homes, occupations and the promise of a future. Now they were nomads, exiled citizens of a capital which no longer existed.

When he reached St Giles's Fields, he saw what looked like the population of a small town, huddled together in sheer bewilderment, torn between protest and resignation, trying to make sense of a tragedy which had struck them so unexpectedly and wondering how they could fend for themselves without a place of work. Clergy moved assiduously among them but their words of comfort went largely unheard by people who were trapped in their private griefs. A thousand different stories of pain and suffering were scattered across the grass. Christopher was deeply moved by the sight of so much undeserved sorrow.

His attention turned to the city itself and he shuddered. Buildings, spires and pinnacles which usually rose above the walls to delight his eye were now wreathed in smoke and all he could make out of the dominating majesty of St Paul's Cathedral was the empty shell of its tower. Christopher tore his gaze away from the devastation and goaded a last burst of speed from his mount as he went along High Holborn. He steeled himself in readiness. It was more than possible that he, too, had been dispossessed. Holborn itself seemed largely undamaged but he could not answer for Fetter Lane until he swung into it. The scene which met him caused Christopher to bring his horse to a sharp halt.

He gaped in dismay. The left hand side of the lane had been gutted by fire at the far end and smoke still curled from the debris. Several of his neighbours were now homeless. Sympathy welled up in him but it was tempered with relief that his own house had somehow escaped. Situated near the Holborn end of the lane, it was marginally outside the circle of damnation: He offered up a silent prayer of thanks then nudged his horse forward.

Christopher was soon admitted to his home by his servant.

'Bless you, sir!' said Jacob, eyes watering with pleasure.

'You've come back at last. I am so glad to see you.'

'And I am so grateful to see you, Jacob.'

'We were spared, sir. God, in His benevolence, took pity on us.'

'I have not observed much sign of benevolence out there,' said Christopher, stepping into the house and closing the door behind him. 'Nor much indication of pity. Every step of the way was lined with poor wretches who have lost the roof over their heads.'

'Sad times!' sighed the old man. 'Sad and sorry times!'

'Tell me all.'

Christopher led the way into the parlour and cast a glance around it to reassure himself that it was completely intact. Only when he saw that his portfolio of drawings was unharmed did he begin to relax. He doffed his hat and turned back to face Jacob. The old man was much more than a servant to him. Honest, reliable and eternally willing, Jacob was a rock in the shifting sands of his master's career and Christopher had developed such an affection for him that he even endured his flights of garrulity without complaint. At a full six feet, he towered over the podgy little servant and had a perfect view of his bald pate. Jacob peered up at him from beneath bushy eyebrows.

'It has been a nightmare, sir,' he said.

'When did the fire start?' asked Christopher.

'Early on Sunday morning.'

'And how long did it rage?'

'Four days.' Jacob sucked in air through his few remaining teeth. 'Four long, terrible days. It would still be burning now if the wind had not dropped on Wednesday. Rain fell and slowed the blaze down. They were able to fight it properly for the first time. Rows of houses were blown up with dynamite to make fire breaks. That stopped it spreading.' He jabbed a gnarled finger towards the window. 'Yet here we are on Saturday and the city is still smoking. They say it will be weeks before the last embers are put out. All is lost, sir.'

'All?'

'St Paul's is gone and over eighty churches with it. There is talk of at least ten thousand houses brought down, probably many more. They are still counting them. The Guildhall went up in flames, so did the Royal Exchange and I doubt if there is a livery hall still standing.'

'What of the Tower?'

'That survived – thank Heaven! It had the wind at its back and the fire never reached it, though much of Tower Street Ward was afflicted. It has been an ordeal for all of us, sir,' said Jacob with a sudden shiver. 'I feared mightily for the safety of this very house for the blaze was moving west with a vengeance on Tuesday. A fire post was set up at the bottom of Fetter Lane but our parish constables with a hundred men and thirty foot-soldiers to help them could not stop some of the houses being burnt down.'

'So I saw.'

'We have been blessed, sir. We escaped.'

Tears trickled down the old man's face and he wiped them away with the back of his hand. Christopher held him in a token embrace then led him across to a stool and lowered him onto it. Jacob was patently harrowed by the experience. The hollowed cheeks and the deathly pallor showed that he had enjoyed very little sleep and there was still a glint of terror in his eyes. Christopher felt guilty that he had not been there to share the ordeal with his servant and help him through it. There was much more to tell and he listened patiently while Jacob unfolded his tale at exhaustive length. As the old man unburdened himself, he was shaking visibly and his whole body twitched at the conclusion of his narrative. Christopher left a long, considered pause before addressing himself to his own concerns.

'What news of my brother, Henry?' he said.

'He has sent word, sir.'

'Was his own house affected?'

'No, sir,' said Jacob, rising to his feet. 'The fire stopped well short of Bedford Street. Covent Garden was untouched. Your brother wants you to call on him as soon as you may. He is most insistent.'

'Henry always is.'

'Messages have come every day.'

'I need to get my breath back before I go running to my brother,' said Christopher, dropping into a chair. 'I have been in the saddle for hours on end. Do we have any drink in the house, Jacob?'

'Yes, sir. The last of that wine is still in the cellar.'

'Fetch a bottle. And bring two glasses.'

'Two, sir?'

'I think you need sustenance as much as I do. Besides, we have something to celebrate. The house is still standing. That is a small miracle. Bring the wine, Jacob. We will raise a glass together.'

'If you say so, sir.'

The servant's face recovered some of its ruddy glow and

his eyes glistened. It was a rare privilege to be allowed – however briefly – to step across the line which separated master from man and Jacob appreciated it. A smile touched his lips for the first time in a week.

'Hurry along,' said Christopher with a flick of his hand. 'I need a restorative drink if I am to face Henry. Conversations with my brother can be wearing at the best of times.'

There was never any danger of Henry Redmayne indulging his servants. He treated them with a lofty disdain, reasoning that they were fortunate enough simply to be in the employ of so august a gentleman and that they deserved no further encouragement lest it give them ideas above their station. Accordingly, the barber who shaved him expected no word of approval, still less any hint of gratitude. Achievement lay in performing his duty without eliciting too many grumbles from his testy customer. His razor moved swiftly but carefully. The sallow face of Henry Redmayne was not one over which he cared to linger. When his work was done, he held up a small mirror while a detailed facial examination was carried out. Henry kept him waiting a long time before giving a dismissive nod.

As soon as the barber quit the room, the manservant entered to help his master to dress. It was a silent ritual in front of a large gilt-framed mirror. Henry preened himself at every stage, lavishing particular attention on his petticoat breeches and his new long multi-coloured waistcoat. When he put on his embroidered coat, he stroked it lovingly with both hands then shifted his stance to look at it from several angles before giving a grunt of satisfaction.

It was only then that the manservant dared to speak.

'Your brother has arrived, sir.'

'How long has he been here?'

'A little while,' said the other tactfully.

'Tell him I will be down in a moment.'

The man nodded and withdrew. He knew better than to interrupt his master while the latter was being shaved or dressed. The visitor had been understanding. He had already waited for almost half an hour. Henry added five more minutes to the delay before he pirouetted in front of the mirror for the last time. When he descended to the parlour, he found his younger brother reclining in a chair and gazing intently at a painting of a naval battle. Christopher was still in his dusty travelling clothes. Henry strode across to him and struck a pose.

'So?' he said with a note of reproach. 'You have come at last. We can always rely on your absence when you are most needed.'

Christopher stood up. 'I had work to do in Oxford.'

'Have you finally discovered the concept of work?'

'Do not be so cynical, Henry. We cannot all have a sinecure at the Navy Office, as you do. Besides,' he added, running an admiring eye over his brother's fashionable attire, 'I had a more personal reason for being in Oxford. Father was visiting the city to attend a convocation there.'

'How is the old gentleman?'

'In excellent health.'

'That means he is still preaching interminable sermons.'

'He spoke much about you, Henry.'

'Fondly, I hope?'

'Alas, no,' said Christopher. 'With some asperity. Reports have reached him that you live a dissolute life in London, quite unbecoming to the elder son of the Dean of Gloucester. The fact that you have reached the age of thirty without the companionship of a wife is also of deep concern to him. In Father's mind, that serves to reinforce the truth of the rumours. He demanded to know if you were indeed the seasoned voluptuary of report.'

Henry winced. 'What did you tell him?'

'What he wanted to hear. That you lead a Christian life which keeps you completely away from the snares of lust and drunkenness. I assured him that you are regular in your devotions and often express regrets that you yourself have not taken the cloth. In short,' said Christopher with an amiable grin, 'I lied outrageously on your behalf.'

'Did he believe you?'

'Only up to a point.'

'Oh dear!' said Henry with a sigh. 'In that case, I will soon receive one of his stern letters, chastising me for my sins and urging repentance. How does he gather all this intelligence about me? Can a man not enjoy the pleasures of the capital without their echoes reaching the cloisters of Gloucester? I will need to be more discreet.'

'Or more restrained.'

'That is out of the question.'

They shared a laugh. It was difficult to believe that they were brothers. Both were tall, slim and well-favoured but the resemblance ended there. Henry's long face was already showing signs of dissipation and the moustache which he took such trouble to cultivate somehow added a sinister quality. Christopher, by contrast, had a more open countenance and a clearer complexion. While he exuded health, his brother looked as if he was well acquainted with disease, especially the kind which might be contracted in a bedchamber. Handsome and clean-shaven, Christopher had dark brown hair with a reddish hue which hung in natural curls. His brother's hair, lighter in colour and straighter in texture, was thinning so dramatically that he had ordered a periwig.

'I am relieved to find you safe and sound,' said Christopher with unfeigned sincerity. 'When I heard news of the fire, I feared that it might have reached this far.'

'Happily, no. It did not progress beyond Temple Bar. But that does not mean I came through the ordeal unscathed,' Henry emphasised, keen to portray himself as a victim. 'For I did not. I shared the misery of many friends who lost their homes and suffered agonies of apprehension on account of my own property. As for the city itself, it was like being locked in Bedlam.'

'What started the fire?'

'That was the problem, Christopher. Nobody knew and so they drew their own conclusions. The blaze was so fierce and so widespread that it seemed to have been started deliberately. Mobs soon formed, believing that London had been torched by Catholics. Passions ran high and the wilder spirits took the law into their own hands. We had open riot.'

'Is there any proof of a Popish Plot?'

'The mobs thought so,' said Henry ruefully. 'They beat confessions out of any Catholic they could find. Innocent foreigners were attacked at random. Frenchmen, Italians and the like who were unwise enough to venture into the streets were set on without mercy. The fortunate ones got away with cuts, bruises and broken bones. I have no sympathy for the Old Religion – remember to tell that to our father – but I do not wish its practitioners to be torn to shreds by an enraged mob. I abhor violence of any kind. It was shameful to behold.'

'Were any arrests made?'

'Dozens. But since most of the prisons were burnt down, there was nowhere to keep the miscreants. It has been a gruesome week.'

'Who, then, did start the fire?'

'Investigations still continue but the finger points to a careless baker in Pudding Lane. That is certainly where the blaze began.'

Christopher gulped. 'A vast city razed by the folly of one man.'

'The fellow denies it hotly but he looks like the culprit.'

'Who will buy bread from him after this?'

'Ship's biscuits. That is what he made. Hard tack. I should know,' observed Henry, straightening his back with self-importance. 'His output helps to victual our fleet. His damnable name has probably passed before my eyes a dozen times at the Navy Office. But enough of the fire,' he said, crossing to rest an elbow on the marble mantelpiece and display himself to full effect. 'It has wreaked its havoc and been brought under control. What we must look to now are the rich pickings it may offer.'

Christopher was puzzled. 'What rich pickings? The city has been reduced to a state of abject poverty.'

'Use your imagination, brother.'

'To what end?'

'Future prospects. One city may have vanished but another one must rise in its place. The opportunities for a talented architect are unlimited. Scores of them will be needed to act as midwives if the new London is to be brought into being.'

'That thought did cross my mind,' admitted the other.

'Seize on it, Christopher. It is the chance you have wanted.'

'I never wanted such wholesale destruction.'

'Nor more did I,' said Henry smoothly, 'but I am alert to the openings it suddenly provides. I know you think me heartless and given over entirely to a life of vice but I do honour my promises. When Father enjoined me to take you under my wing in London, I vowed that I would. I am sure that you will be gracious enough to concede that I have kept that vow.'

'You have,' said Christopher. 'I made much of the point to Father. It was the one honest thing I could say in your favour.'

'Did he have no strictures for you?'

'Indeed he did, Henry. He taxed me with my inability to settle in a career and he was not at all impressed when I argued that I had made my mark in several. As I reminded him, I studied law at Cambridge then became embroiled in anatomy before trying my hand, with some success, at writing poetry. Astronomy was my next love and I prospered in its study until the blandishments of philosophy seduced me away. I spent a whole year among fine minds. I tell you, Henry, there is nothing which thrills the blood so much as a lively debate with fellow philosophers.'

'I would take serious issue with you over that,' said his brother, arching a lecherous eyebrow. 'When I wish to thrill the blood, I do not require the presence of a fine mind. A voluptuous body alone suffices. But come to your latest enthusiasm, brother.'

'It is much more than that.'

'That is what I hoped.'

'Architecture is my obsession.'

'For how many weeks is it likely to last?'

'Indefinitely,' said Christopher with polite vehemence. 'I have found my true *métier* at last. Architecture embraces all the other disciplines. It combines the severity of the law with the fascination of anatomy, the joy of poetry, the mystery of astronomy and the intellectual stimulus of philosophy. When you add the iron logic of mathematics, you have a profession which outstrips all others. An architect is at once an artist and a scientist. What could be nobler?'

'Nobility can wait,' said Henry, strolling across to him. 'All that I am concerned with is securing a regular income for you. I have seen your drawings and was much impressed. They are brilliant. And I know that you have applied yourself diligently to this new interest.'

'Oh, it is not new, Henry. The seeds were sewn long ago in Rome when I chanced to meet Signor Bernini. He designed the Piazza of St Peter's and much else besides. Albeit a Catholic – I have not dared to breathe his name to Father – Bernini opened my eyes to the beauty of architecture. I have been putting my ideas down on paper ever since.'

'To good effect. You are clearly very gifted.'

'It is one of the reasons I went to Oxford,' continued the other as the glow of idealism lit up his features. 'To watch the progress of the Sheldonian Theatre. It is an extraordinary building. Wren is a genius. His design is breathtaking.'

'I am glad you mentioned your namesake. Christopher Wren is indeed a genius. The Great Fire will be the making of him.'

'In what way?'

'He has been invited to prepare a plan for the rebuilding of the city,' explained Henry knowledgeably. 'Wren is not the only one, mark you. I happen to know that John Evelyn will be submitting his own scheme, as will others. I have also caught wind of a notion put forward by a certain Captain Valentine Knight, involving the building of a wide canal from the River Fleet to Billingsgate. Ha!' he sneered with a gesture of disgust. 'Have you ever heard such nonsense?'

'You are amazingly well informed, Henry.'

'I consort with the right company.'

'Which of these many plans will be adopted?'

'That is the one thing I cannot tell you. They will have to be assessed in due course. But my guess is that Wren will emerge as the leading figure. Pattern yourself on him.'

'That is my intention.'

'*Carpe diem*, Christopher. Commit yourself. Study in earnest. It will be months before any rebuilding is allowed and that gives you time to hone your skills. Be ready to help the phoenix rise from the ashes.'

'Nothing would please me more!'

'I will do my share,' volunteered Henry. 'It is astonishing

what information trickles into my ears. When new houses are in demand, I will assuredly learn who wishes to commission some of them. My advice may even be sought in certain cases. How convenient it would be if I could recommend, as an architect, my own brother.'

Christopher was touched. 'Would you do that for me, Henry?' he said, unused to such filial assistance. 'I would be eternally grateful.'

'You can repay me by harping on my generosity when you next write to Father. Play the architect in your correspondence. Design a Henry Redmayne who is more appealing to a Dean of Gloucester.'

'That is a feat beyond even my talent,' said his brother with a chuckle. 'But I will do my best. As for your offer, I embrace it warmly. I will serve a speedy apprenticeship and be ready when the call comes.'

'Then there is no more to be said.'

They exchanged a warm handshake then Henry drifted to the mirror to make a few adjustments to his apparel. Christopher came up behind him with a knowing smile.

'You are going out this evening, I see.'

'I'll not let a fire deprive me of my pleasures.'

'But all your haunts have been destroyed, surely?'

'Some escaped,' said Henry suavely, brushing a fleck of dust from his sleeve. 'Besides, I am bidden this evening to an establishment in Farringdon Without. That ward was unmolested by the fire. Many who fled from the city have taken up residence there.' He turned to face Christopher and gave a quizzical smirk. 'I suppose that it is no use my inviting you to accompany me?'

'No, Henry.'

'A visit to a house of resort might educate you.'

'Love which has to be bought has no value for me.'

'It is the only kind a man can truly rely on, Christopher.'

'Enjoy it in my stead.'

'Are you not even tempted?'

'Not in the slightest,' said Christopher with a grin. 'I have a far more important place to visit this evening.'

'Where is that?'

'The city of London. If I am to help rebuild it, I must first see the full extent of the damage. That is where I will be while the light holds. You seek out the delights of the flesh, Henry,' he said, guiding his brother out of the room. 'I must go forth to meet my destiny.'

CHAPTER THREE

The man moved swiftly. Making sure that he was unobserved, he pushed aside the charred remnants of the front door and stepped into the house. A timber-framed property with a thatched roof, it had been completely gutted by the fire and nothing survived in any of the rooms to tempt a thief. The man was not concerned with the interior of the dwelling. His interest was in the garden. He clambered through to it. Plants and bushes had been burnt away and the little orchard was now no more than a collection of blackened stumps, surrounded by countless shrivelled apples and pears. That did not deter him. The man set about scouring the whole garden, searching the lawn then kicking away piles of ash so that he could examine the scorched flowerbeds. He soon found what he was after – a patch where the earth had recently been disturbed then stamped back into position. A hiding place.

From beneath his coat, he produced a small shovel. Kneeling down, he began to dig quickly but carefully, eager to secure his prize but not wishing to damage it by too vigorous a use of his implement. When he made contact with something solid, he abandoned the shovel and used both hands to scrape the earth away. A first bottle of wine came into view, then a second, then two more, each with the owner's crest upon them. It had to be expensive wine to be worth burying. He dug on until he unearthed a further three dozen bottles of Canary wine, six of brandy and an array of cheeses wrapped up in muslin then stuffed into a wooden box. It was a good haul. What he could not eat or drink himself, he could sell for a tidy profit. He made a mental note to save the Parmesan cheese for his own use.

The man was not finished yet. A property as substantial as this one argued an owner of some wealth. If he vacated the house at speed, he might not have been able to carry away all that he wished. Wine and cheese had been left behind. There was a chance that gold or valuables might also have been buried in the garden to await his return. The man sensed that there were richer rewards still at the bottom of the pit. He reached for his shovel once more. As his hand closed around the handle, however, a large shoe descended on his wrist and pinned it to the ground. It belonged to a brawny constable who loomed over him.

'Have they not suffered enough?' said Jonathan Bale solemnly. 'Their home has already been destroyed by fire. Must they also have their last few possessions stolen by a common thief?'

'They will not miss a bottle or two of wine,' said the man

with an ingratiating smirk, trying to turn his captor into an accomplice. 'Let us each take what we want and nobody will be any the wiser.'

'*I* will, my friend.'

'Then you have it all, Constable.'

'I want none of your stolen goods.'

'It is fine wine and good cheese.'

'The people who bought it are entitled to enjoy it.' Jonathan gave a grim smile. 'That is why you are going to put it back where you found it.'

The man was horrified. 'Put it back?'

'Every last bottle. Every piece of cheese.'

'But it is such a waste.'

'Do as I tell you.'

'There may be gold or valuables down there as well,' said the thief, pointing with his free hand. 'Why not let me dig down to find out? We might both end up as rich men.'

'You will end up in prison, my friend. Trespass is the first charge. Theft, the second. Trying to corrupt a constable, the third. Now, put everything back where you found it before I lose my patience.' He lifted his foot to release the man. 'Hurry up. I will wait.'

Protesting loudly, the man did as he was ordered and replaced the wine and cheese in the pit before filling it with earth then patting it with the flat of his shovel. He stood up to stamp it more firmly into place. His predicament was dire. Caught in the act, he could expect to suffer the full severity of the law. That left him with one last option. Still holding the shovel, he tightened his grip on it and swung it viciously at Jonathan's head. The constable was ready for him. He ducked beneath the tool then countered with a solid punch to the jaw which sent his assailant reeling backwards. As the man fell heavily to the ground, he dropped the shovel and Jonathan kicked it clear. Still dazed, the thief was pulled roughly to his feet and dragged back through the empty house.

The two watchmen who had been stationed outside were elderly men but their combined strength was more than enough to cope with the prisoner now that all the fight had been knocked out of him. Jonathan handed the man over to his colleagues. One of them, Abraham Datchett, a spry character in his sixties, got a firm grip on the malefactor.

'Another thief?' he enquired.

'The worst kind,' said Jonathan. 'He tried to bribe me into silence.'

'More fool him!'

'Take him to the magistrate and see him locked up.'

'We will, Jonathan.'

'I will make a full report when I come off duty.'

'What was he trying to steal?'

'Wine and cheese. Oh, yes,' said Jonathan with a grin, 'and he decided to take my head with him for good measure. But I ducked just in time. Away with the rogue, Abraham. He deserves no mercy.'

The watchmen hauled their prisoner off between them and the constable continued his rounds. Guarding damaged properties was one of his main tasks. Even derelict houses like this one might yield some booty. It was one of the more depressing effects of the Great Fire. Loss for the many had been offset by excessive gain for the few. Watermen, carriers and others who assisted fleeing householders increased their charges to exorbitant levels for customers who were in no position to refuse to pay. There were at least some shards of legality about this practice though it had no moral justification.

But there was nothing remotely legal about the epidemic of burglary which broke out as bold thieves ransacked houses which had been abandoned in the path of the fire or, as now, climbed into the garden of a derelict property to search for items which might have been buried there. When he had not been manning a fire post, Jonathan Bale had spent the past week pursuing and arresting the vultures who preyed on the misfortunes of others. His worst case had been in Knightrider Street where two thieves, gaining access to the garden of a deserted house, dug strenuously until they found a strongbox under the ground. They were so elated that friendship was instantly forgotten and they fought each other for sole possession of the bounty. By the time Jonathan arrived on the scene, only one man was still alive to be arrested.

Fire, destruction, panic, murder, burglary, trespass, mob violence and shameless profiteering. A desperate week for London. Jonathan watched his city mangled out of all recognition. One of the most startling changes was to the distinctive sound of the capital on a Sunday morning. Instead of the jangling harmonies of a hundred or more bells, calling the populace to worship, there was comparative silence. It was eerie. Most churches had been demolished and some of those that survived had lost their congregations temporarily to the outer suburbs. The few bells which did toll had a forlorn and apologetic note to them.

Jonathan's steps took him in the direction of Paul's Wharf and he was soon stopping to gaze wistfully at the ruins of St Peter's Church, once well attended, now deprived of its bell for ever. Those who lay in its little churchyard would be its only parishioners from now on. St Peter's was not the only casualty in the ward. The churches of St Andrew in the Wardrobe, St Mary Magdalene and St Benet Paul's Wharf had also fallen to the flames. The spiritual life of the community had been dealt a series of crippling blows. Jonathan was still looking at the devastation when he heard a familiar voice behind him.

'Do not expect me to mourn its passing, Mr Bale.'

'What is that?' said Jonathan, turning to face the newcomer.

'I am glad that it was levelled to the ground. That is where St Peter's truly belongs. It was a Cavalier church. When the Lord Protector ruled, this was a refuge for the nobility.'

'I know it well, Mr Thorpe.'

'I would gladly have lit the match which set it alight.'

'Then I would just as gladly have arrested you for the crime.'

'Where is the crime in driving out sin?'

Jesus-Died-To-Save-Me Thorpe was a short, slim man in his fifties with a cadaverous face out of which two large eyes shone like beacons. He was dressed in the black garb of the Quakers and wore a high-crowned black hat whose wide brim had been singed by fire. His voice had the natural power of an orator and Jonathan had heard it raised in denunciation many times. The constable enjoyed an uneasy relationship with his neighbour, admiring him for his courage but deploring the extremes to which Thorpe sometimes went. Slight and innocuous in repose, the man could be highly volatile when moved by the Holy Spirit.

'Your attire is too eloquent, Mr Thorpe,' he observed.

'I am not ashamed to be seen for what I am.'

'Take care it does not lead to a beating. There are still mad fools abroad who believe that the fire may have been started by Quakers and who take revenge on any of your sect they encounter.'

'Violence holds no fears for me,' said the other bravely. 'Jesus himself endured many blows in defence of his beliefs. I have done the same before and will do so again.'

Jonathan heaved a sigh and glanced back at St Peter's.

'Whatever you say, it was a fine old church. It will be a great loss.'

'Not to me, Mr Bale. I have a long memory.'

'Too long, I fear. It is time to look forward and not back.'

'Yes,' said the other, 'thou wouldst say that. Thou art a parish constable now with duties and responsibilities. Mr Jonathan Bale upholds the laws of this corrupt Parliament. It pains him to recall that he was once as true a Christian as myself.'

'I still am.'

'No, sir. Thou hast betrayed us and betrayed thyself.'

'That is a matter of opinion.'

'Thou art familiar with mine.'

'It has not been kept hidden from me, Mr Thorpe,' said

Jonathan with a wry smile. 'I hold fast to the beliefs which I have always held. Where you and I differ is in how they are best expressed.'

'Openly and defiantly.'

'That is the shortest route to the prison cell.'

'Why should we suffer punishment that others escaped?' said Thorpe, a bony finger raised in anger. 'Think back, Mr Bale. When this country was ruled by Parliament under the leadership of Lord Protector Cromwell, a due severity was introduced into church services. Not that we could accept the new liturgy ourselves,' he stressed. 'We wait in the grace and the truth that comes by Jesus. We need no liturgy and no priest to act as an intermediary between us and our God. And we were ready to suffer for those beliefs. But what of the congregation of St Peter's?' he demanded. 'Did they obey the law? No, Mr Bale. This church continued the hateful practice of dispensing the sacraments. So many members of the nobility flocked here that they hung the galleries with turkey carpets for the accommodation of those titled sinners. The Lord Protector should have torn the place down.'

'He was not given to defiling consecrated ground,' said Jonathan. 'But I am surprised to hear you speaking with some respect of him. If we must look to the past, let me remind you that the same Lord Protector treated the Society of Friends with great harshness. Hundreds were imprisoned at his command. You were one of them.'

'I wore my ordeal as a badge of honour.'

'What of your wife and children, Mr Thorpe? I venture to suggest that they might have preferred to have you at home with them instead of languishing in a cell with your badge of honour.'

'My family and I are all of one mind.'

Jonathan bit back his rejoinder. There was no point in arguing with a man like Jesus-Died-To-Save-Me Thorpe. He was a combative Christian who thrived on debate. Mocking the established religion was a serious offence, committed by a headstrong man who refused to swear the appropriate oaths and who declined to pay tithes for the maintenance of the Church he despised. A printer by trade, Thorpe was also suspected of writing and distributing religious tracts which fell foul of the law. It was almost as if he was challenging his companion to arrest him. Jonathan refused to assist him in his search for martyrdom. Though the man was profoundly irritating, the constable had a sneaking fondness for him.

'Go home, sir,' he advised softly. 'I have no quarrel with you. In a bleak time such as this, I look for small mercies. I am pleased that you and your family came through the fire without undue loss. Your house was largely spared its ravages. Most of us were not so fortunate.'

'Indeed not,' agreed the other with genuine compassion. 'It has been a time of trial. Thou art a victim, Mr Bale, I know and I am truly sorry. I came past thy house on Addle Hill today and saw again how little of it is left standing. Where are thy wife and children?'

'Staying with my parents in Hoxton.'

'Safe, then? That is good to hear.'

'Thank you for your concern.'

'We are neighbours, Mr Bale. I hoped at one time that

we could also be close friends. But thou hast chosen another path.'

'It leads in the same direction as yours.'

'I would dispute that, sir.'

'Then you must do so alone.'

'Art thou afraid to discuss thy spiritual life?'

'Good day, Mr Thorpe. I must continue my patrol.'

A note of disappointment. 'Thou art not going to arrest me?'

'Not when there are so many real criminals to apprehend.'

Before the man could reply, Jonathan touched his hat in polite farewell and moved away. He escaped lightly. Jesus-Died-To-Save-Me Thorpe was a kind, generous, sincere man of undoubted intelligence but there were times when he could be the verbal equivalent of the Great Fire, raging wildly and consuming everything in his conversational path. Other members of the Society of Friends in Truth waited patiently upon the Lord but Thorpe was altogether too restless to sit in silence. It was only a matter of time before his incendiary disposition landed him behind bars again and Jonathan did not wish to be the man who put him there.

He went north up St Peter's Hill, turned left into Knightrider Street then immediately right into Sermon Lane. Each step of the way took him past ruined houses, empty shops and deserted inns. Yet there were curious survivals – stables which were untouched, a smoke-blackened warehouse with little interior damage, an occasional brick-built property with a tiled roof which had somehow kept the fire at bay. Jonathan wondered if there was any significance in the fact that the home of Jesus-Died-To-Save-Me Thorpe was still standing while his own had collapsed in a heap. Was there some hidden pattern to the Great Fire?

Carter Lane was another scene of carnage, a main thoroughfare which had been largely reduced to rubble, throwing untold numbers of people out of their homes and workplaces, and inflicting a gaping wound on the city. Taverns which had once throbbed with life now lay dead. Civic buildings which had stood like proud sentinels were no more than empty shells. Dozens of people milled about but they looked dispirited and lethargic. The customary bustle of Carter Lane had gone. It was a street of ghosts.

Jonathan picked his way through the debris and went on up to St Paul's churchyard. He was now at the very heart of London, staring in dismay at a cathedral which pumped out the life-blood of the whole city. St Paul's was at once the spiritual centre of the community and its main meeting-place, a venue for buying, selling, preaching, arguing or simply promenading with friends. As the constable knew only too well, it was also the haunt of criminals of all kinds, drawn by the prospect of easy pickings from the large crowds who came there, containing, as they did, such prime targets as gullible countrymen and foreign sightseers. Souls might be saved in St Paul's Cathedral but small fortunes had been lost within its portals and outside in its churchyard.

It was a depressing sight. Jonathan had ambivalent feelings about the great edifice but he felt shocked to see it in such a deplorable state. The roof had burnt and left the whole building exposed in the most undignified manner. What made the fire more damaging was the fact that hundreds of Londoners had used the cathedral as their place of refuge, carrying their goods to what they deemed to be a place of safety and filling the nave with furniture, clothing, curtains, carpets, paintings and other combustible material, unwittingly providing the fuel for a huge bonfire, its heat so intense that it had melted the bells which hung in the tower. The sight of St Paul's in ruins and still smoking provided the most vivid demonstration of the true extent of the catastrophe.

Hundreds of people had congregated around the building. Some came to pray, others to stare, others to walk disconsolately among the gravestones. The person who caught Jonathan's attention belonged to none of these groups. Sitting alone on a stone tomb, he was poring over a sheet of paper supported on a wooden board, sketching with a piece of charcoal and glancing up from time to time at the grim scene before him. The young man, handsome and well-groomed, was dressed almost to the point of elegance and looked incongruous among the shuffling citizens around him. While they were drab and demoralised, the artist seemed to be bristling with excitement. Jonathan's curiosity was aroused.

He was still watching as an old woman slowly approached the man. Dressed in rags, she hobbled along with the aid of a wooden crutch. Straggly hair poked out from beneath the tattered scarf which covered most of her head. Coming up behind the artist, she looked over his shoulder to see what he was drawing then inched closer until she pressed up against him. The woman backed away at once and cringed in apology, expecting at least a reprimand, if not a curse or even a blow. But the young man gave her a smile and beckoned her forward to take a proper look at his work, showing it off with evident pride. After studying it for a minute or so, the woman nodded in approval, gave him a wave of thanks and hobbled off. The artist tossed her a sympathetic glance before returning to his task.

Jonathan Bale showed her far less indulgence. When she drew level with him, he launched himself forward to grab her by the shoulders. A fierce struggle ensured. Dropping the crutch, the woman fought hard to break free and screamed in anger. The constable was just managing to subdue her when the artist came running over.

'Unhand her, you ruffian!' he ordered.

'Stay out of this, sir,' said Jonathan, still wrestling with his quarry.

'Let her go or you'll answer to me.'

The young man accompanied his threat with such a strong push that he knocked the constable off balance and forced him to release his hold on the woman. To the astonishment of all who were watching, she hitched up her skirts and, showing signs neither of age nor disability, ran off at speed towards Paternoster Row. The artist was utterly baffled.

'What's this?' he asked.

'You have just helped a clever criminal to escape, sir,' said the angry constable. 'I was trying to make an arrest.'

'Why?'

'Because I saw him robbing you.'

'Him? I took her for a poor old woman.'

'That is what you were meant to do, sir. But that poor old woman is younger than you. His real name is Tom Fogge and he is as cunning a pickpocket as you will have the misfortune to encounter.'

'A pickpocket?'

'Yes, sir,' said the other. 'While you thought he was admiring your drawing, Tom Fogge was helping himself to your purse.' The young man's hand went immediately to his pocket. 'You will not find it, sir, for I have it here in my hand.' He held it up for inspection. 'I managed to get it from him before you interrupted us. Had you been less rash, I might have recovered all the other things which he probably stole.'

The young man took a step back, spread both arms and shrugged.

'What can I say, Constable? I was foolhardy.'

'That is the kindest word to apply.'

'Choose one of your own.'

'It is the Sabbath, sir. I will not profane it.'

The young man tensed and seemed about to issue a rebuke but the moment quickly passed. Instead, he burst out laughing at himself. He also scrutinised the constable's big, oval face with its prominent nose and its square jaw. Two warts on the left cheek and a livid scar across the forehead turned a pleasant appearance into an ugly one but there was real character in the face. His dark eyes still smouldered.

'I owe you an apology,' said the young man.

'Take your purse back,' said the other, handing it over.

'And you deserve my gratitude as well. Who did you say he was?'

'Tom Fogge.'

'Does he always dress as an old woman?'

'No, sir,' explained Jonathan. 'That would make it too easy for us to pick him out. Tom uses many disguises. I did not recognise him until I saw him brush against you like that. He has a swift hand.'

'Not swift enough to elude you.'

'Foins and foists belong in prison.'

'Foins and what?'

'Pickpockets. St Paul's is one of their favourite places of business.'

'Not any more,' said the artist, turning to gaze at it. 'It is a mere shadow of what it once was. I was trying to capture it on paper before it is knocked down to make way for a new cathedral. It was once one of the largest churches in Christendom and had the tallest spire in the whole world until it was struck by lightning. Even in this parlous state, it has a rare magnificence.'

'All I can see are ruins, sir.'

'That is because you do not have the eye of an artist. Come,' he said, crooking a finger. 'Let me show you.' He led the constable across to the stone tomb on which a sheaf of papers lay. 'Here,' he continued, picking one up to offer to him. 'Does this not have real splendour?'

Jonathan took the drawing and marvelled at it. Though it was executed with charcoal, it had extraordinary precision and verisimilitude. Every detail had been included and, as he looked up at the cathedral once more, Jonathan could find no discrepancy. The one difference between reality and art lay in the spirit which animated the drawing. What the artist had somehow done was to transform a scene of unrelieved desolation into one of strange beauty. His drawing was a celebration of architectural grandeur.

'Well?' said the young man.

'It is good, sir,' conceded the other. 'Very good.'

'Inspiring?'

'To some degree.'

'You like it, then?'

'I find it...interesting, sir,' said Jonathan, unable to tear his gaze away from the drawing. 'You have captured everything there is to see yet added something else besides. What it is, I do not yet know but I will find it soon. Yes,' he murmured. 'It is a fine piece of work.'

'Keep it.'

'Keep it?' repeated Jonathan in surprise.

'As a reward for recovering my stolen purse. It is the least that I can offer you. I can see that you are taken with it. Have it.'

'But it is yours, sir.'

'It is only one of several that I have,' said the young man, indicating the sheaf of papers. 'Do you see? I have two other drawings from this angle and three from the west side of the cathedral. Besides, I have tired of drawing what stands before me and have moved on to what ought to take its place. Look at this.'

He picked up the drawing which lay on the board and held it out for the constable to study it. Jonathan was frankly astounded. He had never seen anything so overwhelming in size and so stunning in conception. Where the old cathedral had a spireless tower, the new one was surmounted by a massive dome buttressed by paired columns. The facade featured a succession of pilastered columns and a portico which thrust out to lend additional sculptural impact. In place of the present churchyard was a vast piazza, enclosed by colonnades which reached out from the main building like giant arms of marble.

Jonathan glanced at the ruins then back at the drawing.

'Is *that* what you could see when you looked up?'

'In my mind's eye.'

'It is…'

'Amazing?' said the artist, fishing for compliments. 'Resplendent, ambitious, uplifting? Be honest, my friend.'

'It is like nothing I have ever seen.'

'That is because you have never been to Rome and imbibed the wonders of the Classical tradition. This is not so much a new design of St Paul's Cathedral as an English version of St Peter's in Rome.' He saw the scowl on the other's face. 'You disapprove?'

'Not of the drawing, sir. Only of its origin.'

'Too Catholic for your taste?'

'I prefer the cathedral we have just lost.'

'Yet that was built when England was of the Old Religion. Roman Catholic genius went into its design and building. True art should have no denomination,' said the young man, laying the drawing down. 'We should be free to borrow from all countries, whatever spiritual dimension they may have. I need to do far more work on the new St Paul's. You keep that drawing of the old one.'

'No, sir,' said Jonathan firmly.

'Why not?'

'I do not deserve it.'

'That is for me to judge. I may have the eye of an artist but you have the much more practical eye of a constable. While I was gazing into the future, you saw a pickpocket taking my purse. Hold on to the drawing in lieu of my thanks.'

'I do not wish to keep it, sir.'

'You are refusing the gift?'

'Yes, sir,' said Jonathan, handing it back to him. 'Excuse me.'

'Wait! You must not do this. It is a form of insult.'

'Then you brought it upon yourself.'

'Anybody else would have been delighted with such a drawing.'

'Give it to one of them.'

He tried to move away but the young man barred his way.

'Are you still angry with me because I stopped you from arresting that pickpocket? Is that what we have here? Pique and annoyance?'

'I could have done without your interference.'

'You had my apology. What more do you want?'

'Nothing, sir. I have duties to carry out.'

'What is to stop you taking my drawing with you?'

'My conscience.'

The constable pushed him gently aside and walked away.

'One moment,' called the other. 'What is your name?'

'Jonathan Bale,' he said over his shoulder.

'I am Christopher Redmayne and I am still grateful, however surly you choose to be.' He raised his voice at the departing figure. 'You are a sound officer. I will remember your name, Jonathan Bale.'

I have already forgotten yours,' said the other to himself.

CHAPTER FOUR

When the cost of the fire was finally counted, chilling figures emerged. Four hundred acres within the city wall had been destroyed along with a further sixty-three acres outside it. Eighty-seven churches perished, as did forty-four livery halls and upwards of thirteen thousand houses. Several million pounds' worth of property went up in smoke. Business and domestic life were severely disrupted. Some trades were virtually expunged. Morale sank to a lower ebb even than during the Great Plague when, as many sourly observed, people were at least allowed to die in the privacy of their own homes.

Death itself, however, had been unusually restrained. Apart from the hapless maidservants in Pudding Lane, it claimed only eight other victims during the blaze, though the number of fatalities increased during subsequent weeks as people died from delayed shock or sheer despair at the enormity of their losses. Confidence shattered, hundreds of Londoners vowed never to return to the city itself and either settled in the outer suburbs or sought a new life further afield. Ruined tradesmen had no choice but to go elsewhere. Unjustly persecuted in the aftermath of the fire, foreign inhabitants thought twice about taking up residence once more in such a vengeful community.

Notwithstanding all this, the capital displayed, in general, a spirit of resilience. If the setbacks were to be overcome, an immense collective effort was needed and most people responded at once. Those whose houses or workplaces had been only partially damaged moved back into them as soon as possible to institute repairs. Within a week of the end of the fire, a man in Blackfriars cleared away the ruins of his old house and began to build a new one on the same site. Others elected to follow suit but their plans were immediately frustrated.

On the thirteenth of September 1666, while the smoke was still rising from parts of the city, a Royal Proclamation was issued, prohibiting any hasty building and empowering the authorities to pull down any structures erected before new regulations were put into place. The haphazard growth of the city over the centuries, with its narrow streets, its close-built dwellings, its superfluity of timber-framed properties, its surviving thatch and its inadequate water supply had contributed to its own demise. It might almost have been designed to assist the rapid spread of a fire. Such a disaster, it was insisted, must never happen again. Safety would henceforth be a prime consideration.

Rebuilding commenced in earnest the following spring.

'We must bear the new regulations in mind,' said Henry Redmayne, sipping his coffee. 'No half-timbering is allowed. The house must be built entirely of brick and stone with a tiled roof.'

'I would accept nothing less,' said his companion.

'Nor must the upper storeys jetty out.'

'Such a style would, in any case, offend my taste.'

'It is gone for ever from our midst, Sir Ambrose.'

'Thank Heaven!'

'I could not agree more.'

'That was an incidental blessing of the fire. It cleared away decrepit old houses that had no right to exist and rid us of squalid lanes and alleys where the poorer sort lived in their miserable holes. Yes,' added the other with easy pomposity, 'I did not support every recommendation put before us by the Commission but, by and large, their suggestions were admirable. I was particularly pleased that noxious trades have been banned from the riverside. Those of us who import goods were assailed by the most unbearable stink whenever we went near the wharf.'

'The brewers and dyers were the worst, Sir Ambrose.'

'Then you have not smelt the lime-burners and the soap-makers when they are practising their craft. Add the reek of the salt-makers and you have a stench that stayed in the nostrils for days.'

'Just like the smoke from the Great Fire.'

'Yes, Henry. Exactly like that.'

'How long has it been now? Six months?'

'Over seven.'

'I still sometimes catch a whiff of that smoke.'

'Memory plays strange tricks on us.'

'Indeed, Sir Ambrose. It may torment us in perpetuity.'

Henry became solicitous. 'Was the coffee to your liking?'

'Excellent.'

'Let us order another cup.'

The two men were sitting in one of the most fashionable coffee houses in the city, swiftly refurbished now that decisions had finally been made about building regulations. Henry was at his most immaculate in a blue coat with extravagant gold braid and a red and green waistcoat. His new periwig lent him an air of distinction which made him even more a slave to his vanity and he kept appraising himself in an invisible mirror. Seated opposite him was Sir Ambrose Northcott, now almost fifty, a man of middle height and corpulent body who defied his many physical shortcomings with the aid of an expensive French tailor. Fleshy jowls were tinged with crimson and the nose was absurdly small for such a large face yet there were no wrinkles to betray his true age and the eyes had a youthful sparkle.

Northcott was an important man. Having inherited his title and a substantial fortune, he determined to improve himself even more and invested wisely in trade. A Justice of the Peace in his native Kent, he was also a Member of Parliament and took a vocal part in the discussions which touched on the future shape and composition of the capital. Henry Redmayne had cultivated him strenuously for years but he now had a more pressing reason to court him. Northcott wanted a new house built.

Henry made an urgent question sound like a casual enquiry.

'Have you had time to study those drawings, Sir Ambrose?'

'I made time, Henry.'

'What was your impression?'

'A most favourable one.'

'I am pleased to hear it.'

'Your brother has remarkable talent.'

'He does,' said Henry, basking in the praise. 'Christopher is a born artist. He has a most cultured hand. It has ever been so. I once saw him draw a perfect circle with a crayon.'

'Does this talent run in the family?'

'Unhappily, no. And even if it did, I would not waste it on a piece of paper. The only perfect circles I would draw would be those I traced with a fingertip around the nipples of a fair lady.'

Northcott laughed. 'Love has its own architecture.'

'With building regulations that are far more appealing!'

They exchanged a polite snigger. Northcott sat back in his chair.

'Tell me more about this brother of yours,' he said.

'That is precisely why I am here.'

'Is he a coming man?'

Henry needed no more invitation. After ordering fresh coffee, he launched into a eulogy which owed far more to fact than to fiction, glad that he was not obliged to lie too much about his brother. Christopher really did possess creative gifts which set him apart from most of his potential rivals and those gifts were allied to a capacity for hard work and a willingness to learn. As he held forth about his brother, Henry came to see just how rich and varied his education had been and how he merely needed something which would concentrate his mind in order for all that study to bear fruit. Delighted with what he heard, Northcott listened intently but he was far too cautious to be rushed to judgement.

'Your brother is very young to have achieved so much, Henry.'

'He is twice the man I was at his age, Sir Ambrose.'

'Yet somewhat lacking in practical experience of design.'

'What could be more practical than the drawings of his that I showed you? A reputable builder could turn any of them into a reality.'

'Some builders still prefer to design their own work.'

'Those days are fast disappearing,' said Henry expansively. 'An architect is indispensable if you wish for the highest standards. Master-builders had their value but they are in decline. Well, Sir Ambrose,' he continued, risking a familiar pat on the man's shoulder, 'can you imagine Christopher Wren working as a mason on St Paul's Cathedral or Hugh May mixing lime mortar for one of those exquisite houses he designs? It is unthinkable. Such men belong to a new and honourable elite – the profession of architect. I am proud to number my brother in their ranks.'

Cups of coffee arrived and Northcott pondered while he tasted his. A large amount of money would be expended on his London abode and a degree of emotional capital would be invested in it as well. It was vital to select the right person to design it.

'What of his character?' he asked.

'His character?'

'Yes, Henry. You have told me much about his history and his ambition. But what manner of man is Christopher Redmayne?'

'Dedicated to his work.'

'That might make him narrow-minded and possessive.'

'Far from it!'

'Is he amenable?'

'Completely, Sir Ambrose.'

'He can take orders? Accept criticism?'

'Christopher is yours to command.'

'What of his discretion?' said the other, lowering his voice. 'I do not want some wagging tongue to voice my business abroad. I require a man who does what he is paid for without asking any unnecessary questions. I need a politic man, willing but prudent. Conscientious and close. Not to put too fine a point on it, I am looking for total obedience.'

'You have just described my brother to perfection!'

'We shall see,' said Northcott with a contemplative nod. 'We shall see. If this paragon really does exist, then I will seriously consider him.'

'Thank you, Sir Ambrose.'

'Arrange a meeting.'

'You will not regret this, I do assure you.'

'Let me see the fellow for myself.'

'How soon?'

'At the earliest possible opportunity.'

Henry's smile broadened and he made an eloquent gesture.

'What a pleasing coincidence!' he said without a trace of irony. 'As luck would have it, I believe that Christopher may be in the next room. You can have the pleasure of meeting him immediately.'

* * *

When the servant rose shortly after dawn, he came downstairs with a taper to find his master slumped across the table, the candle beside him burnt to extinction. Jacob let out a wheeze of disapproval. He put a hand on Christopher's shoulder to shake him gently awake.

'Go to bed, sir,' he whispered. 'Let me help you upstairs.'

'What's that?' said the other drowsily.

'You need some proper rest, sir.'

'Where am I?'

'You fell asleep over your work. Go to bed.'

'No, no.' Christopher rubbed his eyes and shook himself awake. 'I have too much to do, Jacob. Far too much.'

'You have been saying that for weeks, sir. This is the third time in a row that you have stayed up all night to struggle with your drawings.'

'There is no struggle involved. It is a labour of love.'

'Show more love to yourself and less to your work,' advised the old man. 'Flesh and blood can only withstand so much, sir. You need sleep.'

'What I need is food and drink. A hearty breakfast will revive me in no time at all. Then I will be able to finish this last drawing.'

'Let it wait, sir.'

'There can be no delay, Jacob. Sir Ambrose expects the completed set today and he will get them. Everything is riding on this commission. It could be the start of a whole new career for me. That would mean money, Jacob. You would get your wages on time for a change. There is a lot at stake here. And whatever happens, I must not let my brother down. Henry went to great lengths to secure this opportunity for me. I must take full advantage of it.'

'Even if it means slaving away night and day?'

'Architecture is a cruel master.'

Jacob nodded. 'I will prepare your breakfast, sir.'

'One moment,' said Christopher, raising a palm to detain him. 'Open those shutters to let in some light then come and see what I was doing while you were slumbering upstairs. I have not been idle.'

'That is my complaint,' muttered the other.

He opened the shutters, lit a fresh candle with his taper then carried it back to the table. Christopher proudly spread out his drawings.

'Here we are,' he said, beaming at his work. 'What do you think?'

'My opinion is worthless, sir.'

'Not to me, Jacob.'

'I know nothing about designing a house.'

'Just tell me if you would like to live in this one.'

He stood back so that his servant could have a clear view. The old man ran a watery eye over each drawing, moving from one to the other with increasing admiration. He scratched his head in awe. The one over which he lingered most was a drawing of the front elevation of the house. It was a handsome abode with a regular facade, neat rectilinear outlines and square-headed doors and windows. Six stone steps, into which an iron handrail had been set, led up to a portico which comprised elegant pillars with a flat entablature and low pediment. The house bore little resemblance to the Tudor dwellings which proliferated in the city of Jacob's youth and was entirely free from the Gothic extravagances which adorned so many public buildings before the Great Fire.

Jacob was especially impressed with the sash windows, a Dutch invention now taken up with enthusiasm in England. There were eighteen in all, including two which served the attic rooms. The old man wondered how many more windows the house contained and which unfortunate servant would be given the task of keeping them all clean.

'It is pretty, sir,' he said respectfully. 'Very, very pretty.'

'Thank you, Jacob.'

'Anyone would be privileged to live in such a place,'

'I hope that Sir Ambrose Northcott shares your high opinion.'

'If he does not, he must be blind. One question, if I may, sir,' he said, pointing to the first of the drawings. 'Why are the cellars so large?'

'That was the express wish of my client.'

'What does he wish to keep down there?'

'Whatever he wishes, Jacob. Mine is not to question the use to which he puts the cellars. All I know is that Sir Ambrose was most particular about their extent and design. This elaborate vaulting will test the skill of the bricklayers but it is vital in order to support the weight of the house itself. I regard the cellars as a minor triumph. The pity of it is that very few people will ever get to admire the work I put into them.'

'*I* admire it, sir.'

'That is praise enough for me.'

'The whole house is fit for a king.'

'Sir Ambrose would be flattered by such a thought.'

'The only thing is...' He broke off as he peered at the front elevation again. 'I mean no disrespect, sir.'

'Go on.'

'The only thing is, sir, it looks a bit, well...foreign.'

'That is the French influence.'

'Ah.'

'Specifically ordered.' He grinned. 'Like my breakfast.'

'I will get it for you at once, sir,' said Jacob, heading for the kitchen. 'No man can work on an empty stomach. Though I still think that you should take a nap to get your strength back.'

Christopher did not hear him. He was already immersed in his work again, studying each of the drawings with a searching eye to make sure that every detail was correct and that it contributed properly to the overall symmetry of the house. He did not need his brother to tell him how important the commission was. Apart from putting much-needed revenue into his purse, it was a chance for Christopher Redmayne to establish himself as an architect. In a highly visible profession, success was its own best advertisement. If the house for Sir Ambrose Northcott caught the eye and won general esteem, other commissions would assuredly follow and Christopher would be able to play his part in the exciting work of rebuilding a great city.

Close to the ruins of Baynard's Castle, it was a prime site. The new regulations forbade the building of houses along the riverbank itself so the dwelling was set well back from it. Enclosed by a high stone wall, the long garden ran almost down to the Thames and the rear windows of the house afforded an uninterrupted view both of the river and of the one remaining turret of the castle. Sir Ambrose Northcott was thrilled with this prospect, combining, as it did, reality with romance, the busy world of commerce floating past on the water with the noble profile of a derelict fortress. When darkness fell, the lone turret would be silhouetted against the moonlit sky. It would make an evocative neighbour.

When work first began on the site, he visited it every day.

'What progress have you made, Mr Littlejohn?' he asked.

'Small steps forward, Sir Ambrose,' said the other. 'Small but significant steps forward.'

'When will the cellars be completed?'

'According to schedule.'

'Good. I will hold you to that, Mr Littlejohn.'

'You will not find me wanting. May I say what an honour it is to work on such a project, Sir Ambrose?'

'Then do not allow any slacking among your men.'

'There is no danger of that.'

'The house must be ready on time.'

'I have never failed a client yet.'

Samuel Littlejohn was a sturdy fellow of middle years with a rubicund face and a jovial manner. He positively exuded bonhomie. A successful builder even before the fire, he was now in greater demand than ever and Northcott had to include many financial inducements in his contract in order to secure him. Littlejohn not only had a reputation for building sound houses to the exact specifications of his clients, he invariably did so within the stipulated period of time. He was a wealthy man who dressed well but, if occasion demanded, he was not averse to taking off his coat and soiling his hands by helping his employees. He could teach the best of them how to lay bricks and his carpentry was a source of envy. Samuel Littlejohn enjoyed every aspect of his work.

'You have chosen your architect well,' he said approvingly.

'That is what I believe,' returned Northcott. 'I thought about it long and hard before I reached my decision. Because of his youth, I had grave doubts at first but they are fast vanishing.'

'Mr Redmayne understands building.'

'He came with the highest recommendation.'

'It was justified.'

'I am glad that you and he have such an affinity, Mr Littlejohn.'

'It makes all the difference, Sir Ambrose. When an architect and builder do not work happily together, it shows in the finished structure. The opposite is also true,' he added with a chuckle. 'Bricks and mortar glow. Stonework gleams. Windows seem to glitter. When your house is built by men who are in accord, it will have a broad smile on its face.'

'So will I, if it is ready on the date agreed.'

'You have my word, Sir Ambrose.'

'That is good enough for me, Mr Littlejohn.'

The builder was diverted by the arrival of a boat-load of timber and he excused himself to supervise the unloading. Northcott surveyed the site with a deep satisfaction then walked slowly around its perimeter. He could almost see the finished house rising before his eyes. The omens were good. Everything was proceeding exactly as he wished. He strolled across to the trestle table on which Christopher Redmayne had spread out his drawings so that the builders could work from them. Like his employer, the architect was on site every day.

'Do you foresee any problems, Christopher?' asked Northcott.

'Not at the moment, Sir Ambrose,' said the other, looking up. 'We seem to have it all under control. Mr Littlejohn's men work hard.'

'I look to him to keep them at it.'

'He will most certainly do so. You could not have engaged a more experienced builder. In the short time we have been acquainted, I have learnt a great deal from him. He has my admiration.'

'You have certainly earned his.'

'Then I am profoundly flattered.' He glanced towards the river. 'You have selected an excellent site here, Sir Ambrose, and the fact that you have a private jetty is a huge bonus. Materials which would otherwise have to be delivered to some busy wharf upstream can be brought to the very bottom of your garden.'

'It was a feature which attracted me to the property.'

'An appealing situation for a merchant.'

'Trade is only a small part of my life,' said Northcott with a frown. 'I could never be described as a mere merchant.'

'Quite so,' agreed Christopher, anxious not to offend him. 'You have many other arrows to your bow, Sir Ambrose, I know. There must be few men of consequence in London with a quiver as full as yours.'

'Very few.'

'Your talents are so copious. Henry is astounded by your vigour.'

A sly smile. 'Your brother has his occasional bursts of energy.'

'But nothing like your staying-power, Sir Ambrose. He is in awe of you, believe me. Henry has his gifts but he could not do half the things which you contrive to do.'

Northcott was mollified. Christopher had a winning politeness and a readiness to please his employer. Northcott was growing to like him. For his part, Christopher was still too grateful to his companion to have any reservations about his character. Northcott could be peremptory at times and downright rude if there was the slightest questioning of his decisions but the architect took all that in his stride, constantly aware that he who pays the piper calls the tune. Christopher was more than content to play it for him and, in Samuel Littlejohn, he had an ideal musical ally. The two of them worked together in perfect harmony.

'This will be my last visit for a little while,' said Northcott.

'Oh? I am sorry to hear that.'

'I will be away on business for a fortnight or more. When I come back, I hope to see that substantial progress has been made.'

'We will not disappoint you, Sir Ambrose.'

'During my absence, Mr Creech will be in charge of my affairs.'

'Mr Creech?'

'Solomon Creech is my lawyer,' explained the other.

'All monies due to you or to Mr Littlejohn will be released through him. I have also asked him to keep a close eye on developments here so you will very soon be making his acquaintance.'

'I look forward to that. Away for a fortnight, you say?'

'At least.'

'Will you be returning home to Kent?'

'That is my business,' said the other with a note of reprimand.

'Of course, Sir Ambrose,' said Christopher. 'It is not my place to pry into your affairs. I merely wished to know if there was some means of getting in touch with you in the event of a contingency arising here.'

'Speak to my lawyer.'

'Will Mr Creech have ready access to you?'

'He is empowered to act on my behalf.'

'Then nothing more need be added on the subject.'

'Nothing at all, Christopher.'

His remark was buttressed by a mild glare. Christopher accepted the rebuke with good grace and sought to win back Northcott's approval. He drew his employer's attention to the drawings and the two of them were soon bent over the trestle table, discussing every detail of the house. Their mutual enthusiasm for the project quickly repaired the minor rift between them and they conversed for almost an hour. By the time they finished, Northcott's good humour had returned and he even felt able to pat his architect on the back.

'It will be one of the finest houses in London,' he said.

'You must take the credit for that, Sir Ambrose.'

'I had the sense to choose the right architect and the right builder.'

'You also purchased the best possible site,' Christopher reminded him with a sweep of his arm. 'It is so appealing in every way, I am surprised that its previous owner was ready to part with it.'

'When his home went up in the blaze, he lost heart.'

'Could he not build a replica in its place?'

'He lacked the funds to do so,' said the other, 'and, though he will argue his case in the fire court, he can look for very little compensation from that quarter. I seized opportunity by the forelock and made him an offer which he was unable to refuse.'

'I am heartily glad that you did so, Sir Ambrose.'

'So am I – now that we have agreed on the design. Everything is as I would wish. But I must away,' said Northcott, suddenly conscious of the time. 'I have important appointments today and I must call on my lawyer to give him his instructions. He will shortly be in touch with you.'

He waved a farewell then went off for a final word with Littlejohn. Christopher pored over his drawings once more, untroubled by the many compromises he had been forced to make between artistic impulse and the demands of his client. Given a free hand, he would have opted for a slightly plainer style and resisted all of the French flourishes which had been incorporated but it was still a piece of work of which he was quite inordinately proud and it would gain him considerable attention when it finally took its place in the new landscape.

Christopher was still revelling in his good fortune when he became aware that he was being watched. It was not an intrusive surveillance. Indeed, it seemed to wash gently over him like a benign wave and caused him to look up. The young woman was no more than a dozen yards away, her gaze fixed on him, her teeth showing in an open-mouthed smile of admiration. She was slim, comely and elegant in a dress composed of several shades of blue yet there was a slight nervousness in her manner which vitiated her poise. Christopher put her at no more than eighteen or nineteen and he wondered why she was loitering alone in such a place. She held his gaze for a full minute before modestly lowering her lids. His curiosity stirred and conducted an approving scrutiny.

Samuel Littlejohn ambled slowly over to the architect.

'You have made a conquest, I think,' he noted.

'How?'

'Margaret was so enamoured of your design for the house that she insisted she be given the chance to meet you.'

'Margaret? You know the young lady?'

'Extremely well,' said the other with a grin. 'She is my daughter.'

'And a beautiful one at that, Mr Littlejohn.'

His courteous observation drew an immediate response. Margaret Littlejohn met his eyes once more and stared into them with an intensity which bordered on yearning. Christopher was taken aback. The last thing he expected to do amid piles of building materials was to excite the interest of an attractive young woman. A pleasing sensation surged through him and produced an involuntary smile of his own. It was a thrilling moment but it soon passed.

Without quite knowing why, he suddenly sensed danger.

CHAPTER FIVE

The pilfering began almost immediately. Because only small quantities were stolen each time, the theft went unnoticed at first but it eventually became too obvious to ignore. Stone suffered the least. Bricks were taken in dozens and timber, reserved for joists, floorboards, window frames and roof trusses, was spirited away in slightly larger consignments. Expensive lead, destined for the roof, also vanished mysteriously in the night. When the losses came to the attention of Solomon Creech, he howled with rage.

'I blame you for this, Mr Littlejohn,' he accused.

'Why, sir?' said the builder. 'I did not steal it.'

'It is your duty to protect the property.'

'I have tried to do so, Mr Creech, but it still seems to trickle away. We had a nightwatchman on guard last night and even his presence did not deter these villains. Somehow they managed to strike again.'

'Then your nightwatchman is their confederate,' argued the lawyer, waving a scrawny hand. 'Did that not occur to you as a possibility?'

'It was my first thought. I questioned him closely about it but he pleaded innocence.'

'He is innocent of abetting the thefts,' said Christopher. 'I am sure of that. But I suspect he may be guilty of something else.'

'Keep out of this, Mr Redmayne,' snapped Creech.

'I am directly involved in the matter, sir.'

'You only muddy the waters of this discussion.'

'I am trying to help, Mr Creech.'

'Your help is merely a hindrance.'

'Mr Redmayne has the right to an opinion,' said Littlejohn, coming to his defence. 'If there is a delay in the building of the house – or if costs rise sharply because of these thefts – then Sir Ambrose is likely to swinge both me and Mr Redmayne.'

'He will have you hanged, drawn and quartered!' wailed Creech. 'And I will not escape his displeasure. That is why this crime must be solved forthwith and the stolen property recovered.' The scrawny hand fluttered again. 'I hold you responsible for this, Mr Littlejohn. Until you resolve the matter, I will not release any further monies to you.'

'But I need the capital to replace what we have lost.'

'Pay for it out of your own purse.'

'We have a contract, sir.'

'It has been abrogated by your incompetence. Before he left,' said Creech imperiously, 'Sir Ambrose entrusted all his affairs to me. I have discretionary powers with regard to the release of funds and you will not see another penny until my demand is met.'

Christopher had to resist the urge to punch the lawyer and even the builder's geniality was put under severe strain. The two men traded a knowing glance. Neither of them liked Solomon Creech. He was a tall, angular, pigeon-chested man in a crumpled black coat and a misshapen hat. His shoulders had been rounded so much by thirty years in the service of the law that he was almost hunchbacked. Protruding front teeth were the main feature in an unprepossessing face and they were bared in a snarl that morning. By the time he arrived on site to chastise the two men, he had worked himself up into a real fury. Christopher Redmayne and Samuel Littlejohn had to call on their last reserves of patience and tolerance.

The lawyer stamped his foot and sent up a small cloud of dust.

'So?' he demanded. 'What do you intend to do about it?'

'The first thing I will do,' said Littlejohn firmly, 'is to invite a comment from Mr Redmayne.'

'His comments are irrelevant.'

'Nevertheless,' insisted Christopher, squaring up to him. 'I will give them. Were he here, I am sure that Sir Ambrose would want to hear what I have to say. If you do not, close your ears while I speak to Mr Littlejohn.'

'Well?' encouraged the builder. 'You said earlier that you thought the nightwatchman might be guilty of something else.'

'Yes,' said Christopher. 'Drunkenness. He is far too honest to be in league with any thieves but he is also elderly and prone to fatigue. I believe that he drank himself into a stupor here last night. That is why the thieves were able to strike again.'

'What proof do you have, Mr Redmayne?'

'Only this,' said the other, holding up an empty flagon. 'It was hidden under the tarpaulin near the nightwatchman's bench. My guess is that he brought this for companionship, drank it to keep himself awake but found that it only made him slumber more soundly.'

'Dismiss the wretch!' cried the lawyer. I'll bring an action against him for dereliction of duty.'

'That is the last thing we must do,' said Christopher firmly. 'The nightwatchman may be our one asset in this business.'

'Asset!'

'Yes, Mr Creech.'

'A drunken nightwatchman is an *asset?*'

'If he is seen on duty again tonight, the thieves may be tempted to strike *again*. Cover the site with additional guards and they will be frightened away completely.' Christopher gave a shrug. 'What chance will we have then of apprehending them and recovering our property?'

Littlejohn nodded sagely. 'Mr Redmayne has hit the mark.'

'I fail to see how,' complained Creech. 'It sounds like madness.'

'Humour us for one night,' said Christopher. 'We are only dealing with two or three men. That is why they take away the lighter materials and leave most of the stone and the lead. They are limited in what they can carry. They must rob us piecemeal. I have a theory, Mr Creech. Let me put it to the test.'

'And lose even more of our building materials? Never!'

'Nothing else will be stolen, I assure you.'

'How do you know?'

'Trust me, Mr Creech.'

'Why? Will the nightwatchman stay awake tonight?'

'Oh, no,' said Christopher with a smile. 'He will doze off even sooner. I will buy him a flagon of beer myself to make sure that he does not get in anyone's way. The last thing we need is a nightwatchman who actually stays awake throughout the night.'

Over thirty of them attended the meeting but they took care to leave at intervals in twos and threes. Under the terms of the Clarendon Code, a gathering of more than five adults for the purposes of worship was considered to be an unlawful assembly. If they were caught, heavy fines would be imposed. Persistent offenders could be imprisoned or even transported and Jesus-Died-To-Save-Me Thorpe belonged in that category. He was the last to slip out of the house. He had no fears for himself but family responsibilities weighed upon him. His wife, Hail-Mary, was ill and unable to attend the Quaker meeting that night. She needed him to look after her. It was a bad time for him to be apprehended so he was obliged to exercise discretion for once.

There was another reason why he had to avoid arrest. Concealed under his coat were the remaining copies of a pamphlet which he had written and printed for distribution to the Friends. His views *On The Evils Of The Established Church* were trenchant and they would lead to severe punishment if they fell into the hands of the authorities.

Carrying such forbidden tracts on his person gave him a feeling of righteous power but it was tempered by the caution brought on by worries about Hail-Mary Thorpe's illness. Her husband had to get back to her safely. Since she was upset that she had missed the meeting, he decided to console her by reading his pamphlet to her once again. It would be a form of medicine.

It was late as he wended his way home. Part of his journey took him along the riverbank and he could hear the Thames lapping greedily at the wharves. Many warehouses had now been rebuilt and commercial activity restored to an area blighted by the fire. Thorpe walked swiftly, glad that there were so few people about at that hour. He was leaving Queenhithe Ward when the three men lurched out ahead of him. Instinctively he stepped into a doorway, his black garb merging with the darkness to make him virtually invisible. He tightened his hold on the pamphlets beneath his coat.

Evidently, the men had not long come from a tavern. One of them paused to relieve himself against a wall and broke wind loudly at the same time. The others walked on a few paces then stopped. They were close enough to him for Thorpe to smell the ale on their breath and to hear their low whispers.

'Let us go back,' urged one. 'The nightwatchman is alone again.'

'It is too dangerous,' said another.

'Not if the old man is asleep.'

'We may not be so lucky this time.'

'Then we make our own luck,' insisted the first man, fingering the cudgel under his belt. 'We put him to sleep.

One blow will be enough. We could steal every stone from Baynard's Castle before he woke up again.'

'No, I am against it.'

'Are you turning coward?'

'You know me better than that.'

'Then why hold back?'

'If we harm the old man, a hue and cry will be raised.'

'Hours later – when we are well away. I say we do it.'

'Do what?' asked the third man, lumbering over to them.

'Go back again. One more time.'

'Yes,' agreed the newcomer. 'Take all we can and fill the boat. We have never had such easy pickings. The bricks and timber are there for the taking. The house even has its own jetty. What could be better?'

They rehearsed their plans for a few minutes then linked arms before moving off. Jesus-Died-To-Save-Me Thorpe was in a quandary. Wanting to challenge them and denounce them for their sinfulness, he was realistic enough to see the folly of such an action. They would respond with violence. His wife wanted her husband at her side, not lying in a pool of blood in a dark street. Yet Thorpe was impelled to take some action. Everything about the three men offended his sensibilities. A feeling of outrage coursed through him. He watched them go then stepped out of his hiding place. Keeping to the shadows, he trailed them carefully as they made their way towards the ruins of Baynard's Castle.

The nightwatchman was hopelessly confused. When the theft was first discovered, he was all but accused by Samuel Littlejohn of being a party to the crime yet twelve hours later, as he came on duty again, the old man was given a handsome apology by the builder and a large flagon of beer by the architect. It made him resolve to discharge his office with more care that night.

Good intentions were not enough. Loneliness soon began to peck away at his resolution and fatigue slowly set in. He tried to stave off the latter by walking around the site and checking that all was well but his legs quickly tired and his lids began to droop. The flagon of beer was inevitably pressed into service. The first few swigs revived him for a while and he was confident that he could, after all, remain awake at his post all night. He allowed himself one more long drink. It was fatal.

Watching him from the bottom of the garden, the three thieves were growing restless. They had been there for well over an hour now. It was a starlit night and they had a good view of the whole site. They could see the nightwatchman in dark profile, lifting the flagon to his lips. The man with the cudgel took it out in readiness.

'The old fool will never go to sleep!' he grumbled.

'We cannot wait much longer,' said a second man.

'We'll not wait at all. I'll knock him out.'

'Hold!' advised the third man. 'I think he is going to lie down.'

The nightwatchman could no longer maintain the pretence of being diligent. It was good beer and its seductive taste could not be resisted. He emptied the whole flagon. By the time he discarded it, he was barely able to sit upright on his bench. A short nap was urgently required. Summoning up the last of his strength, he hauled himself off the bench and staggered across to a pile of soft earth, dug from the ground to create space for the cellars. It made an inviting bed. No sooner had he stretched himself on its gentle gradient than he fell asleep. Gentle snores rose up into the night air.

After waiting a short while, the man with the cudgel crept furtively up the garden to investigate. Weapon raised, he stood menacingly over the nightwatchman but he was not called upon to strike. The old man was fast asleep and unlikely to be roused by any sounds. After beckoning his companions, the thief made his way across to the tarpaulin which covered the building materials and which had been protection enough until the pilfering began. Stakes had been hammered into the ground so that the tarpaulin could be tied to them and thus rendered safe against high winds. Since it would be their last visit to the site, there was no point in untying the ropes, then later retying them to their stakes, as they had done on previous occasions when trying to conceal their theft. A knife was used to cut through the ropes then two of the men held a corner each of the tarpaulin and drew it back to expose their target.

Expecting to see nothing more than piles of bricks and stacks of timber, they were taken completely unawares when two figures suddenly sprang out at them. Christopher Redmayne unleashed his pent-up rage by flinging himself at one of the thieves and knocking him to the ground. Samuel Littlejohn, sweating profusely from his close confinement beneath the tarpaulin, grappled with another man and showed no mercy. It was not simply a case of apprehending the thieves. Architect and builder alike wanted revenge. They were possessive about their house. It had been defiled by intruders. It made the pair of them rain hard, unforgiving blows on their respective quarries.

Still free, the man with the cudgel did not know whether to save himself or help his fellows. In the event, self-interest won his vote. After a few ineffective swings at Littlejohn with his cudgel, he took to his heels and raced towards the boat which was moored at the jetty. He did not get far. Lurking in the shadows was a bulky figure who stepped out to block his way. The cudgel swung again but the blow was easily parried by a staff. Before the thief could defend himself, the end of the staff jabbed deep into his stomach to take the wind out of him then it clipped him hard on the side of the head. He dropped his cudgel and fell.

Jonathan Bale caught him before he hit the ground.

'Come, sir,' he said. 'Let us get you back to your fellows.'

The constable gave a call and three watchmen came out of their hiding place to take charge of the thief. When they had deprived him of a dagger, they dragged him up the garden of the house.

Surprise had been decisive in catching the other men. Swiftly overpowered, they now lay groaning on the ground. Christopher stood over them with a sword in his hand while Littlejohn used an arm to wipe the perspiration from his brow. Blood dripped from the builder's cheek but it was not his own. It belonged to the man whose lip he had opened with his angry knuckles. Littlejohn was now panting heavily but delighted with his night's work.

'We did well, Mr Redmayne,' he boasted. 'Very well.'

'Not well enough,' said Christopher. 'We only caught two of them.'

'The third is also taken,' announced a voice. 'I had thought to arrest all three myself but it seems that you have done my office for me.'

Christopher and Littlejohn were amazed to see the constable coming towards them with the thieves' accomplice in the grip of the watchmen. They were thrilled that all the malefactors had been caught. In the gloom, Christopher did not at first recognise the constable.

'You came at an opportune moment,' he said.

'I was acting on information, sir,' explained Jonathan.

'Information?'

'Yes, sir. I was roused from my bed and advised that a crime was about to take place on this site.'

'Who gave you such advice?'

'Jesus-Died-To-Save-Me Thorpe'

Littlejohn was baffled. 'Who?'

'A neighbour of mine, sir. A Quaker. He chanced to overhear these rogues plotting their crime. After following them here, Mr Thorpe came straight to my house to warn me.'

'We are most grateful to him,' said the builder. 'And grateful to you as well. These villains have already stolen far too much from this site and they had to be caught. They deserve to rot in prison.'

'They will, sir.'

'We hope we may recover some of the property taken earlier.'

'That depends where it went,' said Jonathan, glancing at the men on the ground. 'These men came by boat so the likelihood is that they had a warehouse nearby where they could take the stolen goods. Do not worry, sir, I am sure they will tell us all we wish to know.'

Jonathan grabbed each of them in turn by the scruff of his neck and pulled him upright. Both were too dazed to resist, let alone to attempt an escape. Two of the watchmen seized a man apiece. The constable was very pleased. In a crime-infested ward, the forces of law and order had achieved a small triumph. Jesus-Died-To-Save-Me Thorpe had been instrumental in securing one arrest. A man who had violated several laws on his own account that night had helped to foil a serious crime.

Christopher took a closer look at the providential constable.

'Do I not know you, friend?' he said.

'No, sir,' protested Jonathan. 'We have never met.'

'Yes, we have. I remember you now.'

'I have no memory whatsoever of you, sir.'

'But you must have,' said Christopher, warming to him. 'You came to my aid once before. It was near St Paul's when a pickpocket robbed me of my purse. Yes, you are Jonathan Bale, are you not?' he recalled. 'I had a feeling we would meet again one day. I am Christopher Redmayne. I offered you a drawing of the cathedral by way of thanks. Surely, you remember me now, my friend? I was the artist whose purse you restored. Christopher Redmayne.'

Jonathan took a deep breath before issuing a polite rebuff.

'You are mistaken, sir. I have never heard that name before.'

* * *

It was almost three weeks before Sir Ambrose Northcott returned to London and he did so in high spirits. They were temporarily dampened when he learnt of the crimes at the site but lifted once more at the news that three thieves were now in custody along with the man who received and paid for their stolen goods. Everything taken from the site was still in the latter's warehouse. Complete restitution occurred. Northcott was delighted that he had suffered no real loss. His only regret was that the malefactors would not appear before him when he sat on the Bench. It deprived him of the pleasure of imposing vile punishments upon them.

Building had continued apace in his absence. The improvement was dramatic. With the cellars complete, the bricklayers were able to start on the exterior walls of the house. Additional men had been taken on by Littlejohn to construct the high wall around the garden, ensuring both privacy and a higher level of security. Though much still remained to be done before skilled craftsmen were brought in to work their magic on the interior of the residence, Northcott was vastly encouraged. The house now bore a much closer resemblance to the one which first began life as an architect's vision on a sheet of paper in Fetter Lane.

Christopher Redmayne earned his employer's warm gratitude. It was his initiative which had helped to ensnare the thieves and which led, indirectly, to the return of the materials which they stole. Northcott pressed the architect to dine with him at a select tavern. Christopher accepted with alacrity though his pleasure was diluted somewhat when he realised that there was a third person at the table with them. He found Solomon Creech more repellent than ever. The lawyer was at his most unctuous.

'Yes, Sir Ambrose,' he said, washing his hands in the air, 'I was most insistent that we solved the crime before your return. I could not have you coming back to find us hampered by such setbacks. I made that clear to Mr Littlejohn and to Mr Redmayne here,' he said, offering a weak smile to Christopher. 'I had perforce to speak sternly to them on your behalf but my firmness paid dividends.'

'So it appears, Solomon,' said Northcott.

'I had half a mind to hide under that tarpaulin with them.'

'Brave man!'

'Age alone held me back.'

'Yet I believe that Mr Littlejohn is older than you,' said Christopher, annoyed at the way in which the egregious lawyer was trying to wrest glory from them. 'Age did not deter him. He fought like a lion.'

'Solomon is more of a fox,' remarked Northcott.

I knew that he was some kind of animal, thought Christopher, but he did not express it in words. Sir Ambrose Northcott was an astute man. He would not be taken in by the lawyer's claims. Christopher could rely on his employer to sift arrant lies from the plain truth.

When the meal was over, Northcott gave a signal and Creech rose to leave, covering his exit with obsequious thanks and bending almost double as he backed out of the room. Northcott turned to his other guest.

'You do not like him, Christopher, do you?' he said.

'I hardly know the man.'

'You know enough about him to despise him. I could see it in your eyes.' He laughed at the other's discomfort.

'Do not be alarmed. I am far from fond of him myself. Solomon Creech can be odious at times but he has one of the shrewdest legal brains in London and that is why I employ him. I always seek out the best men to serve me.' He flicked a finger to order more wine. 'That is why I chose you.'

'Thank you, Sir Ambrose.'

'I have no regrets on that score.'

'Nor I,' said Christopher.

'Come, sir,' teased the other. 'You must have some complaints. When you were engaged to design a house for me, you could hardly have imagined that it would involve spending several hours under a tarpaulin before fighting with a couple of ruffians.'

'I enjoyed every moment of it.'

'So, by all accounts, did Samuel Littlejohn.'

'He is a powerful man when he is roused.'

'As indeed are you, Christopher. Your brother did not just regale me with details of your architectural abilities. He spoke of your physical prowess as well. Henry told me what a fine swordsman you are. And you clearly keep yourself in excellent condition.' The teasing note returned. 'No wonder you have made such an impression on the Littlejohn family.'

'Samuel is a splendid man. It is I who revere him.'

'I was referring to his daughter.'

'Ah.'

'Margaret? Is that what she is called?'

'I believe so.'

'You know so, Christopher. The girl is enthralled by you.'

'Hardly,' said the other, trying to brush an embarrassing subject aside. 'We have hardly spoken two words to each other.'

'She worships you in silence,' said Northcott with a grin. 'I saw her at the site yesterday. Those big eyes of hers never left you for a second. Her father tells me that she was taken with you from the start. Since your exploits with those thieves, she adores you.' He gave his companion a sly nudge. 'What do you intend to do about it?'

'Do about it, Sir Ambrose?'

'Margaret is an attractive creature.'

'Nobody would gainsay that.'

'Then what is holding you back?'

'From what?' Christopher saw the candid lechery in his eye. 'Oh, no, Sir Ambrose. There can be no question of that.'

'Why not? You are young, unmarried and virile.'

'I am wedded to my work.'

'Every man needs to season his labours with pleasure.'

'You begin to sound like my brother.'

'Henry would not hesitate in such a case as this.'

'I am afraid that he would not, Sir Ambrose.'

'So why must you?' pressed the other. 'Margaret Littlejohn is patently entranced by you. Requite her love.' Another nudge. 'Take pity on her, Christopher. Give the young lady what she so earnestly craves.'

'That would be unwise and unfair.'

'Would it?'

Christopher weighed his words carefully before speaking. His first impression of Margaret Littlejohn had proved correct. She was a potential danger. Her admiration of him was now so blatant that he tried to avoid her eye lest even a greeting nod from him be mistaken as a form of encouragement. Christopher had known infatuation himself in his younger days and he understood the lengths to which it could drive a person. His fear was that the builder's daughter would become so enamoured of him that she would discard all propriety and blurt out a declaration of love. That was something which he wished to avoid at all costs.

'Answer me,' insisted Northcott. 'Unwise and unfair, you say?'

'Yes, Sir Ambrose,' explained Christopher. 'It would be unwise for me to become involved with any woman at this time because it would prove a serious distraction. And it would be especially unwise of me to engage the affections of a young lady whose father works alongside me.'

'But the fellow approves of the match.'

'It is not a match. That is the crucial point. Margaret Littlejohn is a charming young lady but I could never requite her love,' he admitted, 'and it would be unfair both to her and her father to pretend that I could. As for the other course of action, it would be quite monstrous of me to take my pleasure then cast her aside when I tired of her. What purpose would be served by that?'

'Ask your brother.'

'Henry and I view these things differently.'

'I am more inclined to side with him.'

'Would you do so if you were involved in a similar situation?'

'What do you mean?'

'Only this, Sir Ambrose,' said Christopher. 'Henry told me that you have a daughter who is little above Margaret Littlejohn's age. Were she to become hopelessly entranced by a young man, would you advise him to take full advantage of her?'

'Leave my daughter out of this!' said Northcott testily.

'I only sought to draw a parallel.'

'It is an offensive one. Let us forget the whole matter.'

'Gladly, Sir Ambrose.'

'My daughter, Penelope, is engaged to be married.'

'Henry omitted to mention that.'

'I will tax him on the subject when I meet him this evening.'

'Please accept my apology. No offence was intended.'

'Enough, man! I will hear no more!'

There was an awkward pause. Another bottle of wine arrived and their glasses were refilled. Christopher waited until his host had taken a long sip before he resumed the conversation.

'I have made enquiries about an artist,' he said quietly.

'Artist?' grunted the other.

'You wanted a portrait painted, Sir Ambrose. To hang in the hall of the new house. You stressed that the artist had to be worthy of such a commission. I have found two men, either of whom would suit you.'

'Who are they?'

Christopher described the two men and praised their work in equal measure. Northcott's interest was engaged once more and his ruffled feathers were gradually smoothed. He insisted on seeing the work of both artists before reaching a decision between them. Talk of the portrait led on to a discussion of furnishings for the house and an hour slipped pleasurably past. The architect was glad that Margaret Littlejohn had faded completely out of their discourse. Northcott had obviously forgotten all about her. Christopher took great care to make no further reference to his host's daughter. He did not wish to provoke more ire.

Northcott regained his buoyant mood. When they parted company, he shook Christopher's hand warmly and thanked him once again for the bravery he had shown in confronting the thieves. Sir Ambrose Northcott was expansive, promising that no expense would be spared on the house and assuring the young architect that he would be among the first guests invited to dine there. Christopher was honoured. The prospect of owning a beautiful new home seemed to rejuvenate Northcott. He walked away with a jauntiness in his gait.

Christopher was struck by the extraordinary vitality of the older man. Sir Ambrose Northcott truly defied his years. He had an inner zest which somehow made light of the passage of time. Though no longer entirely uncritical of his employer, Christopher could not but admire his bounding energy.

As he watched the man go, it did not occur to him for a second that he would never see Sir Ambrose Northcott alive again.

CHAPTER SIX

Sarah Bale was never quite able to relax completely but her load was considerably lightened once she had put the children to bed. Oliver and Richard were boisterous lads who needed a watchful eye kept on them and, in the course of a normal day, their mother was frequently called upon to prise them apart, act as a peacemaker, adjudicate, discipline, amuse, threaten or read to them. Just fifteen months separated the six-year-old Oliver from his younger sibling and the fact that Richard was slightly bigger than him sharpened the edge of his competitiveness, but Sarah's mixture of firm action and warm maternalism usually kept the two boys under control and it was only on rare occasions that their father was brought in to impose his authority. Jonathan was proud of his sons and equally proud of the way in which his wife was bringing them up. Though he took his turn at reading to them from the Bible or telling them stories, it was Sarah who bore the brunt of their education in the home.

The constable was a busy man and the Great Fire increased both his professional responsibilities and his domestic commitments. When not attending to his duties, his main priority was to reconstruct the house in Addle Hill. It was noisy work.

'How much longer will you be, Jonathan?' asked Sarah.

'I am almost finished, my love.'

'The children are in bed at last but they will never sleep while you hammer away like that. Could you not stop now, please?'

'One last nail, then.' The hammer rose and fell with precision until the long nail had been driven deep into the joist, securing yet another floorboard. Jonathan gathered up his tools to put back in their box then examined his hands. Three small blisters decorated one palm.

'I have grown soft,' he said with a resigned smile. 'When I worked as a shipwright, I could hold a hammer all day without getting blisters. My hands were made of leather in those days.'

'I prefer them as they are,' she said, cupping them between her own palms before giving them a gentle kiss. 'When you have washed them, your food will be ready.'

'Thank you, Sarah.'

'See to the boys first.'

'Have they behaved well today?'

An indulgent smile. 'Now and then.'

'Oliver can be a bully sometimes.'

'Richard has been the problem today. He will answer back.'

'I'll speak to them.'

'Not too harshly,' she counselled.

'They must learn, Sarah.'

While she descended to the kitchen, he went off to give his sons a muted reprimand which was further softened by a good-night kiss. He tucked them into their bed. It was a moment in the day which Jonathan always treasured and he was pleased that it could now take place again in their own house. Evacuated to Hoxton by the fire, they had all missed Addle Hill greatly but it was well into the new year before rebuilding could begin. The area had suffered badly and the destruction of the once invincible Baynard's Castle had a symbolic meaning for the whole ward. Like so many others, the Bale household was completely gutted but its exterior walls, though charred in places, remained largely sound. Once they were reinforced with additional brickwork, they became able to bear the weight of new roof timbers and tiles.

As soon as the shell was completed, Jonathan moved in on his own to rebuild the house from the inside, using skills which had been honed by many years in the shipyards. Doing the bulk of the work himself not only defrayed the costs, it gave him a sense of satisfaction. He was able both to rebuild and improve their home. He was particularly pleased with his new staircase, made of seasoned oak and showing evidence of long hours with a plane and a chisel. When the kitchen, parlour and one bedroom were habitable, his family moved back to share the house with him and he continued his renovations around them whenever he could steal a spare hour or two. It was by no means an ideal situation but it was far preferable to living outside the city wall in Hoxton and, in his case, having long walks to and from Baynard's Castle Ward every day.

'I still think that you should have taken it,' remarked Sarah.

'Taken what?' he asked.

'The reward.'

'Oh, no. I could never bring myself to do so.'

'But you earned it, Jonathan.'

'I merely did my duty,' he said solemnly. 'A constable is enjoined to arrest criminals. That is all that I did. It was very kind of Sir Ambrose Northcott to offer me a reward but it had to be refused. If anybody should have received the money, it was Jesus-Died-To-Save-Me Thorpe. It was he who alerted me to what was afoot.'

'Then you should have taken the reward and shared it with him.'

'No, Sarah.'

'Why not?'

'Because my conscience would have troubled me.'

'Jonathan,' she argued, 'we need all the money we can get.'

'Not if it comes from such a source.'

'You prevented a crime being committed on someone's property. The owner was duly grateful. He is entitled to reward you.'

'And I am just as entitled to reject his offer.'

'I would not have done so.'

'You might if you knew the circumstances.'

'What circumstances?'

Jonathan swallowed the last of his food before he answered. Seated in their kitchen, he and Sarah were eating a light salad for supper. He washed it down with a mug of ale then looked across at her.

'A crime was reported to me,' he continued, 'and I took action. I did so with no thought of personal gain. Had the theft been from the meanest house in the ward, I would have responded just the same. I had no notion that the property in question was owned by Sir Ambrose Northcott.'

'But it was, Jonathan, and he was deeply grateful.'

'The size of the reward shows that, my love, but it was offered to me in a way that I found insulting. A lawyer named Solomon Creech sought me out. A scurvy fellow who spoke to me so condescendingly that I was hard pressed to hold on to my temper.'

'Then his manner must have been insulting,' she said, 'for you are the most even-tempered person I have ever met. It takes a lot to rouse Jonathan Bale to anger.'

'Mr Creech managed to do it,' he recalled bitterly. 'He made it sound as if Sir Ambrose was doing me a huge favour when it was I, in fact, who helped *him*. I will not be patronised by anybody, Sarah.'

'Do you think I need to be told that?'

'Least of all by some wealthy Cavalier.'

'Now we come to the truth of it.'

'I felt as if I was being paid off like some menial.'

'Money is money, Jonathan.'

'Not when it is tainted,' he said sharply. 'We need no favours. We will manage on our own somehow. Mr Creech would not believe that I actually refused the award. He began to chastise me and read me a sermon on gratitude. I tell you this, Sarah, if I had not turned on my heel and walked away from the man, I might well have done him an injury. He was truly obnoxious.'

'Would you have taken the money from Sir Ambrose himself?'

'Not a penny.'

'Even though it would have offended him?'

'My refusal would have been polite, Sarah,' he said evenly. 'I look for no reward from Sir Ambrose Northcott, whether direct from him or by means of that damnable lawyer.' He gave a hollow laugh. 'The only consolation is that he did not send that architect of his to transact the business.'

'Architect?'

'A cocksure young man called Christopher Redmayne.'

'How is he involved here?'

'He designed the house for Sir Ambrose and he lay in ambush to catch the thieves. He and the builder, one Samuel Littlejohn, were there that night and helped to catch the villains.'

'That shows rare courage on their part.'

'They have a vested interest in the property. I believe that it is the first house Mr Redmayne has designed. He is a gifted architect.'

'Then why have you not mentioned him before?'

'Because I choose to put him out of my mind.'

'For what reason?'

'I do not like the fellow, Sarah.'

'Is he so unpleasant to you?'

'Quite the opposite,' he sighed. 'Mr Redmayne has tried

to befriend me and that is even worse. I want no dealings with him. He lives in one world, I live in another. That is that. We have nothing in common. It was an unfortunate coincidence that we bumped into each other again.'

'Again?' she echoed. 'You have met him before?'

'Yes. Close by St Paul's.'

'When was this?'

'Several months ago. Just after the fire.'

'Did you take against him then?'

'Very strongly, Sarah,' he admitted. 'It is not so much the man himself as what he represents. He is one of them. When Lord Protector Cromwell ruled, I hoped that such creatures would be driven out of London altogether but they are back in greater numbers than before.'

'Who are?'

'Elegant young gentlemen with their easy manners and easy ways, looking down on the likes of us. Royalists, Sarah. Trailing behind King Charles like his beloved spaniels and soiling the whole city with their droppings. No,' he said as he poured more ale from the jug, 'that was another reason to decline the money. I knew that the architect, too, would doubtless be rewarded for his share in the enterprise. We would have been joint beneficiaries.'

'Is that so terrible, Jonathan?'

'Yes,' he emphasised. 'I would not wish my name to be linked in any way to that of Mr Christopher Redmayne.'

'Christopher!' he yelled. 'Where are you? For Heaven's sake, let me in!'

Henry Redmayne pounded on the door of the house in

Fetter Lane until he heard sounds from within. It was very late and the place was in darkness but he felt certain that his brother would be at home. In the event, it was Jacob who opened the door, taper in hand, and peered out at him. Henry pushed past him to enter the house at the very moment that Christopher was descending the stairs in his nightshirt.

'What on earth is the matter, Henry?' he asked.

'I need to see you,' said his brother in tones of urgency.

'At this hour? Could it not wait until morning?'

'No, Christopher.'

'Very well,' said the other with a yawn. 'Light some candles, Jacob. Then you may go back to bed. I will see to my brother.'

'Thank you, sir,' murmured the old man.

He led the way into the parlour and lit four candles before shuffling out again. Christopher sat down and waved Henry to a chair but the latter remained on his feet. There was a touch of fear in his eyes.

'Sir Ambrose has disappeared!' he announced.

'Disappeared?'

'So it seems.'

'Why come to me?' said Christopher. 'He is not here.'

'But you did dine with him today, did you not?'

'Yes.'

'And he seemed well enough then?'

'In rude health.'

'Then it cannot be illness which kept him away.'

'From what?'

'He and I arranged to meet this evening.'

'Yes,' remembered Christopher. 'He mentioned that.'

'He did not turn up at the agreed time. I went to his house but there was no sign of him there. Feeling alarmed, I called on Solomon Creech, certain that he would know where Sir Ambrose was. But he did not. All that he could confirm was that Sir Ambrose had every intention of keeping his appointment with me. After that—

'Hold there,' interrupted Christopher, still drowsy. 'Did you say that you went to Sir Ambrose's house?'

'Yes. It lies in Westminster.'

'I did not realise he already had a residence here.'

'He bought it several years ago.'

'That is strange,' said Christopher thoughtfully. 'He gave me the impression that he was building the new house in Baynard's Castle Ward in order to have a base in the capital.'

'What of it?' returned Henry evasively. 'Does it matter if he has one, two or three houses in London? Sir Ambrose can have as many houses as he likes. All I am concerned with is his safety.'

'What makes you think that it is under threat?'

'His disappearance.'

'There may be a simple explanation for it.'

'I cannot think of one, Christopher. Nor could Creech. The lawyer was more disturbed by the news than me. Sir Ambrose has his faults but he is very punctual about appointments.' He paced the room. 'It is very worrying. Where can the man be?'

'When was he last seen?'

'By you, apparently. At what time did you part?'

'Well past two o'clock this afternoon.'

'Creech told me that you dined in Holborn.'

'That is so. He ate with us but left early.'

'In which direction did Sir Ambrose go?'

'Towards Newgate.'

'On his horse?'

'No, Henry. He was walking.'

'Did he say where he was going?'

'Not to me.'

Henry came to a halt and stroked his moustache as he pondered. In the pool of light thrown by the candles, Christopher could see that his brother was as immaculately dressed as ever but the fact that his periwig was slightly askew showed how distracted he was. Henry Redmayne was a rare visitor to the house even though he was no stranger to Fetter Lane itself. Until it was destroyed by fire, there was an establishment at the Fleet Street end of the lane which Henry had visited regularly in his endless pursuit of carnal delights and one of the gaming houses he also frequented was still standing. That he should appear on the threshold at all was a surprise. To come at that hour and in such a state of agitation revealed just how anxious he was.

'Might he not have been led astray?' suggested Christopher.

'That is my fear.'

'I imply no danger.'

'Then what is your meaning?'

'Sir Ambrose strikes me as a man after your own heart, Henry. A dedicated sybarite. Given to pleasure, acquainted with excess. I always assumed that that is how the two of you first met. Across a gaming table or in some house of resort.'

'How we met is a private matter,' said Henry testily.

'But you take my point?'

'Of course. And I have visited every one of his known haunts. It has taken me hours. Sir Ambrose has not been near any of them. That is why I came to you to see what light you can shed.'

'None, I fear. You know him far better than I, Henry. Until today, for instance, I had no idea that he owned a residence in Westminster.'

'Forget that. It is not important.'

'I just wonder why it was hidden from me.'

'It was not hidden from anybody,' chided Henry. 'The only thing that we must address at the moment is Sir Ambrose's disappearance. When he is in London, he is a man of regular habits. Such people do not just vanish into thin air.' He bit his lip in meditation. 'Did he give you no clue where he was going when he left you this afternoon?'

'None whatsoever.'

'But he told you that he would be seeing me?'

'Yes, Henry. This evening. You were destined for a reproof.'

'Was I? On what grounds?'

'Indiscretion,' said Christopher with gentle mockery. 'You are in disgrace, Henry. I chanced to make reference to his daughter.'

'Penelope?'

'Yes. Sir Ambrose took exception to my comment. I might as well warn you that he was highly displeased with you.'

'Why?'

'For revealing to me that he had a daughter.'

'In confidence,' said Henry petulantly. 'In strictest confidence. You should have kept it to yourself. Never touch on his family. I told you at the outset how intensely private a man Sir Ambrose was. Your task was to design his house, not to enquire into his background. You have put me in a most awkward position.'

'I am sorry. It slipped out.'

'The damage is not beyond repair, I suppose, but it is embarrassing all the same. Well, that can wait,' he said dismissively, tossing his periwig. 'Our first job is to find him.'

'Is there nowhere else he might be?'

'Not that I can think of, Christopher.'

'What if he had some urgent summons from home?'

'He would never have ridden off to Kent without leaving word for me and for his lawyer.'

'Are you sure?'

'Absolutely. That is not the explanation.'

'Then what is, Henry?'

The question anguished his brother. He flopped down in a chair and stared glassily ahead of him. His face was ashen with fatigue, his brow wrinkled with anxiety. His hands played nervously in his lap. He went through all the possibilities before turning to Christopher and giving a hopeless shrug.

'I dread to think,' he said quietly. 'I fear the worst.'

The night passed without incident. The old man had been replaced with a much younger one, who patrolled the site conscientiously without being tempted in any way either by drink or the blandishments of sleep. He kept a lonely vigil but that did not disturb him. He was being paid well. When dawn began to break, he strolled to the bottom of the garden and stood on a mound of earth to look out across the river as it slowly came into view. The plash of oars told him that a boat was passing but he could not pick it out. A glimpse of a lantern identified another vessel. He watched with interest until the scrunch of feet made him turn.

Someone had come onto the site. The intruder, seen in hazy outline, was making his way around the angle of the house. Drawing his sword, the nightwatchman hurried back up the garden to accost the stranger. His challenge was firm and unequivocal.

'Hold there, sir!' he ordered. 'You are trespassing.'

'It is I, Jem,' said Christopher. 'Put up your sword.'

'Is it really you, Mr Redmayne?'

'The same. Good morning.'

'Good morning, sir.'

Jem was a tall, muscular, ungainly young man with a face as round and expressionless as a full moon. Suspicious by nature, he waited until he was only yards away before he accepted that the unexpected visitor was indeed the architect. He sheathed his sword and cocked his head to one side in curiosity.

'What are you doing here, Mr Redmayne?' he wondered.

'I wanted to see the house.'

'This early?'

'There will soon be light enough.'

'A strange time to come calling.'

'I am hoping to meet someone here, Jem.'

'Mr Littlejohn and his men will not be along for an hour or more.'

'It is Sir Ambrose whom I wish to see, however long I need to wait. He comes to the site every day when he is in London.'

'Yes, Mr Redmayne. He was here yesterday.'

Christopher started. 'You saw him?'

'As I was coming on duty, sir.'

'That must have been well into the evening.'

'It was.'

'Did he say anything to you?'

'Not a word,' said the nightwatchman. 'When I tried to speak to him, Sir Ambrose waved me away. He just wanted to look around, I think.'

'And what time did he leave?'

'Who knows? I was minding my own business.'

'Do you have no idea how long he was here?'

'None, sir.'

'What exactly did he do on the site?'

Jem shook his head. 'I kept out of his way.' He could see the other's concern. 'Is something wrong, Mr Redmayne?'

'That is what I am trying to find out.'

'I was only obeying orders,' said the nightwatchman defensively. 'Sir Ambrose made it quite clear that he wanted me to ignore him. So I turned the other way. He pays my wages, sir. I do as he wishes.'

'Yes, yes,' said Christopher, giving him a conciliatory pat on the arm. 'You did right. I am not criticising you. I just wish you could give me a little more information, that is all. Any detail will be helpful.'

Jem scratched his head vigorously. His face was blanker than ever. Eager to help, he was quite unable to do so and his impotence annoyed him. Christopher was about to abandon the interrogation when the other man hunched his shoulders in apology.

'I am sorry, Mr Redmayne.'

'You are not to blame.'

'I saw nothing after they went down into the cellars.'

'They?' Christopher stepped closer to him. 'Are you telling me that Sir Ambrose was here with someone else?'

'Yes, sir. Another man.'

'Who was he?'

'I do not know, sir. I barely gave him a glance. I know my place.' He ran a tongue over his lips. 'Sir Ambrose was hardly likely to introduce a friend of his to a mere nightwatchman. I was nothing to them.'

'Was the man old or young? Tall or short?'

Jem cudgelled his brain but it was a futile exercise. He was there to guard the site, not to keep his employer under surveillance. Nothing could be dredged up from his memory. He licked his lips again.

'He was a man, Mr Redmayne. That is all I can tell you.'

'I see.'

'Have I been any help?'

'Oh, yes,' said Christopher. 'What you have told me is invaluable. At least, I now know where Sir Ambrose was yesterday evening.' He glanced around. 'Do you have a lantern here?'

'Down by the bench, sir.'

'May I borrow it, please?'

'Why?'

'Just fetch it.'

Jem loped off and Christopher went across to the house, stepping over the lowest point of the exterior wall then walking to the steps which led down to the cellars. He was still staring down into the dark tunnel when the nightwatchman handed him the lantern.

'The candle is burnt right down, sir,' he apologised.

'There is enough light still.'

'Do you want me to come with you?'

'No, Jem. Stay here. I will not be long.'

Holding the lantern, Christopher descended the steps with sure feet. Having designed and supervised the construction of the cellars, he knew every inch of them but there was no time to admire the vaulting or the intricate brickwork now. He was there for an express purpose. His visit was dictated purely by instinct. As he moved from bay to bay, the brittle sound of his footsteps reverberated throughout the whole vault. He still did not know why Sir Ambrose Northcott had insisted on such large cellars and surmised that his employer wished to keep a vast stock of wines down there. The place was empty now though soft, scurrying noises indicated that rats were making their own tour of inspection.

The dank smell began to take on a slightly noisome odour. It puzzled him. Christopher feared at first that someone had dared to use his cellars as a privy and violated their pristine cleanliness. He was outraged at the thought that one of Littlejohn's men might have slipped in there unseen to relieve himself. The further he went, the more distinct became the smell. Yet when he reached the last chamber and raised his lantern, he could see nothing which might produce it. The glow from the candle was too faint to illumine every corner. It was only when he heard a sudden darting movement that he crouched down and swung the lantern across the floor area.

Christopher did not see the rat which had just fled the scene. His attention was monopolised by the figure which lay in the corner of the chamber. The man was on his back, his body twisted in pain and his clothing soaked with blood from gashes in his chest. No respect had been shown to the dead by the rats. They had started to eat the man's face away, removing both eyes and reducing an already small nose to a jagged piece of bone. The crimson jowls were gnawed into shreds. Christopher still recognised him immediately.

Sir Ambrose Northcott would no longer require a new house.

Overcome with nausea, he began to sway and retch. Christopher had to put out a hand against the cold wall to steady himself. For a few minutes, he was completely stunned. He had not expected to find anyone in the cellars, least of all in such a hideous condition. His mind was numb. It was the nightwatchman's voice which jerked him out of his daze as it boomed through the cellars.

'Is everything all right down there, Mr Redmayne?' he called.

'No,' croaked the other.

'What is the matter?'

'Fetch a constable.'

'Why, sir?'

'Just do as I say, Jem. There has been an accident.'

'Have you been hurt?' said the voice anxiously. Heavy feet came down the stone steps. 'Do you need help?'

'I am not injured,' replied Christopher, recovering quickly. 'Do not come any closer. I will stay here while you run for a constable.'

The feet halted. 'If you say so, sir.'

'I do, Jem. It is an emergency.'

'What shall I tell him?'

'Just that. There is a dire emergency.'

'I will go at once,' promised the other, moving off.

'Wait!' shouted Christopher as a thought struck him. The feet halted again. 'Do you live in this ward?'

'Yes, sir. I was born and brought up here.'

'Do you know a man named Jonathan Bale?'

'Very well. Mr Bale lives in Addle Hill.'

'Fetch him. He is the constable I want.'

'Yes, Mr Redmayne.'

'Now, hurry!'

Jem needed no more instruction. The urgency in Christopher's command was enough to send the nightwatchman scrambling up the steps in the half-dark. He was soon trotting clumsily through the streets on his errand.

Christopher was glad that he had gone. Wanting to spare the man the shock of seeing the dead body, he was also keen to have some time alone to take a closer look at the scene of the crime and he could not do that with a horrified nightwatchman on his hands. Jem's presence would have been a definite hindrance. He was best kept in ignorance of what had been found until the constable was summoned.

As the first wave of disgust faded, Christopher plucked up the courage to study the corpse with more care. Kneeling beside it, he held the lantern close and saw that Sir Ambrose Northcott had been stabbed in the chest. A number of wounds had been opened up but the most telling thrust was to the heart. The dagger was still buried deep inside it. He had not been a passive victim. Signs of a struggle were evident from the marks in the dust which covered the floor and there was a piece of material clutched in the dead man's hand, as if torn from his assailant's clothing. Something else caught Christopher's eye. Sir Ambrose's other hand lay open, its palm covered with tiny white flakes. Christopher spotted some more of them on the floor, speckling the dust, but had no idea what they were. He picked a flake up on his fingertip and sniffed it. There was no smell. He blew the flake away again.

Taking care not to touch the body, he ran the lantern from head to toe by way of a cursory autopsy. It yielded little further information. Sir Ambrose was still wearing the apparel in which he had dined though the vivid blood had redefined its colours. Rings still adorned some fingers on both hands. One shoe had come off, its silver buckle glinting in the meagre light. Christopher shook his head sadly, offered up a prayer for the soul of the dead man then rose to his feet.

The implications slowly dawned on him. If Sir Ambrose was dead, what would now happen to the house and to the sizeable fee which the architect was due to be paid for designing it? His personal ambitions suddenly crumbled. Yet he was not only concerned with the prospect of the huge personal loss. How would Samuel Littlejohn react when he learnt that his employer had been murdered? Bricklayers, carpenters, stonemasons, tilers, glaziers and all the other tradesmen engaged to work on the property would have to be laid off instantly. The death would have widespread effects. Christopher did not relish the task of passing on the bad tidings to his brother, still less to Solomon Creech.

Both men had been very alarmed by Sir Ambrose's disappearance. Christopher wondered why. How much did they know? Did they sense that a tragedy like this might occur? Had a shadow been hanging over Sir Ambrose Northcott? Who or what cast it?

Caught up in his reflections, Christopher did not at first hear the approaching footsteps. It was only when a fresh lantern threw more light into the cellar that he realised someone was coming.

'I am here!' he called. 'At the far end.'

'We are coming, sir,' answered a voice.

'Tell Jem to stay back. There is no need for him to see this.'

'Very well, sir. You heard that, Jem.'

'Yes,' said the nightwatchman.

One pair of feet halted but the other came on in purposeful strides. Lantern held before him, Jonathan Bale walked forward until he reached the last chamber and found Christopher blocking his way.

'Why did you send for me, sir?' asked the constable.

'Something terrible has happened, I fear.'

'What is it?'

Christopher stepped aside to reveal the scene of horror.

'See for yourself,' he murmured.

CHAPTER SEVEN

Jonathan Bale did not flinch. He had looked on death too many times for it to hold any shock or surprise for him. His lantern threw a much more searching light over the corpse, enabling Christopher to see details which had been concealed from him earlier. When he tried to look closer, the constable waved him back with an arm.

'Stay clear, Mr Redmayne,' he said. 'I will take charge now.'

'That slight bruising around his throat. I did not notice that earlier. Nor that trickle of blood on his scalp.'

'Did you touch the body at all, sir?'

'No.'

'So it has not been moved?'

'It is exactly as I found it, Mr Bale.'

'Good.'

The constable was methodical. Before he examined the

body itself, he memorised its position and noted the telltale marks all round it on the dust-covered ground. His eye measured the dimensions of the chamber then scoured every inch of it. When he knelt to study the corpse, he ignored the half-eaten face, more interested in the wickedness of man than in the hunger of rats. He carefully opened the flaps of Sir Ambrose Northcott's coat so that he could view each stab wound in turn. The dagger had left ugly red holes in the man's waistcoat and Holland shirt before plunging finally into the heart. Jonathan searched every pocket. It was a long time before he rose reflectively to his feet.

Christopher watched him with gathering impatience.

'Well?' he said.

'This is a bad business, sir.'

'There are obvious signs of a struggle.'

'So I see.'

'He was a strong man. He would have put up a fight.'

'You know the deceased?'

'Of course. It is Sir Ambrose Northcott.'

'Indeed?' Jonathan took a last look at the corpse before turning to appraise Christopher. 'When did you discover the body, sir?'

'Soon after I arrived.'

'And when was that?'

'Dawn was still breaking.'

'An early hour for such a visit, sir.'

'I was anxious to see Sir Ambrose.'

'Did you arrange to meet him here?'

'No, no,' said Christopher. 'But I was confident that he would come to the site at some stage. When he is in London, he calls here every day without fail. I wanted to reassure myself.'

'Reassure?'

'That no harm had befallen him. Sir Ambrose disappeared last night. My brother came to my house in great alarm. Sir Ambrose had promised to meet him that evening but he did not turn up or send an apology for his absence. That is most unusual, according to Henry.'

'Is he your brother, sir?'

'Yes. Henry Redmayne. He is – or, at least, was – a good friend of Sir Ambrose Northcott. Henry searched for him all over the city last night. When there was no sign of him, he became profoundly worried.'

'With cause, it seems,' said the other.

'Alas, yes.'

'What made you come into the cellars, sir?'

'Curiosity.'

'It seems an odd thing to do,' observed the constable with a hint of suspicion. 'If you were hoping to meet someone on the site, the last place you would expect to find him is in a dark cellar. Why come here?'

'Because of what the nightwatchman said.'

'Jem?'

'Yes. He told me that Sir Ambrose called here yesterday evening. I have no reason to doubt his word.'

'Nor me, sir. I can vouch for Jem Raybone.'

'Unfortunately, he was not able to tell me very much but he did remember that Sir Ambrose went down into the cellars.'

'Why?'

'Presumably, to show them off to his companion.'

Jonathan's interest sharpened. 'There was someone with him?'

'Another man.'

'Did Jem recognise the fellow?'

'No, but then he was not encouraged to take a proper look at him. Sir Ambrose made it quite clear that he did not want the nightwatchman peering over their shoulders. Jem made himself scarce.'

'So he *might* have known this other man?'

'If he'd been allowed more than a brief glance.'

Jonathan gazed steadily at him, his tone deliberately neutral.

'Were you the man in question, sir?'

'Of course not!' said Christopher hotly, taken aback. 'I came nowhere near the site yesterday evening.'

'Can you tell me where you did go, Mr Redmayne?'

'This is absurd, man! You surely do not suspect me?'

'I have to consider all possibilities.'

'Well, you can eliminate my name at once,' said Christopher with righteous indignation. 'Sir Ambrose Northcott was my employer. Why on earth should I want to murder him?'

'It may be that you had a disagreement, sir,' suggested Jonathan, fixing him with a stare. 'Over money, perhaps. Or the terms of your contract with him. You tell me, sir. All I know is that it does seem strange for a man to come to the house in the half-dark and go straight to the place where the body lay.'

'I had no idea what I was going to find down here.'

'Really, sir?'

'I was shaken to the core by the discovery. Ask Jem.'

'He says that you would not let him anywhere near you.'

'That is right but he must have heard the upset in my voice.'

'He heard only what you wanted him to hear, sir.'

'Stop this!' exploded Christopher. 'I'll hear no more of it. You have no right to accuse me. Look there, Mr Bale,' he ordered, pointing at the corpse. 'What you see is the body of a murdered man. Do you know what I see lying there? The probable death of my whole career as an architect. Sir Ambrose Northcott gave me an opportunity which few men would offer to a novice like myself. This house would have been a personal monument, a way to advertise my talents to all who saw it. But the likelihood is that it will never be built now. Think on that. Would I be foolish enough to kill the one man who had real faith in me?'

'It seems unlikely, I grant you.'

'Thank you!' said Christopher with sarcasm. 'And if I *had* been the killer, do you imagine I would be stupid enough to return to the scene of the crime like this then send for a constable?'

'That would have been guile rather than stupidity, sir.'

'Guile?'

'Yes, Mr Redmayne. You would be surprised how many times the person who reports a murder turns out to have committed it. There is no simpler way to throw suspicion off yourself.'

More sarcasm. 'It did not work in my case, did it?'

'No, sir. But, then, I am already acquainted with you.'

'What do you mean?'

'I do not trust you,' said Jonathan levelly.

Christopher blenched. 'Why ever not?'

'You are inclined to passion, sir.'

'Passion!'

'You are showing it now.'

'Only because you are provoking me!'

'Are you so easily provoked, Mr Redmayne?'

Christopher turned abruptly away and fought hard to master his temper. There was a lengthy pause.

Jonathan took another look at the corpse. When he spoke again, his tone was more conciliatory.

'I do not believe that you committed this crime, sir.'

'Oh, you've worked that out, have you?' said Christopher, swinging back to face him. 'First you insult me then you exonerate me. What new piece of evidence have you stumbled on?'

'The evidence of my own eyes. You would not take such a risk.'

'Risk?'

'Of being recognised by the nightwatchman. Jem Raybone is a sharp-eyed man. Even at a glance, I think he would pick you out. No,' decided the constable, 'you were not the man who was seen going into the cellars with Sir Ambrose Northcott.' Christopher nodded gratefully and breathed heavily through his nose. 'Do you know if Jem saw one or both men leaving?'

'Neither. He was looking the other way.'

'So the murder could have taken place there and then?'

'Yes, Mr Bale.'

'The condition of the body suggests that it did. I would

like it confirmed by a surgeon,' said Jonathan softly, 'but my guess is that Sir Ambrose was killed at least twelve hours ago. In which case, the prime suspect must be this unidentified companion.'

'Not I,' insisted the other.

'Who is not – I now accept – you, sir.'

A long sigh. 'I am glad that we agree on that.'

'The vital question is this: why did Sir Ambrose Northcott come down here with that man in the first place? Did he sense no danger?'

'Not until it was too late.'

They gazed down soulfully at the corpse. The nightwatchman's voice broke in. He was standing on the cellar steps, guessing what must have been discovered and afraid to venture any closer.

'Mr Littlejohn has just arrived,' he called.

'Keep him out of here,' replied Jonathan.

'What shall I tell him?'

'I will speak to him myself, Jem.' He was about to move off when Christopher's hand detained him. 'You have inadvertently taken hold of my arm, sir,' he said politely. 'I must ask you to release it.'

'Gladly,' said Christopher, retaining his grip, 'when you tell me why you dislike me so much.'

'My opinion of you does not come into it, Mr Redmayne.'

'It informs your whole attitude towards me.'

'That is not true, sir.'

'Something about me seems to irritate you.'

'I am not irritated,' said Jonathan calmly. 'But I will admit that I would rather be in this cellar with someone else.'

'Why?'

'It is a personal matter. Now, please let go of me.'

Christopher released his arm then followed him through the cellars and up the stone steps. Both men were glad to be back out in the fresh air again and they inhaled deeply. Samuel Littlejohn was waiting for them, his face etched with concern. He lurched forward.

'What has happened, Constable?' he said.

'I have sad news, I fear,' said Jonathan. 'Sir Ambrose Northcott has been stabbed to death. His body lies in the cellar.'

Littlejohn recoiled and brought both hands up to his head.

'This cannot be!' he gasped.

'Mr Redmayne found and identified him.'

'It is true, Mr Littlejohn,' confirmed Christopher.

The builder was aghast. 'But what about the house?'

'That is the least of my concerns at the moment, sir,' said Jonathan briskly. 'A murder has been committed. Finding the killer is my priority. Jem,' he continued, turning to the nightwatchman, 'run to the Hope and Anchor on St Peter's Hill. You should find Abraham Datchett and his partner there. Bid them come as fast as they can.'

'Yes, Mr Bale.'

The nightwatchman hurried off. Littlejohn was still stunned.

'What shall I do with my men?' he asked blankly. 'They will be coming to the site very soon, expecting to start work.'

'Send them back home, sir,' advised Jonathan.

'Work must be suspended,' agreed Christopher. 'The

first thing we must do is to inform Solomon Creech. He is responsible for all of Sir Ambrose's affairs and will make decisions on his behalf. Who knows?' he said with forlorn enthusiasm. 'There may yet be some way in which the house can be built. Sir Ambrose's family may take on the responsibility themselves.'

'Is that likely, Mr Redmayne?' asked Littlejohn with a sigh. 'Sir Ambrose was killed here. The property will hardly hold fond memories for his family. We have lost everything.'

'Not necessarily.'

'The project is doomed.'

Christopher tried to console him but his words sounded hollow. In his heart, he shared the builder's pessimism. Construction had to be abandoned. There seemed to be no chance of it ever being resumed. In a city where so much rebuilding was taking place, Samuel Littlejohn would soon find alternative work for himself and his men but Christopher might not. His one venture into architecture had foundered.

Preoccupied with the business implications, Littlejohn also spared a thought for a member of his family. There was real pain in his voice.

'What will become of Margaret?' he asked.

'Your daughter will be upset at the turn of events.'

'She will be distraught, Mr Redmayne.'

'Was she fond of Sir Ambrose?'

'It is not his death which will hurt her the most,' said Littlejohn. 'It is the consequences. If we stop work on the house, how will Margaret see *you*? That is why she came here so often.'

'I see.'

'You must be aware of her feelings for you.'

'Well...yes, Mr Littlejohn.'

'The girl dotes on you, sir.'

Christopher saw that there might yet be a consolation for him. In losing a prized commission, he would also escape the attentions of an amorous young lady. There was an awkward pause. It was broken by a sound behind them and they turned to see Jonathan Bale rolling back the tarpaulin so that he could select a plank of wood.

'I will need to borrow this,' he explained. 'We can use it to carry the body up from the cellar. Will your men bring a cart, Mr Littlejohn?'

'Yes, Constable. Make what use of it you will.'

'Thank you, sir.'

'Will you need a hand to lift the body out?'

'No, sir. The watchmen will help me along with Jem Raybone. But I would appreciate the loan of the cart to take it to the mortuary. How soon will it be here?'

'Very soon,' said Littlejohn, looking rather embarrassed. 'It is a mean conveyance for so august a gentleman as Sir Ambrose Northcott.'

Jonathan was brusque. 'It will suffice, sir. We do not seem to have a coach and horses at hand. Excuse me.'

He carried the plank into the cellar and left the two men to make what they wished of his tart comment. Christopher resisted the impulse to go after the constable in order to confront him. Nothing could be served by an argument with Jonathan Bale at this stage. It would have to wait. He was of far more use in helping Littlejohn to recover from the shock.

The builder was still struggling to come to terms with the tragedy.

'What of his wife, his family?' he wondered.

'They will have to be told as soon as possible.'

'And his friends?'

'My brother, Henry, was an intimate of his. He will pass the word around Sir Ambrose's circle. They will be grief-stricken. Solomon Creech will doubtless inform any business associates of Sir Ambrose.'

'Was he not also a Member of Parliament?'

'Yes, Mr Littlejohn. He will be sorely missed there as well.'

'So many lives affected by this calamity.' He glanced towards the cellar steps. 'May I go and see him?'

'I would counsel against it,' said Christopher. 'You would not recognise the man you knew. It is a gruesome sight, believe me, and it would only unsettle you further. Leave everything to the constable. He seems to know what he is doing.' His jaw tightened. 'Though I wish that his manner was a little more pleasant.'

'Sir Ambrose Northcott murdered? Who could do such a thing?'

'That is what I intend to find out.'

'He was such a generous client.'

'And a very brave one. I was a young and untried architect. He took a huge risk with me.'

'A justified risk, Mr Redmayne. I had no qualms about your talent.'

'Thank you.'

'And my daughter thinks you are a genius.'

Unable to answer his smile, Christopher was glad to be interrupted by the arrival of Jem Raybone and two elderly watchmen. Jonathan emerged from the cellar to beckon all three of them over to him. As soon as they disappeared down the steps, Littlejohn saw the first of his own men approaching the site and he went across to pass on the sad tidings. Christopher could see the horror on their faces. A horse-drawn cart rattled along the cobblestones with four other workmen on board. They were as shocked as their colleagues by the news but all chose to linger rather than to disperse. They felt a loyalty to their former employer. When the body of Sir Ambrose Northcott was brought up from the cellar, Littlejohn and his men doffed their hats in respect.

The corpse lay on the wooden plank. Jonathan Bale and Abraham Datchett carried it between them to negotiate the narrow steps. The watchmen's staves were then placed on the ground so that the plank could be rested on it. All four men now bore the load, lifting up the body and carrying it slowly towards the cart on the staves. Christopher was touched to observe that the constable had removed his coat in order to cover the face and chest of the dead man, sparing him the indignity of attracting any ghoulish interest. Sir Ambrose Northcott's hat rested on his chest. The shoe had been replaced on his foot.

Littlejohn climbed into the cart and used a hand to brush away the accumulated dust. Christopher went over to help them to ease the body into the cart. Everything was done with the utmost care. As other men reported for work on the site, they were told in whispers of the murder.

Jonathan Bale turned to Christopher.

'You will need to give a sworn statement, Mr Redmayne.'

'I appreciate that. First, however, I must contact Solomon Creech. He is Sir Ambrose Northcott's lawyer. It is imperative that he hears about this immediately.'

'Very well,' said Jonathan. 'I have met Mr Creech myself and I would certainly prefer that you spoke to him. The news will come better from you. We will take the body to the mortuary. Find me there, please.'

'I will, Mr Bale.'

'Goodbye, sir.'

Littlejohn climbed out of the cart as the two watchmen clambered into it. Jonathan joined them and took up the reins. A gentle flick sent the horse ambling forward. Christopher and the others watched until the cart and its grim cargo disappeared out of sight. There was a protracted silence. Some of the men gradually began to drift away. Latecomers were turned back with the news. Samuel Littlejohn looked on the verge of tears.

Christopher thought about his daughter and sighed. It was time to go.

Henry Redmayne was in an irascible mood. Everything was conspiring against him that morning. His breakfast had been late, his servants slovenly and his barber had twice drawn blood while shaving him. Other domestic shortcomings annoyed him further. Over-arching these minor annoyances was his intense fear for the safety of a good friend. Henry hoped that Sir Ambrose Northcott would have written to him by now to explain his uncharacteristic absence on the previous evening but no word came. Apprehension deepened at the house in Bedford Street. Even a draught of Canary wine did not relieve it.

The manservant found his master still in his bedchamber.

'You have a visitor, sir,' he said.

'Sir Ambrose Northcott?' asked Henry eagerly.

'No, sir. Your brother.'

'Does Christopher have any news?'

'I am to summon you at once, sir. He said that it was urgent.'

Henry brushed him aside and darted through the door. When he hastened down the stairs, he saw his brother waiting for him in the hall.

'What has happened?' he demanded.

'Can we speak in private?' said Christopher.

'Of course. This way.'

Christopher was shepherded into the parlour and the door was shut behind them. There was no easy way to break the tidings to Henry. He was twitching with anxiety and would brook no delay.

'Well, Christopher?'

'Sir Ambrose has been found.'

'Alive or dead?'

'Dead, I fear.'

Henry's body sagged. 'I knew it!'

'He has been murdered.'

'Dear God!'

Christopher helped him to a chair then stood beside him to relate all the details. Henry winced throughout. His head pounded. The cuts on his face began to smart afresh.

'This is dreadful!' he cried, putting his hands over his

ears. 'I will hear no more. I have lost a dear, dear friend in Sir Ambrose. This is quite insupportable. I will never get over it.'

'You must, Henry. I need your help.'

'Leave me be.'

'No,' said Christopher, gently removing his brother's hands from his ears. 'This is a terrible crime and someone must pay for it.'

'*I* am paying for it!' wailed the other. 'In pity and sorrow.'

'This is no time to think of yourself, Henry.'

'But this is such a blow to me.'

'Strike back at the man who delivered it.'

'How?'

'By helping me to track down the killer.'

'But I have no idea who he might be, Christopher.'

'I think you may,' said his brother, pulling a chair across to sit directly in front of him. 'You knew Sir Ambrose well. I did not. Let us look in the obvious place first. Did he have any enemies?'

'Several. Enemies and rivals.'

'Anyone in particular?'

'Not that I can think of at the moment.'

'I will need some names, Henry.'

'Well, do not come to me,' said the other. 'Solomon Creech is your man. He could give you a full list of Sir Ambrose's enemies.'

'He refuses to do so.'

'You've already spoken to him?'

'I had to tell him the news.'

133

Henry bridled. 'You mean, you kept me waiting while you went off to that lawyer? I am your brother, Christopher. Your sibling. Your closest blood relation. Damnation! You should have come to me *first*!'

'Mr Creech had to be informed. Only he can make decisions about the future of the house.'

'What future? That house will only have a past now.' He turned away and pouted. 'I feel slighted, Christopher. I have been sick with worry yet you kept me in suspense while you trotted off to Solomon Creech.'

'I also had to make a sworn statement before the magistrate.'

'Your brother should have been your first port of call.'

'That is a matter of opinion.'

'You know mine.'

'Yes, Henry,' said Christopher, clicking his tongue, 'and I am sorry if I offended you. It was not deliberate. The facts of the case are these. Sir Ambrose has been murdered. Solomon Creech flew into a panic when I told him and more or less drove me out of his office. He gave me no assistance at all. The wretch would not even undertake to inform Sir Ambrose's family.'

'But they must be told.'

'I will come to them in due course. Let us return to these enemies. You say that Sir Ambrose had several of them?'

'Of course. He was a politician. Such men always have enemies. And he was a very successful merchant. His rivals hated him. Look among them for the most likely killer.'

'Where do I start?'

'I have told you. With his lawyer.'

'Forget him, Henry. Answer me this. When you and Sir Ambrose were together, did he ever express fear that his life was under threat?'

'Never.'

'Are you sure?'

'Quite sure. Sir Ambrose was a brave man. Nothing frightened him. He had such a wonderful lust for life. That is what drew us together. I have never known anyone with such appetites. He will be missed.' He shook his head and rolled his eyes. 'Oh, he will indeed be missed. There are many establishments in this city where his passing will be mourned.'

'Let us turn to his politics.'

'He was a man of some influence.'

'Which party did he follow?'

'He was a close associate of Lord Ashley.'

'The Chancellor of the Exchequer? I had not realised that Sir Ambrose moved in such exalted circles. Was he seen at Court?'

'From time to time.'

'Would his position have aroused envy among rivals?'

'Envy, spite and rancour.'

'Could you name some of those rivals?'

'Not while my head is spinning like this. Good gracious, man!' he exclaimed, glaring at his brother. 'I am in agony. I have just been told that a cherished friend of mine has been murdered in a cellar. You cannot expect me to sit here calmly and talk about his political rivals. Besides,' he added, 'why should you want to know? It is not your business to hunt down the killer.'

'I am making it my business, Henry.'

'Why?'

'Because I owe it to Sir Ambrose,' said Christopher earnestly. 'He gave me hope where anybody else would have offered rejection. And yes, perhaps my ambitions have now run aground but that is no reason to forget what Sir Ambrose Northcott did for me. The least that I can do in return is to search for the fiend who murdered him. And the least *you* can do, Henry, is to help me.'

'But I do not see how.'

'Begin with that list. Reflect on it at your leisure. When you are ready, write down the name of any political opponent with whom Sir Ambrose clashed. Or any other person with whom he fell out. Will you do that for me, please?' He shook his brother's arm. 'Henry?'

'I will try.'

'Excellent!'

'But I will make no promises.'

'Do you have access to Lord Ashley?'

'Not directly but I have friends who do.'

'Use them to question him on this matter. Lord Ashley will have information about Sir Ambrose that could prove crucial. If they were close, I am sure that the Chancellor will be distressed to lose him.'

Henry stiffened. 'And what about me? I am even more distressed. You do not realise what this means to your brother, Christopher. I put years into that friendship with Sir Ambrose. He opened doors for me.'

'I will need to peep inside some of them.'

'Not now, not now. *Please!* Pester me no further.'

'One last request.'

'What is it?'

'I will need Sir Ambrose's address.'

'In Westminster?'

'No, Henry, in Kent. That is where his family live. You mentioned a daughter. That means he has a wife and, perhaps, other children. It is cruel to keep this news from them any longer. Where will I find them?'

'You? It is not your responsibility, Christopher.'

'Do you volunteer to take it on?'

'How can I?' said Henry, getting to his feet. 'I have far too much to do to go riding off to Sevenoaks.'

'Is that where his home is?'

'Near there. A few miles to the east. It is a full day's ride even for such an accomplished horseman as yourself.'

'Have you ever been there?'

'No, but Sir Ambrose often spoke about the onerous journey.'

'What is the name of the house?'

Henry Redmayne needed some time to grope in his memory.

'Well?' prompted Christopher.

'Head for the village of Shipbourne.'

'And the house?'

'Priestfield Place.'

Jonathan Bale had a busy morning. It was hours before he was able to slip back to Addle Hill. Sarah was in the kitchen, slicing up vegetables with a knife before dropping the pieces into a large pot. He took off his coat. When she caught sight of it, she got up anxiously from the stool.

'There is blood on it,' she said in alarm.

'Calm down, my love.'

'Have you been wounded?'

'No, Sarah. It is not my blood. I used my coat to cover the body of a man who was stabbed to death. I did not want anyone to see him.'

'Who was he?'

'It does not matter,' he soothed, easing her back onto the stool. 'I only came back to change my coat and to warn you that I will be out for the rest of the day. Dine alone with the children. I will eat later.'

'But you must have something, Jonathan.'

'There is too much to do.'

'What exactly happened?'

'Nothing that need concern you, Sarah.'

'Is it to do with that summons from Jem Raybone?'

'Expect me when you see me.'

He gave her a kiss on the forehead. The constable never discussed his work at any length with his wife. He was keen to spare her any gory details. He also wanted to allay her fears for his own safety. Even though the population of the city had been reduced by the fire, the streets were still fraught with danger. A watchman had been badly wounded only a fortnight earlier and one of the other constables in the ward had been bludgeoned to the ground when he tried to arrest a felon. Jonathan Bale chose to keep such disturbing intelligence from Sarah. There was another reason for leaving his work at the threshold. His home was a refuge. It was the place in which he could rest from his duties and enjoy the simple pleasure of being a husband and a father.

Hanging his coat on a hook, he took down another and started to put it on. There was a knock on the door. Sarah made to rise but he gestured for her to sit down again. He adjusted his coat and went to the front door. When he opened it, his face fell.

His refuge was being invaded by Christopher Redmayne.

'Mr Datchett told me you might be here,' said the visitor.

'I am busy, sir, and have no time for idle chat.'

'There is nothing idle about what I have to say, Mr Bale.'

'Then please say it quickly and depart.'

'In brief,' said Christopher, 'we are of necessity together in this.'

'I do not follow.'

'Whether you like it or not, I am involved in this murder and have resolved to seek out the killer.'

'Leave that to others more skilled in the work.'

'No,' replied Christopher. 'It is a question of honour. Since neither my brother nor Mr Creech is prepared to do so, I will first ride off to Sir Ambrose's estate in Kent to break the news to his family. They must not be kept in ignorance.'

'That is considerate of you, sir,' remarked Jonathan.

'The visit will have a secondary purpose, Mr Bale. I will gather more information about Sir Ambrose, perhaps even uncover the names of some enemies of his. The more we know about the murder victim, the more likely we are to track down the man who stabbed him. Do you hear what I am telling you?'

'I think so. You will learn things which could be of value to me.'

'But we must strike a bargain.'

'Go on.'

'We need to clear the air,' said Christopher seriously. 'Solving this crime is all-important. You must set aside your inexplicable dislike and distrust of me. In return, I will overlook your surly manner towards me. Then, perhaps, we can pool our resources in the interests of justice.' He looked the constable in the eye. 'Is that fair?'

'Very fair, sir.'

'And you agree?'

'Up to a point.'

'We can help each other. It is the only way forward, Mr Bale.'

Jonathan weighed up the offer. His face was impassive.

'Ride off to Kent,' he said at length.

'Then we are partners in this enterprise?'

'Let us see what you find out first.'

CHAPTER EIGHT

Lady Frances Northcott sat on a rustic bench and surveyed the garden with a glow of pride. Its colour and variety never ceased to delight her and its multiple fragrances were particularly enchanting at that time of the year. Reclining in the shadow of an elm, she looked down an avenue of well-trimmed yew trees and admired the symmetry of the scene. The extensive formal garden at Priestfield Place was largely her creation. It occupied most of her leisure time and kept the small army of gardeners at full stretch. They worked very happily under her serene command. Lady Northcott was a far more amenable employer than her husband.

A tall, gracious woman of middle years, she had the finely sculpted features which seem to improve with age and which were somehow enhanced by the gentle greying of her hair. An air of quiet distinction marked her and even in what she called her gardening dress, she remained unmistakably the mistress of the estate. Whenever any of the gardeners passed, they gave her a deferential nod which was always repaid with a friendly smile. She was herself one of the salient features of the garden. Warm weather invariably brought her out into it.

'I knew that I would find you here,' said a teasing voice.

'Hello, Penelope.'

'You're the patron saint of this garden, Mother.'

'There is nothing I would prefer to be.'

'Is it true that they are going to make another pond?'

'Yes,' said Frances. 'It will absorb some of the overflow from the lake. I've asked them to build sluice-gates to control it.'

'But we already have three ponds.'

'You can never have too much water, Penelope. It brings interest and tranquillity to any prospect. If it were left to me, I would surround the whole of Priestfield Place with water.'

'Like a moat. To keep people out?'

'To keep me in.'

She made room on the bench for her daughter to sit beside her. Penelope Northcott inherited little from her father apart from her name and the fair hue of her hair. For the rest, she was a younger version of her mother with the same high cheekbones, the same elegant nose, the same heart-shaped face and a pair of sparkling turquoise eyes which were interchangeable with those of the other woman. Her admirers often described Lady Northcott as Penelope's older sister. It was a compliment which, politely accepted by the person to whom it was paid, always made Penelope herself giggle.

'I wanted to ask you when Father is coming home,' she said.

'I wish I knew.'

'He has been away for so long this time.'

'Yes,' agreed her mother. 'His business affairs occupy him more and more. His last letter said that he may not return here until the end of the month.'

'That is *weeks* away!' complained Penelope. 'We need him here to discuss the plans for the wedding. How can we make final arrangements if Father is never at home?'

'You will have to be patient.'

'You always say that.'

'Patience is something I have had to learn myself.'

'George is riding over tomorrow,' said her daughter. 'I hoped to be able to give him a firm date for Father's return. He is getting very restless. George is as eager as I am to decide on the arrangements.'

'The most important arrangement has already been decided.'

'Has it?'

'Yes, dear,' said Frances with a sweet smile. 'Penelope Northcott is to marry handsome George Strype. What better arrangement could there be than that?'

'None.' She kissed her mother on the cheek. 'I am so glad that you have started to like George at last.'

A guarded response. 'I have always liked him.'

'Have you?'

'In some ways.'

'Be honest, Mother. At first, you did not approve of George at all.'

'He was your father's choice rather than mine, I admit that.'

'He is *my* choice.'

'Then that is all that matters, Penelope.'

'I want you to love him as I do, Mother.'

'I will try.'

'You must, you must,' urged the other.

'In time, dear. I am sure that I will grow into it in time.'

Penelope squeezed her hand. A breeze sprang up, causing the branches of the elm to genuflect gracefully. Birdsong filled the walks. The two of them simply sat there and luxuriated in the beauty of nature.

A mischievous glint came into Penelope's eye and she giggled.

'I suppose that we could always surprise him.'

'Who? George?'

'No, Mother,' said Penelope. 'Father. If he will not come down to Kent to see us, we could go up to London instead to see him. It would be a real surprise.'

'I am not sure that it is one your father would appreciate.'

'Why not?'

'He likes to keep his home life and business affairs apart.'

'We would not get in his way,' argued Penelope. 'We can stay in Westminster then go into the city to do our shopping. George tells me that there is so much rebuilding going on there now. It is very exciting. I would love to see it. May we go to London, Mother?'

'No, Penelope.'

'But I want to. I crave a diversion.'

'George Strype will provide all the diversion you need once you are married to him,' said her mother easily. 'Concentrate your mind on that. Let your husband take you to London in the fullness of time. I'll not leave my garden for anybody.'

'Not even to see the look of surprise on Father's face?'

'Not even for that.'

'But you used to love London at one time.'

'Those days are gone, Penelope,' she said wistfully. 'I have found other pleasures in life. They have proved more reliable. Come,' she said, rising to her feet and pulling her daughter after her. 'Let us take a stroll. I will show you where I am having the new pond situated. They are to start digging next week. We will have made substantial progress by the time your father returns.' She held back a sigh. 'Whenever that may be.'

Christopher Redmayne threw caution to the winds and set out alone. He was in too much of a hurry to wait for the security of an escort to Kent, trusting instead in a fast horse, a strong sword-arm and an instinct for danger. Only one incident disrupted his long ride south. As the afternoon began to shade into evening, he saw a figure on the brow of the hill ahead of him. Crouched beneath a tree, the man used a crutch to haul himself upright and hobbled to the middle of the road. His hand stretched out in search of alms. Dressed in rags and wearing a battered old hat, he looked like a lonely beggar but there was something about him which alerted Christopher, who took note of the thick bushes nearby. It was an ideal place for an ambush. From that vantage point, anyone approaching in either direction could be seen a long way off. Christopher could not understand why a lame man should drag himself up such a steep hill.

Slowing his horse to a trot, he held the reins in his left hand while keeping the right free. It was a wise precaution. When the rider was only a few yards away, the beggar suddenly sprang to life, shed his apparent lameness and ran forward, lifting the crutch to swing it viciously at his quarry. Christopher's sword was out in a flash, parrying the blow then jabbing hard to inflict a wound in the man's shoulder. Two accomplices leapt out from behind the bushes but they, too, met their match. The first was kicked full in the face and the second had the cudgel struck from his hand by the flashing sword. Before any of the trio could recover, Christopher was galloping hell-for-leather down the other side of the hill.

The remainder of the journey passed without interruption.

Unable to reach his destination before nightfall, Christopher elected to stay at an inn and rest his horse. It was only when he climbed into bed that he realised how tired he was. Before he could even begin to review his day, he was fast asleep. Restored and refreshed, he was up shortly after dawn to eat a simple breakfast. The landlord, a big barrel of a man with flabby lips and a bulbous nose, came across to offer guidance.

'Do you travel far, sir?' he asked.

'I am not sure,' said Christopher. 'I am heading for a place near Sevenoaks.'

'What's the name?'

'Shipbourne.'

'Where, sir?'

'Shipbourne.'

The landlord chuckled. 'There are no ships born around here, sir. We're miles from the sea. I think you must want Shibborn. That's what we call it, sir. Not Ship-bourne. Shibborn.'

'How far away is it?'

'Eight or nine miles.'

'Good. Would you happen to have heard of Priestfield Place?'

'Everyone's heard of it,' said the other, his face hardening. 'The estate belongs to Sir Ambrose Northcott. All five hundred acres of it. Sir Ambrose is well known in this county.'

'Well known and well liked?'

'Ask that of his tenants, sir.'

'What do you mean?'

'They do not speak too kindly of him,' muttered the landlord. 'That is all I am prepared to say. I never met Sir Ambrose myself so I am no judge if he is really as harsh as they claim.'

'How would I find Priestfield Place?'

'Strike off to the left before you reach Shibborn, sir. You will see a signpost to Plaxtol. The estate lies between the two of them.'

'Thank you, landlord.'

'Are you a friend of Sir Ambrose?' probed the other.

Christopher gave a noncommittal nod. He was carrying sad tidings which the Northcott family deserved to hear first. He did not want the news to be spread by means of rumour through the mouth of a portly innkeeper.

Having paid his bill, he set off. It was a fine morning and his ride took him through undulating countryside which offered all kinds of attractive vistas. Christopher saw little of them. He was too distracted by the questions which had haunted him since the moment of discovery in the cellars of the house near Baynard's Castle.

Why did Sir Ambrose Northcott visit the site so late of an evening? Who was his companion? What was the motive behind the murder? Why had Solomon Creech reacted with such fear when he heard of the crime? There were subsidiary questions about the house in Westminster, the whereabouts of Sir Ambrose during his long absence from London and the nature of his political activities. Christopher was reminded time and again just how little he really knew of the man for whom he had designed a house. Why had Henry kept so much from his brother? Sir Ambrose Northcott was hidden behind a veil of secrecy. For what purpose? One final question tugged repeatedly at Christopher's mind.

Why did Jonathan Bale seem to resent him so much?

His cogitations carried him all the way to the crude signpost with the first mention of Plaxtol. Christopher turned his horse down a narrow track which had been baked hard by the sun and which ran between bramble bushes. Riding at a steady canter, he soon found himself entering the outer reaches of Priestfield Place. Most of it was tenanted and those who farmed it were out working in the fields but Sir Ambrose had reserved a vast swathe of land at the very heart of the estate. After passing a herd of cows, grazing contentedly in a meadow, Christopher followed a twisting path through woodland before coming out into open country again. The house positively leapt into view. It still lay over half a mile away but its effect was dramatic.

Set in an elevated position, Priestfield Place was an Elizabethan manor house of the finest quality. It was built of rose-coloured brick which blossomed in the sunshine and which conveyed an impression both of solidity and delicacy. The house was shaped like the letter H, its central portion gabled, its four corners guarded by octagonal turrets which were topped by gilt weather vanes. Climbing to three storeys and roofed with red tiles, it was an imposing edifice which yielded ever more fresh and arresting detail the closer he got to it. Christopher was staggered by the generosity of its proportions and its sheer presence. The new London residence which Sir Ambrose Northcott had commissioned from him was imposing enough. Compared to Priestfield Place, however, it was a mere gatehouse.

When he reached the paved courtyard, he brought his mount to a halt so that he could admire the fountain in which water from sixteen separate invisible pipes played into the huge scallop shell held by the statue of Venus before cascading down again. Then he let his gaze travel to the elaborate porch over which the royal coat of arms had been carved in stone to commemorate a visit by Queen Elizabeth in the previous century. Before he could feast his eyes on the facade, Christopher saw a manservant emerging from the porch. When he introduced himself and announced his business, the visitor was invited into the house while his horse was stabled by an ostler.

Conducted into the Great Hall, he noted the striking pattern in the marble floor, the carved heads on some of the oak panelling and the array of family portraits. Over the mantelpiece hung a large painting of the late master of the house. Sir Ambrose was wearing a breastplate, holding a helmet and striking a military pose. The bold glare was that of a man who considered himself invincible. Christopher sighed inwardly.

Having asked to speak alone to Lady Northcott, he was surprised to see two ladies being shown into the hall. Penelope was keen to hear any news relating to her father and, though neither women yet sensed how devastating that news would be, both seemed to have braced themselves for disappointment. Introductions were made then the two women sat beside each other. Christopher lowered himself onto a chair opposite them. He cleared his throat before speaking.

'I fear that I am the bearer of bad tidings,' he said quietly.

Penelope immediately tensed but her mother retained her poise.

'Go on, Mr Redmayne,' encouraged the latter.

'Has something happened to Father?' asked Penelope. 'Is he ill? Has some accident befallen him? Will he be detained in London even longer?'

'Let Mr Redmayne tell us, dear.'

'I will, Lady Northcott,' he said, 'but I do it with the utmost regret. What I have to tell you is that your husband will not be returning to Priestfield Place at any time. He has passed away.'

Penelope turned white and tears welled in her eyes. Reaching out a hand to steady her daughter, Lady Northcott somehow preserved her own equanimity. She searched Christopher's eyes.

'I think you have softened the news for our benefit,' she decided. 'I have never known my husband to have a day's illness. He was a picture of health.' She gestured to the portrait. 'As you can see for yourself. This was no natural death, was it?'

'No, Lady Northcott.'

'Was he killed in an accident?'

Christopher shook his head. 'It was no accident.'

Penelope's self-control went and she burst into tears, turning to her mother who stood to draw her daughter into her arms. Christopher felt cruel at having to deliver such a shattering blow to them and he averted his gaze from their grief. Lady Northcott seemed calm but there was a deep anguish in her eyes. Penelope was moving towards hysteria and her mother had to hug and reassure her before the sobbing began to case. When her daughter had regained some of her composure, Lady Northcott looked over at their visitor again.

'What are the details, Mr Redmayne?' she said softly.

'I would prefer to spare you some of those, Lady Northcott.'

'Sir Ambrose was my husband. I have a right to know.' She saw the sympathetic glance which he threw towards Penelope. 'We both have a right to know. Hide nothing from us.'

'No,' said Penelope bravely. 'I am sorry to break down in front of you like that, sir. It will not happen again. Please do as my mother bids.'

'Very well.' He rose to his feet and cleared his throat again. 'Sir Ambrose was murdered by a person or persons unknown. His body was found in the cellar of the new house.'

'New house?' repeated Lady Northcott.

'The one I designed for you near Baynard's Castle,'

'Ah, yes,' she said, failing to cover her surprise. 'I was forgetting. *That* house. Please continue, Mr Redmayne.'

Christopher was as discreet and succinct as he could be but the full horror of what had occurred could not be hidden. The two of them held each other throughout and he saw the mother's arms tighten to the point where she was almost supporting her daughter. Lady Northcott's pain was confined to her eyes but Penelope expressed hers more openly, gasping aloud, sagging, swaying then gritting her teeth in an effort to master her emotions. Christopher answered their questions briefly and honestly. Realising that neither of them had any knowledge of a new London house, he took care not to mention it again.

Lady Frances Northcott drew herself up to her full height.

'Thank you, Mr Redmayne,' she said without a tremor. It is very kind of you to ride down here to impart this news. Would you please wait here for a little while? We need to excuse ourselves for a few minutes.'

'Of course.'

He crossed to open the door for them and they went out. Penelope was too absorbed in her own sadness to do anything more than shuffle past on her mother's arm but the latter moved with natural dignity. Christopher shut the door gently behind them. Walking over to the portrait above the mantelpiece, he looked up at Sir Ambrose Northcott and wondered why a man should spend such an immense amount of money on a house while omitting to mention its construction to his wife and daughter. It was baffling. It also put Christopher in the unfortunate position of having to deliver an additional blow to the two women. He consoled himself with the thought that he had probably handled an awkward situation with more tact and sensitivity than Solomon Creech. Had the lawyer travelled to Priestfield Place, he would doubtless have compounded their misery.

Asked to wait briefly, Christopher was left alone for well over half an hour. Though it gave him an opportunity to explore the Great Hall and its many intriguing features, it also left him with the sense that he was now in the way. Some sort of collapse must have taken place, he surmised, as both women struggled with their grief in private. He had a vision of Penelope Northcott, lying on her bed, crying in despair, knocked senseless by the news he had relayed to her. Christopher had an impulse to reach out to comfort her but he sensed that she was beyond solace of any kind and it was not, in any case, his place to offer it. Lady Northcott had maintained her calm in his presence but he doubted if it would last indefinitely. The most probable thing, he decided, was that both of them were so caught up in their distress that they had forgotten all about him. It would be a kindness to them to steal quietly away.

Christopher had almost reached the front door when she called.

'Where are you going, Mr Redmayne?' she asked.

'Oh,' he said, turning. 'I thought that I was perhaps intruding.'

'You were leaving?'

'It seemed advisable.'

'But I must speak to you.'

It was Penelope Northcott who had come down the stairs and not her mother. Though her face was still white and her eyes swollen by a bout of tears, she was now much more controlled and her voice was calm. She took him by the arm and led him back into the Great Hall.

'I must apologise,' she said earnestly. 'It was unmannerly of us to leave you alone for so long but we needed to...' Her voice tailed off. She needed a deep breath before she could speak again. 'Anyway, I am glad that I came down in time to stop you going before I could add my personal thanks. I do appreciate your taking the trouble to ride all the way to Priestfield Place.'

'It was no trouble, I assure you. I felt it my bounden duty.'

'Duty?'

'Your father was very kind to me, Miss Northcott.'

'Ah, yes,' she said distantly. 'The house. You designed it.'

'My first commission.' He felt the need to soothe her. 'Your father obviously planned to surprise you with it when the house was finally built. Sir Ambrose clearly had an interest in architecture. How could he not, living in such a magnificent property as this? Yes,' he said without any real conviction, 'that must have been it. The London house was destined to be a gift to your mother. Or perhaps even to you and your future husband. It would have made a perfect wedding present.'

'Yes,' she said.

But they both knew that the notion was wildly improbable.

'Were you a close friend of my father's?' she asked.

'Not at all. I was just one of many people whom he employed. Sir Ambrose always kept his distance. To tell you the truth, he was a rather mysterious figure to me.'

'Yes,' she murmured.

'The one person who did know him was my brother, Henry.'

'Your brother?'

'Yes,' said Christopher. 'It was Henry who showed some of my drawings to your father and encouraged him to meet me. From my point of view, it was the most wonderful stroke of fortune. Until now.'

Penelope indicated a chair, waited until he was seated then sat next to him. He caught a faint whiff of her perfume. Now that she was alone and much closer to him, he became more conscious of her beauty. Mild excitement stirred inside him. She raised a quizzical eyebrow.

'Why did you bring the news, Mr Redmayne?'

'I felt that you had a right to be informed as soon as possible.'

'But it was not your place to act as the messenger.'

'I believe that it was.'

'Why?'

'Because I was the person who actually found the body,' he said, 'and because the hideous crime took place in a property which I designed for your father.'

'That still does not make it your duty,' she replied. 'Especially as you did not really know my father very well. His lawyer should have brought the news or sent someone in his stead. We are very used to receiving messages from Mr Creech. Father often made contact with us through him.'

'Solomon Creech would not take on the responsibility.'

'But it fell to him.'

'He was shaken by news of the murder. When I told him, he became very agitated. He more or less refused to send word to you so I took on the office. Nobody else seemed willing to do so, including my brother, Henry. To be honest, Miss Northcott...' The scent of perfume drifted into his nostrils again and he paused momentarily to enjoy it. 'To be honest,' he added, leaning a little closer, 'I was grateful for the opportunity. I hoped that it would enable me to learn much more about Sir Ambrose.'

'Why should you want to do that, Mr Redmayne?'

'Because I intend to find the man who killed him.'

'Oh!' she said, blinking in astonishment. 'But surely it is not your task to do so. You are an architect.'

'I *was* an architect. Until yesterday.'

'Must you now turn into an avenging angel?'

'There will be nothing angelic about my vengeance.'

'But think of the danger. The murderer is a ruthless man.'

'I am all too aware of that,' said Christopher. 'I witnessed his handiwork. He must be called to account and I will do everything in my power to catch him. You have my word.'

The turquoise eyes roamed freely over his face, ignited by

a mixture of admiration and apprehension. He basked in her frank curiosity. It was oddly exhilarating.

'Take care, sir,' she said at length.

'I will, Miss Northcott.'

'Do you have any clues as to the identity of the killer?'

'None as yet.'

'Were you expecting to find some at Priestfield Place?'

'As a matter of fact, I was.'

'How?'

'I thought that your mother might at least be able to give me some guidance,' he admitted. 'Lady Northcott would know the names of her husband's enemies and details of any bitter arguments in which Sir Ambrose was engaged. Possibly your father's life has even been threatened in the recent past.'

'If it had been,' she said softly, 'he would not have confided in Mother. Still less in me. The truth is that Father was very rarely here long enough to tell us anything.' She gave a shrug. 'We have not seen him for months.'

'But he was away from London for almost three weeks.'

'Did he tell you that he was coming home?'

'No,' said Christopher, 'but that is what I assumed.'

'We have all made too many assumptions about my father.'

She lowered her head and became lost in her thoughts. Penelope was torn between sorrow at her father's death and regret that she knew so little about the man who had been cruelly murdered at a new house of whose existence she was quite unaware. It was embarrassing to make such a confession to a complete stranger. When she looked up, she tried to mumble an apology but Christopher waved it away.

'Say nothing now,' he advised. 'It was wrong of me to expect any help when you and your mother were still reeling from this dreadful shock. I will trespass on your feelings no longer,' he said, getting to his feet. 'Let me just add this, Miss Northcott. If – in due course – either of you does recall something about Sir Ambrose which might be helpful to me, please send word. A message can reach me in London.'

'Where?'

'Fetter Lane. Number seven.'

'Fetter Lane.'

'Will you remember that address?'

'Yes, Mr Redmayne, but I hold out no promises.'

'Any detail, however minor, could be useful. I need to know about any disputes Sir Ambrose may have had. Problems with tenants, things of that nature. But not now. Forget me until…until you are ready.'

'I will not forget you,' she said, rising to her feet. 'You have been so considerate to us, sir. And now you tell me that you are trying to solve this murder on our behalf even if it means putting your own life at risk. I am profoundly touched and Mother will feel the same when I tell her. You are very brave, Mr Redmayne.'

'I am very determined, that is all.'

'Find him, please.'

'I will.'

'Find the man who killed my father.'

'He will not escape, Miss Northcott.'

She reached out to squeeze both of his hands in a gesture of gratitude and Christopher felt another thrill of excitement. Even in her distress, Penelope Northcott was an enchanting young lady and he had to remind himself that his interest was wholly misplaced. He was there for one purpose alone. It was time to go yet somehow he could not move away from her and the wonder of it was that she seemed to share his reluctance at their parting. He stood there, gazing at her, searching for words of farewell which simply would not come. Christopher felt that such a tender moment justified all the effort of riding down to Kent. The tenderness did not last long.

The door suddenly opened and a young man came striding in.

'Penelope!' he said, descending on her. 'I have just heard the news from Lady Northcott.'

'George!'

'You poor thing!' He enfolded her in his arms. 'What an appalling crime! Someone will be made to pay for this, mark my words!'

The arrival of her fiancé unnerved Penelope and she lost her control for a short while, sobbing into his shoulder. George Strype made soothing sounds and patted her gently on the back. He was a tall man with long dark hair which fell in curls to the shoulders of his coat. Though he was moderately handsome, his costly attire failed to hide the fact that he was running to fat. Christopher noticed the podgy hands and the nascent double chin. He also experienced a surge of envy at a man who was entitled to embrace Penelope Northcott so freely.

George Strype flung an inhospitable glance at Christopher.

'Who are you, sir?' he said coldly.

'My name is Christopher Redmayne.'

'The messenger, I presume?'

'Oh, Mr Redmayne is much more than that,' said Penelope.

'Indeed?' said Strype.

'Yes, George.'

She introduced the two men properly then spoke so warmly about the visitor that Strype interrupted her. Keeping a proprietary arm around her shoulder, he sized the other man up then gave a contemptuous snort.

'So you intend to solve a murder, do you?'

Christopher held his gaze. 'Yes, Mr Strype.'

'How do you propose to do that?'

'This is neither the time nor place to discuss it.'

'In other words, you have no earthly notion where to start.'

'In other words,' said Christopher, 'this is an occasion of intense sadness for Miss Northcott and I would not dare to distress her further by talking at length about her father's murder. It would be unseemly.'

'Thank you, Mr Redmayne,' she said.

'He does not deserve your thanks, Penelope.'

'Yes, he does, George.'

'Why?'

'For showing such tact.'

'What use is tact?'

'And for displaying such courage.'

'There is nothing courageous in a foolish boast.'

'Mr Redmayne did not boast.'

'He is raising false hopes, Penelope, and that is a cruelty.'

'Nothing on earth would induce me to be cruel to your fiancée, sir,' said Christopher courteously. 'I am sorry that my plans meet with such disapproval from you, especially as you might be in a position to render me some assistance. Evidently, I would be misguided if I looked for help from your direction. When the killer is caught – as he will be – you may yet have the grace to admit that you were too hasty in your assessment of my character. You may, Mr Strype, though I suspect that you will not.' He turned to Penelope. 'Please excuse me, Miss Northcott. I have stayed far too long as it is.'

'No, Mr Redmayne,'

'Let him go,' grunted Strype.

'But the least we can do is to offer our guest refreshment.'

'He can find that at the nearest inn, Penelope.'

'George!'

'He is not a guest, Penelope. Merely a messenger.'

'That is very unkind,' she chided.

'We need to be alone.'

'I could not agree with Mr Strype more,' said Christopher, moving to the door. 'I have discharged my duty as a mere messenger and I must away. It is a long and tedious ride back to London. Please give my regards to Lady Northcott and tell her that I hope to meet her in less painful circumstances next time.'

'There is no need for you to meet her at all,' said Strype.

'You are probably right.'

'Goodbye, sir!'

'Goodbye.'

'Wait!' called Penelope as he turned to go.

Christopher hesitated but whatever she had meant to say went unspoken. George Strype exuded such a sense of displeasure that she was visibly cowed and took refuge in his shoulder once more. Her fiancé enjoyed his minor triumph, stroking her hair and placing a kiss on the top of her head. He was lavish in his affection. When he looked up to give himself the satisfaction of dismissing the visitor, he saw that he was too late. Christopher had already slipped out of the house.

As he strolled towards the stables, Christopher asked himself why such a lovely young lady should allow herself to become engaged to such a disagreeable man. Strype looked ten years older than his fiancée and clearly set in his attitudes. He had the arrogant manner of someone whose authority was never challenged. Christopher felt even more pity for Penelope Northcott. At a time when she most needed sympathy, she was in the hands of George Strype. The man's arrival did have one advantage. It robbed Christopher himself of all vain interest in Penelope. She was spoken for and that was that. His mind was liberated to concentrate on the important task of tracking down the man who killed her father.

The stables were at the side of the house but curiosity got the better of him. Instead of retrieving his horse, he went on to take a look at the garden which now stretched out before him. It was breathtaking in its sense of order. Neat rectangular lawns were fringed with colourful borders and dotted with circular flowerbeds. Trees and shrubs grew in serried ranks. Paths criss-crossed with geometrical precision and water met the eye in every direction. Gauging the amount of work which must have gone into its creation and maintenance, he could only marvel.

Its most startling feature was sitting on a bench. She blended so perfectly with her surroundings that at first Christopher did not see her. Lady Frances Northcott was resting in the shade of an arbour as she looked across to the willows edging the lake. Where she might have been tense and doleful, she seemed at that distance to be surprisingly at ease. Christopher could not resist getting a little closer to make sure that it really was the widow of Sir Ambrose Northcott. She had borne the news of his murder with extraordinary composure and Christopher fully expected her to return to him once she had escorted her daughter to her bedchamber. In the event, it was Penelope who came back, giving the impression that it was her mother who was so consumed by grief that she could not face the visitor again.

Lady Northcott was not consumed with grief now. Christopher crept across a lawn until he was only ten yards or so away. Concealing himself behind some rhododendrons, he watched her with fascination for a few minutes. When her head turned briefly in his direction, giving him a clear view of her face, he was shocked. Instead of mourning the death of her husband, Lady Frances Northcott had a smile of contentment on her lips.

CHAPTER NINE

Jonathan Bale ignored the light drizzle as he moved slowly around with his gaze fixed firmly on the ground. It was a long painstaking search but it yielded nothing of real value. He withdrew to the road and studied the site pensively. It was deserted. Work on the house had been terminated and Samuel Littlejohn's men sent home while he looked for alternative employment for them. Most of the building materials had been removed for storage elsewhere. The once busy site had a forlorn air, its ambition snuffed out, its bold design unrealised, its vestigial walls giving it more of a kinship with the ruined households all around it than with the new dwellings which were gradually taking their place. Notwithstanding his reservations about the owner and architect, the constable felt a pang of genuine regret.

It was not shared by the man who strutted up beside him.

'The message could not be clearer,' he asserted.

'What message?' said Jonathan.

'God has spoken. No house should ever be built on this site. It is patently doomed to fall. First, came the Great Fire. Then, the spate of thefts. And now, a foul murder. These are all signs.'

'Of what, Mr Thorpe?'

'God's displeasure.'

'You believe that we have witnessed divine dispensation?'

'What else?'

'Gross misfortune,' argued Jonathan. 'God may be displeased but He would not initiate a murder.'

'It was a punishment inflicted upon the owner of the property.'

'What was his crime?'

'He embodied sin, Mr Bale.'

'Did he?'

'What greater crime is there than that?'

Sensing that Jesus-Died-To-Save-Me Thorpe was in homiletic vein, the constable held back a response. His task was to catch a murderer, not to look for theological significance in what had happened and the last thing he wanted at that moment was an extended sermon from the argumentative Quaker. He ran a ruminative hand across his chin as he scanned the site again. His diminutive neighbour turned to practicalities.

'Have any arrests been made, Mr Bale?'

'Not as yet.'

'Hast thou any indications as to who was responsible?'

'According to you, it was the Almighty.'

'Acting through a human agent.'

'Oh, I see.'

'What clues have been found?'

'I continue to search for them, Mr Thorpe,' admitted the other. 'That is why I came here again this afternoon. I have been over every inch of the site three times now but without much success.'

'I am sorry that I am unable to help thee on this occasion.'

'You prevented one crime, sir.'

'It was my duty to do so.'

'Others would have been too frightened to report what they heard.'

'I am not afraid of common thieves.'

'You deserve great credit. Thanks to your actions, four villains are under lock and key. Those three thieves and their accomplice.' He gave a congratulatory nod. 'I must confess that I thought at first they might in some way be connected to this murder.'

'How?'

'Arrest will cost them dear,' said Jonathan. 'I conceived it possible that a confederate of theirs was sent to exact a dark revenge by killing Sir Ambrose Northcott. On reflection, I dismissed the idea.'

'Why?'

'Because the owner of the house would be an unlikely target. It was I who actually made the arrests with the help of Mr Littlejohn and Mr Redmayne. One of us would have been a more likely recipient of that fatal dagger. Had I been the one,' he said with a philosophical smile, 'it would not have been the first time that I was attacked. Mine is an unpopular job but a necessary one.'

'And necessarily corrupt.'

'How so?'

'Because thou servest a corrupt master, Mr Bale.'

'I serve the citizens of this ward, sir. They include you.'

'Indirectly, thou art a lackey of the King and his vile Parliament.'

'That is not how I see it, Mr Thorpe.'

'Then thou art purblind. One day, perhaps, thou wilt realise the error of thy ways and allow thine eyes to be fully opened to the wonder of God.' He began to move off. 'Farewell to thee.'

Jonathan held up a hand. 'One moment, sir.'

'Yes?' Thorpe halted.

'I am glad that we have met,' said the other, turning up his collar as the drizzle thickened, 'even if it is in such wet weather. It gives me the chance to pass on a word of warning.'

His companion bristled. 'Do I look as if I am in need of it?'

'This is for your own good, Mr Thorpe.'

'I prefer to be the judge of that.'

'Then hear me out,' said Jonathan seriously. 'There are rumours that a seditious pamphlet has been distributed among the Friends. It is said that it pours scorn on the established religion and goes so far as to incite violence. I am sure that you realise the penalty for printing such a document.'

'Only too well.'

'Distributing such material carries an additional penalty.'

'I am familiar with the savagery of the law.'

'Even reading this pamphlet is a crime.'

'If it exists.'

'I believe that it does, Mr Thorpe.'

'Rumours are usually false.'

'This is more than a rumour. I merely wished to say that I hope you are not involved with this publication in any way.'

'Am I accused?'

'Not by name, sir, but we are bound to look to you.'

'Innocence should be its own protection.'

'If – that is – you are entirely innocent.'

'I am, Mr Bale. In my own mind.'

'That is a contentious issue.'

'Then let us debate it here and now.'

'No, sir,' said Jonathan tolerantly. 'We both know where the other stands. While I cannot agree with your position, I respect you for taking it. All that I wish to do here is to give you fair warning that you are under scrutiny. It would be foolish of you to flout the law again.'

'The real folly lies in the law itself.'

'I have said my piece, sir.'

'It did not need saying, Mr Bale,' came the vehement reply. 'Look at thyself, man. Thou art trying to solve the heinous crime of murder. Does the printing of a pamphlet rank alongside that? Canst thou not turn thy attention to real villains and leave us be?'

Jesus-Died-To-Save-Me Thorpe was about to launch himself into a diatribe but his neighbour cut his fulminations short with a kind inquiry.

'How is your wife, sir? I was sorry to hear of her illness.'

The Quaker was checked. 'She is much better.'

'I am glad to hear that.'

'Hail-Mary will soon be able to venture out again.'

'Please give her my regards.'

'Thy own wife hast been very kind,' said Thorpe quietly. 'Mrs Bale brought food and comfort to our house. That chicken broth of hers has done Hail-Mary the power of good.'

'It is Sarah's favourite medicine.'

'A wholesome remedy. I tasted it myself.'

'It can cure many ills.'

'But not, alas, the ones that afflict this city.'

Jonathan took an involuntary step back, fearing another broadside about the moral turpitude of the King and his counsellors, but his little companion instead gave a rare smile.

'I will spare thee my opinions this time,' he said. 'Thy warning was well-intentioned, though no less irritating for that. It deserves a like favour from me. Besides, someone else waits to speak with thee.'

Jonathan looked around. 'Who?'

'Do not keep the ladies waiting, Mr Bale.'

Jesus-Died-To-Save-Me Thorpe touched the brim of his hat in a faint salute then strode off quickly. The constable, meanwhile, looked across at the two women who were hovering a short distance away with their hoods drawn up against the drizzle. The older and plainer of the two was, judging by her attire and her subservient manner, a maid of some kind. Though he could only see half of her face,

Jonathan did not need to be told who the much younger woman was. The resemblance to Samuel Littlejohn was clear. It had to be his daughter. Hands clasped together and lips pursed, she gazed wistfully at the site. Jonathan strolled across to her.

'Did you wish to speak to me?' he asked politely.

Margaret Littlejohn came out of her reverie to look at him.

'Yes, Constable,' she said.

'Well?'

'Are you acquainted with Mr Christopher Redmayne?'

'I am indeed.'

'Do you happen to know where he is?'

'I believe so.'

She reached out impulsively to grasp him by the wrist.

'Please tell me how I can find him.'

Amid the musty books and sheaves of paper in his office, Solomon Creech was bent over his desk, perusing a document with intense concentration. The tentative knock on the door went unheard. When it was repeated, it had marginally more authority. Clicking his tongue, he looked up with a mixture of annoyance and dread.

'Come in,' he snapped.

His clerk stepped into the room and closed the door behind him, keeping his back to it. He gave an apologetic smile.

'Well, Geoffrey?' said the other.

'You have a visitor, Mr Creech.'

'I told you that I would see nobody today.'

'The gentleman would not be turned away.'

'Who is he?'

'Mr Redmayne.'

'Henry Redmayne?'

'His brother.'

Creech gave a mild shudder. 'That is even worse. Tell him that I am far too busy and send him swiftly on his way.' The clerk hesitated. 'About it straight, man! What is keeping you?'

Geoffrey Anger gave a nervous laugh and swallowed hard. Fate had committed a libel when he was named for nobody was less capable of showing anger than the timid clerk. A shy, studious man in his thirties, he peered through spectacles which served as much as a protective screen as an aid to his poor vision. Thinning hair and a pinched face made him look considerably older than his years. He was a conscientious clerk who toiled for long hours without complaint but who was racked with guilt whenever he did anything as violent as swatting a fly off his desk. To expel an unwanted visitor was a Herculean labour to him.

'Go on, Geoffrey!' ordered Creech. 'Do as I tell you.'

'What if the gentleman will not leave?'

'*Make* him leave!'

The clerk let out a cry of alarm and brought a hand to his throat. He did not relish his task in the least. Mustering all of his resolve, he went back into the outer office to pass on the message to the visitor. It was not well-received. Brushing him aside, Christopher opened the door of Creech's office and went in to confront the lawyer. Geoffrey Anger was left bleating ineffectually in his wake.

Solomon Creech had ire enough for twenty men.

'What is the meaning of this?' he said, leaping to his feet.

'I wish to speak to you, Mr Creech.'

'This is my private domain, sir. You cannot come bursting in here like that. It is tantamount to trespass.'

'I was left with no alternative.' Christopher closed the door on the gaping figure of the clerk. 'I came here for some answers and I will not depart until I have them.'

'I am not available to clients today.'

'I did not come here as a client.'

'I am not ready to see *anyone!*'

'Then I will wait until you are.'

The visitor lowered himself onto a chair and folded his arms in a show of determination. Creech lost his temper completely, yelling wildly, waving his hands in the air and threatening to have him evicted. None of his imprecations had the slightest effect on Christopher who simply waited until the storm blew itself out. The lawyer eventually sat down in his chair and frothed with impotent rage.

'I went to Priestfield Place yesterday,' said Christopher at length.

'Indeed, sir?' growled the other.

'Lady Northcott was most unimpressed with your behaviour. She felt that it was your duty to pass on the sad news. You failed her miserably.'

'I was too caught up in events, here, Mr Redmayne. In any case, why should I bother to send word when you were intent on travelling to Kent yourself? But,' he said defensively, 'I have not been idle. The body has at last been released by the coroner. I arranged for it to be transported to Priestfield

173

Place so that burial can take place in the family vault. Even as we speak, Sir Ambrose is making his final journey.'

'He leaves many pertinent questions behind him.'

'I am struggling with some of them now, sir,' the lawyer said, pointing to the document before him. 'This is his will. Its provisions are highly complicated and it demands my full attention.'

'So do I,' insisted Christopher.

'Could we not postpone this discussion until tomorrow?'

'No, Mr Creech.'

'Until later on this afternoon, then?'

'Now, sir! I insist.'

'I will not be browbeaten, sir,' warned the other.

'Nor will I.'

Their eyes locked in a tussle but it did not last long. The lawyer soon saw the futility of trying to defy his visitor. Christopher Redmayne was no fearful and reticent clerk who could be brought to heel with a snarl. He was resolute and single-minded.

Creech resigned himself to the inevitable. He became curious.

'How did Lady Northcott receive the news?' he asked.

'Very bravely. In the circumstances.'

'What do you mean?'

'Well,' said Christopher, 'to begin with, she had to endure the shock of learning that her husband had been brutally murdered. That is ordeal enough for any loving wife. But I inadvertently inflicted another wound when I happened to mention the new house. Neither Lady Northcott nor her daughter had the slightest notion that it existed.'

'Indeed?' mumbled the other.

'You *know* that it is so, Mr Creech. And that is my first question. Why were they not told? What kind of husband keeps something as important as this from his wife?'

'It is not for me to speculate.'

'Sir Ambrose had a reason to conceal that house from them.'

'I suppose that he must have.'

'What was it, Mr Creech?'

'I can only guess,' said the other evasively. 'Sir Ambrose Northcott was a close man. He took nobody into his confidence.'

'Except his lawyer.'

'Only in respect of legal matters.'

'Building a new house *is* a legal matter,' Christopher reminded him. 'You drew up the contracts and visited the site while Sir Ambrose was away. That brings me to another point. Where did he go during those three weeks?'

'It is a private matter, Mr Redmayne.'

'I need to know.'

'Well, I am not able to tell you.'

'But it may have a bearing on his death. Something may have happened during that time while he was away which led to his murder.' He spread his arms questioningly. 'Do you not want this crime solved?'

'Of course.'

'Then give me some help. Where was Sir Ambrose?'

'I wish I knew.'

'Surely he confided in you?'

'I knew only that he was going away on business.

He often did that. I never pressed him for details of his whereabouts.'

'But you must have had some inkling where he went.'

'No, sir.'

'I think you are lying.'

'You may think what you wish.'

'I am minded to shake the truth out of you.'

'If you do, my clerk will fetch a constable to arrest you.'

Christopher stood up abruptly and leant across the desk.

'Who killed him, Mr Creech?'

'How should I know?'

'Because you were closer to him than anyone else. Sir Ambrose trusted you. He told me so himself. His business affairs must have brought in an enormous amount of contractual work for his lawyer.'

'That is true,' conceded the other.

'Then you were more aware of his activities and his movements than anyone else.' He remembered the look of surprise on the two faces at Priestfield Place. 'Far more aware, for instance, than his own family. They were kept wholly in the dark, it seems. Come, Mr Creech. You must have your suspicions about the identity of the killer. Reveal them. Who were Sir Ambrose's enemies? Who were his rivals?'

'Mr Redmayne—'

'With whom did Sir Ambrose do business?'

'That is confidential information.'

'Heavens, man! This is a murder investigation.'

'In which you have no rightful part.'

'Give me some *names!*'

'No!' howled Creech. 'I'll not be interrogated like this!'

'I need your help.'

'Well, you will not get it by forcing your way in here and trying to intimidate me. Nobody is more eager to have this crime solved than I am, believe me. The death of Sir Ambrose Northcott has left me with the most extraordinary amount of work to do on his behalf,' he said, waving a hand at his desk. 'I have to process his will, write countless letters to inform people of his demise and take over the running of his business affairs until someone else is appointed to do so. With all that pressing down on me, I do not have time to indulge in pointless guesswork with you.'

'It is not pointless. You know those names.'

'I know only what Sir Ambrose permitted me to know.'

'What was the motive for the murder?'

'Good day, Mr Redmayne.'

'Where should I start looking?'

'Anywhere but here!' affirmed Creech. 'The only legitimate business you have with me regards the house and I can assure you now that the contract will not be revoked. Though the house will not be built, you will not lose the entire fee. Compensation will be paid.'

'That is the least of my worries at this moment.'

'It is among the most immediate of mine. I like to keep things neat and tidy, sir. It is a rule of mine. Funds will soon be released to all the parties involved. Mr Littlejohn will get his money. So will you. And so will your brother.'

Christopher frowned. 'My brother?'

'Yes, Mr Redmayne.'

'Monies are due to him as well?'

'Did you not realise that?'

An unsettling thought came into Christopher's mind.

'Tell me more, Mr Creech,' he said.

Seated among his cronies at the coffee house, Henry Redmayne held court. Days after the murder of Sir Ambrose Northcott, the event still continued to dominate the conversation and, as a known associate of the dead man, Henry was accorded a great deal of respect and attention. He enjoyed his moment of celebrity.

'I did warn him,' he said airily, sipping his coffee then holding the cup aloft between finger and thumb. 'Sir Ambrose had many enemies but he would go abroad without due care. I offered to be his bodyguard on many occasions but, alas, he spurned the suggestion. Would that he had not, gentlemen! My sword would have saved him. Sir Ambrose would even now be sitting here with the rest of us. I grieve for him.'

Henry gave a theatrical sigh but his grief was short-lived. When he caught sight of his brother, he quickly put down his cup and excused himself from the company. Christopher was bearing down on him with a scowl which promised a stern reprimand and Henry did not wish to receive it in front of his friends. Intercepting his brother, he guided him to an empty table in the corner of the room.

'What a pleasant surprise!' said Henry, taking a seat.

'It is more pleasant than the one I have just had,' returned Christopher, remaining on his feet. 'I come from the offices of Solomon Creech.'

'And?'

'He tells me that you are to receive a percentage of my fee.'

'The treacherous devil!'

'Is it true, Henry?'

'Sit down a moment.'

'Is it or is it not true?'

'I am saying nothing until you sit down,' said Henry, conscious that everyone was now looking at them. 'And lower your voice while you are at it, Christopher. I do not want the whole world to know my business.'

Christopher sat down. 'It seems that you did not even want your brother to know your business. This is appalling.'

'It is normal practice, I assure you.'

'Normal? To steal money from someone else?'

'It was earned and not stolen. Who got you that commission in the first place? Who introduced you to Sir Ambrose? Who made his younger brother sound like a new Christopher Wren?'

'You did, Henry.'

'Thank you!'

'At a price.'

'I was entitled to some reward.'

'Then why did you not ask for it?' said Christopher. 'For it would have been willingly given. I was never involved in this enterprise for the money, you know that. It was the challenge which inspired me. I worked all the hours God sends on those drawings and I was deeply grateful to you for getting me the opportunity to do so. It never crossed my mind that you were conniving behind my back.'

'It was Sir Ambrose's idea,' lied the other.

'Then why does it have the ring of Henry Redmayne to it?'

'That is a slur on my character!'

'Who put it there? In truth,' said Christopher, pulsing with rage, 'this is shabby behaviour even by your low standards. To charge your own brother! Have I ever charged you for any of the countless favours I have done in the past?'

'No, you have not.'

'Do I send you a bill each time I deceive Father on your behalf?'

'Thankfully, no.'

'It gives me no joy to dissemble. Father is a good man and he deserves honesty from his sons but how can I be honest with him when I talk about you? If he knew the true facts about your life, he would come hurrying down to London to exorcise your house.'

'Christopher!'

'And he would certainly cut off his generous allowance to you.'

'Let us leave Father out of this.'

'Why did you do it, Henry?' demanded the other.

'I told you. I felt that some reward was due to me.'

'Did you have to go behind my back to secure it?'

'I was intending to tell you in the fullness of time.'

'Stop lying!' said Christopher, banging the table. 'But for the death of Sir Ambrose, I would never have known about it.'

Henry was bitter. There was no need for you to learn about it now. Wait until I see that piece of excrement who calls himself a lawyer! I'll tear the wretch apart. My contract with Sir Ambrose was confidential.'

'It was an abrogation of trust between us.'

'Do not vex yourself about it so.'

'What do you expect, Henry – a round of applause?'

'Stop shouting. Everyone is staring at us.'

'Whose fault is that?'

'Look,' said the other, trying to mollify him. 'I admit that I was wrong to conceal this arrangement from you but you are an architect. Put it into perspective. It was, after all, only a very small percentage of your fee. And the damage is soon repaired.'

'Is it?'

'Of course. I will repay every penny. Will that suit?'

'No, Henry.'

'Why not?'

'Because I do not want the money,' said Christopher. 'I came here for an honest explanation and a sincere apology. Neither has come from you. Frankly, I am ashamed to call you my brother.'

'But what have I done wrong?'

'You could not begin to understand.'

'An agent is entitled to a fee.'

'A brother is entitled to fair dealing.'

'Without me, you would have had no work as an architect.'

Christopher was still fuming. 'Without me,' he said pointedly, 'you would have had nobody from whom to steal. Imagine how this news will be received at the Deanery in Gloucester.'

'You would surely not tell Father?' said Henry, going pale.

'If he asked me direct, I would not mislead him.'

'But that would be ruinous.'

'To whom?'

Henry was for once bereft of words. The thought of losing his allowance from his father and suffering a punitive sermon at the same time made him quail. Seeing how deeply hurt his brother was, he groped around for a means of deflecting Christopher's anger. An idea came to his rescue and sent his hand to his pocket. He produced a piece of paper.

'I have done as you asked,' he said with an appeasing smile. 'I made enquiries in political circles. Here is a list of six people who were the sworn enemies of Sir Ambrose.' He handed the paper over. 'The other four names are those of his closest associates.'

'I am amazed,' confessed Christopher.

'Why?'

'You have done something useful at last.'

'Show a semblance of gratitude.'

'I am not in the mood, Henry,' said the other, glancing at the names on the list. One jumped out at him. 'George Strype?'

'He is to marry Sir Ambrose's daughter.'

'I know that. You have him down as a close associate.'

'Why, so he is,' said Henry, recovering some of his confidence. 'He was often in London with his future father-in-law. I sometimes drank coffee with the pair of them here.'

'Where else did you imbibe with them?'

'Do I detect a note of suspicion in your voice, Christopher?'

'I ask out of interest,' said his brother. 'When I went down to Kent, I had the misfortune of meeting George Strype.

He was a surly gentleman, affianced to a young lady who deserves better. I would hate to hear that he is yet another denizen of your favourite brothels.'

'I am not familiar with his recreations. All I know is that he was a personal friend of Sir Ambrose Northcott and that the two of them had close business ties. George Strype is a very rich man,' he said with envy. 'He has just inherited a vast estate. In making a match between him and his daughter, Sir Ambrose was bringing off a very successful deal.'

'For whom?'

'All parties. Both men stood to gain.'

'And what of Penelope Northcott?'

'She would acquire a home, a husband and lifelong security.'

'Was she ever consulted about this successful deal?'

'Is that of any consequence?'

'Yes, Henry.'

'Why?'

'Because I pity the woman. Strype is not fit to lick her shoes.'

'Your first impressions of the fellow are very misleading,' said Henry. 'He can be quite engaging and the very fact that Sir Ambrose chose him as a son-in-law speaks volumes on his behalf. He would have weighed George Strype carefully in the balance. Of one thing I can assure you now,' he continued, straightening his periwig before adopting his accustomed pose, 'Sir Ambrose was an excellent judge of men. Why else would he choose me as a friend?'

In spite of himself, Christopher could not suppress a smile.

* * *

It was a crowded morning for Jonathan Bale. After hearing a report from the watchmen who had been on duty the previous night, he gave evidence in court regarding one case, then escorted the convicted prisoner from another and secured him in the stocks in Carter Lane. He then arbitrated in a dispute between bickering neighbours, helped to quell a tavern brawl in Knightrider Street and spent an hour taking further instructions from a Justice of the Peace. It left him little time to slip back to the site once more and institute another vain search for clues to the murder. When he returned to Addle Hill for dinner, he was tired and disappointed. His spirits were not lifted by the sight of the horse tethered outside his home.

Irritation turned to resentment when Jonathan entered the house and found Christopher Redmayne, sitting familiarly in his parlour and talking with the constable's wife. Most galling of all was the fact that Sarah seemed to like the visitor. She was chortling happily at something he had just said. Seeing her husband, she rose instantly to her feet.

'You have a visitor, Jonathan,' she said.

'So I see,' he grunted.

'Mr Redmayne has been waiting an hour or more.' She gave a farewell smile to Christopher. 'Excuse me.'

'I will, Mrs Bale. Thank you for the glass of beer.'

'It was a pleasure, sir.'

Jonathan writhed as his wife gave a faint curtsey before leaving. It endeared him even less to his unexpected caller. He sat opposite him.

'Why did you come here?' he asked inhospitably.

'It was the only way to be sure of finding you.'

'My wife should have sent out for me.'

'She was too busy talking to me,' said Christopher cheerily. 'You have a charming wife, Mr Bale. She was telling me about your sons, Oliver and Richard. I was not surprised to hear that they were named after Lord Protector Cromwell and his son. It explained a lot.'

'What can I do for you, sir?'

'Tell me what you have found out in my absence.'

'Little enough, I fear,' admitted Jonathan, 'though the surgeon confirmed my guess when he performed the autopsy. Sir Ambrose had been dead for at least twelve hours, he said, but he could not be precise about the actual time of the murder. The wound to the heart killed him but the bruises on his neck suggested an attempt to strangle him. Oh,' he recalled, 'one other interesting fact. There was blood on Sir Ambrose's hair.'

'I remember it well. A head wound?'

'No, sir. It did not belong to the deceased at all. It must have come from the man who murdered him.'

'Sir Ambrose fought back hard, then?'

'So it appears.'

'What else did the surgeon say?'

'Nothing of note. You are free to see the coroner's report.'

'Thank you, Mr Bale. I will. It will make gruesome reading but may yet release a valuable clue. Where else have your enquiries taken you?'

'Along the riverbank,' explained the other. 'Sir Ambrose was a person of some note in the mercantile community. And not a popular one at that. The merchants told me straight that they resented a man of his wealth and background forcing his way into their world. He did not belong there, they said. What they really meant is that he competed far too well against them. Sir Ambrose was a cunning trader.'

'So I have discovered.'

'He imported goods from many countries.'

'What sort of goods?'

'I have made a list for you, sir, to study at your leisure.'

'That will be very helpful.'

'What of you? When did you get back from Kent?'

'Early this morning. I spent last night at an inn then rode the final few miles to London.'

'Did you learn anything from the visit?'

'An enormous amount.'

Christopher Redmayne gave him an edited account of his journey to Priestfield Place, including a description of the arrogant behaviour of George Strype but omitting any mention of Lady Northcott's apparent indifference to her husband's death. The image of her, seated so happily in the garden with a smile on her lips, was still vivid in his mind yet he somehow felt the need to protect her from the constable's strong disapproval. What shocked Jonathan the most was the news that Sir Ambrose had kept his wife and daughter ignorant of the building of another London house.

'There should be no secrets between man and wife,' he said.

'I agree with you.'

'Marriage vows are there to be observed.'

'I raised the matter with Solomon Creech,' said Christopher wearily. 'He was the first person I called on when I returned to the city this morning. I taxed him with this deception of Sir Ambrose's. He pretended to know nothing of it.'

'Did you glean anything of value from him, sir?'

'Precious little. The man is running scared. He seemed to be looking over his shoulder all the time. I fear that we can look for no assistance from that quarter. My brother, however, has been more helpful.' He took the paper from his pocket and passed it over. 'Henry compiled a list of the main political enemies of Sir Ambrose. Do these names mean anything to you?'

Jonathan studied the list carefully then handed it back to him.

'No, sir. I do not meddle in politics. These men are strangers to me. The only name I have heard before is that of Mr George Strype.'

'Indeed?'

'He, too, trades in many commodities.'

'Politeness is not one of them.'

'They spoke his name with contempt along the wharves,' said Jonathan. 'He and Sir Ambrose were partners in some enterprises and were equally disliked by their rivals.'

'Would that dislike provide a motive for murder?'

'Possibly.'

'Then ferret away among the merchants,' suggested Christopher. 'I have a strong feeling that the murder is in some way linked to Sir Ambrose's business activities.'

'So have I, Mr Redmayne.'

'Those cellars signify something as well.'

'In what way, sir?'

'I am not yet sure. They are much larger than a house of

that size would normally have. Why? What did he intend to keep there? And another thing,' concluded Christopher. 'Sir Ambrose was last seen going down into those cellars with a man who was, in all probability, the killer. Why did he take his companion there if not to show him the extent of the cellars? That man must have been a business associate of his.'

'Not any more,' sighed Jonathan.

'No, Mr Bale. His character underwent a complete change once he was below ground. He entered those cellars as a friend of Sir Ambrose and emerged from them as his killer.'

'What happened to bring about that change?'

Christopher rose to his feet, eyes glistening with determination.

'When we catch the villain,' he said grimly, 'we will ask him.'

CHAPTER TEN

When he finally caught sight of his home, Christopher Redmayne gave a mild groan of relief. A tiring day had begun with an early departure from the inn where he spent the night. In his eagerness to confront Solomon Creech, he had ridden past Fetter Lane on his arrival back in London and gone straight to the lawyer's office in Lombard Street. The bruising exchange with his brother at the coffee house had been followed by the meeting with Jonathan Bale, after which he was drawn back inescapably to the scene of the crime. Searching the cellars for clues, he lost all track of time and only abandoned his examination when the candle he was using dwindled to a pale flicker. It was now well into the afternoon. Christopher began to realise that what he needed most was a restorative meal and a period of reflection. He was confident that the trusty Jacob would provide the first without hesitation then melt discreetly away while his master enjoyed the second. The house had never looked more like a haven of peace.

As he dismounted and unsaddled his horse, he consoled himself with the thought that progress of a kind had been made. He certainly knew far more about Sir Ambrose Northcott than he had when he set out on his journey and none of the new information was remotely flattering. Tenants at Priestfield Place and rivals in the mercantile community shared a general dislike of the man and Christopher was disgusted by the way that he had deceived his wife and daughter over the building of the new house. He was still puzzled by Lady Northcott's ambiguous reaction to her husband's death but his chief memory of the visit to Kent concerned Penelope Northcott, to whom he had felt strongly attracted from the start. His protective instincts were aroused by her supercilious fiancé's treatment of her and he was already beginning to wonder how he could prise them apart and save her from an unfortunate marriage. The fact that her late father had encouraged the match with the odious George Strype left yet another stain on the paternal character.

Reluctantly, both Solomon Creech and Henry Redmayne added fresh detail to the posthumous portrait of Sir Ambrose and it made nowhere near as impressive a painting as the one which hung with martial dignity in the Great Hall at Priestfield Place. Truth was a more reliable artist. It worked with honest colours. Christopher realised that natural sympathy for a murder victim should not obscure the fact that he was a deeply flawed human being. It remained to be seen how many more defects came to light.

Christopher's mind turned to Penelope once again.

Everything about her delighted him. He just wished that they could have met in more propitious circumstances. Penelope Northcott was a much more rewarding subject for meditation than her father and he mused fondly about the chances of meeting her again one day. Accepting that it would probably never happen, he decided to address more immediate matters such as the rumbling noise from his stomach. After stabling his horse, he walked around to his front door and found Jacob waiting for him. The look on his servant's face told him that he had a visitor.

'Who is it, Jacob?'

'A young lady, sir.'

His hopes rose. 'Miss Northcott, by any chance?'

'No, sir. Miss Margaret Littlejohn.'

Christopher was at once startled and dismayed. Nobody was less welcome in his house and in his life at that moment than the builder's daughter. However, courtesies had to be observed so he steeled himself before going into the parlour. Margaret Littlejohn was accompanied by her maidservant and both rose from their chairs when he entered. They exchanged pleasantries. In response to his invitation, Margaret resumed her seat but Nan, the maidservant, hovered watchfully in the background.

'What brings you here, Miss Littlejohn?' he asked politely.

'I wanted to see you, Mr Redmayne,' she said, blushing slightly.

'How did you know where to find me?'

'Mr Bale told me that you were expected back in London today and my father mentioned that you lived in Fetter Lane.

He did not tell me which number,' she said with a breathy laugh, 'so Nan and I had to knock on several doors before we found you.'

'Why did you not ask your father the number?'

'Because he would not have given it to me. Father has always guarded your privacy. He warned me that I was not to bother you in any way but I simply had to come here.'

'I see.'

'You are not angry with me, are you, Mr Redmayne?'

'Of course not.'

'I like to think that we are friends.'

'Yes, yes,' he said gallantly.

'You will not tell my father that I called here, will you? He would not approve. I can trust Nan,' she said with a glance at her companion. 'She will say nothing. I hope that I can trust you as well.'

'Implicitly.'

'Thank you.'

Margaret Littlejohn was both embarrassed and elated, bashful in the presence of the man she adored yet savouring the experience all the same. Christopher was glad that the maidservant was there, hoping that his visitor would not blurt out any declaration in front of a third person. His mind was already grappling with the problem of how he could get rid of them without undue rudeness.

'Father kept most of it from me,' explained Margaret. 'He did not want to upset me with the nasty details. All that he told me was that Sir Ambrose Northcott had met with an accident and that the building work had been stopped.'

'In essence, that is the truth.'

'But the poor man was *murdered*.'

'Alas, yes.'

'What happened to him is too horrible to contemplate.'

'That is why Mr Littlejohn protected you from it.'

'I shudder every time I think about the way Sir Ambrose died.'

'Try to put it out of your mind.'

'But I was *there*, Mr Redmayne,' she confessed, eyes widening with consternation. 'On the day that he was killed, I was there at the site.'

'So were the rest of us. The place was humming with activity.'

'I am talking about that evening. When...' Her voice died and she needed a moment to compose herself. 'When it happened,' she continued. 'What I saw may be of no use at all, of course, but I felt I had to tell you about it just in case. I feel guilty at holding it back.'

'You saw something?' he pressed, moving in closer. 'You were at the site on the evening when Sir Ambrose was killed?' She nodded. 'Did you see him arrive with another man?'

'No, Mr Redmayne. When we got there – Nan was with me – the only person we saw was the nightwatchman. He was in the garden, well away from the house itself. He was pulling the tarpaulin over the bricks and the timber,' she recalled. 'He did not see the man leave.'

'What man?'

'The one who came out of the cellar.'

Christopher crouched down before her. 'You saw a man come out of the cellar?' he said. 'On his own?'

'Yes.'

'Did you recognise him?'

'Unhappily, no. I hoped for a moment that it might be...'
She blushed again but covered her coyness with a swift
recital of events. 'I have never seen him before. He was tall,
well-dressed and wore a wide-brimmed hat that was pulled
down over his face. We were too far away to see much more
than that, Mr Redmayne. I was afraid to venture too close
in case the nightwatchman saw me and reported it to my
father.' She tossed a look over her shoulder at Nan. 'I misled
him. He thought that I was visiting my cousin but I was near
Baynard's Castle instead.'

'If I understand you correctly,' recapitulated Christopher,
sensing that the girl had invaluable information, 'you saw
a man coming out of the cellar and leaving before the
nightwatchman could descry him?'

'He took care that it would not happen, Mr Redmayne.'

'What do you mean?'

'Well,' she said, 'he crept up those steps and peeped around
to make sure that nobody could see him. Then he put down
the lantern he was carrying and hurried off quickly. Oh, did
I say that he was carrying a stick? I do remember that. A tall
man with a hat and a stick.'

'Did he notice you and your maidservant?'

'No, Mr Redmayne. We were hiding behind the corner.'

'Which way did he go?'

'Towards the river. I think he had a boat waiting.'

'Did you see a boat?'

'No,' she said, delighted at his interest and keen to
maintain it. 'The wall of the house blocked him from sight
for most of the way. But I did catch a glimpse of the top of

his hat when he reached the landing stage beyond the garden. Why else would he go there?'

'Quite so, Miss Littlejohn.'

'After that, it was time for us to leave ourselves.'

'So you saw nothing else?'

She shook her head. Christopher took her carefully through each detail of her story once again and fixed the approximate times of her arrival and departure. Her evidence dovetailed with that of Jem Raybone. The nightwatchman saw two men enter the cellar. Christopher was certain that the one whom Margaret Littlejohn observed leaving was the killer. The probable time of the murder was confirmed.

'Was I right to come to you?' she asked.

'Oh, yes. I am most grateful.'

'Father said that you were determined to solve this crime. I hoped that I could be of some little help to you.'

'You have been of great help,' said Christopher, standing up.

'Thank you, sir. Do not think too badly of me.'

'Badly?'

'A dutiful daughter should have told all this to her father,' she admitted. 'But I could not do that or he would have known that I deceived him about where I was that evening. Please do not betray me.'

'I would not dream of it.'

'The simple truth is…' She reached out to touch his arm. 'The simple truth is that I hoped against hope that *you* might be at the site that evening. That is why I came. That was why I always came.'

Margaret Littlejohn suddenly burst into tears and flung

herself clumsily forward. Christopher had no alternative but to catch her. It put him in an awkward predicament, compounded by the fact that Nan had mysteriously disappeared from the room as if by some pre-arranged signal. Margaret sobbed, clung tightly to him, felt the comfort of his arms then turned a tearful face up for some return of affection. Christopher managed a smile but his emotions were swirling. He was still wondering how he could detach himself from her when Jacob came to his rescue.

Materialising out of the kitchen, the old servant was resourceful.

'I see that the young lady is unwell, sir,' he said, moving her gently away from his master and easing her towards the door. 'I take it that you would wish me to accompany her back home at once?'

Margaret felt profoundly cheated and Nan appeared in the doorway with a look of exasperation on her face but Christopher was so relieved that he vowed to give his servant a handsome reward.

'Thank you, Jacob,' he said in a tone of the utmost consideration. 'Your offer is most timely. See them to the very door of their house and take especial care of Miss Littlejohn who is a trifle upset. She has just given me the most enormous amount of help. I am so glad that she made the effort to come here.'

Partially appeased, Margaret Littlejohn stemmed her tears with a lace handkerchief and bestowed a yearning smile of farewell on her host before going out with her maidservant. Neither woman overheard the urgent command which

Christopher whispered into Jacob's hairy ear.

'Never – never, ever – let them across my threshold again!'

The Jolly Sailor belied its name that evening. It was half-empty when Jonathan Bale arrived and the atmosphere felt curiously flat. Most patrons were either too drunk to exhibit any jollity or too sober to get drawn into a song. The constable did not mind. During his years as a shipwright, the tavern had been a favourite of his. He felt comfortable among seafaring men, sharing their concerns, understanding their problems and talking their language. His office might have given him a new sense of responsibility but it did not deprive him of his love of the sea or of those who made their living in its capricious bosom.

Jonathan talked easily to six or seven sailors before he chanced upon one who could really help. The man was on his own in a corner.

'You have heard of Sir Ambrose Northcott, then?' said Jonathan.

'Oh, yes,' replied the other before spitting dramatically on the floor. 'I know the rogue only too well.'

'Why is that?'

'Because I sailed aboard his ship.'

'For how long?'

'Almost two years.' Jonathan smiled. 'Let me fill your tankard for you, my friend.'

'I'll not try to stop you.'

The constable sat opposite him at a rough wooden table and called for more beer. When both their tankards were full, they clinked them before taking a long sip apiece. Appraising his companion, Jonathan realised why the man chose to lurk in a shadowy corner of the tavern. He was a short, solid individual in his forties with huge scarred hands. His face was so ugly that it had a kind of grotesque fascination. Nature had contrived the misshapen features and an occasional brawl accounted for the broken nose and the swollen ear but these were minor distractions from the dozens of large, hideous, red boils which swarmed across his cheeks, chin and forehead like so many enraged wasps.

'Do not look too close, sir,' said the man. 'Take pity on me.'

'Have you always had this condition?'

'It came on me this last year.'

'Is there no cure?'

'I have not found one yet so I am instead trying to cure people of staring at me like a freak.' He bunched a menacing fist. 'The only thing which seems to work is to loosen their teeth with this.'

'I am sorry,' said Jonathan, averting his gaze. 'You mentioned a ship. I had heard that Sir Ambrose owned a vessel.'

'That is right. The *Marie Louise*.'

'A strange name for an English ship.'

'It was called *The Maid of Kent* when I sailed in her.'

'*Marie Louise* does not sound much like a maid of Kent.'

A throaty laugh. 'More like a whore of Calais!'

'When was the name changed?'

'Some time last year, they tell me.'

'And did they say why?'

'No,' replied the man. 'Some whim of Sir Ambrose Northcott's. He was always doing things like that. Making decisions, changing things around. And he was a loathsome passenger to have aboard. Real tyrant, he was. Never stopped harrying the crew. Many's the time I'd have liked to push him overboard.'

'Where did you sail?'

'Anywhere and everywhere. Spain, Portugal, France, Holland, even Norway on occasion. As soon as one cargo was unloaded here, we would set sail to collect another. *The Maid of Kent* was a trim vessel, I'll say that for her. When we clapped on full sail, she could outrun most of her rivals. Yes,' he sighed nostalgically, 'when Sir Ambrose was not aboard, I had some good times on that ship.'

'And since then?'

'I joined the crew of a coastal vessel, bringing coal down from Newcastle. Miserable work until I was forced out of it.'

'Forced out?'

'This face,' said the man, jabbing a stubby finger at it. 'There's no better way to lose shipmates than to sprout a crop such as I did. They could not bear to look on me lest they catch some disease. When the captain discharged me, I could not find anyone else to take me on. It is just as well, really. The sea spray used to make these boils sting so much I felt that my face was on fire.'

He took a long, noisy sip from his tankard then wiped his lips with the back of his arm. Jonathan coaxed as much detail as he could out of the man about his time on Sir Ambrose Northcott's vessel. He was surprised to hear how often the owner went on the voyages. War did not seem to hinder his business. He traded covertly with countries which were nominally at odds with his own.

'Sir Ambrose sounds like a doughty privateer,' said Jonathan.

'I'd sooner call him a black-hearted bastard.'

The man's reminiscences became harsher as he retailed examples of what he saw as the iniquities of Sir Ambrose Northcott. By the time his companion had finished, Jonathan had been given some valuable insights into the commercial activities of the dead man. He memorised the details so that he could pass them on to Christopher Redmayne. Whatever his doubts about the latter, he had to admit that the architect had dedicated himself to the pursuit of the killer in the most selfless manner. Working with him might not turn out as unpleasant a task as he feared.

A degree of jollity at last entered the Jolly Sailor. Drink was flowing more freely, raucous ditties were being sung, customers were flirting with the landlady and two of them were trying to dance in the middle of the floor. Jonathan decided to leave before the first brawl started but he paid to have the other man's tankard filled first.

'Will you not drink with me?' said the sailor.

'I still have a drop left here, my friend.'

'Then let us have a toast.'

'Gladly.'

'To my future health!' said the man.

'I'll drink to that,' said Jonathan, raising his tankard before emptying it with one long gulp. 'I hope that you soon find the cure for your ailment and get back to sea where you belong.'

'I have one last chance.'

'Last chance?'

'When I take my boils to the finest physician in London.'

'And who might that be?'

'Why,' said the man proudly, 'His Majesty, of course. They say that the King's Touch can cure any disease. Tomorrow, I am to present myself to Mr Knight, His Majesty's surgeon, who lives in Bridges Street at the sign of the Hare in Covent Garden. When he has examined me, I will be given a ticket to join those other sufferers who will receive the King's Touch the next day.'

'I wish you luck, my friend!'

'I put my faith in His Majesty.'

'That is more than I would do,' murmured Jonathan.

'Many men have felt the King's Touch.'

'And many women, too,' said the other under his breath. 'I have heard tell of miracles taking place this way,' he added aloud. 'I pray that you will be cured by one.'

'I have to be,' said the man with an edge of desperation. 'This face of mine is cursed. I'll not endure the pain for much longer. Mind you, I will admit this. There are other poor souls in a worse condition than me. Most of those who will go before His Majesty are stricken with the King's Evil, as they call it. Scrofula. A cruel disease. It can turn a beautiful face into vile ugliness. I have seen men whose skin looked as if they have been flayed alive and some have been so stricken that they went blind.' He drank some more beer, then belched. 'Have you ever seen anyone with the King's Evil?'

'Oh, yes!' said Jonathan ruefully. 'Indeed, I have, my friend. I have seen a whole city afflicted with it.'

'A whole city? What is it called?'

'London.'

The ceremony was held at the Banqueting House. Since it was his first visit there, Christopher Redmayne took the opportunity to study what was, architecturally, the most striking part of Whitehall Place. He found it pure joy to view the work of Inigo Jones at such close quarters. Faced with Portland stone and built at a cost of over fifteen thousand pounds, the Banqueting House was the first exclusively Renaissance building in the capital and, in the opinion of most observers, still by far the best. The scale of the interior filled Christopher with awe and his eyes took in every lush detail. He spent so much time gazing up at the ceiling, adorned by a Rubens painting in celebration of the benefits of wise rule, that his neck began to ache. Sheer scale once again hypnotised him.

'Look at the size of those figures,' he urged, pointing upwards.

'I have seen them before,' said his brother airily.

'The cherubs must be almost ten feet high.'

'I prefer my cherubs lying horizontally on a bed.'

'Henry!'

'Pay attention. I brought you here to watch the ceremony and not to goggle at the ceiling like some country bumpkin on his first visit to London.' A loud murmur of interest went up. 'Ah, here is the King.'

Preceded by two priests in their vestments, Charles II entered at the head of a stately procession and made his way up the steps of a small dais to take his seat on the throne. Christopher was at the rear of the hall but, even from that distance, he thought that the King cut an impressive figure. Charles was a tall, dignified man with long, black, curly, shining hair and a black moustache. A leader of fashion, he was dressed in the French style with a long scarlet vest beneath his coat and black shoes offset by scarlet bows. It was the first time that Christopher had ever seen him in person and he was irresistibly reminded of the reward placard which he saw on display after the Battle of Worcester in 1651 and which described the royal fugitive as 'a tall, black man upwards of two yards high.'

There was a swarthiness about the kingly countenance which gave him a slightly foreign air but his bearing was that of a Stuart monarch with a firm belief in the Divine Right of his rule and in the importance of the ceremony in which he was to officiate. The face was striking rather than handsome and it wore such a grave expression that Christopher found it difficult to reconcile the man whom he saw before him with the rampant satyr of common report. A royalist by instinct, he felt a surge of pride in his monarch and admired the graceful ease with which he presided over the assembly.

When the priests had read from the Book of Common Prayer, the King's surgeons brought in the diseased supplicants to present them to him. There were almost five hundred of them in all and they gave off a communal odour of sickness. Some limped, some hobbled, some had to be carried into the royal presence. Most were afflicted with scrofula, the King's Evil, which blighted them with swollen glands and unsightly skin conditions. More advanced cases of the disease could lead to blindness and other frightening disabilities. As they shuffled in strict order towards the dais, the Gospel was read by one of the priests and the stirring words of St Mark echoed through the chamber.

'Afterward he appeared unto the eleven as they sat at meat, and upbraided them with their unbelief and hardness of heart, because they believed not them which had seen him after he was risen. And he said unto them, Go ye into all the world, and preach the gospel to every creature. He that believeth, and is baptised, shall be saved; but he that believeth not shall be damned. And these signs shall follow them that believe; in my name shall they cast out devils, they shall speak with new tongues. They shall take up serpents; and if they drink any deadly thing, it shall not hurt them.'

He raised his head to signal the first diseased man forward.

'They shall lay their hands on the sick, and they shall recover.'

As the words were spoken, the King laid both hands fearlessly upon the kneeling supplicant before him then waited for a second person to take his place. Each time a different man, woman or child knelt in hope before him, the King's Touch was accompanied by the same verse from the Gospel.

'They shall lay their hands on the sick and they shall recover.'

Christopher found the whole event profoundly moving. Touched by the simple faith of those who waited so patiently in line, he was full of admiration for the way in which the King conducted himself. Charles did not shrink from even the most repulsive cases. Each one of them was treated with gentle consideration as they knelt to receive the Touch which might yet redeem them from the misery of their illness. When the long queue of people had eventually filed past, the ceremony was only half over. More prayers were offered then a second reading was taken from the Gospel of St John.

'In the beginning was the Word, and the Word was with God, and the Word was God. The same was in the beginning with God. All things were made by him; and without him was not anything made that was made.'

Christopher knew the words by heart and chanted them under his breath in unison with the speaker. Reared in the shadow of Gloucester Cathedral and fed daily on the Gospels, he found them endlessly inspiring though he sensed that his brother, Henry, who was also mouthing the verses beside him, was doing so out of force of habit rather than from any inner conviction.

'That was the true light, which lighteth every man that cometh into the world.'

The words were repeated each time one of the supplicants knelt for the second time before the King. Showing no signs of fatigue or loss of dignity, Charles hung an azure ribbon around the necks of all those whom he had touched. From the ribbon was suspended a gold medallion stamped with his image. Christopher was enthralled.

'What is he giving them, Henry?' he whispered.

'A gold angel.'

'Such a generous gift!'

'Too generous,' said the other sharply. 'When the Commons added up the Crown's expenses last year, they found that five thousand pounds had been spent in angel-gold. Five thousand, mark you! Why give them gold, when base metal would suffice? They have been cured by the King's Touch. That should be reward enough.'

'And have they been truly cured?'

'Some of them.'

'What of the others?'

'They lack faith,' said Henry irritably. 'The fault is never in the King but in the wretch who kneels before him. Everything depends on having enough faith in His Majesty.'

'So I see.'

'Let us steal away, Christopher. The smell offends me.'

'But I want to watch the whole ceremony.'

'You have seen all that matters. I brought you here to meet some of those enemies of Sir Ambrose Northcott. They will come out of their holes when the King returns to court. We must be there to study them.'

'You are right, Henry. But I am most grateful to you for bringing me here. It was an extraordinary event. The only surprise is that it takes place in the Banqueting House.'

'Where else?'

'Anywhere but here, I fancy,' opined Christopher. 'This building holds such terrible memories for the King. It was from here that his father stepped out before that bloodthirsty crowd to have his royal head struck from his body. The King must be highly aware of that. It shows great courage on his part to come here for the sake of his subjects' health and to behave with such equanimity.'

'I prefer the King in more humorous vein.'

'You might not do so if you suffered from scrofula.'

'Enough of disease!' said Henry, ushering him out. 'And

enough of the execution of a lawful King! What concerns us now is the murder of Sir Ambrose Northcott. Adjourn to Court with me and I will introduce you to some of those politicians who have delighted in his death. Sound them out for yourself, Christopher. But beware of their wiles.'

'I am used to dealing with cunning minds.'

'From whom did you learn that skill?'

'From you, Henry.'

'Me?'

'Where could I find a better tutor?' said his brother with a grin. 'You are the most devious and artful man in the whole of London. You are so steeped in craft and so wedded to guile that even the King's Touch could not cure you.'

The ship lay at anchor in the middle of the Thames but there was much activity abroad. Watching from his vantage point on the wharf, Jonathan Bale realised that the *Marie Louise* was about to sail on the evening tide. She was a three-masted merchant vessel with the kind of sleek lines and impressive fittings which would ordinarily have held his attention for hours but he had no leisure to expend on such an exercise. Built for speed, she had top-gallant sails for the main and fore masts, an unusual addition to the standard rig of a middling craft. She was clearly able to defend herself and Jonathan counted the number of cannon along the starboard side, wondering why a ship that was designed to carry cargo needed such artillery. When the sails were unfurled and the crew weighed anchor, Jonathan reached forward involuntarily as if trying to hold her back, but it was a vain gesture. The *Marie Louise* had other plans.

It was only a matter of time before her canvas caught the first smack of wind and she creaked into motion.

By the time that Christopher Redmayne arrived, the vessel was already a hundred yards downriver. The newcomer was alarmed.

'Has she set sail already?'

'I fear so, Mr Redmayne.'

'Did you manage to get aboard her?'

'Alas, no,' said Jonathan, turning to him. 'The captain would not let me aboard nor come ashore so that I could question him here. I was told that I would need the written permission of Mr Creech before I would be allowed on the *Marie Louise*.'

'Did you seek such permission?'

'Three or four times, sir. But the lawyer was never at his office. His clerk told me that he was busy elsewhere and that I had to come back.'

'Solomon Creech is not busy, Mr Bale. He is hiding.'

'From what?'

'From any enquiries which relate to Sir Ambrose Northcott,' said Christopher resignedly. 'I have called on him myself a number of times in the past few days and collected the same annoying excuses from that clerk of his. Still,' he said, brightening, 'a great deal has happened since we last met and I have much to tell you. Judging from your message, you have much to tell me as well.'

'Yes, sir,' said Jonathan. 'Thank you for coming so promptly. I am sorry you did not get here in time to take a proper look at the *Marie Louise*. She was a handsome craft, a credit to those who built her.'

'Your letter mentioned that the ship changed its name. Why?'

'I hoped to find out by talking to the captain.'

Jonathan gave him a detailed account of his researches along the wharves and in the taverns frequented by sailors. Christopher took especial note of the man who purported to seek the King's Touch to rid himself of his boils. It was his cue to relate his own movements. He talked excitedly about the ceremony at the Banqueting House but it elicited only a cynical scowl from his companion. When Christopher talked about meeting certain political figures, however, Jonathan showed real interest.

'Did any of them have a motive to murder Sir Ambrose?'

'Each and every one of them.'

'Was there some sort of conspiracy?'

'Unhappily, yes,' sighed the other. 'Once they realised why I was asking so many questions, they closed ranks and refused to say any more. And the worst of it is that Solomon Creech belongs to this conspiracy. The one person to whom we should be able to turn for enlightenment has hidden behind a wall of silence.'

'Where does he live?'

'Close by his office but he is not at home. I have been there.'

'What do we do, sir?'

'Wait until he appears,' decided Christopher. 'I'll repair to his office first thing in the morning and sit there all day, if need be. Mr Creech must make contact with his clerk at some stage or he will not be able to conduct any business.'

'Ask him about the destination of the *Marie Louise*.'

'It is one of a hundred questions I have for him.'

'That ship holds many secrets, I am sure of it.'

'We need to plumb them somehow.' They watched the vessel slowly shrinking to invisibility in the distance; then Christopher remembered something. 'But I have a question for you as well, Mr Bale.'

'Oh?'

'Is the name of Mrs Mandrake familiar to you?'

'Do you speak of Molly Mandrake?'

'Yes. Do you know her?'

'Better than I would wish to, sir. I once arrested the lady.'

'I think I can guess why.'

'She had a house in my ward,' he explained. 'One of three which she owned in the city. The last I heard of her, she had moved to Lincoln's Inn Fields to be outside the city jurisdiction.' His gaze narrowed. 'What is your interest in the lady, sir?'

'It is more a case of my brother's interest,' admitted Christopher. 'I forced him to tell me how he had first met Sir Ambrose. Apparently, it was in an establishment run by this Mrs Mandrake. Henry spoke well of her. He has a high opinion of the young ladies whom she employs.'

Jonathan was brusque. 'As to that, sir, I could not say. I have no knowledge of such creatures nor do I wish to. What I can tell you is that Molly Mandrake is very proficient at her trade. Heavy fines and a spell in prison have not deterred her. She has made a veritable fortune from the likes of Sir Ambrose Northcott and your brother.'

'It pains me to link the name of Redmayne with hers.'

Jonathan made no comment but his expression was eloquent. He still could not bring himself to regard Christopher as a friend but he no longer treated him with such suspicion. The latter's honesty about the shortcomings of Henry Redmayne was quite disarming. Of the two brothers, the younger was the only one whom Jonathan would ever find at all tolerable but he was still not at ease in his company. For his part, Christopher was warming to the constable.

'I am glad that we are working in harness,' he said.

Jonathan was guarded. 'Are you, sir?'

'It is too big an assignment for one person. Together we have made big strides forward. The beauty of it is that each of us can visit places which are closed to the other.'

'Can we?'

'Yes, Mr Bale. While you trawl the riverside taverns, I mix with men of consequence at Whitehall Palace. Between us, we are able to cover the whole of London society from top to bottom.'

'Which is which?' asked Jonathan with a sardonic smile.

Christopher laughed. 'A fair comment,' he conceded. 'But tell me more about this Mrs Mandrake.'

'Your brother knows the lady more intimately than I, sir.'

'That is precisely why he was so defensive about her. But he did confess that Sir Ambrose was once a regular client of hers. Why?'

'Do you really need to ask?'

'There are many houses of resort available. What is so special about hers? What did Molly Mandrake offer that made her establishment so popular with men like Sir Ambrose? We must look further into it, Mr Bale. Talk to the lady and we may learn something of interest about Sir Ambrose Northcott.'

'I leave that office to you, sir. It is not one which I would relish.'

'What sort of a creature is she?'

'Molly Mandrake? A cheerful sinner.'

'Henry called her one of the seven wonders of the world.'

'I am glad that he is not my brother.'

Christopher laughed again then made plans to meet the constable on the following day. Taking his leave, he mounted his horse and rode home thoughtfully to Fetter Lane, trying to sift through all the new information which he had just acquired.

Jacob had a meal waiting for him and Christopher ate it at the kitchen table, still deep in cogitation. He did not hear the rumbling of a coach outside the house nor the knock on his front door but Jacob's voice was as clear as a bell.

'Please come in,' he said politely. 'I will call Mr Redmayne.'

The words cut through Christopher's reverie and made him sit up in mild alarm as he sensed who the unexpected visitor might be. When the servant came into the kitchen, he gave an apologetic smile.

'A young lady has called to see you, sir,' he announced.

'I told you not to let Miss Littlejohn in!' hissed Christopher. 'I am not in a mood to see anybody right now, least of all her.'

'Miss Littlejohn is not the visitor in question, sir.'

'Oh? Then who is?'

Jacob made him wait then savoured his master's surprise.

'Miss Penelope Northcott.'

Chapter Eleven

Christopher Redmayne's astonishment was matched by his unabashed delight. Jacob watched with wry amusement then stood aside as his master surged out of the kitchen and through into the parlour. Penelope Northcott was standing in the centre of the room, gazing around it with distant curiosity. In his eagerness to see her again, Christopher had forgotten that she was in mourning for the death of her father and he had to school his own excitement when he was confronted by the subdued figure in sober attire. She gave him a tired smile.

'I am sorry to descend on you unannounced, Mr Redmayne.'

'Not at all, Miss Northcott,' he said, pleased to find that she was alone. 'You are most welcome. Do sit down.'

'Thank you,' she said, lowering herself onto a chair. 'It has been a taxing day and I must confess that I am weary.'

'May I offer you some refreshment?'

'Not for me, Mr Redmayne, but I daresay that Dirk would be very grateful for something to slake his thirst.'

'Dirk?'

'My coachman. He waits at your door. It has been a long drive and the poor fellow must be close to exhaustion.'

'Then we must revive him at once.'

Christopher turned to call Jacob but the servant was already at his elbow. Having taken his instructions, he left the house by the kitchen door to see to the needs of the coachman. Christopher perched on a chair and appraised his visitor with admiration.

'You came all this way in one day?' he said.

'Dirk drove the coach. All that I had to do was to sit in the back of it and count the bumps in the road. There were thousands. But, yes,' she said wearily, 'we left before dawn in order to get here by nightfall. Fresh horses were waiting for us in Orpington.'

'Would it not have been more comfortable to break the journey?'

'Infinitely more comfortable, Mr Redmayne. But my business in London would brook no delay.'

'I see.'

'In view of that, I hope that you will overlook what may appear to be somewhat indecent behaviour.'

'Indecent?'

'My father was buried only two days ago,' she said quietly. 'Most people would think it highly improper for his daughter to go haring off to London when she should be grieving in the privacy of her home. You may well take such a view of my conduct yourself.'

'Never!' he affirmed. 'You will hear no word of criticism from me, Miss Northcott. Though we only met once, I judged you to be a person who would do nothing without a good reason. Something has clearly impelled you to come here. I look forward to hearing what it is.'

His warm smile was intended to encourage her but it seemed to have the opposite effect. Penelope was suddenly discomfited and her hands fidgeted in her lap. Evidently, she was having second thoughts about her impulsive action. He tried to come to her rescue.

'I am still on the trail of the killer,' he promised her. 'Would you like to hear what progress we have made?'

'We?'

'A constable named Jonathan Bale is helping me.'

'Do you know the identity of the murderer?'

'Not yet, Miss Northcott. But we get ever closer to him.'

Suppressing any unfavourable details about her father, Christopher gave her a full account of their investigations. Though her face was lined with fatigue, she listened intently throughout. He noticed the blush which came to her cheeks at the mention of the *Marie Louise*. When his recital was over, she spoke with great feeling.

'You have done so much on our behalf, Mr Redmayne. Mother and I cannot possibly repay you for your sterling efforts.'

'Finding the man responsible will be reward enough.'

'That is what I have been telling myself.'

'What do you mean?'

'Arresting the guilty man takes precedence over everything,' she said solemnly. 'The end justifies the means.

Even if those means involve some personal embarrassment.'
She leant forward. 'Mr Redmayne, I will have to rely on your
discretion.'

'Do so with complete confidence.'

'May I?'

'Whatever you tell me will remain within these four
walls.'

'It must needs spill out beyond them, I fear,' she sighed.
'Let me explain. Before you left Priestfield Place, you asked
me to make contact with you if we remembered anything
about Father which might be germane to your investigation.
You gave me this address.'

'I am glad that I did so.'

She became more hesitant. 'What brought me here today
was not something which either of us remembered,' she said
slowly, lowering her head, 'but something which I found. Most
of Father's private papers are kept in a safe at his lawyer's
office but a few were locked away in a desk in the library at
Priestfield Place. I prised the lock open to find them.'

'That was very enterprising of you, Miss Northcott.'

'My enterprise led to a rude awakening.'

'In what way?'

'Judge for yourself,' she said, bringing a small bundle of
letters out from beneath her cloak. 'I assume that you read
French?'

'Tolerably well. I lived in Paris for a while.'

'These were sent to Father by someone called Marie
Louise.'

She handed him the letters. Written on scented paper, they
were held together by a pink ribbon. Christopher had some

idea of what he might find and consideration for Penelope's feelings made him hold back until she gestured for him to read one of the missives. It did not take him long. The first letter was short, explicit and couched in the most loving terms. Marie Louise was patently entranced by Sir Ambrose Northcott. She had a fine hand and a turn of phrase which was subtly erotic.

'Read the next one,' urged Penelope.

'Do I need to, Miss Northcott?'

'An address is given in Paris. And the lady's full name.'

Christopher opened the next letter. Marie Louise Ollier was even more explicit this time, recalling the delights of a week spent together with her lover in Calais and looking forward with enthusiasm to their next rendezvous. In the meantime, she sent an address where she could be reached in Paris.

When he glanced up, Christopher saw the look of intense embarrassment on Penelope's face and his heart went out to her. Coming on top of the news of her father's murder, the discovery of the letters must have been a crushing blow to her and he could only imagine the pain it must now be costing her to show them to a stranger and make her anguish public. He offered them back to her.

'Keep them, Mr Redmayne,' she said. 'Read them all.'

'Later,' he decided, putting them on the table.

'I do not wish to touch them again.'

'That is understandable.'

'It was an effort to refrain from burning them,' she admitted. 'For that is what I did with the portrait of her.'

'Portrait?'

'It was no more than a sketch, attached to one of the letters, but it must have been a good likeness or my father would not have kept it.' Her voice began to falter. 'That is what hurt me most of all, Mr Redmayne.'

'What was?'

'Marie Louise Ollier is…a young woman. If the sketch is to be believed, she is not much above my own age.'

The full horror hit her once again and she closed her eyes to absorb the blow, biting her lip as she swayed to and fro. Christopher moved across to put a comforting arm around her and her head fell gratefully onto his shoulder. Joy and sadness were intermingled as he enjoyed the brief intimacy and shared her sorrow, inhaling her perfume and consoling her with soft words. When another young woman had been in his arms, fear had consumed him but the embrace felt wholly natural this time. Penelope Northcott was everything that Margaret Littlejohn could never be. She was wanted.

As soon as he felt her rally, he released her and stood back. She thanked him with a nod then dabbed at her eyes with a handkerchief. Christopher resumed his seat, touched that she felt able to express her emotions in front of him. She regarded him seriously.

'Will you be honest with me, sir?' she asked.

'Of course.'

'Were you entirely surprised by what I have disclosed?'

He shook his head. 'No, Miss Northcott.'

'Why not?'

'My brother, Henry, was a friend of your father's. That fact alone,' he said, searching for a kind euphemism, 'hinted at a degree of moral laxity. Henry has always sought pleasure in abundance. I assumed that he and Sir Ambrose were birds of a feather. My brother has admitted as much.'

'Yet you made no mention of it to me.'

'I hoped to keep such details from you.'

'That was very kind of you,' she said, 'but I have no illusions left to shatter. When I heard that he had been killed, I thought I had lost a dear and loving father. It was like a knife through the heart to realise what sort of man he really was.'

'Was your mother equally wounded?' he said.

'Why do you ask that?'

'She may have noticed things which you did not.'

'Go on.'

'When I was leaving Priestfield Place, I chanced to see Lady Northcott in the garden. Your mother was not exactly overwhelmed with grief.'

Penelope nodded. 'I think that Mother had guessed what was going on and learnt to live with it. Father's absences grew longer and longer. A wife is bound to draw conclusions. The garden has always been a great consolation to her.'

'Did you show her the letters?'

'Of course.'

'What was her reaction?'

'She refused to read them.'

'Does Lady Northcott know that you brought them to me?'

'It was my mother who urged me to find you.'

'And what of your fiancé?' he asked tentatively. 'Does Mr Strype know that you are here?'

'No,' she said bluntly. 'He would have stopped me coming.'

'Why?'

219

'That is a personal matter, Mr Redmayne.'

'Then I will not pry.'

Christopher turned the conversation to more neutral topics, asking about her coach journey and whether or not she found London an exciting city to visit. Penelope gradually relaxed. Having unburdened an unpalatable family secret, she could actually start to enjoy her host's company. She had no doubts about the wisdom of what she had done and knew that she could trust Christopher with her family secrets.

He was drawn to her more strongly than ever. What she had done would have been courageous in a mature woman. In a young lady, fragile and vulnerable after a bereavement, it was an act of sheer bravado, enhanced by the fact that she was concealing her movements from the man she was engaged to marry. Time flowed past so freely and pleasantly that neither of them noticed the shadows lengthening. It was only when Jacob brought in additional candles that they realised how late it must be. As the servant quit the room, Penelope rose to her feet in a flurry of apologies.

'I have stayed far too long, Mr Redmayne. Do forgive me.'

'There is nothing to forgive.'

'Dirk must have been waiting for hours.'

'Do not worry about your coachman. Jacob will have looked after him, I am sure. Where do you plan to spend the night?'

'I had thought to go to the house in Westminster.'

'Had thought?' he repeated, hearing the doubt in her voice. 'Has something happened to change your mind?'

'Yes, sir. That bundle of letters.'

'Do you fear that you may find more in Westminster?'

'It is possible,' she said with a shiver. 'When you read the rest of those missives, you will see that Father was building the house near Baynard's Castle for this French lady of his.' Bitterness intruded. 'It was not enough to have her name painted on the side of his ship and to correspond with her. He was planning to live with her in London. To keep one abode here for his family and another for his mistress.'

'I had already made that deduction, Miss Northcott.'

'Then you will understand my reluctance to visit the house in Westminster. Its atmosphere would not be conducive to rest. No,' she said, reaching a decision. 'I will stay at a reputable inn. If there is one which you can recommend, I would be most grateful.'

'As it happens,' he began, responding to a sudden idea, 'there is such a hostelry. But I hesitate to name it because it falls so far short of the kind of accommodation to which you are accustomed at Priestfield Place. It is clean, decent, totally safe and there is nowhere in London where you will be looked after with more care. But,' he added with a shrug, 'it is small and limited in the comforts it can offer you.'

'All that I need is a warm bed, sir. I will dispense with comforts.'

'Then I recommend an establishment in Fetter Lane.'

'Where will we find it?'

'You are standing in it, Miss Northcott.'

Penelope was startled. 'You invite me to stay here?'

'As my honoured guest.'

'Oh, no, Mr Redmayne. It would be an imposition.'

'Jacob will have a room ready for you instantly.'

'An inn might be a more suitable place.'

'I leave the choice to you.'

Christopher's engaging smile helped to weaken her reservations. Exhorting the coachmen to make all due speed, she had suffered the consequences in the rear of the vehicle. Her bones were aching and fatigue was lapping at her. She did not want to endure a further drive to Westminster and the prospect of staying among strangers in an inn was not appealing. There was another reason why the house in Fetter Lane took on a lustre for her but she was not yet ready to acknowledge it.

'Thank you, Mr Redmayne,' she said at length. 'I accept your offer with gratitude. Will you tell my coachman to bring in my things?'

'Jacob has already done so.'

She smiled for the first time.

When he got back to the house in Addle Hill, his wife was waiting for him in the kitchen. Sarah Bale looked up from the table without reproach.

'You are late,' she observed.

'I had much to do, my love.'

'You have been saying that every night for a week, Jonathan. The children miss their bedtime kiss from you. How much longer will this investigation go on?'

'Until an arrest is made,' he said. 'As you well know, my own duties occupy most of the day. It is only in the evening that I can take up my search for the man who murdered Sir Ambrose Northcott.'

'Where did that search lead you this time?'

Jonathan Bale lowered himself onto the chair opposite her. 'It began with a meeting,' he explained. 'I sent word to Mr Redmayne to find me at the wharf near which the *Marie Louise* was anchored. He has been as busy as I have so we had much news to exchange. When he left, I scoured the taverns to see if I could pick up any more details about Sir Ambrose's ship.'

'I can smell the beer on your breath,' she said tolerantly.

'At least I now know where she is sailing.'

'Good. How was Mr Redmayne?'

'Civil.'

'He could never be less than that,' she chided. 'He is a perfect gentleman. It pains me that you cannot bring yourself to like him.'

'We were cast in two different moulds, Sarah.'

'So were he and I, yet I find him very affable.'

'Then you speak for yourself,' he said. 'I do not have time to find the man affable or not. We are investigating a murder together. It is a solemn undertaking. The most it leaves room for is companionship.'

'You are softening towards him,' she teased. 'I can see.'

'Then you see more than I feel.'

'So be it. Let us forget Mr Redmayne for the moment,' she said briskly. 'Someone else demands your attention. I hoped that you'd be home earlier because she sat in this kitchen with me for hours.'

'She?'

'Hail-Mary Thorpe.'

'What did she want?'

'To speak to you, Jonathan.'

'Why?'

'Her husband has been arrested.'

'On what charge?'

'She is not certain. He was taken from the house while she was visiting a neighbour. Mrs Thorpe thinks that it might be for refusing to attend church and to pay tithes.'

'Let us hope that she is right.'

'Why?'

'Because those offences carry a mild punishment, Sarah. If he is lucky, he may get away with a fine. My fear is that he could be arraigned for a far more serious offence.'

'What is that?'

'Printing and distributing a seditious pamphlet,' said Jonathan. 'I am fairly certain that he is the culprit and tried to warn him of the dangers he faced. But you know Jesus-Died-To-Save-Me Thorpe. He enjoys danger. The man welcomes arrest.'

'His wife does not welcome it. She has only just recovered from a serious illness. Mrs Thorpe needs her husband beside her.'

'I made that point to him.'

'Would that he had heeded your advice!'

'It is not in his nature.'

'What will happen to him?'

'That depends on the charge brought against him,' said her husband, stroking his chin. 'If that pamphlet were found on his premises, it will go hard with him. Mr Thorpe could face a long prison sentence or even worse.'

'Worse?'

'Transportation.'

'God forbid!'

'What state was his wife in?'

Sarah heaved a sigh. 'She was very agitated, poor dear! It took me an age to calm her down. Mrs Thorpe was hoping that you might be able to help her in some way.'

'There is little enough that I can do, I fear.'

'Could you not find out with what he is charged?'

'Yes, Sarah. That is easily done.'

'Mrs Thorpe would be most grateful.'

'Who made the arrest?'

'Tom Warburton.'

'I could wish it was any other constable,' said Jonathan with a grimace. 'Tom Warburton does not like Quakers. If it were left to him, every member of the Society of Friends would be hurled into prison.' He hauled himself up. I'll walk to his house now. There is a good chance that Tom will still be up. He can tell me what charges Jesus-Died-To-Save-Me Thorpe faces.'

'What of Mrs Thorpe?'

'If I see a light in her house on my way back, I will call on her and tell her what I have learnt. Otherwise, I will have to leave it until first thing in the morning.'

'Either way, she will not get much sleep tonight.'

'It is not the first time her husband has been taken.'

'That makes no difference,' she said, rising to her feet

and reaching out to touch his arm. 'She is suffering badly. I know that you must perform your duties without fear or favour but they have been good neighbours to us. Try to help them, Jonathan. There must be something you can do for Mr Thorpe.'

'There is, Sarah.'

'What is it?'

'Pray.'

At intervals throughout the night, Christopher came awake with a smile as he realised that Penelope Northcott was sleeping only yards away from him. While he basked in his good fortune, he was also troubled by anxieties about her, fearing the consequences she might have to face. George Strype would be angry enough when he learnt that she went to London without even telling him. If her fiancé discovered that she had spent the night in a house in Fetter Lane, he would be outraged. Christopher could imagine the kind of recriminations which would ensue. That she should take such risks argued daring on her behalf and, he hoped, hinted at slight affection towards him. In the privacy of his bedchamber, he was ready to acknowledge far more than slight affection on his side.

He rose at dawn and, by the light of a candle, read the letters which she had given him. They disclosed a relationship which had being going on for the best part of a year. Sir Ambrose Northcott had not stinted his mistress. Each time she wrote, she thanked him for some lavish gift and she was flattered when he changed the name of his ship to *Marie Louise*. The constant theme of the letters was the desire to spend more time with her lover and she looked forward to the moment when they could move into the new London residence together.

Christopher had designed the house. He was jolted by the thought that his career as an architect had begun in the lustful embraces of Sir Ambrose and his mistress. He was also angry that his brother had not warned him of the existence of Marie Louise Ollier. It was one more sin of omission with which to tax Henry Redmayne.

The correspondence raised a brutal question. It was easy to see what a middle-aged man like Sir Ambrose Northcott found so tempting about a beautiful young Frenchwoman but what did she see in him? His charms were hardly overpowering. Love was expressed in every one of the letters but Christopher had no means of judging how sincere it was. After a second reading of the *billets-doux*, he could still not decide whether he was looking at the tender outpourings of a woman in love or the guileful prose of someone in pursuit of Sir Ambrose's wealth. No false note was sounded by Marie Louise Ollier, however, and he slowly came to see her as the innocent victim of an older man's lechery. Whatever the true nature of their relationship, one thing was clear. She deserved to know that it had been brought to a premature end.

After a fruitful hour of reflection, Christopher dressed and went downstairs. He was surprised to see that Penelope Northcott was already up, seated at the dining room table over the breakfast which Jacob had prepared for her. He sensed an element of discomfort.

'Good morning, Miss Northcott,'

'Good morning.'

'Did you sleep well?'

'Extremely well, Mr Redmayne. The bed was very soft.'

'You were welcome to stay in it much longer,' he said. 'Did you have to rise so early?'

'My coachman will be here for me soon.'

'I am disappointed that you cannot tarry.'

'So am I,' she said, meeting his gaze. 'But I have imposed on you enough. Besides, I have business elsewhere.'

'Do you plan to return to Kent today?'

'No, Mr Redmayne. I will be staying in London for a few days.'

'My home is entirely at your disposal.'

'A kind offer, sir, but one which I must decline. Before I fell asleep last night, I reached a decision. It is vital that I visit our house in Westminster because it may contain clues which will be of great help to you. That being the case, I am forcing myself to go there.'

'I would be happy to accompany you,'

'That will not be necessary,' she said almost primly. 'I would prefer to be alone. Dirk will take me there in the coach.'

Christopher took a seat opposite her as Jacob brought him his breakfast. They ate in silence until the servant left the room. Penelope was a trifle nervous. He noticed that she avoided his eyes.

'I hope that you have no regrets, Miss Northcott,' he said.

'Regrets?'

'About staying under my roof.'

'None at all, Mr Redmayne,' she said, looking up at him. 'And it was convenient to have an inn around the corner in

Holborn where my coach and coachman could be lodged for the night.'

'You give me the impression that you would have preferred to spend the night there yourself.'

'That is not the case at all, I promise you, and I am sorry if my manner suggests otherwise. You have been generosity itself but my mind is in turmoil over recent events. Please excuse me if I appear at all rude,' she said with a penitent smile. 'I am merely preoccupied.'

'Of course.'

'Is there anything you wish to ask before I leave?'

He grinned. 'I have questions enough to detain you for a week.'

'You will have to save them until a more fit time.'

'I will,' he said. 'Just remember that I am always here. If you need help of any kind while you are in London or, more to the point, if you do uncover what you conceive to be useful evidence at your house in Westminster, you know where to find me.'

'At the sign of the Kind Landlord.'

'Is that what I am?'

'You keep a comfortable inn, sir.'

'It has been blessed by your presence, Miss Northcott.'

His frank admiration unsettled her slightly and she was grateful when the rumble of wheels was heard outside. A glance through the window confirmed that her coachman had arrived. Showering him with more thanks, she rose from the table and crossed to the door. He followed her until a thought made her stop.

'There is something which deserves my particular thanks, sir.'

'Is there?'

'Your discretion,' she said. 'When we talked last night, you refrained from asking what anybody else would have asked at the outset.'

'And what was that?'

'How much of what I told you my fiancé must have known.'

'Nothing at all, surely.'

'I hope that is the case, naturally, and my heart assures me that it is. But you are more aware than I of how closely Mr Strype's business affairs were intertwined with my father's. They met frequently here in London. It must have crossed your mind that Mr Strype may have stumbled on some unpleasant facts about his future father-in-law.'

'It never entered my thoughts,' he lied.

'I do not believe you.'

'Then let me put it another way, Miss Northcott. It does not concern me. I consider it a matter between you and your fiancé.'

'Your tact is appreciated.'

Jacob opened the front door to let her out and Christopher helped her into the coach. When she settled into her seat, she spoke to him through the window.

'Please let me know if your investigations start to bear fruit,' she said.

'They already have,' he said with a smile which he instantly changed to an earnest frown. 'I will, Miss Northcott. But how will I reach you? I do not have your address in Westminster.'

'You will find it in my note.'

'What note?'

'The one I left for you in my bedchamber,' she said, 'thanking you for your hospitality. As you may imagine, I had great qualms about this visit but I feel reassured now. I just hope that some of the information I brought you may prove useful.'

'It is invaluable.'

'What will you do next?'

'Go straight to Mr Creech's office in Lombard Street to confront him with your findings. He must have known about this Marie Louise Ollier all along. And there is much else which that lawyer has been concealing from me. Not any more, Miss Northcott,' he vowed. 'You have given me the ammunition I need. I will make him divulge everything. I'll not leave his office until I have got the full and unequivocal truth out of Solomon Creech.'

The body was floating in mid-stream. It had lain beneath the water for some time before bobbing back to the surface in so bloated a condition that it was hideous to behold. The passengers in the boat turned away in disgust but the watermen were used to such sights. One of them shipped his oars and uncoiled the rope which lay at his feet. When he and the others resumed their journey across the Thames, the boat was towing the dead man by his ankle.

An hour later, the corpse was lifted onto a slab at the morgue to be examined by a surgeon. It was a gruesome task. Even though the chamber was sweetened by herbs, the stink was nauseating. The man's face was swollen to twice its original size and so distorted that his closest friends would never recognise him. Birds had started to peck at his face, rendering it even more repulsive. The trunk and limbs were also grotesquely inflated, splitting open his apparel in several places. Spewed up by the River Thames, he was one huge ball of putrefaction.

The surgeon turned to his assistant with a sigh.

'Cut off his clothes and we will make a start.'

'Do not prevaricate!' warned Christopher. 'Tell me where he is.'

'I do not know, sir. That is the truth.'

'You must know. You are Mr Creech's clerk.'

'He simply told me that he was going away for a few days.'

'To hide from me.'

'Your name was not mentioned, Mr Redmayne.'

'What of the name of Sir Ambrose Northcott?'

'That was at the forefront of his mind,' admitted the other. 'The last thing he said was that he would have to go aboard Sir Ambrose's ship to transact some business with the captain.'

'What was the nature of that business?'

'I can but guess.'

Christopher saw that no purpose would be served by haranguing the clerk. Geoffrey Anger was a harmless individual, loyal to his employer but quite unable to lie convincingly on his behalf. He cowered before the interrogation which his visitor inflicted on him and Christopher felt a twinge of guilt. He adopted a softer tone.

'I am sorry to make demands which you cannot meet, Mr Anger,' he said quietly, 'but you must understand my position. Mr Creech is in possession of certain facts which will help me track down the man who killed Sir Ambrose.

That is why I must speak to him. Urgently.'

'I would value some urgent conference with him myself,' bleated the other. 'I need his approval on a dozen matters.'

'How long have you been his clerk?'

'Seven and a half years, sir.'

'Do you like the work?'

Geoffrey Anger was cautious. 'I find it very rewarding, sir.'

'Mr Creech has a high reputation.'

'He has more than earned it.'

'You must have made some contribution towards it.'

'I, sir?'

'Come, Mr Anger. I have dealt with many lawyers. They are only as good as the clerks who toil at their elbow. If you have been here so long, you must have a good insight into Mr Creech's business.'

'I like to think so.'

'Then answer me this,' said Christopher. 'Does the name of Marie Louise Ollier strike a chord in your mind?'

'I am not at liberty to discuss our clients, sir.'

'Then the lady is a client?'

'I did not say that, Mr Redmayne.'

'Then what are you saying?' pressed Christopher, reverting to a more combative approach. 'Are you telling me that you do not wish the man who murdered Sir Ambrose to be caught? Are you deliberately holding back crucial facts from me? I can see from your expression that you recognised the name. You *knew* that Mademoiselle Ollier was linked to the new house which was being built. Well? Did you not?'

'Yes, sir,' came the faint reply.

'And you also knew that Sir Ambrose's ship bears her name.'

'That is true.'

'Then it follows that you were privy to the relationship between this lady and your client. I have seen the letters which she wrote to him and they leave no room for doubt. The lady was his mistress.'

The clerk was shocked. 'No, sir!'

'Those missives were not penned by a nun, Mr Anger.'

'I have not seen them,' said the other. 'Nor do I wish to, sir. The fact that a lady's name is conjoined to a particular property does not of itself mean that there is some liaison between her and Sir Ambrose. He owned another house occupied by a lady yet I have heard no suggestion of impropriety between them.'

'Another house?' Christopher was intrigued. 'Do you refer to the residence in Westminster?'

'No, sir. In Lincoln's Inn Fields.'

'Sir Ambrose owned a property there? Why did he need to build a third house when he already owned two? Surely, he could have installed Mademoiselle Ollier in Lincoln's Inn Fields?'

'It was leased out to someone else.'

'Who is it?'

'Mrs Mandrake.'

'*Molly* Mandrake?'

'That is the lady, sir.'

Christopher needed a moment to take in the information and to remind himself that he was dealing with a man of remarkable naivety. The name of Molly Mandrake had passed across the desk of Geoffrey Anger on many occasions but he had no idea who she was or what sort of a house she kept. His blinkered life protected him from the darker pleasures of the city. The fact that someone was a client of Mr Creech was enough for him. Their character was never suspect.

Christopher marvelled at his innocence and treated him gently.

'How many other properties did Sir Ambrose own?' he said.

'Just these two, sir.'

'One in Westminster, one in Lincoln's Inn Fields.'

'And a third that was never built.'

'As I know to my cost, Mr Anger!' said Christopher ruefully. 'Did Mademoiselle Ollier ever visit this office?'

'No, sir.'

'Was Sir Ambrose a frequent caller?'

'Mr Creech always met him away from here.'

'Why was that?'

'You will have to ask him yourself, sir.'

'I intend to. What do you know of the *Marie Louise*?'

'Little beyond the fact that it was owned by a client of ours.'

'All of his commercial transactions must have gone through his lawyer. Were you not handling contracts for him all the time?'

'Mr Creech took care of those himself,' explained the other. 'I had no direct contact with Sir Ambrose's business affairs.'

'Was Mr Creech in the habit of keeping things from you?'

'No, sir.'

'So why was he so secretive about Sir Ambrose Northcott?'

'It is not my place to say.'

'You must have had some idea.'

'I assure you, sir, I did not.'

'Where does Mr Creech keep his papers?'

'Locked up in his office, sir.'

'Do you have a key to it?'

'No,' said the clerk. 'And even if I did, I would permit nobody to go in there without Mr Creech's express permission.'

'But there are important documents in there which I need to see,' said Christopher with irritation. 'What is to stop me breaking in now and looking for them?'

'Oh, sir! You would never do that.'

'Why not?'

Geoffrey Anger's quiet reply had a devastating power.

'You are a *gentleman*, sir.'

When he cut open the stomach with his scalpel, the surgeon turned away as the noisome contents poured out. The dead man had eaten a hearty meal before he drowned and its remains were now scattered all over the stone slab on which he lay. When the surgeon and his assistant looked back at the glutinous mess, they saw something which glinted in the light of the candles. The surgeon reached down to pick it up. After dipping it into the basin of water, he held it up to examine it.

'What was a gold ring doing in there?' he wondered.

CHAPTER TWELVE

'Woe into the bloody city of London! It is full of sinful and ungodly men!'

Jesus-Died-To-Save-Me Thorpe was preaching to a small, hostile congregation from an unlikely pulpit. Head and hands trapped in the pillory, he was a target both for the cheerful abuse of the onlookers and the various missiles which they threw at him for sport. A rotten tomato struck him on the forehead and bled profusely down his face but it did not interrupt the torrent of words which flowed from his mouth. Being locked in the pillory was a hazardous punishment. It exposed the victim to vile taunts and, in some cases, vicious behaviour by spectators. More than one person had been stoned to death while immobilised by the rough, chafing wood. Thorpe was more fortunate. The worst blow that he had to suffer came when a dead cat was hurled at him and split open to dribble with gore.

'Turn to God in truth and humility or ye are all doomed!'

His denunciation continued unchecked until someone pulled away the box on which he was standing and almost broke his neck. Thorpe's head was suddenly jerked backwards and he had to stretch hard in order to touch the ground with his toes. The pain was agonising. Without a box to stand on, he was virtually dangling from the pillory. All the breath was knocked out of him and the crowd bayed in triumph. Too proud to beg mercy from them, the little Quaker closed his eyes in prayer.

It was soon answered. He heard a grating noise as the box was put back in position beneath his feet and his pain eased at once. The jeers of the crowd also subsided and most people began to drift away. When he opened his eyes, Thorpe saw the solid figure of Jonathan Bale standing between him and further humiliation. Only when the audience had largely dispersed did the constable step out from in front of the pillory and turn to his neighbour. He used a handkerchief to wipe the worst of the mess from the Quaker's face.

'Thank ye, Mr Bale,' said Thorpe. 'It is a strange world indeed. One constable puts me in the pillory and another comes to my aid.'

'You have only yourself to blame for being here.'

'I suffer my punishment willingly.'

'You need not have suffered it at all,' said Jonathan. 'Your offence was to be caught working on a Sunday. Had you expressed remorse, you might have got away with a fine. But you were too truculent. According to Tom Warburton, you more or less challenged the Justice of the Peace to pillory you. From what I hear, you were lucky that he did not order your ears to be nailed to the wood.'

'I do not respect corrupt justice.'

'Then try to avoid it, Mr Thorpe.'

He retrieved his neighbour's hat from the ground and set it on the man's head to shade his eyes from the late afternoon sun. Jonathan had sympathy for any man imprisoned in the pillory but it was difficult to feel sorry for someone who actively gloried in suffering. The constable's real sympathy was reserved for Hail-Mary Thorpe and her children. He was just about to remind the Quaker of his family responsibilities when the approaching clatter of hooves made him swing round.

Christopher Redmayne was in a hurry. As he pulled his horse to a halt, he dropped from the saddle and beckoned Jonathan across to him. They stepped into the privacy of an alley to converse.

'I thought we arranged to meet this evening, sir,' said Jonathan.

'My news would not wait that long.'

'Then tell it me straight.'

'Solomon Creech is dead,' said Christopher. 'Murdered.'

'How?'

'First bludgeoned then flung into the Thames to drown. They found the body this morning. It had been in the water for days.'

'Then it must have been in a sorry state,' said Jonathan. 'The river changes a man beyond all recognition. How did they identify Mr Creech?'

'From his clothing. The name of his tailor was in his coat

and the fellow remembered for whom he made the garment. Corroboration came from a gold ring they found in the dead man's stomach.'

'His stomach?'

'That is why his clerk was so certain it must be him.'

The constable blinked. 'Mr Creech swallowed a gold ring?'

'Deliberately, it seems,' explained Christopher. 'The ring was a wedding gift from his late wife and he treasured it above all else. He told his clerk that he would sooner part with his life than with that ring and that, if ever he were set upon by robbers, he would swallow the token of his wife's love.' He shook his head sadly. 'I wronged Mr Creech. I never took him for a married man, still less for one with such a romantic streak. His clerk recognised the ring at once. It was inscribed with his employer's initials. That put the identity of the body beyond all question.'

'And is that what happened?' asked Jonathan. 'He swallowed the ring because he was set on by robbers?'

'No, Mr Bale. His purse was untouched and his watch still on its chain. This is no murder for gain unless it be to gain his silence.'

'Where was he last seen?'

'Leaving his office some days ago. He told his clerk that he had business aboard the *Marie Louise*. No word was heard from him after that. This was no random killing. It is linked in some way to the death of Sir Ambrose. The river binds both men together. Solomon Creech was pulled out of it and the man who killed Sir Ambrose was last seen at that landing stage. I am forced to wonder if the murderer was waiting to be rowed out to the *Marie Louise*.'

'I found out a few more things about that vessel.'

'So did I, Mr Bale.'

'It was bound for France.'

'Everything seems to lead there.'

Christopher told him about Penelope Northcott's unheralded visit to his house, omitting the fact that she spent the night there in order to avoid any misunderstanding. Jonathan clicked his tongue in disapproval when he heard about the love letters from Marie Louise Ollier but held back from adverse comment. At the end of the tale, he reached the same conclusion as Christopher himself.

'Your brother should have warned you about this.'

'I mean to tax him on that very topic.'

'He must have known that the new house was being built for this Marie Louise. It would have been a kindness to tell you.'

'I think I can see why Henry kept the truth from me.'

'Supposing he had not, Mr Redmayne?'

'What do you mean?'

'Supposing that you *knew* your house would be lived in by a rich man and his mistress. Would you still have agreed to design it?'

'Yes,' said Christopher without hesitation.

'In your place,' said the other steadfastly, 'I would have refused.'

'Then you will never make an architect, my friend. My commission was simply to design a house, not to examine the morals of the people who might inhabit it.'

'But that is exactly what you are forced to do now, sir.'

'That irony has not been lost on me, Mr Bale.'

A jeer went up nearby. Now that the constable had moved aside from the pillory, a small knot of people had gathered around it again. Jesus-Died-To-Save-Me Thorpe found his voice once more and upbraided them sternly. Christopher moved to the corner to look across at him.

'I thought that Quakers were men of peace.'

'Not this one, sir. He is too belligerent for his own good.'

'What was his offence?'

'Working on the Sabbath.'

'I may be guilty of the same crime myself this Sunday.'

'You, sir?'

'Yes, Mr Bale,' said Christopher. 'Before I call on my brother, I will find the quickest way to sail to France. I am convinced that the answers we seek lie with Marie Louise Ollier or with the ship that carries her name. Sunday will find me working hard to track down a killer. Is that a sinful labour on the Sabbath?'

'No, Mr Redmayne.'

'Would you arrest me for it?'

'Only if you fail.'

'Why on earth did you not tell me about this, Penelope!' he yelled.

'Because you would have obstructed me.'

'And quite rightly so. You had no business to come here.'

'I believed that I did. Mother agreed with me.'

'Lady Northcott was distraught over your father's death When she urged you to come to London, she did not know what she was doing.'

'Yes, she did, George.'

'It was madness, to go driving off like that.'

'We both felt that it was imperative.'

'You should have discussed it with me first.'

'Why?'

'Because I am your fiancé! I have certain rights.'

'You do not have the right to stop me coming here.'

'I would have persuaded you of the folly of your action.'

'It was not folly. Those letters were vital evidence. I had to put them into Mr Redmayne's hands as soon as possible.'

'That was the last thing you should have done, Penelope.'

George Strype was puce with rage. Having ridden to London in pursuit of her, he had found Penelope at the Westminster house. It irked him that she was showing no regrets about her intemperate action. Making an effort to control his temper, he guided her across to a settle and sat beside her on it. He took her hand to give it a conciliatory kiss.

'Listen to me,' he said softly. 'When you accepted my proposal of marriage, we agreed that there would be no deception between us. We would be completely open with each other. Do you remember that?'

'Yes, George.'

'Then why have you gone back on that promise?'

'I was forced to,' she said.

'Why?'

'Because I was afraid of you.'

'Afraid? Of the man who loves you?' He stroked her hand. 'What afflicts you, Penelope? You need never be afraid of me.'

'You would have stopped me coming to London.'

'Yes,' he argued, 'but for your own good. Do you not see that? When you found those letters, it must have been a dreadful shock for you. I can understand that. But your father is dead now. His ugly secret belongs in the grave with him. The last thing you should have done was to expose it to the public gaze.'

'I merely showed the letters to Mr Redmayne.'

'It amounts to the same thing.'

'No, George. I can trust him to be discreet.'

'He is not family. I am – or soon will be. And my instinct is to close ranks in a case like this. In betraying Lady Northcott, your father made an appalling mistake. I admit that. But,' he insisted, squeezing her hand, 'that mistake should be buried in the past where it belongs. Think of the shame it might otherwise cause.'

'I was prepared to withstand that shame.'

'Well, I am not.'

'Mother and I discussed it.'

'Without me.'

'We put our faith in Mr Redmayne.'

'But I do not!' he roared, leaping to his feet. 'Christopher Redmayne has no cause to poke his nose into this. What is he? An architect, that is all. A man whose task is to design houses. Why does he presume to set himself up as an officer of the law? We want no bungling amateur.'

'He is trying to discover my father's murderer and needs all the help he can get.'

'Not from me!'

'How else can the culprit be arrested?'

'This investigation should be left to the proper authorities.'

'Mr Redmayne is working with a constable.'

'Dear God!' wailed Strype. 'Another pair of eyes peering into our private affairs! How many more people will see those letters, Penelope? You might as well have taken them to a printer and had copies made to be sold at every street corner!'

'Why are you so concerned, George?'

'Someone has to protect your father's reputation.'

'What reputation?'

'The one that the world sees.' He took her by the shoulders. 'What your father did was unforgivable, Penelope. In our eyes, his reputation has been badly tarnished. But we do not need to spread his peccadilloes abroad. We keep them hidden from public gaze. Everyone then benefits. Let me be candid,' he told her seriously. 'I want to marry into an unblemished family, not one which is pointed at and sniggered over. Do you understand me?'

'Only too well, George.'

'We have to exercise common sense.'

'Is it common sense to suppress evidence in a murder inquiry?'

'The family name must always come first.'

'You mean that George Strype must always come first,' she said angrily, brushing his hands away as she got up. 'It is disgraceful! You are less worried about catching a man who killed my father than you are about your own position here.'

'*Our* own position, Penelope. Do you want to begin a

marriage with this kind of scandal sticking to us? No, of course not. You have too much pride. Too much self-respect.' He paced the room in thought. 'I must find a way to retrieve the situation in which you and your mother have so foolishly landed us.' He snapped his fingers. 'The first thing is to get those letters back.'

'But I gave them to Mr Redmayne.'

'Mistakenly.'

'He said that they were vital clues.'

'I am not interested in what Mr Redmayne said. It is high time that someone put him in his place. His duty was done when he brought the news of Sir Ambrose's death. We do not need him any more.'

'I do,' she said quietly.

He turned to stare at her. 'What did you say?'

'I trust Mr Redmayne.'

'I heard more than trust in your voice, Penelope.'

'Did you?'

'Is that the way the wind blows?' he asked with suspicion. 'Can you have developed an interest in the fellow on so slight an acquaintance?'

'I look upon him as a friend.'

'How did you know where to find this friend?'

'He gave me his address when he came to Priestfield Place.'

'Did he, indeed?'

'Mr Redmayne asked me to get in touch if anything came to light which might help him to trace Father's murderer.'

'If you believed those letters were so important, why did

you not send them to him? It was not necessary to bring them yourself.'

'I felt that it was.'

'Why?'

'Because I was too ashamed to put them in anyone else's hands.'

'You gave them to Redmayne.'

'That was different.'

His tone hardened. 'When did you arrive in London?'

'Yesterday evening.'

'Yes, but at what time?' he pressed. 'It was afternoon when I called at your house and learnt about your flight. I followed you at once but had to stay overnight at an inn.' He moved in towards her. 'Your mother told me you left before dawn. It must have been close to nightfall by the time you reached London.'

'It was.'

'Did you go straight to Redmayne's house?'

'Yes.'

'Where did you spend the night?'

'Does it matter?'

'Very much.'

Thrown on the defensive, Penelope shifted her feet and glanced around. Not wishing to deceive him, she feared the consequences of telling the truth. George Strype was impatient.

'Well?'

'Do not glower at me so, George.'

'I asked you a question.'

'You have no cause to interrogate me like this.'

'Give me a simple answer,' he demanded. 'Or must I get it from your coachman? He will tell me if you stayed in this house or at an inn.'

'Neither,' she said bravely.

Strype was simmering. 'You spent the night under *his* roof?'

'Mr Redmayne was kind enough to invite me.'

'I am sure that he was!'

'He treated me with the utmost respect,' she said calmly, 'which is more than you are doing at the moment. Jacob prepared a room for me and I spent a comfortable night there.'

'Jacob?'

'Mr Redmayne's servant.'

'And did this Jacob remain on the premises?'

'Of course.'

'How do I know that?'

'Because it is what I tell you, George. Why should I lie?'

Grinding his teeth, he watched her shrewdly for a few moments.

'Where does he live?'

'That is immaterial.'

'Where does Redmayne live?' he demanded. 'I wish to know.'

His manner was so intimidating that Penelope felt obliged to fight back. George Strype was not behaving like the considerate man who had courted her so diligently and indulged her so readily. Stress and anger were revealing another side to his character.

'Why did you not tell me about Father's ship?' she asked.

'What?'

'You must have known that he changed its name.'

'Indeed, I did,' he said, caught unawares by her

vehemence. 'But I thought it of no great consequence.'

'Did you know *why* it was called the *Marie Louise*?'

'No, Penelope.'

'Is that the truth?'

'Your father was a capricious man. He often changed things.'

'Renaming a ship is much more than caprice,' she asserted. 'He would need a very strong reason to do something like that. Did you never ask him what that reason was?'

'I may have done.'

'Your goods are carried on that vessel. Were you not curious that it suddenly ceased to be *The Maid of Kent*?'

'Naturally,' he said, recovering his poise. 'But when I questioned your father, he explained it away as a fancy which seized him. He was prone to such things. As for telling you about it, there was no point whatsoever in doing so. Sir Ambrose and I were at one in keeping our business and private lives separate. It was not a case of hiding something from you, my darling. I simply did not think that it would have any relevance to you.'

'When I found those letters, it had the utmost relevance.'

'How was I to know that?'

He saw another question trembling on her lips and pre-empted it.

'No, Penelope,' he said firmly. 'I had no idea that your father had formed a liaison with this woman. Had I done so, I would have done everything in my power to bring it to an end and to remind Sir Ambrose of his marital vows. I am saddened that you could even think such a thing of me.'

'I needed to hear your denial, that is all.'

'Then you have it.'

George Strype looked so hurt by her doubts about his integrity that she softened towards him immediately. Her eyes moistened and she moved forward into his arms, apologising for her suspicion and telling him how glad she was that they were together again. He held her tight and kissed her gently on the forehead but his resolve was not weakened.

'Now,' he murmured, 'tell me where Redmayne lives.'

Henry Redmayne was in the last place where his brother expected to find him. When Christopher ran him to earth, he was working late at the Navy Office in Seething Lane, a building which had escaped the Great Fire by dint of being upwind of it. Bent over his desk, Henry was inspecting the designs for a new ship and he did not welcome the interruption.

'What do you want, Christopher?' he said peevishly.

'To search that murky vault known as your memory.'

'Your sarcasm is in bad taste.'

'And so are your lies, Henry,' said his brother, confronting him. 'Why did you not tell me that the house I was designing for Sir Ambrose was destined for him and his mistress?'

'Was it?' asked the other, feigning surprise.

'You know quite well that it was. You also knew that he changed the name of his ship to the *Marie Louise* in honour of her. Yet somehow you failed to mention either of these things to me.'

'I did not think them pertinent.'

'Well, they are extremely pertinent now,'

'Are they?'

'Yes,' said Christopher tartly. 'But let us begin with news

which has evidently not reached you. Solomon Creech has been murdered.'

Henry jumped to his feet. 'Creech? When? How?'

'His body was dragged out of the river this morning.'

'Poor devil!'

'It explains why Mr Creech was so terrified when Sir Ambrose was killed. He clearly feared for his own life – and with good cause.'

'Do they have any idea who killed him?'

'Not yet. I believe that he is the second victim of the same man. First Sir Ambrose, and now his lawyer. How many more victims must there be before you start to help me?'

'I have helped you,' stuttered the other.

'Only fitfully.'

'Tell me more about Creech. How was he found?'

Christopher recapitulated the facts and watched his brother's reaction carefully. To his credit, Henry was genuinely remorseful and he managed to say a few kind words about Solomon Creech by way of a valedictory tribute even though he had never liked the man.

'How did you learn of this, Christopher?'

'I was at Mr Creech's office when the ring was brought.'

'It must have made his clerk turn white with fear.'

'He almost fainted at the sight of it, Henry, but he was able to confirm whose it was and how it came to be in such an unlikely place.'

'Did he have any idea why his employer was murdered?'

'None whatsoever.'

'Do you?'

'Oh, yes,' said Christopher. 'I think he was killed because

of his close association with Sir Ambrose Northcott. Nobody knew as much about his business affairs and his private life as Solomon Creech. Some of that information was too dangerous to leave in his possession. That is why he had to be silenced.'

'Is this fact or supposition?'

'A blend of both.'

'So you could be wildly wrong?'

'I could be, Henry. But my instinct tells me otherwise. However, let me come back to you,' he said, fixing his brother with a stare. 'You lied to me about receiving a percentage of my fee and you lied to me about the real purpose behind the building of that house. Why?'

'I did not lie, Christopher. I merely withheld the truth.'

'It amounts to the same thing.'

'Oh, no. There is a subtle distinction.'

'I shall be grateful if you can explain it to me.'

'A lie is a deliberate act of deception,' said Henry, 'and I would never knowingly foist one on my brother. If, on the other hand, I felt there was something which he had no real need to know, I would conceal it.'

'Such as your theft from me.'

'It was not a theft, Christopher. It was fair payment.'

'For what?'

'I do not want to have that argument all over again,' said the other, waving an irritable hand. 'Put it behind us and concentrate on what brought you here. Why did I not tell you about Marie Louise Ollier? Simple. Because it was none of your business.'

'It was, Henry.'

252

'In what way? Does it matter if Sir Ambrose intended to share that house with his lawful wife or with a harem of naked women? He could have leased it out to a tribe of piccaninnies with rings through their noses and flowers in their hair. He hired you as an architect, not as a parish priest.'

'I still feel that you might have mentioned it to me.'

'Sir Ambrose chose you precisely because I did *not* need to mention such matters to you. It was a first condition of hiring you. He insisted on absolute discretion.'

'That was beforehand,' Christopher reminded him. 'Once he was dead, there was no need to hide the truth from me. It would have saved me valuable time if I heard about Marie Louise Ollier from you and not from another source.'

'What other source?'

'It does not matter.'

'I want to know.'

'Well, I am not in a position to tell you.'

'Ah, I see,' said Henry with a lift of his eyebrow. 'You accuse me of concealing information yet you are happy to do so yourself. There is one rule for me and another for Christopher Redmayne. What is your purpose?'

'I am trying to protect my brother's life.'

Sudden panic. 'My life?'

'Do you not realise that it may be at risk?'

'No. Why should it be? I have done nothing wrong.'

'You were an intimate of Sir Ambrose Northcott's. That may be enough. We are dealing with a ruthless killer, Henry. If his motive is revenge, he may not stop at Sir Ambrose's lawyer. Close friends could be his next targets.'

'Why?' gulped Henry.

'Perhaps you know too much. Like Solomon Creech.'

'I know nothing!'

'Be honest, Henry.'

'Sir Ambrose was a chance acquaintance, that is all.'

'Yet he entrusted you with secrets denied to others,' reasoned Christopher. 'To his wife and daughter, for instance. You shared his passion for gambling and for women. You dined with him, discussed the affairs of the day with him, even went to Court with him. That is more than a chance acquaintanceship, Henry.'

'You really think that I am in danger?'

'Until this villain is caught.'

'What must I do, Christopher?'

'Be more truthful with me. The longer you hold back secrets, the more you imperil yourself. I need to know *everything* about your relationship with Sir Ambrose, especially where the new house is concerned. It is no accident that he was murdered on the premises. That property had a vital significance. Help me to find out what it was.'

'How?'

'Go back to the start, Henry. Tell me how and when Sir Ambrose first decided to commission another house. Why did he choose that site? And how did you persuade him that your brother was the ideal architect for him to employ on the project?'

Henry sat back down again to gather his thoughts. Having failed to get the answers he wanted, Christopher had decided to frighten them out of him. He did not really believe that his brother was at risk but it was the only way to ensure his full cooperation.

His ruse worked. Important new information gushed out of Henry in a continuous stream and further aspects of the character of Sir Ambrose Northcott were laid bare. Henry knew far more about the man's political activities than he had hitherto disclosed and, it transpired, had once sailed with him in the *Marie Louise*. When the confession came to an end, Christopher told him the one thing about his friend which he obviously did not know. Henry paled.

'Sir Ambrose owned that house in Lincoln's Inn Fields?'

'I had it on good authority.'

'Why did he never tell me?' said Henry, wounded that such a fact had been kept from him. 'We went there several times together yet he never even hinted that he was the owner. I always assumed that the house belonged to Molly Mandrake.'

'What sort of an establishment is it?'

'A wondrous edifice in every way.' A beatific smile spread over Henry's face. 'We were fortunate enough to see Molly Mandrake in her prime. What a truly extraordinary woman! The most remarkable piece of architecture in London. Such symmetry, such proportions!'

'I will take your word for it, Henry.'

'She would inspire any artist.'

'That is a matter of opinion,' said Christopher with a tolerant smile. 'I just hope that the name of Mrs Mandrake does not come to Father's ears. I doubt that he would appreciate her architectural pre-eminence. But enough of the lady,' he continued. 'I will have to ask Mr Bale to take a look at her establishment in my absence.'

'Mr Bale? Is that the constable you have mentioned?'

'Yes, Henry. A staunch fellow. Jonathan Bale is a dour Roundhead but as solid as a rock for all that. He and I have been working together. I sail from Deptford tomorrow on the morning tide. While I am in France, he can follow up other lines of enquiry here.'

'And what of me?'

'Study Sir Ambrose's political enemies more closely.'

'I am talking of my safety. What must I do?'

'Go armed, brother.'

'I will, I will.'

'And do not venture near the river on your own.'

'I will immure myself in my house.'

'There is no need for that,' said Christopher. 'Sensible precautions will suffice. And you must go to Court. How else can you keep a wary eye on those politicians?'

When he left the Navy Office, he was confident for the first time that Henry had been completely honest with him.

Christopher collected his horse and rode to Addle Hill to acquaint Jonathan Bale with what he had just learnt and to suggest that he kept a certain house in Lincoln's Inn Fields under surveillance. The constable accepted the assignment with some reluctance then surprised Christopher by warning him to look after himself while in France.

'I will, Mr Bale. We reach Calais on Sunday.'

'Desperate men do not respect the Sabbath.'

'Nor do desperate women,' said Christopher with a grin. 'I suspect that activity will continue unabated in Lincoln's Inn Fields. If your feet take you in that direction, you may learn something of interest.'

'I am no Peeping Tom, sir.'

'We must both look through keyholes if we are to get to the bottom of this, Mr Bale. I must find Mademoiselle Ollier and you must renew your friendship with Mrs Mandrake.'

'The lady is no friend of mine.'

'In time she might become one,' advised Christopher mischievously.

'A century would not suffice,' said Jonathan proudly. 'I am a married man and more than happy with my lot.'

'You have every right to be. Mrs Bale is a delightful woman.'

'Then no more jests, sir.'

'I am sorry if I appear to treat the matter lightly,' said the other seriously, 'for I am in earnest. The bedchamber seems to have been the natural milieu of Sir Ambrose Northcott. Neither of us must shrink from peeping into it.'

'Necessity will dictate.'

Jonathan showed him to the door and waited while he mounted.

'Good luck, sir!'

'Thank you, Mr Bale.'

'When will I hear from you again?'

'As soon as may be. Farewell!'

Christopher rode off through the darkening streets, pondering the mystery of Jonathan Bale. The investigation which had drawn the two of them together allowed him to see the constable's merits and compassion yet some kind of impassable barrier remained between them. Sarah Bale was open and friendly towards him but her husband was somehow unable to follow her example. Christopher wondered why.

Speculation took him all the way back to Fetter Lane

where he stabled his horse and came round to the front of the house. He was just about to go inside when he saw a coach lurching up the street out of the gloom. His spirits soared as he recognised it as belonging to Penelope Northcott. He waited until the coachman brought the vehicle to a halt then reached out to open the door for her, smiling broadly in welcome.

But it was George Strype who glared out at him. He was the sole passenger and he took note of Christopher's evident disappointment.

'Were you expecting someone else, Mr Redmayne?' he asked.

'No, Mr Strype.'

'I see that you remember my name.'

'I can hardly forget it.'

'You seem to have forgotten that it is linked with the name of Penelope Northcott,' said the other pointedly. 'She and I are engaged to be married. I take a dim view of any man who lures my betrothed into spending a night beneath his roof.'

Christopher tried to douse the man's smouldering anger.

'Perhaps you would care to step inside my house,' he said with great courtesy. 'We can discuss this like gentlemen and I promise you that I will be able to put your mind at rest.'

'I did not come here to discuss anything with you, Mr Redmayne.'

'Then what is the purpose of this visit?'

'To retrieve those letters.'

'Miss Northcott entrusted them to me.'

'She now wants them back.'

258

'I beg leave to doubt that.'

'Give me the letters, man!'

'They are valuable evidence. I need them.'

'Miss Northcott wishes to have them back!'

'Do you have a written request to that effect?'

'Of course not.'

'Then I will not return them.'

'She empowered me to speak on her behalf.'

'I find that unlikely, Mr Strype,' said Christopher evenly. 'When the letters first came to light, Miss Northcott chose to keep their existence from you. I can see why.'

'Damn you, man! Hand them over.'

'Not unless she comes here in person.'

'Must I *take* those letters from you?'

George Strype hauled himself up and stood menacingly in the doorway of the coach, back crouched and head thrust forward. One hand closed on his sword and he drew it halfway from its sheath. Christopher did not move an inch. When their eyes locked, his were glistening with quiet determination.

'You are most welcome to try to take them, Mr Strype,' he said.

His pugnacious visitor ducked out of the coach then paused on the step when he saw that Christopher did not budge. He was almost inviting attack. Strype noticed his hand, resting on the handle of his own sword with the nonchalance of a man who knew how to use the weapon. The prospect of a duel in the street suddenly lost all appeal. There was a long pause while the visitor reviewed the situation. With a snort of anger, George Strype then stepped back into the coach and slammed the door behind him. Christopher gave him a cheery wave.

'I will return!' warned Strype.

Then he ordered the coachman to drive off.

Arresting prostitutes was not a duty Jonathan Bale ever enjoyed. He did not mind the violent altercations which often ensued; but the propositions troubled him. Many women whom he apprehended tried to buy their freedom with all manner of favours and it pained him to put any woman in that position, however immoral her life might be. Though he always refused such favours, he was insulted that they should even be offered and was ashamed to be taken as the kind of man who might succumb to them. Besides, he had lived in London long enough to know that brothels could never be entirely eradicated. To him, they were a symbol of the capital's decay and he believed that their numbers had proliferated since the restoration of a Stuart king. He habitually referred to Whitehall Palace as the largest house of resort in the city.

On the long walk to Lincoln's Inn Fields, he had to remind himself of the importance of the work he was undertaking. Something of real value to a murder investigation might be learnt. Molly Mandrake's establishment would cater for a much higher standard of clients than those who rutted in the stews of Clerkenwell or caroused in the brothels of Southwark but position and place did not absolve them in his eyes. Whether artisans or aristocrats, men who frequented such places were uniformly corrupt. They deserved arrest just as much as the women who served their carnal appetites.

As he strolled down Fleet Street, he felt a twinge of guilt about lying to his wife. Instead of admitting that he was going to keep vigil outside the abode of the infamous Molly Mandrake, he had told Sarah that he was visiting the riverside taverns again. It puzzled him that he had found such deceit necessary. He wondered what he should say to her when he got back home. As he turned right into Chancery Lane, he was grateful that he would only have the role of an observer. The area lay outside city jurisdiction and he would not need to enforce laws which could not be ignored within his own ward.

It was dark when he reached Lincoln's Inn Fields but a half-moon threw enough light to guide his footsteps and to dapple the buildings around him. He did not take long to find the house. It was the largest and most palatial on view, rising to three storeys with extensive gardens at the rear. Jonathan paused when he saw a coach stopping outside the house ahead of him. Two men alighted and went swiftly inside. Torches burnt beneath the marble portico and a sunburst of candlelight spilt out when the front door was opened. It was no place to lurk unseen. Keeping to the shadows, he went instead around the side of the building and chose a vantage point from which he could keep the road under surveillance.

Traffic was fairly steady. Most clients arrived in coaches or on horseback. Only a few approached on foot. They came in pairs or in small groups, all caught up in a mood of anticipatory delight, laughing, joking and, in some cases, very inebriated. Jonathan recognised only one of them by sight – a Justice of the Peace from Queenhithe Ward – but he heard many names being trumpeted in Molly Mandrake's distinctive voice as she welcomed each new visitor to her abode. Skulking in the darkness, the anomaly of his position troubled the constable but he memorised all the names with care. He chose to forget the boastful and obscene comments he overheard from some of those who tumbled out happily into the night when they had sated themselves.

Molly Mandrake's popularity knew no bounds. Well after midnight, fresh clients were arriving to replace those who had already left. Jonathan decided that it was time to vacate his post and return to the sanctity of the marriage bed. Before he could do so, however, he heard footsteps on the cobblestones and withdrew into his hiding-place. Arriving alone, the newcomer ignored the front door and came to the side of the house where Jonathan was waiting in the shadows. The man looked around furtively to make sure that he was unobserved then produced a key to let himself in through the side door.

At first Jonathan only saw him in silhouette. Tall and slim, he carried a walking stick. His movements were lithe and he was clearly on familiar ground. When the door opened, enough light poured out to give Jonathan a brief glimpse of his face. It was an eerie moment. What he saw beneath the broad-brimmed hat was a long, white, tapered, impassive countenance with a flat nose, a narrow mouth, slit eyes, a slight bulge in place of eyebrows and a smooth complexion which had the most unnatural glow to it. At first, he wondered if he was looking at a ghost. It took him a full minute to realise that the visitor's entire face was covered by a mask.

Chapter Thirteen

Christopher Redmayne was an indifferent sailor and it was only the necessity of reaching Paris which made him cross the Channel with any enthusiasm. He marvelled at the fearless way in which the crew handled the ship, especially when it came out from the shelter of the estuary to be met by stronger winds and more purposeful waves. His queasy stomach eventually settled down and drowsiness soon took over. The salt spray which so many found bracing had the opposite effect on Christopher and he spent most of the time below deck, huddled in a corner, drifting in and out of sleep, rocked like a baby in a giant cradle. Food and drink were never even considered. How long he slumbered he did not know, but he came awake to the sound of yelling voices above his head, the cry of gulls and the distant chiming of church bells.

When he ventured up on deck again, he saw that they were

about to enter the harbour at Calais. The prospect of dry land and his intense curiosity spared him any further discomfort and he was able to remain at the bulwark throughout. He scanned the harbour but was disappointed to find no sign of the *Marie Louise* among the assorted vessels moored there even though Calais had been its designated port of call. When he disembarked, he made enquiries at the quayside and learnt that he had arrived too late. Having taken a cargo of wine on board, the *Marie Louise* had sailed back to England and must therefore have passed Christopher's own craft in the night. It was galling.

He was glad that England was finally at peace with France, albeit an uneasy one. It turned him from a nominal foe into a welcome friend and his command of the language drew approving smiles from everyone he met and set him apart from most of the other English passengers who stepped off the ship onto French soil.

Paris still lay a long way off and he elected to travel most of the way by coach, withstanding the noisy conversation and the bad breath of his companions in return for a journey of relative comfort and assured safety. Fond thoughts of Penelope Northcott filled his mind throughout the first day on the road and he wondered how she would react when she learnt of George Strype's bold but failed attempt to retrieve the letters from him during what Christopher was certain was a visit unauthorised by her. At the inn where he spent the night, he fell asleep with the contentment of a man who had helped to sow discord between the engaged couple.

Awake at cockcrow, he tried to picture the moment of discovery when Penelope prised open her father's desk. To a sensitive young lady, the disillusion must have been searing as all her certainties about her father were ripped asunder. Christopher was bound to speculate on the motives which drove her to institute the search in the first place and to take it upon herself to break into a locked drawer. Another thing puzzled him. Given the nature of the letters, why had Sir Ambrose Northcott kept them at Priestfield Place and not in his possession? It was almost as if he wanted them to be found.

As the coach rumbled off again, Christopher realised that he was following a trail which Sir Ambrose himself must have taken many times. It meandered gently through the enchanting landscape of Picardy and provided scenery to divert the most jaded travellers. Trees were in full bloom, grass was green and lush, sheep and cattle grazed in the sunshine, hedgerows were fringed with pert wild-flowers and a playful breeze turned the sails of the occasional windmill. Yet Christopher took no pleasure from the journey. Eager for action, he was instead surrounded by rural tranquillity. Anxious to reach Paris, he was forced to sit in a stuffy coach with gaping passengers as it kept up a steady speed.

They passed through Amiens early on the third day and the sight of its magnificent cathedral did tear him away from his preoccupations and make him admire it afresh. Christopher believed that it was an even finer piece of ecclesiastical architecture than Notre Dame and its ornate detail bewitched him long after the coach had driven out of the town. When they reached Beauvais, he decided to abandon the coach and complete the last leg of the journey alone. Shortly after dawn on the next day, he was cantering on a hired horse along the road to Paris.

What lay before him he did not know, but he was spurred on by memories of what he had left behind. Two murders and a series of unpleasant revelations had trapped him in a kind of labyrinth. He was hoping that Marie Louise Ollier might somehow teach him the way out.

He knew Paris well and it always struck him as a strange mixture of beauty and ugliness, of effortless splendour rooted in filthy streets. When he eventually reached the French capital, what first greeted him was the high wall which encircled the city and which was in turn ringed by an earth dyke. He entered through the Porte de St-Ouen and plunged into its narrow, congested streets, dwarfed by the endless churches, colleges and religious houses built with a grey stone which was stained by time. The city's characteristic stink rose up to attack his nostrils and he put a hand to his face as he picked his way through the milling crowd.

The sense of being lost in a labyrinth became stronger than ever.

Arnaud Bastiat owned a fine house in the Faubourg St Germain. Alone in the room which served as a library and study, he sat at his table, lost in contemplation. The book which lay open before him was unnoticed and the booming of the nearby church clock went unheard.

Bastiat was a rotund man of middle years with a pale face which was pierced by two intelligent blue eyes and a high forehead which was covered in a network of veins. Lank grey hair hung to his shoulders, complemented by a small grey beard. Dressed largely in black, he had white cuffs and a white lace collar which spread its intricate pattern across his barrel chest. When his servant knocked and entered, it took Arnaud Bastiat a while to become fully aware of his presence. The servant, a compact young man with a dark moustache, stood there in silence until his master spoke.

'Yes, Marcel?'

'You have a visitor, monsieur,' said the man.

'I am expecting no callers this evening. Who is it?'

'A young man from England.'

'From England?' said the other guardedly. 'Did he give a name?'

'Christopher Redmayne.'

'I do not know him. What business can he have with me?'

'He did not come in search of you, monsieur.'

'Oh?'

'The person he seeks is Mademoiselle Ollier.'

Bastiat sat back in surprise and stroked his beard. He signalled that the visitor was to be brought in then rose from his chair, closing the book gently before walking around the table. When Christopher entered, his host was standing in the middle of the room, composed but alert, his eyes and ears now attuned to what was in front of him. Introductions were made and each man tried to weigh up the other as they spoke in French.

'You have come all the way from England?' began Bastiat.

'Yes, monsieur. A long journey but an unavoidable one.'

'Why is that?'

'I must see Mademoiselle Ollier at the earliest opportunity.'

'And your reason?'

'That is a matter between myself and the young lady.'

'What brought you to this address?'

'It was the one given in a letter which Mademoiselle Ollier sent to a mutual friend of ours.'

'Have you seen this letter?'

'I carry it with me,' said Christopher, tapping his pocket.

'May I look at it?'

'No, Monsieur Bastiat. It is of a very private nature. I will only show it to Mademoiselle Ollier to establish my credentials.'

A lengthy pause. 'This mutual friend,' said Bastiat at length, 'are you able to tell me his name?'

'I am afraid not.'

'Then it is a gentleman of whom we speak?'

'My tidings are for Mademoiselle Ollier.'

'May I at least know your relation to this mutual friend?'

'I was employed by him as his architect.'

'An architect? An exalted position for a messenger.'

Christopher tired of his probing. 'The message I bring is of the most urgent nature, monsieur,' he said. 'I implore you to tell me where I can find the young lady.'

'Mademoiselle Ollier does not live here.'

'So I deduce.'

'But she could be sent for in an emergency.'

'I believe that this qualifies as an emergency.'

'Why?'

'I am sure that the young lady will tell you in due course.'

Bastiat raked him with a shrewd gaze then moved to the door.

'Excuse me one moment, monsieur.'

Christopher noted that he went out to speak to the servant instead of summoning him and giving him instructions in front of the visitor. Evidently, a private warning was being sent to Marie Louise Ollier and Christopher wished that he could hear what it was. He took advantage of his host's brief absence to look at some of the books which filled the shelves. Bastiat was clearly a studious man. Before the other returned, Christopher was just in time to observe that the volume which lay on the table was an edition of the Bible.

'Mademoiselle Ollier will be here soon,' said Bastiat.

'Thank you, monsieur.'

'I take it that you will have no objection if I am present during your conversation with her?'

Christopher was adamant. 'I object most strongly,' he said, 'and I suspect that the young lady will do likewise when she realises the nature of what I have to reveal to her.'

'But I am her uncle, Monsieur Redmayne.'

'Were you her father, I would still bar you from the room.'

'Then your message must be of a very delicate nature.'

'It is.'

'Can you give me no hint of its content?'

'None, monsieur.'

Bastiat continued to fish for information but Christopher would not be drawn. Having braved a taxing journey, he was not going to spill his news into the wrong pair of ears. Besides, he was there to listen as well as to inform and he sensed that he would learn far more from Marie Louise Ollier if they were alone than if her uncle were in attendance. Bastiat was a quiet, softly spoken man but he exuded an authority which was bound to have an influence on his niece. The size of the house suggested that its owner was a man of some means but it was not clear what profession he followed. He did not look to Christopher like a person who lived on inherited wealth. There was an air of diligence about him. He was also very circumspect. Probing for detail about his visitor, Bastiat gave away almost nothing about himself.

It was twenty minutes before the servant returned and tapped on the door. Bastiat excused himself again and Christopher could hear him conversing in a low voice with someone in the hall. When he reappeared, he brought in Mademoiselle Ollier and performed the introductions, lingering until his niece was seated and assuring her that she only had to call if she wished to summon him.

Left alone with the newcomer, Christopher needed time to adjust his thoughts because Marie Louise Ollier bore no resemblance whatsoever to the person of his expectations.

Penelope Northcott had made a judgement about her based on a rough portrait which she had seen but Christopher realised that no artist could possibly have conveyed her essence in a sketch. Marie Louise Ollier had the kind of striking beauty which was all the more potent for being unaware of itself. She was a tall, slender, almost frail young lady with a fair complexion and fair hair which was trained in a mass of short curls all over her head. The blue and white stripes on her dress accentuated her height and poise. Its bodice was long and tight-fitting and the low *décolletage* was encircled with lace frills. The full skirt was closely gathered in pleats at the waist then hung to the ground. On her head was a lawn cap with a standing frill in front and long lappets falling behind the shoulders.

The two things which struck Christopher most were the softness of her skin and her aura of innocence. Marie Louise

Ollier was not the coquette whom he thought he saw on a first reading of her letters. She was much nearer to the victim who seemed to emerge from a closer perusal of them. Yet she was not timid or submissive. Framed in the window, she sat there with great self-possession as she appraised him through large pale green eyes. Christopher took note of the small crucifix which hung on a gold chain around her neck. Marie Louise Ollier was a porcelain saint. The idea that she could be entangled with a man like Sir Ambrose Northcott seemed ludicrous.

'You must excuse my uncle,' she said softly. 'He is very protective. Since my parents died, he believes that it is his duty to look after me.'

'I see.'

'He was afraid to leave me alone with you.'

'Are *you* afraid, mademoiselle?'

'Yes,' she admitted.

'Of me.'

'Of what you have come to tell me.'

'It is not good news, I fear.'

'I know.'

'How?'

'Because I sense it, monsieur. He has not written to me since he left for England. That is a bad sign. Something has happened. Something to stop him sending a letter. Is he unwell?' Christopher shook his head. 'Worse than that?'

'Much worse,' he whispered.

She gave a little whimper then tightened her fists as she fought to control herself. Her eyes were filled with tears and her face puckered with apprehension but she insisted on hearing the truth. Christopher broke the news to her as gently as he could. Her body convulsed and he moved across to her, fearing that she was about to faint, but she waved him away and brought a lace handkerchief up to her face. She sobbed quietly for some minutes and all that he could do was to stand and wait. When she finally mastered her grief, she found the strength to look up at him.

'Why did you come to me?' she asked.

'I felt that you had a right to be told.'

'Thank you.'

'I know how much Sir Ambrose meant to you.'

'Everything,' she murmured. 'He was everything.'

The bundle of letters suddenly became like a lead weight in his pocket. He took them guiltily out, feeling that he was intruding into a private relationship simply by holding them. He offered them to her.

'You might want these back.'

She took them sadly. 'Did you read them?' He nodded. 'They were not meant for anyone else's eyes. They were for him. Only for him.'

'I realise that, mademoiselle. But I needed to find you. It was one of the letters which brought me to Paris.'

'I am glad you came.'

'It was not a welcome undertaking.'

'You are very considerate, monsieur.' She used the handkerchief to wipe away a tear and looked at him with more interest. 'So you are the architect,' she said with a wan smile. 'Ambrose talked so much about our house. He was delighted with what you had done, Monsieur Redmayne. I was so looking forward to living in London. I dreamt of nothing else. What will happen to the house now?'

'It will probably never be built.'

'That is such a shame.'

She stroked the bundle of letters with her fingers and he noticed for the first time the handsome diamond ring on her left hand. Marie Louise Ollier went off into a reverie and he did not dare to break into it. He waited patiently until she blinked as if suddenly coming awake.

'Do please excuse me, sir.'

'There is nothing to excuse.'

'How did you find the letters?' she asked.

'I did not, mademoiselle. They were given to me.'

'By whom?'

'Sir Ambrose's daughter.'

'Daughter?' She recoiled as if from a blow. 'He had a daughter?'

'Did you not know that?'

'No, monsieur. Ambrose told me that his wife died years ago. There was no mention of any children. I was led to believe that he lived alone.'

'You were deceived, I fear,' said Christopher, distressed that he had to inflict further pain. 'Sir Ambrose owned a house in Kent which he shared with his wife and daughter. Lady Northcott did not die. I have met her and she is in good health.'

'But he was going to marry *me*,' she protested.

'That would not have been possible under English law.'

'Nor in the eyes of God!'

Her hand went to the crucifix and Christopher began to wonder if he had misread her letters. A close physical

273

relationship was implied in them yet he was now getting the impression that Marie Louise Ollier was far from being an experienced lover. If that were the case, a startling paradox was revealed. After years of consorting with ladies of easy virtue, Sir Ambrose Northcott had become obsessed with a virgin. He could only attain her with a promise of marriage.

'Mademoiselle,' he said, sitting beside her, 'you told me earlier that you sensed something was amiss because Sir Ambrose had not written to you since he went to England.'

'That is so.'

'Was he recently in France, then?'

'Yes, he spent ten days here.'

'Together with you?'

'Some of the time,' she recalled. 'He stayed here at my uncle's house. Before that, he had business to transact in Calais and Boulogne. And, of course, he had to travel to the vineyard.'

'Vineyard?'

'In Bordeaux. It is owned by my family.'

'Is that where Sir Ambrose bought his wine?'

'Most of it.'

'And is that how you met?'

'No,' she said wistfully. 'We met in Calais. He was so *kind* to me.' She turned to Christopher. 'I know what you must think, monsieur. A young girl, being spoilt by a rich man who takes advantage of her innocence. But it was not like that. He was attentive. He treated me with respect. He just liked to be with me. And the truth of it is, I have always felt more at ease with older men. They are not foolish or impetuous.' She gave a little shrug. 'I loved him. I still love him even though he lied to me. He must have planned to leave his wife,' she continued, as if desperate to repair the damage which had been done to a cherished memory. 'That was it. He was working to free himself from this other woman. Proceedings must already have been under way. They had to be. Ambrose was mine. That house in London was not being built for anyone else. It belonged to *us*. He encouraged me to make suggestions about it.'

'I remember commenting on the French influence.'

'That came from me, monsieur.'

'So I see.'

She gazed down at the ring and fondled it with her other hand.

'Ambrose gave this to me,' she said.

'It is beautiful.'

'I will never part with it.' She looked at the bundle of letters which lay in her lap. 'Why did you bring these to me, monsieur?'

'I felt that you would want them back.'

'I do but there was no need for you to bring them. A courier could have been sent. That is how Ambrose kept in touch with me. By courier.' She stared up at him. 'Why come in person?'

'Because I hoped to break the news as gently as I could.'

'Was that the only reason?'

'No, I wanted to meet you.'

'Why?'

'I need your help, mademoiselle.'

'What can I do?'

'Tell me about Sir Ambrose,' he explained. 'I owe him a

great debt and it can only be repaid by tracking down the man who killed him. I have dedicated myself to that task.'

'That is very noble of you, monsieur.'

'His death must be avenged.'

'Oh, yes!' she exclaimed. 'The murderer cannot go unpunished. He must be caught quickly. Do you know who he is?'

'No, mademoiselle.'

'But you have some idea?'

'I feel that I am getting closer all the time,' he said with a measure of confidence. 'The trail led to Paris.'

'Why here?'

'That is what I am hoping you can tell me.'

'But this was where Ambrose came to escape. To be with me.'

'When did you last see him?'

'Let me see...'

Christopher plied her with questions for a long time and she gave ready answers but none of them contained any clues as to why Sir Ambrose was murdered and by whom. Marie Louise Ollier had been kept largely ignorant of his business affairs and he had told her nothing whatsoever about the true nature of his domestic situation. Time spent together had been limited, taken up for the most part with discussions about the new house and its furnishings. She made flattering comments about his design and Christopher realised that some of his earlier drawings of the house must have been shown to her. The man she described was very different from the confirmed rake who sought pleasure in the company of men such as Henry Redmayne.

As he listened to her fond reminiscences, Christopher was left in no doubt about the fact that she truly loved him and he could understand very clearly why Sir Ambrose had been besotted with her. Now that he was so close to her, he could see that she was perhaps a few years older than Penelope Northcott but she had a childlike charm which made her seem much younger.

Having described her own history, she asked him about his memories of Sir Ambrose. Christopher searched for positive things to say about the man, concealing anything which might strike a discordant note. It was only when she gave a slight shiver that he realised something was amiss.

Marie Louise Ollier was sitting in the chair closest to the open shutters and an evening breeze was disturbing her headdress. When there were more comfortable chairs in the room, it seemed odd that her uncle should conduct her to that one. The library looked out on the garden at the rear of the house and it suddenly occurred to Christopher that anyone standing outside could eavesdrop on them with ease. He was about to stand up and investigate when she reached out to grab his arm.

'Will you send word to me, monsieur?' she begged.

'Word?'

'When you catch the man who killed him, please let me know.'

'I will.'

'Send word to this address.'

'Even though you do not live here?'

'It will reach me.'

'Would it not be easier if I had your own address?'

277

'No, monsieur.'

'Is your own house nearby?'

'Send word here.'

Christopher detached her hand and got up to cross to the window. When he glanced out into the garden, he could see nobody but he still had the uncomfortable feeling that they had been overheard.

'Evening is drawing in,' he announced. 'I must away.'

'Will you not stay the night in Paris?'

'No, mademoiselle. It is a long ride. I would like to put a few miles between myself and the city tonight.'

'I understand. Wait here while I call my uncle.'

She moved to the door and let herself out, leaving the room still inhabited with her presence and charged with her fragrance. Christopher had a moment to compose himself. Though he had not been given the valuable clues he sought, he had discovered much that would be useful once he had sifted carefully through it. Yet he was still left with many imponderables. Before Christopher could rehearse them, Bastiat came into the room on his own. There was concern in his voice.

'My niece tells me that you are leaving, monsieur.'

'I fear that I must.'

'You are most welcome to spend the night here as my guest.'

'That is very tempting, Monsieur Bastiat, but I must begin the homeward journey tonight.'

'Are you sure?'

'I have no choice.'

'Where will you stay?'

'There is an inn which I passed on the way here,' said Christopher. 'It must be ten or twelve miles along the road to Beauvais. I will lodge there and make an early start in the morning.'

'Very well. I can see that there is no point in trying to persuade you against your will.'

'None at all.'

'You are a determined young man, Monsieur Redmayne.'

'Of necessity.'

'Why?'

'Your niece will explain.'

'Then I bid you adieu.'

He conducted his visitor out into the hall and opened the front door for him. Christopher looked around in disappointment.

'I would like to take my leave of Mademoiselle Ollier.'

'That will not be possible, monsieur.'

'Why not?'

'She is deeply upset by the terrible news which you brought. In your presence, she held up bravely but it has taken its toll. She wishes to be alone with her grief now.' He hunched his shoulders. 'There is darkness in her heart. It would be a cruelty to intrude.'

'Say no more, monsieur. I understand.'

'It was good of you to come all this way.'

'I felt that it was an obligation.'

'An obligation?'

'Nobody else would have come here.'

'You deserve our thanks,' said the other. 'My niece did not need to tell me why you travelled to Paris. I saw it in her face.

Poor creature! She is suffering badly.' He touched his guest's shoulder. 'I hope your journey will not be too onerous. Do you sail from Calais?'

'Yes, Monsieur Bastiat.'

'You will have much to reflect upon, I suspect.'

'Oh, yes,' said Christopher warmly. 'I did not simply come on an errand of mercy. I was in search of guidance.'

'Indeed?'

'Thanks to Mademoiselle Ollier, I found it.'

Jonathan Bale had always believed that honesty was the best policy, especially where matrimonial exchanges were concerned. He was proved right once again. Unskilled in hiding anything from his wife, he told her exactly where he went when he returned from his first night's vigil in Lincoln's Inn Fields. Sarah was at once critical and curious, disapproving strongly of places such as Molly Mandrake's establishment yet wanting to know exactly what happened inside their walls and who patronised them. Her husband was reticent about activities within the house but he gave her several names from the memorised list of visitors. That list had been committed to paper and added to substantially as a result of two subsequent visits.

As Jonathan prepared to set out for Lincoln's Inn Fields for a fourth time, he sat in the kitchen of his home and consulted his list of names once again. It contained one earl and more than a scattering of baronets. In his view nothing more clearly mirrored a degenerate aristocracy. He stuffed the paper into his pocket and rose to leave. His wife got up from the table with him.

'At least you had time to put the boys to bed this evening,' she said gratefully. 'When shall I expect you back?'

'I have no idea, Sarah.'

'As long as you do not get lured inside that place.'

'It holds no attraction for me.'

'Even though it must be filled with gorgeous young ladies?'

'They are poor women, led astray,' said Jonathan sadly. 'Besides, I could never afford to keep company with them. They charge more for one night than most men earn in a month.'

'How do you know?' teased his wife.

He grinned. 'That is a secret.'

'What happened to that man with the mask?'

'I only saw him on that first visit.'

'Has he not been back to the house?'

'Not while I have been there, Sarah.'

'Why would a man wear a mask like that?' she said.

'To conceal his identity. I guess him to be a person of high rank who does not wish anyone to know that he frequents the place. Who knows? It might even have been the King himself.'

She was shocked. 'He would never sink so low!'

'Do not put it past him, my love. The rumour is that he tires of his mistresses on occasion and seeks entertainment elsewhere.'

'Well, it is a scurvy rumour and I will not believe it.'

He was worried. 'I hope you are not turning into a royalist, Sarah.'

'Of course not,' she said stoutly. 'I deplored the Restoration as much as you did. Life was better under the Lord Protector. But while we have a King on the throne, I prefer to give him the benefit of the doubt. Now, off with you and prove me wrong.'

'I may well do so.'

She gave him a kiss then walked with him to the front door.

'When is Mr Redmayne coming back?' she wondered.

'I do not know.'

'He has been gone for days now. Why did you not offer to go with him, Jonathan? It is dangerous for someone to travel all that way on his own. You could have been his bodyguard.'

'Mr Redmayne can look after himself, Sarah. He would never have considered taking me and I would certainly not have enjoyed spending so much time alone with him.'

'It would have given you chance to get to know him better.'

'That was my fear.'

He let himself out of the house, gave her a wave and strode off. The route was familiar now and he seemed to arrive in Lincoln's Inn Fields sooner than ever. Clouds drifted across the moon to keep the whole area largely in darkness. It enabled him to slip into his accustomed hiding-place with no danger of being seen. Revellers soon began to arrive. Some were regular visitors whose names had already been recorded but others were memorised for the first time. When another coach arrived, its lone passenger was given an especially warm welcome by Molly Mandrake as she opened the door to greet him. It was a French name and Jonathan doubted if he would be able to spell it correctly when he added it to his list.

The most interesting snatch of dialogue which he overheard came towards the end of his stay in the shadows. A man arrived on horseback, tethered his mount then pulled the doorbell. Caught between the two torches under the portico, he gave Jonathan a clear view of his profile and the constable was forced to ask once again why yet another elegant young gentleman had to pay for pleasures which he could more properly enjoy within a lawful marriage. When the door swung open, light blazed out and brought Molly Mandrake's rich voice with it.

'Why, Mr Strype!' she said happily. 'This is a pleasant surprise.'

'Have you missed me, Molly?'

'We all have, sir. Desperately.'

'I have not been able to visit London for some time.'

'More's the pity!' A deep sigh followed. 'We were so shocked to hear about what happened to Sir Ambrose.'

'A dreadful business, Molly. Quite devastating!'

'I hope that it has not dragged you down too much, sir.'

'I must confess that it has.'

'Are you sad and lonely?'

'Sad, lonely and in need of jollity.'

'Then step inside, Mr Strype,' she said with a ripe chuckle, taking him by the arm. 'We have the cure for your malady right here. Nobody is allowed to be sad or lonely in my house. Jollity reigns supreme.'

'Lead me to it, Molly.'

One door shut in Jonathan's face but another one had ju opened. It gave him something to think about on the back home.

* * *

283

Christopher was a mile away from his destination when he realised that he was being followed. He slowed his horse and listened for the sound of hoofbeats behind him. Only one rider could be discerned. When he came to a stand of poplars, he reined in his mount and waited among the trees. The hoofbeats had stopped. After waiting a few minutes, he decided that the other horseman must have turned off the road and taken another route. Christopher continued on his way but instinct told him that he was still being trailed. He doubted if it was a highwayman. Such men usually operated in bands and lurked in ambush. There was no attempt to catch him up. Whoever rode behind him was content to keep an appreciable distance between them.

Knowing how treacherous the roads could be, Christopher was well armed, carrying a loaded pistol as well as a rapier and dagger. He hoped that he would not be called upon to use any of the weapons.

When the lights of the inn finally came into sight, he kicked a last burst of speed out of his horse. Clattering into the courtyard, he dropped from the saddle, handed the reins to the ostler who came running and noted to which stable his horse was taken. Then he shook off the night and went into a hostelry which blazed with dozens of candles.

the landlord gave him a cheerful

ny old man with a ragged beard

walk

the night, monsieur?'

st room.'

overlooks the stables.'

'As you wish.'

'And I will need something to eat before I retire.'

'My wife will see to your needs, sir.'

There were no more than half a dozen other guests in the taproom and most took no notice of him, engaged either in desultory conversation or in the important ritual of sampling the hostelry's stock of wine. Christopher found himself a table in a corner from which he could watch the door. The landlord's wife brought him bread and cheese. A full-bodied red wine helped to wash it down and revive him after his travels. Nobody came or left. After an hour, Christopher paid his bill in advance and followed the landlord up a rickety staircase and along a narrow passageway to his room. His host opened the door and set down the lighted candle on the table beside the bed.

'You will be comfortable enough here, monsieur.'

'Thank you,' said Christopher, giving the room a cursory glance. 'This will be most adequate, landlord. Good night.'

'If you need anything else, just call.'

'I will.'

When the man went out, Christopher closed the door behind him and saw that there was no bolt on it. He crossed to the window to gaze down into the courtyard. It was deserted. Only the occasional whinny from the stables disturbed the silence. There was no sign at all of the mysterious rider who had shadowed him. Closing the shutters, he took a closer look at his room. Small, musty and simply furnished, it had a low ceiling and undulating oak floorboards but it was reasonably clean and its bed looked inviting. Christopher was annoyed that he would not get to sleep in it because a sixth sense rearranged his accommodation.

After making up the bed to look as if it were occupied, he took the solitary chair into the corner behind the door and settled down on it. None of his apparel was removed. His sword rested within reach against the wall and the pistol was on the floor at his feet. The dagger remained in its sheath at his belt. He closed his eyes for a few moments then opened them again as if disturbed and crossed to the bed in four short strides. Confident that he could do so again in the dark, he blew out the candle and returned to his position in the corner. The chair was hard but he endured the discomfort willingly.

With so much to ponder, he found it difficult to keep his mind alert for sounds of danger and fatigue began to steal over him. Eventually he dropped off to sleep.

The creaking of the floorboards in the passageway brought him out of his slumber. His hand went swiftly to his belt, to the wall and to the floor. Dagger, sword and pistol were all there. A faint glimmer of light came under his door, then it inched slowly open. Candlelight illuminated the bed for a second before the flame was snuffed out. Christopher heard the sound of the candle-holder being set down on the floor; a murky figure entered the room and surged towards the bed.

The man's dagger flashed but its point found nothing more than a couple of blankets which had been rolled up. There was an angry grunt from the intruder then a gasp of surprise as Christopher jumped on him from behind and knocked him forward onto the bed. He tried to jab behind his back with the dagger but Christopher already had a firm grasp on his wrist and he twisted it until the man let his weapon go with a cry of pain. Before he could struggle, the intruder felt the point of Christopher's own dagger pricking the nape of his neck and he froze.

'Who are you?' demanded Christopher.

'Let me go,' begged the man. 'Do not kill me, monsieur.'

'Tell me who sent you.'

'Nobody sent me. I saw you on the road.'

'What were you after?'

'Your purse, monsieur. That is all.'

'Don't lie!'

Christopher stood up and dragged the man after him by the hair, spinning him around and buffeting him across the face with his arm. The man rocked back but quickly recovered, aiming a kick at Christopher's legs and scything him to the floor before flinging himself on top of him. A firm hand closed on the wrist which held the dagger and the weapon was twisted inexorably around until its point threatened Christopher's eye. Though he could barely see it in the gloom, he felt its proximity and the sweat of fear began to flow. The man exerted additional power then suddenly put all his strength into a downward thrust. Christopher's head rolled out of the way just in time as the dagger sank into the floorboards.

Releasing the weapon, he grappled with the man and rolled him over on his back, getting in a relay of punches which took some of the energy out of his assailant. When Christopher felt a thumb trying to gouge his eye, his temper flared and he smashed a fist into the man's nose, splitting it open and sending blood all over his face. Rage served to revive the intruder and he found enough strength to hurl Christopher off before groping around in the dark for the dagger. Christopher was too quick for him. As he fell against the chair in the corner, he knew exactly where his rapier was standing and his hand closed gratefully on it. He hauled himself quickly to his feet.

The intruder saw only the outline of his body in the darkness. When he found the dagger on the floor, he leapt up and ran straight at Christopher, intending to stab him viciously in the chest. Instead, he let out a long agonised wheeze as he found himself impaled on a sharp and merciless sword. He dropped the dagger, flailed uselessly at Christopher with both hands then slumped to the floor on his side. As the sword was withdrawn, he remained motionless. Christopher waited for a couple of minutes to see if the noise of the brawl would bring anyone running but he was relieved that nobody came. He did not relish having to explain the situation in which he had unwittingly been caught.

Stepping over the fallen body, he groped his way to his candle and lit the wick. He then held the flame over his visitor and saw that the man was comprehensively dead, islanded by a sea of blood. Turning him over on his back, he let the candle illumine the man's face. The shock of recognition made him reel for a second. He had met the man before.

The dark moustache was unforgettable. It was the servant Marcel, who had admitted him to the house of Arnaud Bastiat.

CHAPTER FOURTEEN

Lady Frances Northcott snipped the stem of a rose then placed the flower carefully alongside the others in her basket. It was late morning and bright sunshine was buttering the whole garden. Birds sang from their perches and insects buzzed happily over petals and ponds. Lady Northcott looked across at the wisp of smoke that was curling up into the sky from behind a hawthorn hedge. Putting her basket on a stone bench, she went around the hedge and walked across to the fire that was burning quietly in the shadow of a wall. She bent down to toss some more fuel onto its dying flames then used a hoe to rake the embers. When the fire came once more to life, she returned to the rose bush again.

'Do you never tire of this garden, Mother?' said a voice.

'No, Penelope. This is my idea of heaven.'

'What does that make me?'

'One of the angels.'

Penelope gave a tiny smile. The garden which her mother found so idyllic somehow only made her feel restless and dissatisfied. It was the older woman's universe, filled with everything she could want and changing with the seasons to provide movement and variety. Yet it seemed curiously empty to Penelope. As a girl, she loved to play on its lawns, to climb its trees, to explore its countless hiding places, to plunder its orchard, to watch the fish in its ponds and the wildfowl on its lake. Looking around now, she realised that it was not the garden which was deficient. Under her mother's guidance, it had been greatly enriched and enlarged. The emptiness lay inside Penelope herself.

'Sit down a moment,' said her mother, indicating the bench. 'We need to have a little talk.'

'I am not in a talkative mood, Mother.'

'You have been fending me off for days. Now, come here.'

'Well, just for a moment.'

Penelope sat beside her mother, who took her by the hand.

'What is the matter?' she asked.

'Nothing, Mother.'

'I am not blind, Penelope. Since you got back from London, you have been deeply troubled about something. You hardly ventured outside your room on the first day home.'

'I was tired.'

'Well, you are not tired now. And you have had ample time to get over whatever it was that upset you in London. Are you ready to tell me about it now?' Penelope bit her lip and lowered her head. 'Why not?'

'Because I still do not understand it myself.'

'Understand what?'

'Why I feel this way, Mother. So hurt. So melancholy. So lonely.'

'Lonely? In your own home?'

'I cannot explain it.'

'Grief takes strange forms sometimes,' said the other softly. 'I know that from personal experience. In the sudden excitement of rushing off to London, you were not able to mourn your father's death properly. You put it out of your mind. Now that you are back in Priestfield Place, all your memories of him come flooding back.'

'Unhappy memories.'

'Some of them, perhaps, but not all. You may have reservations about him – we both have – but he was still your father, Penelope.'

'I know that.'

'Then you are bound to grieve.'

Her daughter raised her head and gazed straight in front of her.

'I am still very unsettled by what happened to Father,' she said quietly, 'and by the things which we discovered after his death. It is like an open wound which will not heal. But there is another side to my grief. I have been trying to make sense of it.'

'Does it concern George?'

'Yes.'

'Did you have an argument?'

'Several.'

'Did you patch up your differences before you came home?'

'Not really, Mother.'

'Was he unkind to you, Penelope?'

'No,' sighed the other. 'Not exactly unkind.'

'Then what? Aggressive? Domineering?'

'He was George.'

'Why did you come back to Kent alone?'

'He had business in London.'

'When he left here,' recalled her mother, 'he was furious. He told me that he was going to bring you straight back. Yet you stayed on in London for a few days. Why?'

'I did not like the way he ordered me about.'

'You have always tolerated it before, Penelope.'

'It was different then. He used persuasion and charm. I was content to agree with what he suggested.' She pursed her lips in irritation. 'I blame myself for being so naive. George is a domineering man, and I have allowed him to govern all my decisions.'

'He was not the only one.'

'What do you mean?'

'Many of his decisions were influenced by your father.'

'I know. George admired him so much.'

'Does he still admire him?'

'Yes, but not in quite the same way.' She turned to her mother. 'He swore to me that he knew nothing about Father's secret life with…that other person. I believe him. George has always been honest with me.'

'Has he?'

'You know he has.'

'I have always had my doubts about George Strype.'

'He is a wonderful man,' said Penelope defensively. 'Strong

and loving and everything I could wish for in a husband. He has many fine qualities when you get to know him. He is dependable. I keep reminding myself of that. But...'

Her mother waited. 'Go on,' she coaxed at length.

'I had not realised that he could be so jealous.'

'He loves you, Penelope. He is very possessive.'

'It was more than that.'

'Was it?'

'He became almost demented when I told him that I had given those letters to Mr Redmayne. He insisted on getting them back. I tried to stop him but it was no use. George ignored me. The next thing I knew, he had taken my coach and gone to demand the letters from Mr Redmayne.'

'Did he get them?'

'No, and that made his temper fouler than ever.'

'You must have been very angry yourself.'

'I was, Mother,' said Penelope. 'It cost me a lot to show those letters to Mr Redmayne and he was most discreet and understanding. George was quite the opposite and I told him so. I was incensed at the way that he commandeered our coach as if it were his own.'

'What did he say?'

'That everything in a marriage should be shared.'

'But you are not yet married to him.'

'According to George, I am. He kept telling me that I must do as I was told. That was when the argument really flared up.'

'How was it resolved?'

'It was not. He stormed out of the house.'

'Did he not come back the next day to apologise?'

'No, he was still sulking somewhere.'

'So you did not actually see him before you left?'

'Not in person,' said Penelope. 'But he sent a servant with a basket of flowers from his gardens to sweeten the carriage for my journey. They arrived on the morning that I was leaving.'

'What did you do with them?'

'I left them at the house.'

'Oh, I see.'

'I wish I had brought them with me now.'

'Why?'

'George was trying to make peace.'

'Was he?'

'It was his way of saying that he was in the wrong, Mother. And they were beautiful flowers. You would have appreciated them. I should at least have sent him a note to thank him.'

'Why didn't you?'

Penelope shrugged. 'I don't know.'

'Do you miss him?'

'Of course.'

'And do you still love him?'

'I think so.'

'What made him leave the house in Westminster in such an ill temper?'

Penelope winced at the memory. 'Something I said to him. I was so angry when he told me where he had been. I pointed out just how much Mr Redmayne was doing to catch the man responsible for Father's death. He has gone all the way to Paris on our behalf. I asked George why he could not act more like Mr Redmayne and actually search for the killer.'

Frances made no comment. She could see the doubt and anguish in her daughter's face and did not wish to add to it. She asked another question which she had been saving up for some time.

'When you were at the house in London, did you find anything?'

A slight pause. 'No, Mother.'

'Did you search?'

'In truth, no.'

'Were you afraid that you *might* find something?'

'Probably,' said Penelope, anxious to quash the topic. 'I am beginning to wish that I had not found those letters here. They have turned everything sour.'

'No,' murmured the other. 'Sourness was already there.'

Rising to her feet, she pulled Penelope gently after her.

'Let us go for a walk,' she suggested.

'Very well. Some fresh air would benefit me.'

'Let me attend to something first.'

When they came around the angle of the hawthorn hedge, she strolled across to the fire. Picking up the last few books from the pile, she tossed them into the heart of the blaze. Penelope was shocked. She recognised the beautiful calf-bound volumes at once. They were treasured items from the library.

'You're burning all of Father's books!' she protested.

'No, dear,' said her mother. 'Only the ones written in French.'

Though he would never admit it to anyone else, Jonathan Bale was missing him badly. It was over a week since Christopher

Redmayne had set sail for France and the constable wished now that he had gone with him, both to act as his bodyguard and to join in the search for clues that would help to solve two murders. At the same time, however, he saw the value in remaining behind to explore other avenues on his own. He had amassed a lot of information about the house in Lincoln's Inn Fields and it irked him that he was not able to pass it on to Christopher. There was another reason why he wanted the other to return soon. It would put a stop to Sarah's solicitous enquiries about the young architect.

Heavy rain swept the streets that morning. As Jonathan ate his breakfast with his wife and children, he did not look forward to going out in the storm. When there was a knock at the door, Sarah went to open it.

'Why, Mr Redmayne!' she exclaimed. 'Look at the state of you!'

'Good morning, Mrs Bale. Is your husband here?'

'Yes, he is. Come in out of the wet.'

'Thank you.'

Jonathan was as surprised as his wife to see his visitor. Drenched by the rain, Christopher also bore some reminders of the fight at the inn. One side of his face had been badly grazed by the rough floorboards, discouraging him from even attempting to shave. Bruises still showed on his temple and his right eye was rimmed with yellow. His coat was sodden and Jonathan also noticed that it was spattered with bloodstains. Choppy waves had made the Channel-crossing an especial ordeal for him, leaving Christopher pale and drawn. Sarah clucked maternally over their visitor and insisted on making him some broth to warm him up. Conducting him into the little parlour, her husband shut the door behind them. He waved his guest to a chair and Christopher dropped gratefully into it, removing his hat to reveal tousled hair.

'I did not expect you today,' said Jonathan. 'They told me that no ship would arrive from Calais until Thursday at least.'

'I sailed from Boulogne.'

'Why?'

'It is a long story, Mr Bale.'

Having raked over the details many times in his mind, Christopher was able to give a full and lucid account of all that happened to him in France. Jonathan listened without interruption. The narrative reached the point where Christopher was fighting for his life at the inn when Sarah came in with a bowl of broth. Though the visitor did not feel that he would ever eat anything again, he thanked her graciously and assured her that he was in a much better condition than he looked. A warning glance from her husband sent Sarah back to the kitchen where the two boys were disputing ownership of an apple. Their noisy bickering was soon silenced by their mother.

'Go on, sir,' said Jonathan, keen to hear the rest of the story. 'You were forced to kill the man in self-defence. What then?'

'I lit a candle to look at his face.'

'Did you recognise him?'

'Yes, Mr Bale. He was the servant who answered the door at the home of Monsieur Bastiat. I think his name was Marcel.'

'Why should *he* follow you?'

'I did not stop to consider,' said Christopher. 'The fact was that I had killed him. If I was found standing over a dead body, nobody would believe my version of events. So I left immediately.'

'Where did you spend the night?'

'On the road, for the most part. I snatched a couple of hours' sleep under the trees then pressed on to Beauvais at dawn. When I returned my horse, I took the first coach which was heading for the coast. I had a good start,' he said, watching the steam rise from the broth, 'but I was taking no chances. Monsieur Bastiat knew that I was travelling to Calais. He took the trouble to ask me where I would lodge for the night. Just in case he sent someone else after me, I made for Boulogne to throw them off the scent.'

'That was a wise decision.'

'At least it means that I returned in one piece.' He managed a grin. 'More or less, anyway. I am sorry to turn up on your doorstep in this fashion.'

'I was thankful to see you again, sir.'

'It was touch and go at that inn, Mr Bale.'

'You acquitted yourself well.'

'I could not rely on French justice to take that view.'

'In your place, I would have done exactly the same.'

'Then we agree on something at last.'

Jonathan smiled. 'What does it all signify, Mr Redmayne?' he asked. 'Have you manage to puzzle that out yet?'

'I have spent days trying to, my friend, and I have been able to draw some conclusions. Before I tell you what they are, let me hear your news. Did you do what I asked?'

'Yes, sir. I went to Lincoln's Inn Fields a number of times.'

'What did you learn?'

It was Jonathan's turn to take over. His report had a plodding slowness to it but nothing was left out. The constable had been vigilant. Christopher listened attentively and even found the appetite to sip at the broth. He sat up at the mention of a French visitor to the house though Jonathan's garbled pronunciation of the name led to some confusion. It was the man with the mask who really held his attention.

'You say that he let himself into the premises?'

'Yes,' confirmed Jonathan. 'By the side door.'

'Mrs Mandrake's clients would not have a key. What makes this man so special? And why did he need to conceal his identity by wearing a mask?' He ran a hand through his hair. 'A tall man with a hat and a walking stick. That description fits the person whom Margaret Littlejohn saw going into the cellars with Sir Ambrose.'

'It also fits thousands of other men in London, sir.'

'True.'

'And there was no mention of a mask by Miss Littlejohn.'

'She was too far away to see it and the man kept his head down. Besides,' mused Christopher, 'he may not have been wearing the mask on that particular evening. We must not rule him out. It is a pity that he was the one visitor to Lincoln's Inn Fields for whom you do not have a name. The rest, you say, are all noted?'

'I have the list here, Mr Redmayne.'

Jonathan thrust a hand into his pocket and extracted a piece of paper which he handed over. Five separate nights had found him lurking outside the house and his findings were tabulated day by day. The list was a revelation. Christopher recognised many of the names on it but one in particular sprang off the page.

'George Strype?'

'Yes, sir.'

'Are you quite certain?'

'I heard Molly Mandrake talk to him.'

'What did he look like?'

Jonathan gave a brief description. Christopher was left in no doubt that Penelope Northcott's fiancé had gone in search of pleasure at the house. It made him smart with anger on her behalf. At the same time, it opened up a new line of thought. If George Strype was a patron of the establishment owned by his late father-in-law, he must have known more about Sir Ambrose's life in London than he admitted. Penelope's faith in the man was sadly misplaced. Christopher was confronted by a moral dilemma. Did he inflict more pain by telling her the truth or did he hold his peace and allow her to marry a man who had already betrayed her?

He studied the list again. His finger stopped at another name.

'Who is this?'

'Where, sir?' Jonathan peered. 'Ah, the Frenchman.'

'Sharonta?'

'That is what it sounded like.'

Christopher was bewildered for a moment then light dawned.

'Could it possibly have been Charentin?'

'Yes, sir. That was exactly it. Sharonta.'

'Cha – ren – tin,' enunciated the other. 'No first name?'

'Molly simply called him Mussyer Sharonta.'

'Or something akin to that,' said Christopher with a kind smile. 'Well, Mr Bale, you have done wonders. I know you found it demeaning to spy on the establishment but it has yielded results. Mrs Mandrake is even more popular than I thought. Some of the most illustrious names in the government are recorded here. There is even a senior churchman or two. Red faces would light up London if this list were ever made public.'

'How does it help us?'

'I am not certain yet. What we have to establish is the link.'

'Between what?'

'One house in Paris and another in Lincoln's Inn Fields.'

'Sir Ambrose Northcott was one such link.'

'There has to be another.'

'Mr Strype?'

'He must certainly be looked at and so must Monsieur Charentin. The search evidently begins in Mrs Mandrake's house. One of us must pose as a client to get inside it.'

'Not I, sir!' cried Jonathan, baulking at the notion.

Christopher laughed. 'Do not worry, Mr Bale,' he said. 'This is not an office which I would thrust upon you. I know it would compromise your principles simply to step across the threshold of that sinful place. And I must confess that I do not look forward to the experience myself but it is an absolute necessity.'

'I begin to think that you may be right.'

'Be frank with me. Should I go there with a face like this?'

'You do not look at your best, Mr Redmayne.'

'Then I will wait a day or so until these bruises fade. When I look presentable again, I will prevail upon my brother to introduce me to Mrs Mandrake. Henry owes me a favour.'

'Do you wish me to go with you, sir?'

'You?'

'To guard your back,' said Jonathan seriously. 'There has already been one attempt on your life. You survived that but only because you killed your assassin. Next time, you might not be so fortunate.'

'I am relatively safe now that I am back in England.'

'Sir Ambrose was murdered here.'

'Only because he was taken unawares.'

'Every man can use an extra pair of eyes.'

'It is a kind offer, Mr Bale, but I will not take advantage of it. I was attacked in France because I was on the right trail. Monsieur Bastiat wanted me killed before I found out anything else.'

'He may have confederates in England.'

'I am certain that he does,' said Christopher, 'but I do not intend to hide from them. I want to draw them out into the light. When I went to France, I was inclining to the view that Sir Ambrose's death had some political implications and I still believe that is the case. But I am now convinced that something else provided the real motive behind it.'

'What is it, Mr Redmayne?'

'What I saw in Monsieur Bastiat's face, on the shelves

of his library and hanging around the neck of Marie Louise Ollier.'

'Around her neck?'

'Religion.'

The weight of responsibility which at first threatened to crush Geoffrey Anger instead brought out unseen strengths in the clerk. Once he had grown accustomed to the death of his employer, he realised how much freedom it suddenly gave him. After years of tyranny by Solomon Creech, he was now temporarily in charge of the office, winding up its business before closing the premises and searching for another lawyer. Papers which had hitherto been hidden from him now lay at his disposal. Clients whom Creech had jealously kept to himself were available for his inspection. Going through the contents of the safe was an education to Geoffrey Anger. The sense of power helped him to grow in confidence. He was still very shocked that Solomon Creech had been murdered but, he now saw, it was not an undiluted tragedy.

When Christopher called at the office next day, his appearance had markedly improved. Jacob had bathed his face and shaved him with such care that he felt no pain. The bruising had largely disappeared. Even the colouring around his eye had paled to a faint tint. He was both surprised and pleased to find the timid clerk in a cooperative mood. After giving him a brisk welcome, Anger escorted him through to the inner office and offered him a chair. The clerk then settled into the seat which had been sculpted over the years by the buttocks of Solomon Creech.

'I have been expecting you to call, Mr Redmayne.'

'Good.'

'This is what you have come for, I think.'

'What is it?'

'The verdict of the coroner's jury on the death of Mr Creech.'

'It is certainly something which I would like to see, Mr Anger.'

'Feel free to peruse it, sir.'

The clerk handed over the document which had been lying on the desk. It did not take Christopher long to read it. The report bore a close resemblance to the one issued after the post-mortem was carried out on the body of Sir Ambrose Northcott. It recorded an unsolved crime.

The verdict of this jury is that a certain person or persons unknown did feloniously, wilfully and with malice aforethought, batter Mr Solomon Creech and throw him into the River Thames to drown. In the opinion of the jury, Mr Creech would not have survived the brutal injuries which were inflicted upon him by the aforesaid person or persons but the actual cause of death was drowning.

After glancing through the rest of the judgement, Christopher put the document back down on the desk and looked into the solemn face before him. He wondered just how helpful the man was prepared to be. Geoffrey Anger's occupation of his employer's office had already yielded reforms. Christopher noticed that it was substantially tidier than before and that fresh air had been allowed to disperse the worst of its smell.

'You have been busy in here, Mr Anger,' he commented.

'It has been hard but rewarding work, sir.'

'I hope to profit from it myself. Have you learnt anything

about the business affairs of Sir Ambrose Northcott?'

'A great deal, Mr Redmayne,' said the clerk, patting the safe to his left. 'Most of the documents locked away in here related to those affairs.'

'I would value a sighting of them.'

'That is asking too much, sir, but I did anticipate your interest and am desirous of being helpful. To that end, I have made a record of certain transactions in which Sir Ambrose engaged.'

'Do they relate to France?'

'Almost exclusively.'

'Do they involve contraband?'

'You cannot expect me to impugn Mr Creech's reputation.'

'Would you rather that his murder went unsolved?'

The clerk hesitated. 'Some of the transactions stray outside the strict limits of the law but that is all I am prepared to say.' He opened a drawer to take out a document. 'Here it is, Mr Redmayne. I hope that it will assist you in some small way in bringing the killer to justice.'

Christopher took the paper from him and ran his eye over it. The neat calligraphy of Geoffrey Anger uncovered a whole history of trading between Sir Ambrose Northcott and certain French merchants. Among them was the name of one Jean-Paul Charentin of Paris. Christopher felt a buzz of excitement. Links were slowly being forged.

'This is most obliging of you, Mr Anger,' he said.

'I have had it waiting for days.'

'My search took me across the Channel and I have only just returned.' He tapped the piece of paper. 'May I have some elucidation?'

'If you wish.'

Christopher took him line by line through the document, asking for clarification even where he did not need it. The clerk's confidence got the better of him. Thinking that he was being discreet, he instead revealed far more than he intended, enjoying a rare moment to show off his knowledge of commercial transactions. By the time they had finished, Christopher could see why Sir Ambrose and his lawyer had been so secretive. Much of their legitimate trading was no more than a mask for some profitable smuggling. The architect remembered the extensive cellars which he had designed for the new house – the ideal place in which to store contraband goods unloaded from the *Marie Louise* and brought to the private landing stage.

'I have one last thing to ask you, Mr Anger.'

'There is nothing more that I can tell you,' said the other, rising to indicate that the interview was over. 'You will understand how much work I have to do. Let me show you out.'

Christopher remained seated. 'In a moment,' he said. 'Answer me this first. When you opened that safe, did you find a copy of Sir Ambrose Northcott's will?'

'I did.'

'Is it still on the premises?'

'That need not concern you, Mr Redmayne.'

'Is there no chance that I might see it?'

'None at all, sir,' said the other with a sudden pomposity. 'The last will and testament of a client is the most confidential of all documents. I could not possibly divulge any of its contents.'

'I am only curious about one tiny provision.'

'Your curiosity must go unsatisfied.'

'Must it?' said Christopher with a smile, getting to his feet. 'You have given me so much help today. I am overcome with gratitude and I applaud your thoroughness. Mr Creech did not appreciate you.'

'That was my opinion, too,' confessed the other.

'You would have made a worthy partner to him.'

'Oh no, sir,' said the clerk piously. 'I could never have condoned some of the transactions which went on in this office.'

'With regard to the will...'

'It is a closed book to you, Mr Redmayne.'

Christopher nodded. 'So be it. Knowing the extent of Sir Ambrose's interests and property, I am sure it is such a complicated document that even you could not remember all of its provisions. There is no point at all in my asking to whom the house was left.'

'Which house?'

'The one in Lincoln's Inn Fields,' said Christopher artlessly. 'Sir Ambrose would hardly leave it to his family or they would become aware of the nefarious activities which took place there. He would protect his wife from such a shocking discovery. On the other hand,' he added, watching the clerk's expression, 'he would be unlikely to bequeath the property to the lady to whom it is leased, Mrs Mandrake.'

Geoffrey Anger's lip twitched. Christopher had his answer.

* * *

Penelope Northcott sat on the edge of the bed and held the objects in her hands. She had not dared to show them to her mother. It had never even occurred to her to share her discovery with George Strype. Whether from fear or consideration of another's feelings, she kept them hidden and lied to her mother about their existence. Found during her search of the Westminster house, they had caused her intense unease yet she could not bring herself to throw them away and forget that they ever existed. They were too important for that. As she laid them on the bed, she saw the objects as yet another part of a troublesome legacy. If she gave them to her mother, she suspected, they would only end up on a fire in her beloved garden.

Lady Northcott was quickly learning to live without her husband. It would be cruel to open yet another gaping wound in her past. Penelope elected to carry the revelation inside her until it could be divulged to the one person who might find it instructive. Sir Ambrose Northcott was a private man but even his daughter had not expected this level of secrecy. She wondered how long this particular deception had been sustained.

A tap on her door forced her to abandon her contemplation.

'Penelope!' called her mother. 'Are you there?'

'One moment!' she answered, hiding the objects under the pillow.

'May I come in?'

'Of course, Mother.'

Lady Northcott entered with a look of concern on her face.

'Why have you stayed in your room all afternoon?'

'I was tired.'

'Well, I expect some company this evening,' warned the other. 'I would like to continue the conversation we had in the garden yesterday.'

'Yesterday?'

'About George.'

'Indeed?'

'I think that you should consider postponing the wedding.'

Penelope nodded. 'It has been at the forefront of my mind.'

'Have you reached a decision?'

'No, Mother. It would be unfair to do that before I speak to George.'

'And when is that likely to be?'

'I am not sure.'

'You cannot tarry for ever.'

Penelope nodded, moving to the window in thought. She looked into her future with trepidation then remembered the possessions of her father which she had just concealed beneath her pillow. When she came back to her mother, there was an apologetic note in her voice.

'Would you mind if I did not join you this evening?' she said. 'I will retire early so that I can leave at dawn tomorrow.'

'Where are you going, Penelope?'

'Back to London.'

Her mother stiffened. 'To see George Strype?'

'No,' said her daughter. 'Mr Christopher Redmayne.'

* * *

The request amused Henry Redmayne so much that he could not stop laughing. It was the last thing he expected to hear from his brother when the latter called on him in Bedford Street. Shaking with mirth, he almost dislodged his periwig.

'So!' he said. 'You have come to your senses at last. You want to acknowledge your manhood and enjoy the delights of the flesh.'

'No, Henry,' said Christopher. 'I merely wish to meet Mrs Mandrake and take a look inside her premises.'

His brother sniggered. 'Moll has the most commodious premises I have ever seen. Warm and welcoming to the few who can afford her. If you board her, dear brother, beware. Once you are inside, you will wish to stay there in perpetuity.'

'The lady has no appeal for me in that way.'

'Then you must choose one of her stable, Christopher, for they are fine fillies, each one of them. Damarosa is my favourite, an inventive wench, but you might prefer the gentler touch of Betty Hadlow. There is also a pretty Negress with a rump which could raise the Lazarus between the legs of a saint and two fresh-faced sisters called Poppy and Patience, who will share your bed together and take it in turns.' He gave a smirk. 'But you may not be ready for anything as demanding as that.'

'I am not ready for any of the things you imagine, Henry.'

He explained the purpose of his request. Henry was disappointed to hear that he would be there solely as an observer but agreed to help. He just hoped that the presence of his younger brother would not inhibit his own pleasure at the house. Christopher was given strict advice about what to wear and how to behave. Before he left, he tossed a name into Henry's ear. His brother's nose wrinkled with disgust.

'Jean-Paul Charentin!'

'Do you know the man?'

'Yes,' sneered Henry. 'A contemptible Frenchman. A sly, thin-faced, leering fellow with no breeding. Had not Sir Ambrose brought him to the house, I doubt that Molly would have admitted him. She maintains the highest standards, as you will see. Monsieur Charentin is some kind of merchant from Paris. Whatever he trades in, it is not grace and fashion.'

'How often have you met him there?'

'Once or twice. Three times at most.' Henry stared at him. 'What's your interest in the rogue?'

'His name has come to my attention.'

'Wait until Molly's paps come to your attention. Mountains of pure joy. You will have no interest in a scurvy foreigner when they are bobbing away before your eyes. I could watch them for hours.'

'*Chacun à son gout, mon frère.*'

'I'll wager that you are equally entranced by her.'

'We shall see,' said Christopher, heading towards the door.

'Wait. You have not yet told me about your visit to Paris.'

'No, Henry. I have not and do not intend to.'

'Did you meet that dog, Charentin, while you were there?'

'Not in person,' said Christopher, 'but I am wondering if I encountered an acquaintance of his.'

* * *

311

Molly Mandrake was more than just a notorious whore. She was an excellent businesswoman who ran her establishment efficiently and profitably. Attention to detail was her guiding principle. Before any of her guests arrived that evening, she made a tour of the house to inspect every room and to issue instructions. None of the whores was allowed to meet any clients until Molly had scrutinised each woman and made slight adjustments to her hair or her attire. Cosmetics and perfume had to be used with great subtlety before she would approve.

When the first coach arrived, Molly Mandrake stood at the door to welcome the two gentlemen who sauntered in and to collect their fulsome compliments about her own appearance. She was a shapely woman of medium height with a vitality which shone out of her like sunlight. Her silk gown was emerald green in colour, its close-fitting boned bodice dipping to a deep point in front to suggest a slimmer waist than she actually possessed. The neckline was low cut in a rounded shape which encircled the *décolletage* and bared her shoulders. Huge breasts all but escaped their moorings, the left one bearing a beauty spot which matched another high on her left cheek. The handsome face consisted of one big smile, the teeth white, the lips sensuous, the nose attractively upturned and the brown eyes awash with roguish delight. She favoured a *coiffure à la ninon* with hair pushed back from the face and bunched curls on each side of her head, falling in ringlets to her shoulders.

'Why, Mr Redmayne!' she said with a warm grin. 'How agreeable to see you once again, sir! And who have you brought along with you?'

'This is my brother, Molly.'

'Two Redmaynes in one night. We are honoured. Your name, sir?'

'Christopher,' he said with a polite smile. 'I am pleased to make your acquaintance, Mrs Mandrake. Henry has told me much about you.'

'I wish that he had mentioned you before now,' she said, running a practised eye over him. 'You are a proper man, young sir. Do come in.'

She took Christopher's arm as he passed and gave it a meaningful squeeze. Dressed in his most fashionable apparel, he did his best to appear relaxed and sophisticated but there was an immediacy about Molly Mandrake's charms which was almost overwhelming. She took the two of them through into a large room with a round table at its centre. Set out on the table were decanters of wine and goblets made of Venetian glass. A selection of salted meats was carefully displayed on a series of oval dishes. A black manservant was in attendance, wearing dark blue livery with gold buttons. He bowed to the newcomers and handed them goblets of wine. Their hostess ushered them across to some upholstered chairs in a corner and chatted for a few minutes until the sound of the doorbell drew her away.

Christopher sipped his wine and looked around the room. Soon a few other guests arrived and took seats against the far wall, vying for the attention of a tall, stately young woman with fair hair which brushed her alabaster shoulders. Henry identified her with an obscene comment which his brother chose to ignore. The room was elegant and well-appointed but what Christopher admired was the clever positioning of the candelabra. Subdued light created a feeling of intimacy. He watched the fair-haired woman opposite. Like trained actresses, both she and Molly Mandrake knew exactly where to stand in relation to the flames in order to show themselves off to best advantage.

The wine was rich and Henry's glass was soon empty. Without waiting for it to be refilled, he went off to intercept a buxom woman who had just sailed into the room wearing Egyptian costume. Christopher was not left alone for long. Having guided the newcomers to the table, Mrs Mandrake beckoned someone from the shadows then led her by the hand towards Christopher. He rose politely from his chair.

'I would like you to meet Sweet Ellen,' she said with a knowing smile. 'She is worth five guineas of any man's money.'

The doorbell rang again and she wafted out of the room. Sweet Ellen eased Christopher back into his seat and nestled beside him. Her manner was at once familiar and reserved. Christopher could see why she had been chosen for him. Sweet Ellen was younger and more slender than any of the women he had so far seen. There was nothing gross or threatening about her. Framed in auburn hair, her face had a kind of demure beauty. Christopher was fleetingly reminded of Marie Louise Ollier. While his companion interrogated him gently, Christopher saw the manservant pour more wine liberally into his goblet. Sweet Ellen probed on. When she learnt Christopher's name, she giggled and cast an affectionate glance across at his brother.

'Why have we not seen you here before?' she asked.

'It was a terrible oversight on my part.'

'I hope that you will visit us again often.'

'I have every intention of doing so,' he lied.

'Are you enjoying our company?'

'Very much.'

'Do you work at the Navy Office with your brother?'

'No, Ellen.'

'What is your profession?'

'I am an architect.'

'Ah!' She was impressed. 'You design houses and churches?'

'Whatever I am commissioned to do.'

'Then you have an eye for fine buildings,' she said, putting a hand on his wrist. 'What do you think of this house, Mr Redmayne?'

'Most elegant. I would love to see more of it.'

'Then you shall, sir.'

With a little laugh, she got to her feet and led him across the room, collecting an approving nod from Molly Mandrake, who was arm in arm with the latest arrival. Sweet Ellen flitted along on her toes and showed Christopher all the rooms on the ground floor with the exception of the kitchen. She paused at the bottom of the staircase and simpered.

'Would you like to see where I sleep?'

'Very much.'

'Then I will show you.'

As she took him upstairs, she squeezed his hand and rubbed her naked shoulder softly against him. He took a long sip of his wine.

'How long have you been in the house, Ellen?'

'Long enough, sir.'

She simpered again and guided him along the landing. Some of the bedchambers were clearly occupied and telltale noises came through the doors. Raucous laughter from inside one was followed by urgent grunts from inside the next. Sweet Ellen turned down a corridor then opened the door at the end of it. Christopher was swept into a small, neat room which was dominated by a four-poster and lit by a candelabrum. A heady perfume invaded his nostrils. When the door was shut behind them, he heard the key turned in the lock.

'Do you like my little apartment, sir?' she asked coyly.

'It is perfect.'

'Are you glad that your brother brought you here tonight?'

'Yes,' he said, 'but it was a friend who recommended the house.'

'A friend?'

'Monsieur Charentin. Do you know Jean-Paul?'

'Oh, yes, of course. I always enjoy it when he visits us. Jean-Paul is a most generous man. But tell me more about yourself, Mr Redmayne,' she said, easing him down on a chair. 'You are an architect, you say. A house in London is always expensive to build. You must work for some very wealthy men.'

'When I have the opportunity.'

'Where do you meet them?'

'Chiefly in the coffee houses.'

'And at Court, perhaps?' she enquired.

'Naturally,' he said. 'Henry takes me there.'

Her face ignited. 'Have you ever met His Majesty?'

'Well, yes. In a manner of speaking.'

'Tell me about him.'

Sweet Ellen seemed inordinately interested in the King and his circle and her questions poured out. Christopher obliged her with ready answers, giving the impression that he was a seasoned courtier with access to the royal ear. He also took care to find out as much as he could about the running of the establishment. As they talked, Sweet Ellen slipped behind a screen in the corner of the room and spoke from behind it. Christopher was so caught up in their conversation that he did not realise what she was doing. When she reappeared wearing nothing but a petticoat, he almost choked on the wine he had just drunk.

She rushed forward solicitously to pat him on the back.

'Oh, you poor man!' she soothed. 'Are you all right, sir?'

'No,' he said, seeing the polite way to escape. 'I am unwell.'

'Let me nurse you. Come and lie on the bed.'

'Not now, Ellen. I fear I shall disgrace myself.'

He clutched his stomach with both hands and went off into such a frenzy of coughing that she backed away from him. Taking some coins from his purse, he tossed them on the bed, gestured his apologies then unlocked the door to leave. When he got downstairs, he made his way to the side door so that he could slip away unobtrusively. Christopher was glad that he had come on foot. A bracing walk would help to clear his head and allow him to assimilate all that he had learnt from Sweet Ellen. She had been a most helpful tutor but there was a critical point beyond which he could not allow her lesson to go. He tried to work out why she had reminded him of Marie Louise Ollier.

A busy mind and a long stride combined to get him back to Fetter Lane before he realised it and he was astonished when his house came into sight. He got no closer to it. Two figures suddenly emerged from the shadows to attack him with cudgels. Before he could defend himself, he was felled by a blow to the head then beaten and kicked by both men. Curling into a ball, he brought his arms up over his head to ward off the worst of the attack but it ceased as abruptly as it had started. Someone came running over the cobbles to hurl one man aside and to deprive the second of his cudgel. Before he could inflict injury on them, a peremptory voice came out of the darkness.

'Leave him be! We have taught him a lesson!'

The two attackers ran gratefully from the scene and their master went after them on his horse. Jonathan Bale watched them go then reached down to help Christopher up from the ground.

'Are you hurt badly, sir?'

'No,' said Christopher, still slightly dazed. 'But my pride is.'

'I warned you that you needed a bodyguard. It is just as well that I followed you from Lincoln's Inn Fields or you might be lying dead.'

'No, Mr Bale. They were not paid to kill me.'

'How do you know?'

'I recognised the voice which gave the order.'

'Who was it?'

'A man with a score to settle. George Strype.'

CHAPTER FIFTEEN

Jacob was alarmed to hear of the attack on his master and insisted on examining him for broken bones, removing Christopher's coat to feel his way over arms and ribs then gingerly testing both legs for signs of fracture. Christopher submitted unwillingly to the kindly intentions of his servant. When it was seen that he had suffered no more than severe bruising and a large bump on the head, he sent Jacob in search of the one bottle of brandy in the house. Even Jonathan Bale consented to drink a glass of it. Christopher took that as a hopeful sign. He could see that the constable was uncomfortable in strange surroundings. It was the first time he had visited Christopher's house and he compared its superior size and furnishings with his own more modest abode in Addle Hill. The first sip of brandy helped to smother his natural resentment but Christopher could still detect no sense of friendship.

'What must I do, Mr Bale?' he said wearily.

'Do, sir?'

'You stopped me from being robbed outside St Paul's and you have just saved me from a savage beating. Do you have to rescue me from drowning before you can treat me as an equal?'

'We can never be equals, Mr Redmayne.'

'Why not?'

'I think you already know.'

'Tell me.'

'Because I come from humbler stock.'

'That has nothing to do with it, man.'

'It must have, sir,' said Jonathan, glancing around the room. 'You would not deign to live in a house like mine and I could not afford to own a house like yours.' He tapped his glass. 'While you drink brandy, I have nothing stronger at home than my wife's chicken broth.'

'Then you are right,' agreed Christopher. 'Equality is out of the question. Mrs Bale's broth is infinitely better than my brandy. It brought me alive again after that fearful voyage. I raise my glass to her.'

Jonathan almost smiled. 'Then I will join you.'

'One other thing. I do not own this house, I rent it.'

'A fine place, nevertheless.'

'Only so long as I can pay my landlord.' He sipped the brandy and felt it course warmly through him. 'What made you come to Mrs Mandrake's house this evening?'

'I had a feeling that you might need me, sir.'

'And I did. But why not disclose yourself when I left the premises? You must have followed me all the way back here.'

'From a safe distance. I remembered what you said.'

'About what?'

'Staying visible, Mr Redmayne. To draw enemies out into the light.'

'I certainly did that,' said Christopher, feeling the lump on the back of his head. 'Had I not been wearing my hat, that ruffian would have cracked my skull open.'

'Why should Mr Strype want to assault you?'

'A personal matter.'

'I was a witness. A warrant can be taken out for his arrest.'

'Oh, no. This is something which must be settled between the two of us. I do not want the law getting in the way – much as I appreciated its intervention out in the street. Well,' he added thoughtfully, 'if you saw me arrive and leave, you know that I spent only a limited amount of time inside the place. Too short a stay to sample any of the fare.'

'Were you not tempted to do so?'

'I am sorry to disappoint you, Mr Bale, but I was not. Henry will no doubt succumb joyfully but I was there to gather information.'

'What did you find out, sir?'

Christopher described his visit to the house and could not resist including a few lurid details in the hope of scandalising his companion but Jonathan's face remained expressionless. Having arrested Molly Mandrake in the past, he could not be shocked by any revelations about the house of ill repute which she kept in Lincoln's Inn Fields. His main interest was in the French merchant, Jean-Paul Charentin.

'He is the link between that house and the one in Paris.'

'There must be others, Mr Bale.'

'Did you discern any?'

'Not yet but I sense that they are there.'

'You also sensed that religion was somehow involved,' observed Jonathan drily, 'yet I heard no mention of it in your account.'

'No,' admitted Christopher. 'Mrs Mandrake did not celebrate Mass with her guests. However, when Sweet Ellen went behind the screen to disrobe, I am sure that she said grace with Christian zeal before coming out to devour me for supper.' He saw the other scowl with disapproval. 'That was uncalled for, Mr Bale. I apologise.'

'I am becoming accustomed to your levity, sir.'

'It is the reason my father never encouraged me to enter the Church. I lacked solemnity. In Henry's case, of course, there is a much more insurmountable barrier to ordination.' He swallowed the last of his brandy. 'To return to that link between the two houses. We have ignored a more obvious one.'

'Have we?'

'The *Marie Louise*.'

'That is the means of communication between the two.'

'I have a sneaking suspicion that we will find it is the ship which brings Monsieur Charentin to and fro. Could we get aboard, I am certain that we would find out much more of interest.'

'It is no longer anchored in the Thames.'

'But it sailed for England just before I arrived in France.'

'Yes,' replied Jonathan. 'I saw it arrive. One cargo was unloaded, another taken on board and off it went again before I could get anywhere near it. But there was talk of it coming back again soon.'

'Keep a weather eye out for it, Mr Bale.'

'I will, sir. What of you?'

'That list of yours will come back into play. Now that I have been inside the house, I have some idea of its potential uses. I do not believe that Mrs Mandrake is there solely to satisfy the appetites of lustful men. She has a darker purpose.'

'What is it?'

'I am not sure but I feel that the answer may lie in that list of names. There is a pattern there, if I could but recognise it. I knew some of those names; Henry will know them all. You act as lookout for the *Marie Louise,*' he suggested, 'and I will lean more heavily on my brother.'

'You may be brothers in name, sir, but the two of you are as unlike as chalk and cheese.'

'Do you mean that you could grow to *like* Henry?'

Jonathan smiled. 'I must return home.'

'Tell your wife to give you a hero's welcome.'

'She always does, Mr Redmayne. That is why I married her.'

'Even *before* you tasted her chicken broth?'

Jonathan got up and drained his glass before setting it on the table. When Christopher had seen him out, he went into the kitchen and found Jacob dozing in a chair. He touched him on the shoulder.

'Go to bed, Jacob. I am sorry that we kept you up.'

'But I had to tell you about your visitor, sir.'

'A visitor?'

'That young lady called again.'

'Miss Northcott?' he said eagerly.

'No, sir. Miss Littlejohn. She asked where you were.'

'What did you tell her?'

'That you had gone to France.'

'Did you not say that I had returned?'

Jacob grinned. 'It slipped my mind, sir.'

Penelope Northcott was surprised how pleased she was to see him again. When he called on her at the house in Westminster that morning, George Strype was in a penitent mood. Instead of sending a servant with flowers, he brought them himself. Where he might have upbraided her for quitting London without telling him, he simply told her how delighted he was that she had returned to the city. Inhaling the scent of the flowers, Penelope took her fiancé into the parlour. She put the basket on the table.

'How did you know that I was back?' she wondered.

'I paid the housekeeper to send word the moment you returned.'

'We did not arrive until late evening.'

'The message came first thing this morning.' A note of reproach sounded. 'Though I would have preferred it to come from you rather than from the housekeeper here.'

'I was not sure that you were still in London.'

'Would you have tried to find out?'

'Of course, George.'

'Is that why you came back? In the hope of seeing me?'

'That was part of the reason.'

'Good!'

He took her in his arms and pulled her close. Penelope allowed the embrace without really enjoying it. The rift between them could not be mended quite as easily as that. He stepped back to appraise her.

'You look wonderful, my darling!'

'Thank you.'

'London has been so dull without you.'

'How have you occupied yourself while I was away?'

'Attending to my business affairs,' he said evasively. 'Your father's death has left things in a very confused state. There has been so much to disentangle, Penelope. It will take me weeks.'

'You and Mr Creech together.' His face clouded and he looked away. 'George, what is the matter?'

'You have still not heard?'

'Heard what?'

'About poor Mr Creech.'

'What has happened to him?'

He turned back to her. 'His body was pulled out of the river.'

'Oh, no!' she cried, bringing her hands up to her face. 'Mr Creech, murdered as well? This is dreadful news!'

'It has certainly complicated things for me,' he said irritably. 'All of my commercial transactions went through his office.'

'When did you discover this?'

'Some days ago.'

'Before I left London?'

'Yes, Penelope.'

'Why ever did you not tell me?'

'Because I did not wish to distress you any further. You

325

were still shocked by your father's death and by the discovery of those letters. I tried to spare you another blow. Besides,' he continued, trying to shift the blame to her, 'you spent all of the time arguing with me. I had no chance to tell you about Creech.'

'You should have *found* the chance,' she scolded. 'He was our lawyer. We had a right to know. It was wrong of you to keep this from me. I cannot understand why you did it.' He reached out to take her by the shoulders but she pushed his hands away. 'No, George. Leave me be.'

'Penelope, I am sorry.'

'An apology will not cover what you have done.'

'I merely withheld unpleasant news out of consideration to you.'

'You would have shown more consideration if you had told me the truth. I am not a child. Heavens, it was crucial that I knew. Mr Creech was responsible for my father's will. All our affairs were in his hands. And now he has been murdered. Why?'

'They are still searching for the killer.'

'Is it the same man who murdered my father?'

'Who knows? It may be.'

'What motive could anyone have to kill a harmless lawyer?'

'Do not agitate yourself about it.'

'But you lied to me.'

'No, Penelope!'

'You deliberately held the information back.'

'Only because it would have upset you too much.'

'I am much more upset now that I realise what you have

done. It was cruel. I had planned to see Mr Creech while I was here. Mother asked me to call on him. It is one of the reasons that I came.'

'But not the main reason.'

'No, George.'

'You came back to London to be with me, didn't you?' he said with a grateful smile. 'And I am so pleased to see you again. You came here so that we could put all those silly disagreements behind us and start afresh.' He reached out once more but she took a decisive step back. 'Penelope!'

'I did not come here to see you,' she said levelly.

'Who else?' His anger was instantaneous. 'Not *him* again!'

'I need to speak to Mr Redmayne.'

'I have already had words with him myself.'

'This is a private matter, George.'

'Oh, no, it is not!' he yelled. 'I am directly involved and I made that abundantly clear to him. You are my future wife, Penelope. He needed to be forcibly reminded of that. Mr Christopher Redmayne will not try to come between the two of us again.'

'What do you mean?'

'He will be too busy licking his wounds.'

'Wounds?' she repeated in alarm. 'Is he hurt?'

'It was no more than he deserved.'

'What did you do to him?'

'Forget Redmayne. You will never hear from him again.'

'But I must,' she said, concern blending into affection. 'If he is injured, I must go to him at once. He *cares* about us. He has been a light in all this darkness.' She headed for the door.

'If you have hurt him, George, I will never forgive you.'

Fuming with rage, Strype moved quickly to block her exit.

'Let me pass, please,' she said firmly.

'You will go nowhere, Penelope.'

'Will you dare to stop me?'

'If need be.'

She had never seen such menace in his eyes before. It helped to confirm a decision with which she had been toying ever since their earlier argument. Penelope felt remarkably cool. There was not the slightest regret. Crossing to the table, she picked up the basket of flowers and carried them across to him. She held them out with contempt.

'Take them away, George.'

'But I brought them for you.'

'I want nothing of yours in this house. Ever again.'

Infatuation gave her no respite. Having thought about him constantly for well over a week, Margaret Littlejohn had been drawn back as if by a magnet to Fetter Lane. Even though she had been told that Christopher Redmayne was not there, his house still held a magic for her. She would never forget the one time she had been inside the building and the one glorious moment when she had been held in his arms. That memory prompted her to pay yet another visit to Fetter Lane.

It was late morning when she and Nan arrived. Simply being back in his street was exciting enough. When she saw his house again, Margaret Littlejohn flushed with joy. She envisaged him coming out to welcome her then escorting her inside. Her companion was supportive but cautious. Nan advised against getting too close to the house, lest they be seen by the manservant. Accordingly, the two of them lingered a small distance away, diagonally opposite the building.

They waited there for half an hour before they noticed the man. Like them, his interest was in Christopher Redmayne's house. Walking past on the opposite side of the road, he stopped and looked back at it with intense curiosity. He was thirty yards away from the two women and they could only see him from the rear but they thought there was something familiar about him. When they realised what it was, they exchanged a look of fear. Tall, slim and wearing a broad-brimmed hat, the man was carrying a walking stick. They recalled the figure they had seen emerging from the cellars at the building site.

When the man came towards them, they held their ground and pretended to converse. Taking no notice of him at first, Margaret waited until he was level with her before shooting him a glance. She gulped with horror as malevolent eyes glared at her through two slits. The man's whole face was covered by a white mask. When he vanished around the corner, she needed a few moments to collect her thoughts. Sensing that the man she loved might be in danger, she was desperate to warn him somehow. She decided to tell his manservant that the house had been watched by a sinister man whom she believed she might have seen before. If nothing else, her concern would endear her to Christopher Redmayne.

But she was not able to express it. Before she could move, a coach came rumbling up the lane from Fleet Street and stopped outside his house. Margaret watched in despair as the man whom she thought was in France came eagerly out of his front door to offer his hand to the young lady as she alighted from the coach. Even at that distance, she could see the studied affection in his manner. Margaret felt utterly betrayed. Not only had Christopher told his manservant to lie to her, he was paying court to someone else. The impulse to warn him disappeared beneath a welter of emotions. Supported by Nan, she went off in tears.

'But what happened to you, Mr Redmayne?' she said. 'Were you hurt?'

'Not really, Miss Northcott.'

'George boasted to me that you had been assaulted.'

'I was,' said Christopher, fingering the back of his skull, 'and I still have a lump on my head to prove it. Beyond that, the only injuries I suffered were a few bruises. The aches and pains will soon wear off.'

'How can you dismiss it so lightly?'

'Oh, I am not doing that, I assure you.'

'George could be arrested for attacking you like that.'

'Mr Strype did not actually touch me,' he explained. 'He paid two ruffians to do so. Fortunately, I had help nearby. Mr Bale frightened them off before they could inflict any real damage.'

'I am so *sorry*, Mr Redmayne,' she said, tormented with guilt.

'It was not your fault.'

'But it was, indirectly. If I had not come here with those letters and then spent the night under your roof, this would never have happened.'

'I would take any beating for the pleasure of seeing you again.'

Christopher's declaration came out so easily that it took them both by surprise. She smiled uncertainly and he became self-conscious. Waving her to a chair, he sat opposite her and offered up a prayer of thanks that he had been at home when she called. Penelope searched his face for signs of injury and felt glad that she had broken off her engagement to George Strype. He had deliberately given her the impression that he had fought with Christopher himself but, she now learnt, he had taken the more cowardly option of hiring bullies to do his work for him. Having removed one man from her life, Penelope was now able to appreciate the depth of her feeling for another.

'When did you return from France?' she asked.

'Some days ago.'

'Did you find anything out?'

'A great deal, Miss Northcott,' he said with enthusiasm. 'In spite of everything, the journey was very worthwhile.'

'In spite of everything?'

'The trip was not without incident.'

Christopher gave her the salient facts about his visit to Paris. His face was taut as he talked about Marie Louise Ollier but it creased into dismay when he described the attempt on his life at the inn. Penelope sat forward on the edge of her chair.

'Why did they try to kill you, Mr Redmayne?'

'Because I stumbled on the truth,' he said. 'Or part of it, anyway. I knew too much. Solomon Creech was murdered for the same reason. He was your father's confidante, the one person in London who knew the full details of your father's liaison with Mademoiselle Ollier.' He checked himself. 'I take it that you have heard about Mr Creech?'

'Belatedly. It came as a hideous shock.'

'One advantage has followed. His clerk has been able to release information to me which Mr Creech refused to divulge. I now know a great deal about Sir Ambrose's commercial transactions with France.'

'George could have told you about those,' she began, then her voice faded away. She shook her head. 'Perhaps not. He might not have proved very forthcoming.' A thought pricked her. 'You do not think that *he* is involved in all this, do you?'

'No, Miss Northcott. I do not have the highest opinion of Mr Strype but I can absolve him of any involvement here. Sir Ambrose kept him ignorant of too many things. Besides, he would hardly collude in the death of his partner and future father-in-law.' He noticed the glint in her eye. 'Have I said something out of turn?'

'Our engagement has been terminated,' she said quietly.

He smiled inwardly. 'This is a surprising development.'

'I prefer not to talk about it, Mr Redmayne. There are more important topics to discuss. Tell me more about *her*.'

'Marie Louise Ollier?'

'Was she very beautiful?'

'Some might think so,' he said tactfully.

'How old was she?'

'Not as young as you thought.'

'Describe her to me.'

Choosing his words with care, Christopher drew his own sketch of the striking young woman whom he had met in Paris, astonished at how much it varied from his first impression of her. He no longer saw Marie Louise Ollier as the complete innocent who had sat before him in Arnaud Bastiat's house. His visit to Lincoln's Inn Fields had helped to revise that assessment. Sweet Ellen had shown him how easy it was to feign childlike purity.

It distressed him to talk about someone whose existence gave Penelope such obvious pain. Though she pressed him relentlessly for details, she winced when she heard them and her cheeks coloured at the mention of the claim made by Mademoiselle Ollier.

'She intended to *marry* my father?'

'That is what she told me.'

'But how? He already had a wife.'

'Sir Ambrose led her to believe that your mother had died.'

'He would never do that!' she protested.

'I am only reporting what I heard.'

'Did you believe her?'

'At the time.'

'And now?'

'I am not so sure,' said Christopher. 'I suspect that I was too ready to accept her word. My opinion of her changed radically when I realised that she was keeping me talking so that her uncle could eavesdrop on us and discover exactly how much I knew. I begin to wonder how sincere her love for Sir Ambrose really was.'

'You read her letters. They were vastly sincere.'

'Save for one thing, Miss Northcott.'

'What is that?'

'I am not even sure that she wrote them.'

'But they bore her signature.'

'Her hand may have penned the words,' he said, 'but I think that someone else may have dictated them.'

'What do you conclude, Mr Redmayne?'

'Your father was duped. Sir Ambrose loved her deeply, of that I am certain. He would not have changed the name of his ship to the *Marie Louise* unless he were wholly committed to her. But love throws people off guard. It makes them vulnerable.'

'To what? Blackmail?'

'I fancy that this goes deeper than that,' said Christopher, rubbing his chin. 'Mademoiselle Ollier insisted that he told her he was a widower and therefore free to marry. But she would never consider marriage to a man like Sir Ambrose.'

'Why not?'

'She is a devout Roman Catholic.'

Penelope stiffened as she remembered the purpose of her visit. Opening the bag which lay in her lap, she took out two objects and handed them to him. Christopher looked in astonishment at the rosary beads and the Catholic missal.

'I found them at the house in Westminster,' she said.

'Was your father planning to convert?'

'In view of what you have said, it seems a possibility.'

'More than that, Miss Northcott. In all likelihood he had been taking instruction. It shows how far he was prepared to go to meet the demands of Mademoiselle Ollier. It is strange,' he murmured. 'I never took Sir Ambrose for a religious man.'

'Then you mistake him,' she said with unexpected loyalty. 'In the light of his infidelity, this may seem an odd thing to say but my father took the spiritual side of life very seriously.'

'Did he?'

'That is why he was so proud of our house in Kent.'

'What do you mean?'

'Look what it is called, Mr Redmayne.'

'Of course,' he said. 'Priestfield Place.'

Jonathan Bale was thrilled to see the return of the *Marie Louise*. After sailing up the Thames, it anchored in midstream to unload its cargo. As its crew brought casks and boxes ashore, he tried to engage them in conversation but they would tell him little beyond the fact that they had sailed from Calais and would be returning there within a few days. Certain that the vessel held important secrets, Jonathan did everything he could to contrive a visit to it but all his requests were met with blank refusal. The *Marie Louise* would allow no strangers aboard. Even a London constable would need a warrant before he was permitted to inspect the craft. A law-abiding man was forced to contemplate the disconcerting notion of trespass.

'Where are you going?' asked Sarah.

'Back to the wharf.'

'At this time of night? It is almost dark, Jonathan.'

'It needs to be, my love.'

'Why?'

'I am going out on the river.'

'Is that why you are leaving your hat and greatcoat behind?'

'It is part of the reason.'

Jonathan would say no more than that. Kissing his wife goodbye, he let himself out and began the long walk, grateful that the darkness was slowly throwing its blanket over the city. Dressed in the clothes he once wore as a shipwright, he felt a sense of release. Anonymity liberated him and gave him the confidence to do something which he would never even attempt in the guise of a constable. When he reached the river, he could see the myriad lights of Southwark on the opposite bank. He went down the steps and onto the landing stage.

The boat had been borrowed from a friend and he had no qualms about rowing it until he was caught up in the current. He had forgotten how treacherous the river could be. It took him some time to master its swirling rhythms and his bare forearms were soaked in the process but he persevered until old skills returned. Craft of all kinds dotted the river and he had to pick his way through them in order to reach the *Marie Louise*. She towered above him. The ship was largely in darkness but lanterns burnt on deck and he could see light in some of the cabin windows. Most of the crew were still ashore but some surely remained on watch. Stealth was vital.

He shipped his oars and moored his boat to the sheet anchor. When he was certain that nobody on deck had seen him, he went hand over hand up the cable, grateful that it was not too slimy to allow a firm grip. It was slow work which made demands on his muscles but he eventually reached the bulwark. Climbing over it, he rolled behind the windlass then peeped out to take his bearings. Several lanterns burnt at strategic intervals. Two men were on watch, chatting together outside the fo'c's'le, taking it in turns to swig from a flagon of beer to offset the tedium of their duty. Their casual attitude suggested that they did not expect visitors.

Though Jonathan had never been aboard the *Marie Louise* before, he had an intimate knowledge of its design. He had helped to build three almost identical vessels and could feel his way around them in the dark. Keeping low and hugging the bulwark, he crept past the two men and made his way towards the cabins at the stern. He was tempted to search the hold while he was there but saw the folly of that without a lantern. His real target was the captain's cabin where the ship's log book and manifest were kept. It well might yield up other secrets about the ship. Jonathan felt certain that the captain would be ashore. No red-blooded sailor would spurn the delights of London for a lonely night aboard a merchant ship.

Voices came up from below to warn him that one of the cabins was occupied. He moved with extra care, descending the wooden steps very slowly, glad that his movements were disguised by the gentle creaking of the timbers.

Inching his way towards what he took to be the captain's cabin, he tried the door and found it predictably locked. He slipped his dagger from its sheath and used its point to explore the lock. There was a loud click and the door gave before him. He sheathed his dagger and stepped inside, grateful for the lantern which swung from the beam. It cast an uncertain light but he was able to see that it was not the captain's cabin at all. Jonathan was disappointed yet his visit brought him one reward. Lying on a bunk and staring up at him with sightless eyes was an object he felt he might have seen before.

It was a large white mask.

Before he could take a closer look at it, something hard and cold was thrust against the side of his head. He heard the pistol being cocked.

'What are you doing here?' growled a voice.

'Is this the *Peppercorn*?' asked Jonathan, thinking fast.

'No!'

'Then I have come aboard the wrong ship, friend.'

'That is certainly true. Turn round so that I can see you.'

It was his only chance of escape and he took it bravely. As the man stepped back to allow him to turn, Jonathan swung round quickly to knock the barrel of the pistol upwards so that it discharged its bullet harmlessly at the ceiling. His other fist sank into the man's stomach and took all the wind out of him. Thrusting him roughly aside, Jonathan went scrambling up the steps and raced across the deck. The sound of the pistol alerted the two men on night watch and they came running towards the stern with muskets in their hands but they were far too slow. All that they saw was a bulky figure, diving headfirst into the river. When they hung over the bulwark with a lantern, they could see no sign of him. He had disappeared beneath the water.

The visit of Penelope Northcott left him in a state of mild exhilaration for the rest of the day. In bringing the rosary beads and the missal, she had given him some crucial guidance but it was the news of her broken engagement which really stirred him. It was not simply that it freed her from what he felt was an unfortunate match; it also removed any scruples Christopher had about confronting a beloved fiancé. He could now avenge himself on George Strype with a clear conscience though that pleasure had to take its turn behind other priorities. Having spent the morning and much of the afternoon with Penelope, he had called on his brother early that evening to press him into service again.

Back in Fetter Lane once more, he was able to review the new facts which had come to light and to reflect on the enchanting character of Penelope Northcott. Other daughters in her position would have been so paralysed by grief at the death of their father that they would have felt unable to move, let alone begin a systematic search of his private papers. Anyone else learning such an unpleasant secret about a parent they respected would have kept it hidden from view out of a sense of shame but she overcame her mortification to bring the letters to Christopher. Her trust in him was inspiring. It made him redouble his efforts to catch the man who killed both Sir Ambrose Northcott and, in all probability, his hapless lawyer.

Seated in the parlour, Christopher went through the sequence of events once again, fitting each piece of evidence neatly together. A fierce knocking at his door interrupted his cogitations and sounded an alarm bell. Waving Jacob away, Christopher reached for his sword and went to answer the door himself. If it was an enraged George Strype, he would be more than ready for him. Determined to support his master, Jacob came up behind him with a candelabrum in one hand and a stick in the other. When Christopher opened the door, however, he found himself staring at the most unlikely caller.

Jesus-Died-To-Save-Me Thorpe delivered his message bluntly.

'Ye are to come at once, Mr Redmayne!'

'Where to?'

'Addle Hill. Mr Bale is in need of you.'

'Why?' asked Christopher anxiously, knowing that nothing short of an emergency would make the constable summon him. 'Is he injured?'

'He does not have breath enough to tell us,' said Thorpe. 'When he got back home, he was like a drowned rat. It was Mrs Bale who sent me.'

'I will come immediately,' said Christopher, then he looked more closely at the messenger. 'Wait, sir. Have I not seen you before? Yes,' he recalled, taking the candelabrum from Jacob to hold it closer to his visitors face. 'You were locked in the pillory. Mr Thorpe, is it not?'

'It is, sir. Neighbour to Mr Bale. He was kind to me when I was unjustly pilloried. I am glad to be able to help him in return. But hurry, Mr Redmayne. Ye keep the poor man waiting.'

Having delivered his message, Jesus-Died-To-Save-Me Thorpe vanished into the darkness. Jacob brought a lantern and helped his master to saddle the horse. Within minutes, Christopher was cantering in the direction of Baynard's Castle Ward, wondering what had happened to the constable and feeling guilty in case he had endangered the man's life with the orders he had given him. When he reached the house, he leapt from the saddle and was still tethering the animal when Sarah Bale came bustling out to greet him.

'Thank goodness you have come, Mr Redmayne!' she said.

'What is amiss?'

'Jonathan has been in the river. He would not tell me why.

You are the only person who can get the truth out of him.'
She ushered him into the house. 'Excuse his rudeness. He did
not want me to send for you.'

Christopher soon saw why. When he went into the parlour,
the constable was lying in a chair, wrapped in a blanket. His
hair was still wet, his face pale and his fatigue apparent.
Jonathan Bale was far too proud a man to let anyone but his
wife see him in such a condition and he glared inhospitably
at his visitor before shooting Sarah a look of reproach. She
gave him a smile and backed out of the room.

'What are you doing here, sir?' asked Jonathan grumpily.

'Your neighbour, the quarrelsome Quaker, urged me to
come.'

'Mr Thorpe?'

'The same. A case of Jesus-Came-To-Call-Me. Here I am.'

'There was no need. As soon as I had dried myself off, I
intended to come straight to you. I am recovered now.'

'Mrs Bale obviously thought otherwise,' said Christopher,
'and I prefer to rely on her opinion. Now, tell me what
happened. You have been swimming on the river, I hear.'

'Not from choice. I got aboard the *Marie Louise*.'

'How?'

'Under cover of darkness.'

Jonathan told his tale and mellowed as Christopher
interjected compliments and congratulations. The discovery
of the mask was seen as a critical piece of evidence. Jonathan
felt certain that it was the one worn by the nocturnal visitor
to the house in Lincoln's Inn Fields.

'Then he may well be the killer,' decided Christopher.
'He has been placed at Mrs Mandrake's house, on the *Marie*

Louise and, I suspect, in the cellar where Sir Ambrose met his death. He links all three locations.'

'Since he has access to the ship, he must have been aboard when Solomon Creech visited the vessel. I guess that is where Mr Creech was killed.'

'But the body was nowhere near where the *Marie Louise* had been anchored. It was found some way downriver.'

'Currents, sir,' said Jonathan ruefully. 'They carried him along. I have known bodies coming to the surface a mile from where they were dumped in the water.' He gave a shiver. 'I was almost one of them.'

'Did you swim to the bank?'

'No, Mr Redmayne. I went under the hull of the fishing smack nearby and hid behind that for a long time. When I was sure they had stopped looking for me, I swam back to retrieve my boat.' He pulled the blanket around him. 'It is not easy to row when you are soaking wet.'

'Your sacrifice was worthwhile, Mr Bale. You may have found the most valuable clue of all. When is she due to sail?'

'Within a few days.'

'Then we must act quickly.'

'To do what, sir?'

'Bait the trap.'

'I do not understand.'

'You will, my friend,' said Christopher. 'But first let me tell you what I learnt today. I had another visit from Sir Ambrose's daughter. She found something which helps to confirm what my visit to Paris suggested.'

'And what is that?'

'The real worm in the bud here is religion.'

Jonathan listened with fascination as the architect constructed his argument with the same punctiliousness he would give to the design of a house. It took on definition and solidity before his admiring eyes. Though still incomplete, the structure began to look impressively sound. The constable gave a grudging smile.

'You have put much thought into this, sir,' he observed.

'It is important to me, Mr Bale.'

'And to me,' the other reminded him. 'A wonder that it is not more important to Mr Strype. You might think that he would have a stronger reason than any to want the murderer caught. When Sir Ambrose was killed, Mr Strype lost a friend, a business partner and a future father-in-law.'

'I am sure that he desires the arrest and conviction of this man as much as anyone,' said Christopher blandly. 'What upsets Mr Strype is the idea that *I* might be the person to catch the villain.'

'Is that why he had you attacked the other night?'

Christopher thought of Penelope and a smile ignited his face.

'No, Mr Bale. That was over something else.'

By the time that Christopher left the house, Jonathan Bale had rallied, overcome his resentment at the visit and even risen to an expression of gratitude. Sarah added her own thanks as she saw their guest to the door; then she went back in to cosset her husband.

Christopher left the city by Ludgate and rode slowly as he reflected on events. He was desperate to speak to his brother but he did not relish having to search for Henry through a

343

series of gaming houses at that time of night. Resolving to call at Bedford Street early next morning, he let his horse take him back towards Fetter Lane.

In one day, he felt, they had made substantial progress in their investigation but he did not let his sense of satisfaction distract him. He realised that George Strype had even more cause to assault him now, blaming him – at least in part – for the broken engagement. One hand on his sword, Christopher was vigilant as he trotted up Fetter Lane. There was no sign of any ambush but two horses were tethered outside his house. He wondered who would call at such a late hour. While his master was dismounting, Jacob came scurrying out of the front door with a lantern and a look of apology.

'I had to let them in, sir,' he explained.

'Who?'

'Miss Littlejohn has come back.'

'What?' said Christopher in annoyance. 'I told you never to let her across the threshold again. This is too much, Jacob. Stable my horse.'

He tossed the reins to his servant and marched into the house, determined to eject Margaret Littlejohn with such courteous firmness that she would never again bother him. When he went into his parlour, however, the person who stood up to greet him was Samuel Littlejohn. The builder seemed embarrassed. He licked his lips and gestured to his daughter, who was squirming with discomfort on a chair.

'Please excuse us calling, sir,' said Littlejohn, shifting his feet. 'But I simply had to bring Margaret here at once.'

'Why?' said Christopher uneasily.

'She has something to tell you.'

CHAPTER SIXTEEN

Propped up in bed, Henry Redmayne was still not fully awake. There was a fuzziness inside his skull which he could not quite dispel. His cheeks were sallow, his eyes bloodshot, his mouth unpleasantly dry. Breakfast lay on the tray beside him but he could not muster enough enthusiasm to look at it, still less to try to eat it. A late night had left him feeling delicate. He simply wanted to be left alone to recover in privacy. When the door of his bedchamber burst open, therefore, he shrieked in dismay at the figure who came bounding towards him.

'Go away! I am not receiving any visitors today!'

'I am not a visitor,' said Christopher. 'I am your brother.'

'My house is closed to *all* of my relations. Especially to younger brothers who show neither respect nor consideration. Away with you!'

'Wake up, Henry. This is important.'

'So is the sanctity of my bedchamber.'

He let out a groan as Christopher sat on the edge of the mattress and caused it to tilt. Henry brought a hand up to his pounding head.

'This is pure torture!'

'Listen to me,' said his brother, putting a hand on his arm. 'I am sorry to call on you so early and so unannounced but I was left with no choice. My life is in serious danger.'

'You may be sure of that!' growled Henry. 'If I had a weapon in my hand, you would already be dead.'

'Somebody is planning to do the office for you.'

'What are you talking about?'

'Stop thinking only of yourself,' ordered Christopher, 'and I will tell you. Margaret Littlejohn called at my house last night.'

Henry showed a measure of curiosity for the first time.

'So that is it. You have come to boast of a conquest.'

'Do not be so obtuse!'

'You baulked at the challenge of Sweet Ellen and preferred a more sedate ride on the builder's daughter. How was she?'

'Covered in confusion. Her father brought her.'

'Why?'

'Because she saw the man who means to kill me.'

'You see him before you, Christopher.'

'Stop that!' said the other, shaking him. 'I am serious. Do you want to be put in the position of writing to Father to explain that his younger son was murdered because you were too lazy to help him? I can imagine what the good Dean of Gloucester would say before he closed his purse to you for ever.' Henry came wide awake. 'That is better. Now that

I have your attention, let me also share your breakfast for I left before Jacob was able to prepare mine.'

He took an apricot from the platter and popped it in his mouth.

'What is all this to-do about Margaret Littlejohn?' asked Henry.

'She was outside my house yesterday when she noticed a man spying on it. The same person, she believes, whom she saw leaving the cellar at the building site around the time that Sir Ambrose was killed. Margaret was eager to warn me but, for reasons of her own, decided against it. Fortunately for me, Nan has scruples.'

'Nan?'

'Her maidservant.'

'Where does she enter the story?'

'She was waiting near my house with her mistress.'

'Why?'

'Let us not go into that,' said Christopher wearily. 'The fact of the matter is that Nan sensed I might be in peril and would not hold the discovery back. She spoke to Samuel Littlejohn.'

'Was he lurking in Fetter Lane as well?'

'Of course not.'

'Has the whole Littlejohn household congregated there?'

'No,' said Christopher, 'and thanks to yesterday's episode, Margaret will never be allowed near me again. Her father was enraged that she had disobeyed him and that she had not warned me about the man watching my house. He made her tell me everything that she saw. I have no doubt that the man in question murdered both Sir Ambrose and Solomon Creech.'

'What makes you so certain?'

Christopher told him. He described the sighting of the man at Molly Mandrake's establishment and the appearance of his mask aboard the *Marie Louise*. For the first time, he also gave his brother a full account of his visit to Paris and of the ensuing attempt on his life. Even Henry's befuddled brain acknowledged the degree of peril faced by Christopher.

'What can I do to help?' he asked.

'That is what I came to tell you. Have you studied the list?'

'List?'

'The one I gave you yesterday,' said Christopher, shaking him again. 'The one that Jonathan Bale compiled for me.'

'Oh, that list,' said Henry loftily. 'Yes, I studied it closely. When I saw some of those names, I could not forbear laughing. No wonder Moll was so pleased to see me entering her portals once more.'

'What do you mean?'

'She would have had lean pickings from the clients on that list. Half of them are too old to manage anything more energetic in bed than a mild fart. Sir Patrick Compton is so fat that he has not actually seen his organ for several years, let alone manoeuvred it into action. Lord Halgrave is about as virile as a dead mongoose. And there was, I am told, a cruel prescience in the christening of Sir Roger Shorthorn.'

'Did you do what I asked you?'

'Yes, Christopher. I added names of others I have seen there.'

'And did you arrange them as I requested?'

'In the exact order you specified.'

'Excellent fellow!

'Does that mean I can go back to sleep again?'

'No, Henry,' said Christopher, selecting another morsel from the platter. 'You must get up immediately and send for your barber. Then you must put on your finest apparel. We must have you looking at your best for a royal audience.'

His brother's jaw dropped and the bloodshot eyes goggled. 'Royal audience?'

'Yes,' said Christopher. 'You must introduce me to the King.'

The meeting was held in one of the warehouses which had not yet been rebuilt after the Great Fire. Largely destroyed, it had one bay which was still roofed and with walls thick enough to muffle the sounds of Christian witness which rose up within. When the meeting was over, the Quakers left singly or in pairs so that nobody would realise they had attended an illegal gathering. Among the last to venture out of the stricken warehouse was Jesus-Died-To-Save-Me Thorpe and his wife. Hail-Mary Thorpe was a small, bird-like woman who seemed to hop along the ground on the arm of her husband. She had a tiny face with pin-prick eyes and a blob of a nose. It was she who first spotted their neighbour.

Jonathan Bale was gazing at the Thames when they came up.

'Good day to thee, Mr Bale!' said Hail-Mary Thorpe.

The constable turned and touched the brim of his hat in greeting.

'I had supposed thou hadst thy fill of the river last night,' observed Thorpe with a grim smile. 'Art thou recovered, neighbour?'

'I am, Mr Thorpe. Thank you for your help.'

'It was the least I could do for thee.'

'Mrs Bale and thee have been good to us,' said his wife. 'We could not have better neighbours. Many a time when thou might have hadst cause to arrest us, we were sent on our way with a kind warning from thee. It was always appreciated.'

'Though not always heeded, alas,' said Jonathan with a twinkle.

'We are what we are,' announced Thorpe.

'Nobody has been left in any doubt of that, sir.'

'Remember us for our honesty before God, if for nothing else.'

'Remember you?'

'Yes, Mr Bale. We are leaving thee and this sinful city.'

'But we will miss our neighbours,' added his wife. 'Mrs Bale has been my doctor so many times now. I was blessed in her loving kindness.'

'You depart from London?' said Jonathan.

'Before we are forced to,' replied Thorpe. 'We have decided to join the brave new community which has been set up in America. I thought it best to sail away from this country in a state of freedom or this cruel government would have me deported in chains. We go to New England, sir. New life, new hope, new challenges.'

'You will meet many of those, I suspect,' said Jonathan. 'But I wish you both well. It takes courage to cross the ocean.'

'That is the only part which worries me,' confessed Hail-Mary Thorpe. 'I have no fears about what we shall find when we get there but the voyage itself is fraught with danger. Tell us, Mr Bale, for most of thy life has been spent among ships and those who sail in them. What is the best thing to take on such a long and arduous voyage?'

'Belief in God. He is a master mariner.'

'Then we are saved.'

'Just as I told thee, Hail-Mary,' said her husband solicitously. 'We have no need to fear if we put our trust in God.'

Their decision produced a confused response in Jonathan. He was not sure whether to sigh over the loss of such decent neighbours or to rejoice at his escape from the burden of arresting them from time to time. New England might be a more amenable place for assertive Quakers.

'Is London so hateful a place that you must flee it?' he asked.

'It is since the cloven hoof returned,' said Thorpe.

'Cloven hoof?'

'I speak of the Devil who rules this city and corrupts it with his own wickedness. He is the real reason why we must quit this swamp of iniquity.' Thorpe raised an admonitory finger. 'Ask of us who is sending our little family thousands of miles away to enjoy a more godly existence and we will tell thee straight. It is that Lord of Hell,' he asserted with withering scorn. 'King Charles.'

Whitehall Palace consisted of a motley collection of buildings scattered over a large acreage. If the Banqueting House formed its architectural pearl, it was surrounded by many semi-precious stones, some of which were badly chipped. The royal apartments were situated in the southern half of the palace, looking out across a well-trimmed green sward which swept down to the river. Christopher Redmayne and his brother entered through the Palace Gate and made their way towards the Great Hall. When they entered the building, a guard was waiting to lead them through a bewildering maze to the royal Drawing Room.

Henry glided into it with the confidence of a man who was at his ease in the palace but Christopher looked in awe at the opulence around him. The room was a fruitful source of study for any architect and he quite forgot the purpose of their visit. He was still trying to estimate the cost of the superb chandeliers when his brother's cough alerted him to the presence of the King. Charles entered from a door at the far end and posed before the fireplace. After bowing politely, the brothers approached.

Proximity filled Christopher with the glow of privilege. The King had been imposing when viewed from the rear of the Banqueting Hall but he was much more striking when only yards away. It was not just the exquisite apparel and the dignified posture. There was a grandeur about the man which set him above ordinary mortals. Christopher found it faintly disappointing when the glorious demi-god before him resorted to something as mundane as human speech.

'What is this nonsense about a Popish plot?' he asked.

'It is not nonsense, Your Majesty,' said Henry. 'At least, I hope that it is not, for all our sakes. My brother will explain.'

Christopher inclined his head respectfully. Charles regarded him.

'An architect, I hear?'

'That is so, Your Majesty.'

'What do you think of my palace?'

'May I be candid?'

'I will accept nothing less from you.'

'You are worthy of something much finer.'

'That is what I tell my Parliament year after year but they will not give me the money to improve it. Kings need kingly surroundings. Parts of this palace make me feel more like a tradesman than a monarch.' He beckoned his visitor forward. 'Stand here by me, Mr Redmayne. I await your explanation of this alleged conspiracy.'

Christopher took a couple of steps forward, noting that he had been placed within earshot of the door. The King was alone but Christopher had a strong feeling that someone else was listening. It did not hamper his recitation of the facts.

'Your Majesty,' he began, 'will be aware of the cruel murder of Sir Ambrose Northcott, stabbed to death by an unknown assailant. Shortly afterwards, a second victim, Mr Solomon Creech, fell to the same killer. Mr Creech was Sir Ambrose's lawyer and privy to the many secrets in his life. I have been trying to unravel those secrets and they have brought me to a stark conclusion.'

'Give it to me in one concise sentence,' ordered Charles.

'The murders were preliminaries to your assassination.'

'That is a bold claim, Mr Redmayne.'

'So I told him, Your Majesty,' said Henry, determined not to be left out. 'But he convinced me. Listen patiently and I am quite sure that my brother will convince you as well.'

Charles looked pained. 'I am not easily convinced.'

'May I go on, Your Majesty?' asked Christopher.

'If you must. A warning, however.'

'Your Majesty?'

'It is time for my walk. Be brisk.'

Christopher needed no second invitation. His account was succinct but persuasive. It was the mention of Paris which took the cynicism out of the royal gaze and the discovery aboard the *Marie Louise* made him stroke his moustache reflectively. When Christopher stopped, the King gave him an approving nod.

'You can present a cogent argument, sir.'

'Thank you, Your Majesty.'

'I have done my share,' said Henry plaintively.

Charles ignored him. 'Where is this list?' he asked.

'I have it here, Your Majesty,' said Christopher, taking the document from his pocket to pass it over. 'When I first saw the names, I did not realise their full significance. It was only when Henry arranged them in order for me that I could see just how many members of Your Majesty's government have responded to the blandishments of Mrs Mandrake.'

Charles was torn between amusement and surprise.

'Everyone but the Earl of Clarendon is here,' he said, studying the names. 'By Jupiter! Can Sir Roger Shorthorn really have the gall to visit a house of resort? What do the ladies do with him – take it in turns to search for his missing member?' He became serious. 'But you are quite correct, Mr Redmayne. There is a pattern here.'

'Yes, Your Majesty,' said Christopher. 'Over half of the men on that list are in a position to divulge sensitive information about affairs of state. When I visited the house myself, the young lady assigned to me showed more than interest when I pretended to be a regular visitor at Court. She positively interrogated me about you.'

'What was her name?'

'Sweet Ellen.'

'She always takes charge of newcomers to the house,' explained Henry. 'It was Sweet Ellen who favoured me on my first visit there. I was so busy enjoying myself that I thought her endless questions were simple curiosity. Now I know otherwise.'

'My brother was being pumped, Your Majesty,' said Christopher. 'Subtly but effectively. And I am certain that many of the other men on that list had a similar experience. Quite unwittingly, they have been parting with all kinds of state secrets to Mrs Mandrake and her ladies.'

'And where do those secrets end up?' said the King.

'In France. Carried there by Monsieur Charentin aboard the *Marie Louise*. That is why he is so generous a benefactor. He is not just paying for any services which the ladies render. He is rewarding his spies.'

The King examined the list again then strolled to the door. Without a word, he let himself out. Christopher and Henry watched with growing dismay as the minutes past.

'Have I said something to vex him?' asked Christopher.

'I hope not.'

'Where has he gone, Henry?'

'For his daily walk, by the look of it.'

The door suddenly opened again and Charles strode in to take up the same position. They noticed that he no longer carried the list.

'Tell me, Mr Redmayne,' he said slowly. 'Was Sir Ambrose

Northcott party to this deceit among the bedclothes?'

'No, Your Majesty,' replied Christopher. 'I believe that he was killed before he could find out. If he had known that his house was being used for the purposes of spying, he would sooner have razed it to the ground than condone the intrigue.'

'I find that reassuring.'

'Why so, Your Majesty?'

'Because, on more than one occasion, he invited me to visit the establishment. Sir Ambrose was most insistent. I, of course, invariably declined,' he said airily. 'I would never dream of setting foot in such a disreputable place.'

'Yet that was ever Molly Mandrake's theme,' recalled Henry. 'She begged me to entice you there, Your Majesty. In order to give her house royal approbation.'

Charles was aloof. 'Quite out of the question.'

'Is it, Your Majesty?' said Christopher. 'I think that it is perhaps time to answer her plea.'

'Why on earth should I do that?'

'I will tell you. Might I first make a suggestion?'

'What is it?'

'Leave the door ajar so that we can be heard more easily. I know that someone is listening to every word we say.'

Charles burst out laughing. 'I have a better idea,' he said, putting a hand on Christopher's shoulder. 'Join me on my walk. This subject is best discussed in the Privy Garden. Only the birds will eavesdrop there.'

Penelope Northcott knew that he would try again. George Strype was far too conceited a man to accept rejection lightly.

The social consequences would be extremely painful to him. Stung by her rebuff, he would do everything in his power to make her reverse her decision before it became public knowledge. To keep him at bay, she gave instructions that he was not to be admitted to the Westminster house on any pretext. In the event, he did not even turn up and she began to feel even safer.

Penelope felt able one day to venture into the city. She was taken completely by surprise when she left Mr Creech's office and found her discarded fiancé waiting for her outside in Lombard Street.

'George!' she exclaimed.

'You still deign to talk to me?' he said with a tentative smile.

'Only to wish you well.'

'Do I deserve no more from you than that?'

'I am busy,' she said. 'You will have to excuse me.'

He was insistent. 'Listen to me, Penelope. I followed you here and I waited for an hour in the street for you to come out. I am not to be shaken off now.' He indicated her coach. 'Why do we not continue this conversation in some privacy?'

'No, George.'

'Are we to stand out here like haggling tradesmen?'

'You may but I will not,' she said. 'Goodbye.'

'Wait!'

'We have said all that we need to say to each other.'

'Will you not at least let me apologise properly to you?' he pleaded. 'I spoke out of turn at your house. It was ungentlemanly. Your censure was justly deserved and I make no complaint about it. But,' he said earnestly, 'was my behaviour really so bad as to justify a complete rift? I love you, Penelope. I want to spend the rest of my life with you. Think of all those plans we made together, all those ambitions we had. What a terrible waste for you to throw it all away now.'

'I am not the person who threw it away, George.'

'All I ask for is a second chance.'

'It is too late,' she said, opening the door of her coach. He touched her arm. 'Please take your hand off me.'

'Not until you hear me out.'

'Supposing I refuse?'

'Penelope!'

'What will you do – set those ruffians onto me as well?'

'So that lies behind all this, does it?' he sneered, releasing her arm and stepping back. 'Redmayne has been telling tales. Well, let me tell you something about him. Did you know that he has been here to this office to pester the clerk for details of your father's transactions? He had no right to do that. It is intolerable. Do you want Sir Ambrose's private affairs to be scrutinised by an interfering architect?'

'I have every faith in Mr Redmayne.'

'Is that what you told him when you saw him?'

'He knew it already,' she said, getting into the coach.

'Next time you meet him, give him a message from me.'

'I am not your courier, George.'

'Warn him, Penelope!' he snarled. 'And take a last look at that pretty face of his before I redesign his features.'

'How many bullies will you pay this time?'

'One person will be enough. Me.'

The coach rolled off and left him smouldering with rage.

Molly Mandrake was in her counting house, seated at her desk as she assessed the takings from the night before. Business had been brisk and money rolled in with encouraging ease. Every payment was entered in her ledger. Only a small percentage of the income would go to the girls whose bodies had helped to earn it. They understood that. In taking them into her service, Molly was their benefactress. She had rescued them from cruder establishments where disease and violence could bring an early end to their careers, and she introduced them to clients from the very pinnacle of society. In her opinion, they should be paying her for the privileges she had bestowed on them.

There was a tap on the door and she broke off from her work.

'Come in!'

The door opened and the black manservant entered with a letter.

'This has just arrived for you, Mrs Mandrake,' he said.

'Who sent it?'

'Henry Redmayne. The messenger is awaiting your reply.'

'Why?'

When she read the letter, she understood. Letting out a cry of joy, she reached for some writing paper.

'Give this to the messenger at once,' she said, scribbling away with excitement. 'When you have done that, send Damarosa to me.'

'Damarosa?'

'Tell her that I have some wonderful news for her.'

* * *

Sarah Bale could usually discern the cause of her husband's long silences but this time she was baffled. As he put on his coat, Jonathan was tense and preoccupied. She tried once again to initiate a conversation.

'I will be sorry to see them go,' she said. 'We could have had far worse neighbours than the Thorpe family, even with his ranting. It is disgraceful when God-fearing people like them are forced to emigrate.' She clicked her tongue. 'New England! All that way when they have no idea what they will find when they get there. It is frightening, Jonathan. I could never face a journey like that.'

'I could,' he muttered.

'What did you say?'

'Nothing.'

'Why are they leaving? Is there no way to persuade them to stay? Hail-Mary Thorpe is not a robust woman. How will she survive the long voyage? And think of those poor children of theirs.' She shook her head. 'They must be desperate to take such a course as this.' He reached for his hat. 'Do you have no opinion at all to offer?'

'Not tonight, Sarah.'

'Why? What ails you?'

'I have to go.'

'Where? Not back into the river, I hope.'

'No.'

'Then where?' He gave her a token kiss.

'I will tell you on my return.'

'Is it such a big secret? Surely, you can tell me.' She followed him to the door. 'Jonathan, what is going on? You have hardly said a word to me all evening. I am your wife. What have I done to upset you?'

'Nothing, Sarah.'

'Then why are you so morose? Anybody would think that you were walking off to your own execution. Are you looking forward so little to your duties tonight?'

He opened the door then turned to look back at her.

'Yes,' he confessed. 'I am.'

Henry Redmayne was in his element. He had always wanted to ride in a coach with the King of England. Wearing his periwig and accoutred in his finery, Henry went over the arrangements once again.

'I chose Damarosa for you, Your Majesty,' he said. 'Not simply because she is my favourite. A voluptuous creature in every particular, I do assure you. Breathtakingly so. No, the main reason that I specified Damarosa in my letter was that she has a room on the ground floor. When we enter by the side door, you can slip into her bedchamber without being seen by anyone else.' He emitted a high laugh. 'Not that anyone would recognise you because your disguise is too cunning. I am not sharing a coach with King Charles at all but with Old Rowley.'

'Quite so,' said the other.

His companion used a thumb and forefinger to smooth down his black moustache. A black periwig hung to his shoulders and obscured much of his swarthy face. Flamboyant attire had been sacrificed for more homely garments yet there was still a touch of distinction about him.

'Tell me about this room again, Henry.'

'As you wish, Your Majesty.'

'Old Rowley,' corrected the other.

'How could I forget?'

Henry babbled on happily until the coach drew up outside the house in Lincoln's Inn Fields. When the coachman opened the door for him, Henry alighted and went across to the house with a swagger. He did not see Jonathan Bale lurking uncomfortably in the shadows. Knocking at the side door, he waited until Molly Mandrake herself opened it.

'Is everything in readiness, Moll?'

'Everything,' she said, beaming. 'Exactly as you asked.'

'Where is Damarosa?'

'Waiting in her room.'

'I will fetch...' He checked himself. 'Old Rowley is in the coach.'

Molly's grin broadened as she watched Henry helping the other passenger out of the coach. When they went past her, she mumbled a welcome and dropped a curtsey. The King rewarded her with a gentle squeeze on her arm before he was led down a corridor by his guide. Henry paused outside a door, knocked sharply and received a summons to enter from a female voice. He opened the door to usher his companion in then closed it gently behind him, strolling back to Molly Mandrake who was watching excitedly from the end of the corridor.

'Let us leave them to it, Moll.'

'Did he really ask for Damarosa?'

'At my suggestion.'

'Why did you not let *me* entertain him?'

Henry ogled her. 'Because I save the best for myself.'

* * *

Damarosa was seated in profile on a chair in front of a large mirror, using the glow from the candles to artful effect. She was a full-figured young woman in a blue gown which was cut low in the front and which, as the mirror was revealing, plunged almost to the waist at the back. Still in her early twenties, she suggested a blend of youth and experience which was titillating. She had a Mediterranean complexion and cast of feature. Large brown lascivious eyes sparkled with uncompromising zest. Dark hair hung in ringlets. Diamond earrings and a magnificent diamond necklace glittered in the candlelight.

When her guest entered, she rose to curtsey but he waved her back to her seat. He wanted no acknowledgement of his royalty. Sweeping off his hat, he instead gave her a complimentary bow.

'Old Rowley at your service, ma'am.'

'Will you take wine with me, sir?' she said, indicating the seat opposite her. 'I think you will find it palatable.'

'I am sure I shall,' he said, closing one eye and letting the other rove admiringly over her. 'Damarosa, is that your name?'

'Yes.'

'It becomes you, my dear.'

She poured the wine and handed him a glass, raising hers to him in a silent toast before taking a small sip. He tasted his own wine before setting the glass down on the table and taking a swift look around the room. It was exactly as it had been described to him, large, plush, well appointed and possessing a second door. The four-poster took precedence but the decorated screen also made an arresting feature. It stood in the far corner, close to the other door. Old Rowley was very satisfied with his inventory. The only thing which he had not been warned about was the bewitching perfume which filled the air. Damarosa was fragrance itself.

'Your reputation runs before you,' he said.

'Does it?'

'Oh, yes, Damarosa. You were highly recommended.'

'I am flattered.'

'Nothing less than you would suffice for me.'

'Good,' she said, smiling over the top of her glass. 'I am delighted to see you here at last. It is an honour.'

'From what I hear, it is I who have the honour.'

She gave a playful giggle. He watched the dimple in her cheek. Damarosa was slightly nervous and he detected a slight tremble in her hand. He could not decide if she was in awe of his perceived status or if something else was making her tense. Picking up his glass, he tried to put her at ease.

'You will have to teach me, Damarosa.'

'Teach you?'

'I am a new pupil on my first visit here,' he said with boyish candour. 'I do not know what to do and what to say. Tell me, Damarosa. What do the others say?'

'The others?'

'Guests who have been fortunate to make your acquaintance already. When you bring them in here, of what do they speak?'

Another giggle. 'Themselves.'

'Wild boasts and foolish promises?'

'Yes,' she said. 'Most of them like to talk about their work so that I know how important they are. They want me to know how privileged I am. That is beforehand, anyway.'

'And afterwards?'

'It is very different.'

'In what way?'

'They say the nicest things imaginable.'

'I will remember that.' He pondered. 'Damarosa.'

'Yes?'

'I do not like the sound of beforehand.'

'Oh?'

'It is such a waste of time,' he said, reaching out to stroke her hair. 'And I am certainly not ready for afterwards yet. Why do you not show me what happens in between the two?'

She nodded eagerly. After taking a long sip of her wine, she kissed the fingers of one hand then touched his lips with them before flitting off behind the screen. He rose from his seat and turned his back, watching in the mirror out of the corner of his eye and noticing that she opened the other door to slip silently out. He put his glass down and adjusted his periwig. When he heard a sound behind him, he realised that his earlier inventory had been incomplete. It had omitted the third person who had remained in the room with them throughout.

The man came slowly out from behind the screen and crept towards him with a long scarf held between his hands. He got within a yard of the King, intending to slip the scarf around his neck in order to throttle him. But his quarry was prepared this time. The assassin was not dealing with an unsuspecting companion in a dark cellar or with a puny lawyer aboard a ship. Before he could slip the scarf into position, the man was struck by such a powerful blow that he was knocked off balance and fell to the floor. His victim then flung himself on top of him and tore the scarf from his grasp. They wrestled furiously. The disguise could now be abandoned.

Christopher Redmayne could be himself now, strong, supple and determined. As he straddled the man's chest, he held him by the wrists and looked down at a livid white mask.

'I have been waiting for you to come, my friend,' he said.

'I'll kill you!' roared the other.

'Who is paying you this time? Monsieur Bastiat?'

The man tried to throw him off but Christopher had too firm a purchase on him. His assailant twisted, turned, bucked and kicked in order to get free, his head flailing so violently that it beat out a rhythm on the carpet. There was a snapping sound and the mask suddenly went rolling across the floor, exposing a face so hideous that Christopher froze momentarily in disgust. It was red, raw and oozing with malignancy. Skin was peeling readily and he was reminded of the tiny white flakes he saw near the dead body of Sir Ambrose. It was the final confirmation of guilt.

The royal assassin was afflicted with the King's Evil.

Christopher's pause was a mistake. Taking full advantage of it, the man threw him off, leapt to his feet and dived behind the screen to grab his walking stick. With a flash, he had extracted the sword that was concealed inside it. Christopher acted with speed himself, clambering up and snatching the wine decanter to throw its contents over the other's face. It produced a cry of fury. Temporarily blinded, the man lashed out viciously with the sword but Christopher stepped out of range. When he was able to see properly again, the assassin was not facing an unarmed King who was completely off guard. He was up against a resourceful young man who had pulled out a dagger from inside his boot and who was crouched in readiness.

They circled each other warily, looking for an opening.

'Who *are* you?' hissed the man.

'A friend of Sir Ambrose. I have much to thank him for.'

'So have we,' said the other with a harsh laugh. 'He made it all possible. Sir Ambrose was a fool. Every man can be led by the pizzle if you find the right woman and we chose the ideal one for him.'

'Marie Louise. I met her.'

'She had him eating out of her hand.'

He jabbed at Christopher but the thrust was expertly parried.

'Was it her idea to make him convert?' said Christopher.

'That was another ruse to buy time. Marie Louise told him that she would never share his bed until he became a Roman Catholic. Only then would she consent to be his mistress.'

'Mistress. Was there no talk of marriage?'

'She already has a husband.'

'A *husband*?'

'She is Marie Louise Charentin.'

Christopher was taken aback. The man saw his chance and jabbed with his sword again. Christopher stepped to the right but he was too slow this time and his left arm was caught by the blade. It cut through his coat and opened up a gash. The pain revitalised him and he went on the attack, stabbing at his adversary with his dagger and fending off the answering thrusts of the sword. Blood was now gushing down his left arm but he still had enough strength in it to snatch off his periwig and hurl it into the man's face. The assassin stumbled backwards, his sword flailing. Christopher ducked beneath it to strike at the man's sword-arm with his dagger. As his flesh was pierced to the bone, the man gave a yell of rage and dropped the weapon.

Kicking it out of reach, Christopher used the handle of his dagger to club the man to the floor then dropped on top of him to pound away with his fist. The flaking skin was soon dripping with blood. Though he fought hard, the man had nothing like Christopher's manic strength and willpower. A final punch knocked him senseless and his head lolled. Christopher moved swiftly to bind his hands with the scarf; he used the bed hangings to secure his prisoner to the four-poster. It was only then that he slipped off his coat to attend to his wound, stemming the flow of blood by winding a handkerchief around his arm. Putting on his coat again, he replaced his periwig, adjusted it in the mirror and stepped out through the door with regal dignity.

Two figures watched furtively from the end of the corridor. Molly Mandrake and her companion were dismayed when they saw the King emerge, apparently unscathed. The man with Molly was a stranger but Christopher guessed his identity at once. Henry's description of the Frenchman had been very accurate.

'Monsieur Charentin?' challenged Christopher.

Gripped by panic, the man took flight, pushing Molly Mandrake unceremoniously aside and darting for the side door. He unlocked it and rushed out only to find that he had gone straight into the arms of Jonathan Bale. There was the briefest of struggles before the constable overpowered him and held him tight. Christopher stood in the doorway.

'Well done, Mr Bale!'

Jonathan recognised his voice and gaped at him.

'Is that you, Mr Redmayne?'

'Who did you think it was?' said Christopher with a grin. 'Be of good cheer, my friend. You did not have to act as a royal bodyguard, after all. I know that office would have ruffled your Roundhead feathers.'

'Why did you not tell me?'

'I just did, Mr Bale. Hold on to Monsieur Charentin. His accomplice is trussed up inside. Unmasked at last.'

'You have caught him?'

'The murders are finally solved.'

An agitated Henry came trotting up behind his brother.

'Is everything in hand, Your Majesty?' he asked deferentially.

'It is now, Henry.'

'You should have called me, if you needed help.'

'I never need help in a lady's bedchamber.'

'Word somehow leaked out of your presence here,' said Henry, who had clearly been unable to resist boasting about it. 'Everyone wanted to know how I persuaded Your Majesty to come here. I was just explaining to Mr Strype the blandishments I used.'

'Mr George Strype?'

'The same.'

Christopher eased him aside and went straight to the parlour. The black manservant stood dutifully beside the table, serving food and drink. An ancient guest was being pampered by a young prostitute. Two other men were bartering for the favours of a second woman. George Strype was talking airily to Sweet Ellen, guzzling his wine and boasting loudly about his prowess as a lover. When he saw the stately figure enter, he at once became subservient. He gave Christopher a deep bow.

'This is a pleasure, Your Majesty.'

The uppercut caught him on the chin and sent him sprawling.

'So was that,' said the other cheerfully.

Strype rubbed his jaw and looked up in utter bafflement.

'Your Majesty?'

'Christopher Redmayne sends his compliments.'

Penelope Northcott was so overjoyed that she could not stop smiling. As she sat in the parlour of the house in Westminster, she showered her guest with compliments and kept asking him to repeat certain details of his story. She was distressed that he had been wounded in pursuit of her father's killer but accepted his assurance that it was a minor scratch even though his left arm was in a sling. Christopher had told her a very diluted version of the truth, recounting the events in Lincoln's Inn Fields but making no reference to the fact that Sir Ambrose Northcott once owned the house. Indeed, he went out of his way to supply her father with a mask of his own.

'Your father was foolishly led astray,' he said. 'Marie Louise was not his mistress at all but simply a means of ensnaring him. He was the victim of a conspiracy.'

'Why did they have to kill him?'

'Because he had served his purpose, Miss Northcott. And because he was in danger of stumbling on the conspiracy.' He gave a shrug. 'In some small way, I suppose that I am to blame.'

'You, Mr Redmayne?'

'The house was his undoing. Marie Louise insisted on its being built as proof of his commitment even though she had no intention of ever living there. But the work on the house proceeded faster than they anticipated because I urged the builder on. That forced their hand,' he explained. 'Sir Ambrose had to be removed before the house was completed or the situation would have been awkward.'

'He would have expected her to move in with him.'

'When she was, in fact, living with her husband in Paris.'

'It is so complicated, Mr Redmayne. I do not understand.'

'Do not vex yourself with the details,' he advised. 'All that you need to know is that the killer and his accomplice have been arrested. They are now behind bars and will face the sternest interrogation.'

'Thanks to you!'

'And to Mr Bale. Do not forget him.'

'I would like to meet this constable one day.'

'He is a curious fellow.'

'Mother and I owe him a great deal.'

'So do I, Miss Northcott,' he said with feeling. He adjusted the sling for comfort then gazed admiringly at her. 'I am glad the business is concluded. Even if it does mean that we shall lose you.'

'Lose me?'

'You will no doubt wish to return to Kent with the good news.'

'A messenger has already done that, Mr Redmayne. I propose to stay in London for a while to see something of the rebuilding.'

'Indeed?'

'I find the creation of a whole new city very inspiring. Mr Wren has been commissioned to rebuild St Paul's, I hear, and dozens of new churches are to rise up from the ashes.' She became more hesitant. 'Yet I lack a knowledgeable guide. Someone who could take me around London and explain things to me. Mr Redmayne,' she added softly, 'you once recommended the most excellent accommodation to me. I wonder if I might trespass on you again?'

'As often as you wish, Miss Northcott.'

'Could *you* suggest the name of a guide?'

Jonathan Bale was at his most relaxed. Having dined heartily, he played with his sons in the tiny garden then went indoors to sit with his wife in the kitchen. Sarah was pleased at the dramatic improvement in his mood.

'Is that why you were behaving so strangely last night?'

'Yes, my love.'

'You thought you were mounting guard on the King?'

'That is what I was led to believe.'

'Why did you not say so?'

'The very idea made me feel sick.'

'Any other man would have been proud of such an honour,' she argued. 'Look at Mr Redmayne. He put his life at risk for His Majesty. He was even prepared to impersonate him.'

'Would he have been quite so ready to impersonate Oliver Cromwell in the same circumstances? Not that the Lord Protector would ever go anywhere near a house like that,' he said quickly, 'but my point holds. Mr Redmayne has his hero and I have mine.'

'You and Mr Redmayne are the real heroes.'

'We caught them, Sarah. That is all that matters.'

'Both of you survived. That is what matters to me.'

'Yes.'

'Are you glad that it is all over?'

'Very glad.'

'So am I, Jonathan.' She smiled fondly. 'Though I will miss seeing Mr Redmayne. He brought some colour to Addle Hill. We shall probably never see him again.'

'It is of no consequence, Sarah.'

'Stop pretending,' she scolded with a playful nudge. 'I can read your mind. Deep down, you like Mr Redmayne. Admit it.'

'All that I will admit is that I no longer *dislike* the man.'

'It comes to the same thing.'

'Not in my book.'

'I think that you will miss him as well.'

'Yes,' he agreed willingly. 'I will miss watching his back. I will miss all the footwork I did at his request. I will miss standing outside a brothel in the dark and swimming in the river at night. And I will be very glad to miss having a pistol put to my head. Is that what you meant about him bringing colour to Addle Hill?'

There was a knock on the door. Jonathan tensed.

'I'll go,' said his wife, getting up.

'If it is Mr Redmayne, say that I am not at home.'

'I would never lie to a gentleman like that.'

Jonathan heard the door open. An unfamiliar voice spoke and Sarah replied. A few moments later, she came back into the kitchen with a letter in her hand.

'This has come for you, Jonathan.'

He took it from her and opened it at once. His face whitened.

'What on earth is the matter?' she asked.

'I am bidden to the Palace,' he croaked. 'To meet the King.'

King Charles II swept into the Drawing Room with his spaniels swirling about his heels like the hem of a robe. When he took up a stance in front of the fireplace, the dogs yapped and fought to lie at his ankles. He gave an indulgent laugh at their antics.

'Such delightful creatures! Their loyalty is a joy to me.'

He raised his eyes to look across at his guests. They formed an incongruous trio. Affecting nonchalance, Henry Redmayne wore his new vest and coat for the occasion, beaming as if he were about to receive a knighthood and fondling his periwig with an idle hand. Christopher, by contrast, wore plainer attire and had his wounded arm in a sling. There was no hint of his brother's triumphalism in his manner. Stiff and grim-faced, Jonathan Bale stood between them, visibly suffering.

'I brought you here to thank you,' said the King with an expansive gesture. 'You have served me well and I will not forget you.'

'It was a privilege, Your Majesty,' said Henry with a low bow.

'I am glad that you recognise your true king,' teased Charles. 'I am told that last night you switched your allegiance to another one.'

'His Serene Highness, Old Rowley.'

'Do not labour the point.'

'An apposite nickname, if I may say so,' continued Henry. 'Old Rowley is the most famous stallion in the royal stud. You have rightly adopted it for yourself. In fact—'

Charles cut him off with a warning glare then turned his gaze upon Christopher. 'You were wounded in my service, sir. That entitles you to a reward. What shall it be?'

'The only reward I seek is the knowledge that wicked men will pay for their crimes,' said Christopher. 'Have they confessed, Your Majesty?'

'It is taking time to draw the truth out of them but we will have it in full before we are finished. I have skilful interrogators. In brief, sirs,' he said, casually flicking away a spaniel which tried to mountaineer up his leg. 'The assassin's name is James Lovett, a damnable Catholic. He was paid to murder Sir Ambrose and to dispose of his lawyer. That left him free to concentrate on the loftier target you see before you. Thanks to your good selves, his attempt on my life failed.'

'Let the rogue be hanged, drawn and quartered!' urged Henry.

'He will be duly punished, I do assure you. James Lovett was working in harness with Monsieur Jean-Paul Charentin, a merchant of Paris, who won the confidence of Sir Ambrose in order to worm his way into Mrs Mandrake's house. Charentin cleverly drew that formidable lady into the practice of espionage.' His eyebrow arched meaningfully. 'Naked men can be very indiscreet. Female wiles can elicit secrets which no amount of torture could extract. I have the names of Mrs Mandrake's clients and I will be castigating each of them in turn for their folly.'

'Do not spare them, Your Majesty!' said Henry.

'They include you,' warned the other, 'and I will take you to task at a later time, Henry. No doubt you have parted with your share of Court gossip while lying between the thighs of some harlot.'

Henry quailed, Jonathan was shocked and Christopher smiled.

'What of Molly herself, Your Majesty?' asked Henry tentatively.

'She is in prison and the house has been closed down.'

'Not for ever, I hope?'

'Control your passions, sir. They blight your character.'

'There remains the question of Monsieur Bastiat,' said Christopher. 'What of him, Your Majesty? James Lovett and Jean-Paul Charentin were merely his agents. I believe that it was Monsieur Bastiat who devised the plot to ensnare Sir Ambrose.'

'You may well be right,' returned the other. 'We have agents of our own in Paris and their reports have mentioned the name of Arnaud Bastiat more than once. He was a Jesuit priest at one time but has clearly turned to a more bloody occupation. You did well to escape his clutches when you visited Paris. What I wish to know,' he said, picking up one of his dogs to caress it, 'is how you followed such a tortuous trail. I would have had no idea where to start.'

'In the cellars, Your Majesty.'

'Cellars?'

'Of the house I designed. Sir Ambrose was murdered

there. He would never have gone into them with someone he feared might attack him. His companion, this James Lovett, must have posed as a business partner and asked to be shown where contraband goods would be stored.' He grimaced. 'I thought that I was creating a fine house for Sir Ambrose and his family. Yet what I was really designing was a hiding place for his mistress and a potential haven for smuggled goods.'

'There will be other commissions,' Henry reassured him.

The King turned to Jonathan, whose impassive countenance had remained unchanged throughout.

'You are strangely silent, Mr Bale,' he observed.

'Am I, sir?'

'Your Majesty!' whispered Henry in correction.

'From what I hear,' said Charles, collecting a second dog from the floor, 'you must take your share of the credit.'

'Indeed, he must, Your Majesty,' interposed Christopher. 'My efforts would have come to nought without Mr Bale. His boldness in getting aboard the *Marie Louise* provided a vital clue.'

'As did my list of clients,' said Henry.

'Your work has been exemplary,' said Charles, ignoring Henry and looking at the others. 'What impressed me most was the bravery and discretion with which it was carried out. Bravery is not uncommon. Discretion is in shorter supply, as we have seen from the unguarded follies committed in Lincoln's Inn Fields.'

Henry nodded. 'Your Majesty is right to close the place down.'

'Be silent, man!'

'If you wish, Your Majesty.'

'I do, Henry.'

The King replaced the two dogs on the floor then stood up again.

'Bravery and discretion are a rare combination,' he said, 'and I value the man who shows both. To have two such men at my command is heartening. I will look to employ them again.'

'As what?' gasped Jonathan.

'My loyal servants.'

'But I am an architect, Your Majesty,' said Christopher.

'And I am a constable,' added Jonathan.

'Continue in your chosen professions,' encouraged the King. 'You will not be summoned often. From time to time, however, certain situations may arise which call for exactly the qualities which you have displayed. I will send one of my minions to you.' His eye alighted on Henry. 'The very person stands before me. Henry Redmayne will be my go-between. Neither brave nor discreet himself, he can at least carry a message efficiently.'

Henry looked hurt. Beside him Christopher blinked and Jonathan shuddered.

'Well?' said the King. 'I have just offered you a post as royal agents. With appropriate remuneration, of course. Are you not pleased to be given the opportunity to serve your king again?'

'Why, yes, Your Majesty!' said Christopher. He nudged Jonathan in the ribs. 'We are delighted, Mr Bale, are we not?'

'Yes,' said Jonathan through gritted teeth. 'Your Majesty.'

A smile of regal satisfaction spread over the King's face.

'Then it is settled,' he said, striding towards the door with his spaniels in close attendance. He paused to look back at the three men. 'All that you have to do is to wait for my call.'

The Restoration series

The young and ambitious architect Christopher Redmayne is never short of work; following the Great Fire of London a few years previously, much of the capital city is in need of restoration or rebuilding, and Christopher is keen to make his mark on London's developing landscape. But a bustling city in latter half of the seventeenth century is a hotbed of crime, and Christopher cannot stand by when he witnesses an injustice. Along with his good friend the Puritan Constable Jonathan Bale and Christopher's dissolute brother Henry, Christopher seeks to right wrongs and provide justice for the victims. Searching for the truth whilst rebuilding the pride of a city destroyed would be a taxing task for any man, but it is one Christopher Redmayne is happy to undertake.

The Amorous Nightingale
The Repentant Rake
The Frost Fair
The Parliament House
The Painted Lady

The Railway Detective series

London, 1850s. With the development of the railways comes a new breed of criminal, one who chooses train travel as the fastest means of escape, or who takes exception to the mounting interest in the engineering triumphs of the advancing rail network and attacks the cargo, carriages or – worse – the people on board. But to tackle these criminals there is a new type of policeman: the Railway Detective. The dapper Detective Inspector Robert Colbeck and his good friend Sergeant Victor Leeming are the front line against all crimes involving the railway. Travelling across the country, they witness firsthand the changes wrought by the progress of technology – and not all of it is for the good...

The Captain Rawson series

Introducing Captain Daniel Rawson – soldier, spy, charmer...
It is 1704 and Europe is at war. The dashing young captain
is called upon to undertake many dangerous missions in
the course of his duty, including leading his men into battle
against the French enemy and travelling in disguise. He must
succeed at all costs – the future of England is at stake. But
no adventure is too big for Daniel, and as he and his soldiers
march across the Continent, Daniel is delighted to find
distraction in the various ladies he meets along the way...

a&b